Falstaff

Gets

Found

Falstaff Gets Found

Or

Bad People Do Bad Things

Chris Loblaw

Dedication

For K, always

1

The cold of the desert at night numbed the complaints of his beaten body. He shivered in the low sweeping breeze and thought about the sunrise. When the heat of the day came down with all its weight, he was going to die.

An hour ago, he had been on the tail end of a good run at the hold 'em poker table, riding a good mixture of chemicals that put his mind at ease. Winning just enough to make it fun, but not enough to bring attention. And then he saw a nervous tic flitter across the dealer's face as a floor manager walked by. He couldn't help himself as he blurted out a crack about the dealer fucking the manager. The manager stopped dead in her tracks. The dealer went pale. Then security showed up.

They investigated him for 30 minutes with gloved punches and barefoot kicks. The owner of the two-bit casino, the manager's wife, did not like being publicly humiliated as a cuckquean. She had used a hammer on his ribcage and back until she grew too tired to swing it again. Like always, he had stayed conscious through the beating.

The security guards had driven him outside of the city limits after the "investigation" was done and thrown him into the scrap yard dirt. The driver shouted "have a fun walk home, nigger!" as he drove off.

It took very little to coax out the racism buried deep in the heart of ugly America. Falstaff was used to it, used to be being the personification of whatever bias they held. Through their jaundiced eyes, they saw traces of their most hated group. His darker skin, the shape of his eyes, the curl in his hair, the movement of his hands when he spoke. As a kid, he would argue against any epithet hurled at him. It never stopped the fight, because the truth does not matter. They liked to hate.

Hitting the ground had jarred his consciousness loose for the first time that evening. Falstaff regained his senses some time after being left in the sand, laying at the base of an old family restaurant sign that had been dumped, just like him, in the desert to be forgotten. The sign was made of cracked neon and faded circus paint. The picture in the middle of the sign was a wide eyed and smiling cowboy marionette, a knockoff Howdy Doody waving the kids into the discount family-friendly buffet. He turned his head away from Howdy and tried to crawl to a safe spot but his arms and legs refused to follow simple instructions.

The rough circle of dirt that he lay in the middle of was ringed with discarded artifacts of failed businesses. Old cracked vinyl booths from a 50s-themed burger shack were butted up against the scavenged shells of old slot machines. Broken marquee signs from cabaret shows and burlesque houses made empty promises of entertainment and titillation. A sun-bleached plastic dome from an old payphone lay curved up to the sky with 4 inches of dirty runoff water pooled in the bottom, just a dozen feet from him. Falstaff decided he just wanted one last drink before he died.

He flailed his arms and legs towards the holy dirty water. Something inside of his chest ground up against something sharp, and his vision went into a grey tunnel. He gave up moving and stared up to the sky as he pleaded for relief. Howdy leered down at him. He tilted his head to the side to let the weak stream of phlegm and blood ooze out of the corner of his mouth and spoke a whispered prayer.

"Bless me Saint Howdy, patron saint of the Faded American Empire, for I have sinned. I fucked up. I saw the darkness coming and I ran away. When the shadow fell over me, again and again, I turned tail. That girl in the tobacco field was the first one I left behind. I might have loved her. I brought her into the circle and she got caught up in something that she couldn't handle. I could have tried to help her. I left instead. I paid a penance of being alone. But that's not enough. How could it be?

The impartial sun will be my executioner, but I'm already half-dead. Have been for years. Caught between the honestly wicked and the denialists with their hidden deviances. I lied. I stole. I self-medicated with reckless abandon. I'm high right now, did you know that, Saint Howdy? Every drug I took was meant to keep the ugliness of people blocked out, even my own. So, what I need to know now is can I be forgiven for all of this? Can I die in the dirt in peace?" He looked directly at the faded cowboy smile and heard no response at all. He licked his lips with his sandpaper tongue and waited meekly for death to come.

He slipped in between sleep and fever, fading in and out of the world around him. The rasping uneven sound from his chest accompanied his vigil. The rasp was joined a while later by a distant noise, car tires crunching on the gravel and dirt road outside of the scrap yard. Two cars pulled to a stop, one after the other. The survival instinct grabbed his throat and tried to shout for help. The sound was a weak croak that died on his lips. He threw himself onto his left shoulder and tried to push himself to a sitting position. The exertion and pain made him pass out again.

The stink of smelling salts brought him back to wakefulness. He gagged on the stench but couldn't muster the energy to vomit. He panted to avoid breathing the smell in any deeper. The person who had administered the smelling salts scurried back, leaving him alone with the second man standing above him. He looked at the man's tasselled caramel-colored loafers, followed the leg up to the sheer white dress socks peeking out from under the high cuff cream trousers. Then up to the round girth of the man's waist. Suspenders snaked up from the other man's wide white belt, over his vest and under his velvet beige sportscoat. Perched on top of the torso was a chubby and cheery pink faced man with a white beard and tiny round spectacles.

Staring into the face of the man above him he said "you're not real."

The chubby man smiled and answered in a rich German accent "of course I am real, silly boy."

The beaten man croaked out a plea for water, pathetically smacking his chewed up chapped lips together for emphasis. The German waved two fingers in a gesture of benediction. In response, the smelling salts carrier returned with a plastic bottle of water. The fat man bent down with great care and caution and put the opened bottle to the beaten man's lips. "Slowly" he urged. He tipped the bottle to pour a meagre mouthful through and over Falstaff's lips. The German ignored the beaten man's mewling when the bottle was pulled away.

"Swallow."

Falstaff battled his gorge as it rose to revolt against the water. He managed to keep it down and whispered "more". Dutifully, the fat man doled out mouthfuls until Falstaff could speak clearly. He looked up at his benefactor and smiled through cracked lips. "Traded Howdy Doody for a Vegas lounge Santa. I'm moving up in the world."

The fat man laughs. "I have been called Santa before, you may be surprised. In America that is the only story they have for a fat man with a beard. My name is Herr Muenster. I am from Germany, and I work now in Washington. I would like to offer you an opportunity."

The beaten man looked with wild eyes at the fat man spouting nonsense. "Isn't muenster a cheese?"

"It is. And a town in Germany where my great-grandfather was born. And there is even a small village in Canada with the same name. But maybe we can avoid wasting time talking about nothing? You are going to die soon without help. What name should I use for you, by the way? You have a history of assumed names. Would you prefer to use your favourite one? Or the name you had at birth?"

The beaten man sputtered and interrupted the German before he could say the name. "No, stop. Leave that name. Call me Falstaff. John Falstaff."

Herr Muenster poured another sip of water into Falstaff's mouth and mused about the name.

"Falstaff, ja? From Shakespeare."

"Can we skip to the practical part? Small talk makes me nauseous."

"No story for me? Oh well. I have a story for you, instead. Lucky boy. It is a story about a country. It was very strong and very rich for a very long time, but then it started to slow down. The people chose leaders that promised a return to glory. But these leaders, they were not the men they said they were. These men traded in secrets and forbidden actions. Secrecy surrounded them. They led the country to war, twice. The people were outraged, but still these men held power for another 4 years. On their exit, the mastermind who controlled the darkest secrets of the administration erased every trace of their acts. The records of the people involved, the places they went and the terrible operations they did on behalf of the government, all vanished.

But the bad men were gone from office. A good man was in their place. The problem is fixed, yes? A wave of hope washing racism and hate from the American fabric? No. This is not how humans work. Your country was teetering towards collapse. Trust in government was nonexistent. The ignorant and angry were arming themselves for their very own civil war. This was the dissolving nation that your new president was handed a few months ago. A country pulling apart at the seams. Those erased operations I mentioned, the dirty forgotten deeds, they are the holes in the middle of the seams. And the loose threads around those forgotten sins are the ghosts of those operations. The men and women of grim conviction who did what they were ordered to do. Though the new administration had no record of these operatives, they were able to find most of them, the safe ones. But there are others. Anomalies. Faint echoes of the past that show up in the present. These ghosts do not want to rest."

The German paused and watched Falstaff laying on the ground. His half-closed eyes made it look like he was on the way out of the land of the living. The German called for the attendant to bring the smelling salts again. Falstaff held up his right hand and weakly waved away the help.

"Still here, for now. Why are you telling me this?"

"How do you find a ghost, John? There are no records to research. No evidence to compare to. Only word-of-mouth from the people who have witnessed the ghosts."

"What witnesses? Didn't the big bad government get rid of them too?"

The German sighed loudly and took out a brass cigarillo case. He lit a short cigarillo and exhaled a cloud of fragrant smoke. Falstaff caught the edge of the cloud and inhaled it deeply.

"John, the ghosts have not finished with the living. They hate the living and want their revenge."

"These aren't real ghosts, are they? I'm dying, so this could all be in my imagination. Ghosts, goblins, vampires."

"Metaphor, dummkopf. Please follow along. These 'ghosts' are contractors who were formerly trained and employed in secrecy by the U.S. government. They are not good people. Now they have been left abandoned by their employer. They will do awful things again. It is their nature. And when the American public learns of these awful things, and the past deeds done in their name, the fabric of the American dream will tear in two. No more country. War in the streets. To avoid that war, you need to help us find those ghosts."

"Pass. Let me die here."

"Do you know what an 'impact projection' is, John? The Intelligence Community uses it to assess the potential for unexpected…deviances in behaviour from government assets. Those are spies and agents, contractors and soldiers. For everyone of those assets, the IC determines the likelihood of a rogue event. What are the odds that the person will become uncontrollable and cause collateral damage? This is the vital question they ask. And when they have that number, they estimate the number of collateral deaths that will result. These are innocent people who will die, John.

Lucky for us, we have a fragment of the Impact Projection for the lost operatives. A single line that has no clues to the identities of orphaned assets. The good news for you is that most of the assets are safe. Those are the ones who have been brought home already.

But the malevolent ghosts are not safe. They are all 85% likely to become unstable and deviate. And when they do, each will accrue a body count. Dozens, in most cases. Hundreds, in a few. Minimum. So, who will be responsible for those deaths, hmmm? The killers, to be sure. And the men who set them on their bloody path. But what about the man who could have found the ghosts so they could be stopped, but chose not to? What happens to the soul of that coward, John? How many deaths do you want on your head?"

An angry groan escaped through Falstaff's clenched teeth.

"Leave me alone. I can't save anyone. I'm not a fucking detective or spy or what the fuck ever you're trying to get me to be."

The German walked the perimeter around Falstaff. He beckoned the attendant to his side and took a manila folder from his hands. Muenster made a great display of walking slowly around the ruined furniture while reading the file inside the folder. He stopped by the Howdy sign and clucked his tongue disapprovingly. The German stopped again by the booth with the cracked vinyl seats and sat down dramatically.

"Those boys. That poor girl. Dead for no reason. So very tragic."

"What boys? What girl? Is it better to die for a reason? Dead is still dead. Stop being cryptic. My lungs are filling with blood."

"You have to tell me the answer to that, John. Is it better to die without purpose?"

Falstaff heard his heartbeat thundering in his ears. The rush of blood through his body was filling the space after each beat. He felt both hot and cold. The pain in his torso crawled up to his chest and started squeezing. He drew in as much breath as his broken ribcage would allow.

"It's pointless, anyway. I won't be able to stop the killers."

"No, you do not stop them. You merely find them. A bluthund. Bloodhound. You sniff them out and leave everything else to others. You have a talent that will make this possible." The German imitated the snuffling of a bloodhound on the scent, but the sound was closer to a pig's snorting.

Falstaff coughed up a wad of bloody phlegm. It took effort to regain enough breath to keep talking.

"Some fucking talent. I can see the worst in people, even when they try to hide it. The way their faces tic when they talk, the flush of blood to their cheeks when they think about their unspeakable desires, their little verbal hiccups. They might as well be shouting 'I am a piece of shit and here's the reason why.' So if you want me to run around and guess the secrets of random people, then maybe someday we'll get fucking lucky and find one of your bad guys."

Falstaff watched the German raise himself out of the seat and amble back to him. The pains in Falstaff's right arm were in sync with the German's steps, building in intensity as he got closer. Falstaff made a guess.

"There's already been a killing, hasn't there? Shit. This isn't hypothetical. There are actual bodies somewhere."

"And more to come, I fear. I think you will not be around to hear about the next murders. You do not look well."

"I'm fucking dying, asshole."

The German smiled and nodded his head.

"You're the goddamned devil."

"No Mr. Falstaff, I am an entrepreneur with a job offer. And you a man running out of chances."

The different pains across his body gathered together to assault his chest in concert. In the background of the agony squeezing the life out of him, Falstaff felt his heart miss one beat, then 3, then 5. He gritted his teeth as judgement day came charging at him and he made a choice to get out of the way.

"I'll do it."

The last word left his lips as his heart stopped completely.

2

Falstaff came back to life in the back of a private ambulance. The EMT pinned him down to keep him on the gurney, and then a fresh flush of pain meds sent him back to unconsciousness. Falstaff woke up again, briefly, when he was moved from the ambulance to a private plane, and then again while the plane was in the air. He had screamed in terror when he woke up to the empty darkness outside of the nearest window. Every time he came to, the blurry form of the attendant beside him would hold him down and wait for the wave to pass. It kept passing.

The second ambulance trip started with another resuscitation. This time, Falstaff was awake as the defibrillator restarted his heart. The smell of burnt body hair and singed skin filled the ambulance until the windows were cranked down to let the cold spring air to rush through the vehicle.

The ambulance stopped at the delivery dock of the Allegheny County Medical Examiner. Falstaff was conscious again when he was wheeled through the back door. The haze of sedation wore off to leave an ocean of pain and nausea behind. The EMT ran another quick check of Falstaff's vitals. He shook his head and said "he'll live for now. He should be in a hospital to rest."

"That will do. Give him space. Are you with us, John?"

Falstaff turned his head and looked into the eyes of a dead stranger with an ugly red gouge in his neck, lying flat on a steel table beside him. "Hey handsome, you've had better days" he said to his new friend.

Falstaff tested out his body by putting his hands on the sides of the gurney and slowly pushing himself up into a sitting position. The pains from his chest and torso fought to keep him immobile, but he managed to get upright. His head swam from the change in position. Falstaff ignored the dire warnings his battered body was screaming at him and scanned the room.

Arranged around him on autopsy tables and cadaver carts were 5 dead people: 4 men, 1 woman. The man closest to him, his new friend, had been choked to death by something that had bitten deep into the flesh of his neck. Falstaff couldn't see the causes of the other 4 deaths from his seated position.

Like a baby deer trying to stand for the first time, he put one foot tenuously on the floor, followed by the second. Holding on to the gurney for dear life, he put his weight down and stood up. The world spun for a moment. His body tried to betray him by collapsing into a heap, but he pressed on and willed the pain into the background. The EMT ran back over to catch him, but Falstaff waved him away.

"I'm okay. Buzz off."

The German clapped his hands in delight. "Well done. You are very resilient."

"It's a gift. Takes a whole lot to keep me down."

The contents of his stomach churned together, and the taste of bile rose in his throat. With as much dignity as his battered form could muster, Falstaff leaned over the wastebasket beside his gurney and vomited.

"Oh, that is a disappointing surprise. Your past suggests that dead things do not bother you? Your time in the abattoir gave you no tolerance for dead things?"

"Not the corpses making me sick. The chemicals in my blood aren't getting along. Too much sedation is my guess."

The EMT came over to Muenster, sputtering in his own defence. He claimed that he followed standard protocol. He only gave the patient the minimum dose required to make it possible to treat him. Falstaff looked past the protesting EMT to the other ambulance attendant lurking at the door.

The thin man with the deep-set eyes looked familiar in a distant way. He called the man over and asked for a bottle of water to clear out the phlegm and puke in his mouth.

"Do I know you, bud?" he asked after taking a cautious swig of the water bottle.

The nervous man shook his head and retreated to the edge of the room. The other EMT repeated his claim that there was no chance of unforeseen drug interactions or over-medicating.

"That's assuming I was sober when you found me. I was on something. Seven somethings, actually. The party was well in progress before you showed up with new party favors."

"You see, sir? I am blameless" the EMT announced.

For his reward for being right, Muenster ordered the EMT to go dispose of the wastebasket and clean up any trace evidence associated with it. That took the wind out of the EMT's sails. He glowered at Falstaff continuously as he walked out of the room with the puke-tainted bucket. Falstaff found his legs and walked slowly around the table to look at the other corpses.

"Hey, this new job that you talked me into: does it make me a military employee? I assume that's the part of the government you actually work for, but I could be wrong. Or have I been drafted? Am I a soldier, because I would be a very shitty soldier."

"No, John. You are an independent contractor, hired by me. I am also a contractor who is employed by a strategic solutions firm. They have, in turn, been hired by a series of other companies. Those companies have received grants through many small, boring government agencies. You, however, take instructions exclusively from me."

Falstaff lifted the sheet over the next corpse and pulled back in reaction to the gaping hole in her face. With as much respect as his trembling hands could muster, he gently lay the sheet back down over the poor woman. He moved to the next one to see its face was intact.

"What do I put on my business card- 'independent contractor for an independent contractor to a bunch of shell corporations, in charge of shadowy mystery-solving'? That won't really fit."

"Not at all, Herr Falstaff. Here."

The German held out an ID badge and a small stack of business cards. Falstaff shuffled over to him and took the items for examination.

"What the hell is a 'logistics systems analyst'?"

"A job title that is bureaucratic and boring. We do not want people wondering about you. The less attention you demand, the better. Be a little cog in an incomprehensible machine."

"I should get a phone too."

"No phone for now."

"What? That's weird. Not a great show of trust."

"Here. Let us proceed."

The German shoved the manila folder into Falstaff's hand and began lecturing.

You are in the Allegheny County Medical Examiner's office. This is the morgue for the city of Pittsburgh and the surrounding area."

"Pittsburgh, huh? Never been."

"The 5 deceased people on display were murdered approximately 8 hours ago. The woman was a local prostitute with a lengthy criminal record, who was killed with a close-range gunshot wound to the face. The man with the deep laceration around his neck was a small-town drug dealer, also with a long criminal record. The other 3 men were from small towns that are less than an hour's drive from Pittsburgh. They all had minor criminal records. All 3 were shot twice in the centre of their torsos. Early investigation revealed that all the gunshot victims were heavily sedated at the time of being shot. One of them may have even been dead due to an overdose before the wound was inflicted. The toxicology report will not be ready for several days in the best-case scenario, but we can safely consider the early results as accurate."

"You didn't say how the neck wound victim died."

The German gave Falstaff a long, sneering glare before answering.

"The victim with the neck wound was choked to death. The choking device used was a wire garrote that cut into the upper layers of skin as he was strangled."

"Was that so hard? Just trying to be thorough."

"Do you have any other obvious questions?"

Falstaff turned his back to the German and walked between the corpse tables. He stopped at each to pay respects to the dead.

"Only this poor woman was from the city. The men were all from the country, right? They all had a history of run-ins with the law. I guess that they all had a drug of choice. What's the big thing out here? Probably oxy. It's big everywhere, now. So the killer wanted to execute the dudes, make an example of the dealer, and erase the woman's identity. Range of emotional commitment to the crimes. The woman's death is hateful. The dealer's death is rage-fueled. Don't know what the 3 guys did to deserve death. Maybe wrong place and time. My question is how does any of this relate to your fairy tale about the dark secrets of the big bad previous government?"

"This is the connection."

Muenster placed a 6-inch-long cylinder of metal and plastic onto the nearest table for Falstaff to examine.

The dull grey and green color of the tube was accented by a notice, written in raised block letters, warning that the contents within were dangerous and should not be administered by unauthorized personnel.

"It is an auto-injector designed for battlefield use for your U.S. Army. It delivers a generous dose of morphine. A dose large enough to incapacitate most individuals, so that they can be quickly and effectively evacuated from the site. The unofficial explanation for its existence is to lessen the suffering of the gravely injured soldiers, the "kiss of mercy". As with any of their valuable and dangerous supplies, the auto-injectors are kept under tight inventory control. Each serial number is recorded and tracked closely. And yet, the serial number of this unit does not exist in those records. Odd, is it not? The manufacturing date on the injector places it within a batch created 5 years ago for the Iraq and Afghanistan mission that your government is still caught up in. When we had the manifest for those injectors reviewed, we discovered a gap in the serial number record. 500 of these units have vanished from the records, as if they have never existed. And yet, here is one on the table. Would you like to wager that the needle has DNA traces that match one of our victims here? This is your first clue. The killer found these injectors and is using them to commit their crimes. 5 have been used. 495 potential victims. Is this enough motivation for you?"

"4" Falstaff replied as he leafed through the police reports.

"Excuse me?"

"The strangled man wasn't injected. That's what the first responder report said. But let me confirm."

He walked back to the strangled man and pulled up his right hand. Falstaff gingerly twisted the stiff wrist to show Muenster the deep cuts on the fingertips.

"See? He might have been doped up, recreationally speaking, but he was functional enough to fight back against the garrote by prying his fingers underneath it. Didn't help at all. The killer is pretty good at choking people to death. Good, and motivated."

The second ambulance attendant came back into the room and warned the German that the coroner's assistant was on their way down to begin processing the bodies. Muenster nodded curtly and told Falstaff to follow him. The disgruntled EMT moved to his side to help him walk, but Falstaff pushed him away and shambled forward under his own steam.

They slipped out through the tiled hallways in silence. Halfway down a hall Falstaff stumbled into the wall to keep from falling outright. The world went grey, then back to colour, and he kept moving. They made it outside to the back alley. The EMT and the second attendant scurried back into the private ambulance and sped off without another word.

"Not to complain or worry too much, but there's still a chance I could keel over. Maybe some ongoing medical attention would be in order? My heart did stop twice."

"3 times. You were legally dead for a few minutes during the flight. Over Minnesota, I believe the pilot said."

"Okay, I was dead in Minnesota. That's a first."

"And you will have continued medical care. Jakob?"

At the sound of his name, a massive mountain of a man opened the door of the drab grey sedan parked nearby and stepped out. He was at least a foot taller and wider than Falstaff. His hands looked like boulders hanging off his arms.

"He's a doctor?"

"He will be your medical caregiver and investigative assistant. I assure you that he is very well suited and trained for both."

Falstaff tried to take a step towards the hulking brute but could not force his trembling legs forward.

"Goddamn you're a big one. But not a doctor, according to that non-answer. A nurse, I guess. Well, Nurse, are you instructed to follow my orders?"

The German laughed loudly.

"Of course not. You have no authority anywhere. Who would put the bloodhound in charge? Now, off we go."

A flicker of movement from the big man sent Falstaff lurching sideways to escape his grasp. Falstaff fell against the passenger door of the sedan and fumbled it open. The big man gracefully slipped into the driver's seat and drove away from the darkened alley, leaving the German standing and smiling all alone in the half-light.

3

The fat right hand of the driver pushed Falstaff into his seat. The pressure was enough to aggravate the multiple bruises covering his chest and back, and push his broken rib grinding against itself. He sputtered in protest.

"What are you doing, meathands? Let me go."

The man spoke one word softly, "Seatbelt" and pushed even harder.

"Alright, alright. Back off the fucking muscle, okay? I'm mostly mushed up blood and guts right now. You'll pop something that I need to live."

Falstaff clicked the seatbelt in place and the arm restraining him retreated.

"You cannot be a real medical professional. I'm recovering from a vicious beating and 3 massive heart attacks and you're manhandling me like a rowdy drunk. I'm fucking delicate."

"You complain too much. I will ensure you are alive and functional."

"And pain-free? Can we aim for that lofty goal, Nurse?"

Nurse stared at the road ahead with a completely blank look on his face. Falstaff goaded him with the same question repeatedly. Finally fed up, Nurse mashed on the brake, sending Falstaff straining against the seatbelt. He groaned from the internal impact.

"Your comfort is not a priority."

Falstaff sulked against the door and looked out the window.

"You know what? You're a shitty nurse. The shittiest. Bet you got fired. If you even graduated nursing school. Worst nurse ever."

The muscle under Nurse's right eyelid twitched a single time. Falstaff noticed it and smirked. Nurse sucked saliva through his front teeth, filling the car with a disgusting squeak.

"Nervous habit, Nursie? Bet you suck on your teeth whenever you're irritated by something."

"I was a field medic. I am good at my job."

"Whatever you say, nurse. Where are we going now, huh?"

"Safehouse."

"That sounds exciting and clandestine. Hey, take the scenic route. Let's get a sense of the city."

"It is a city and you are trying to waste time."

Falstaff turned to study Nurse's face. The eye-twitch was gone, but now every muscle on his face was rigid. He was transitioning from irritated to angry. Falstaff didn't want to see him angry.

"Listen, I'm sorry for fooling around. But I have a legitimate reason for touring the city. The murder site is on the way, right? I'm guessing, anyway. We should see what that neighborhood is like, and what the area the hooker came from was like. The report here has an address for her. Big picture, the people with answers about this crime aren't 9-5 clerks and homemakers. I got to find the underbelly of the city and get to know the grubs and vultures that feed there. Context, man. I need city context. If I get a sense of the place, I can connect with the citizens and find some answers."

"Will you shut up for the rest of the drive?"

Falstaff smiled a crooked smile and slouched in his seat. "Deal. Ow. Fuck."

The streets rolled by outside the window, lit by the conflicting mix of dying streetlights and pre-dawn light. Each crumbling pothole they drove over shook Falstaff's wounds awake. The few people still walking the streets were a mix of the resilient and the lost: tired hookers, desperate junkies, hopeless hobos, and lurking low-ranking predators.

The neighborhood transitioned from the ugly fringe of the city to the discount tourist trap. Drunken stragglers wandered the sidewalk, thrown out of the closing bars to fend for themselves. A block further down the tourist element vanished. Here was a rough stretch, filled with pawnshops, cheque cashing bloodsuckers, and broken window storefronts. They pulled up to a red light, and Falstaff made eye contact with a dealer standing on the corner, looking for customers. Trying not to draw attention to himself, Falstaff searched his pockets for money or goods he could use to score. He came up empty. The light turned green and Falstaff sadly watched the dealer disappear.

Through the dark urban streetscape they drove, into the industrial warehouse district along the dirty bend of the river. They turned a corner and Nurse pointed down the block to a warehouse that looked identical to the ones on either side.

"There" he said. Falstaff looked at the warehouse and noticed the police officer leaning against the door. A pair of squad cars parked across the loading bay lit the area with their flashing lights.

"That's the murder scene,eh? The chances of anyone being around here to witness the murder are fucking low. There's no reason to be out here, unless you're breaking in to a warehouse to loot it."

Nurse drove past the crime scene and continued out of the district and into a rundown suburb. The car eventually came to a stop in the driveway of a grubby bungalow with pale yellow shutters and olive-green siding. The rest of the neighborhood was filled with similar single-family homes. The one unique house on the block was the house across the street from theirs. The front of the house was haphazardly lit by patio lanterns and Christmas lights cluttered along the porch roofline. Falstaff stepped out of the car and heard music floating across from the lit-up house. Nurse walked up to the front door and unlocked it while keeping an eye on Falstaff.

"Relax. I'm coming."

Falstaff slowly walked his battered body up the driveway and into the house. As soon as he had crossed the threshold, Nurse closed the door and locked it shut. Falstaff stood under the glare of the white light filling the hallway and took in his surroundings.

The first thing he noticed was the awful collection of odors rising from his body. The stench of drying puke was crusting into the torn remains of his shirt held together with safety pins. Sweat and blood coated his upper body. He was pretty sure he had pissed himself at least once during the desert event and ambulance adventure. He looked around the room for a sign of where he could get cleaned up and proceeded to wander aimlessly down the hallway headed off to the right. Nurse stepped to intercept him.

"First door on right, bathroom. Across from it, your room. Second bedroom, off limits. Clear?"

"Jesus Christ why did you not tell me how bad I smelled? We were in that car together for what, an hour, and you didn't say a single fucking thing."

Nurse refused to respond. Falstaff marched slowly down the hall and into the bathroom, leaning against the thin hallway walls for support.

In the bathroom, Falstaff leaned heavily on the cheap laminate vanity and stared at his reflection in the mirror. He took stock of the network of bruises and contusions covering his face and neck, wondering how many additional scrapes he had brought upon himself while writhing around on the desert floor.

Falstaff gingerly stripped off his jacket and tattered shirt but stopped halfway through when he heard an out of place noise. He dug through all his pockets again with frantic intensity and was rewarded with the sound of plastic crinkling. In a pocket-within-a-pocket of his cheap nylon jacket was a dimebag with a little bit of powder left in it. He wasn't sure what the powder was, but that wasn't important. He tossed the jacket and his filthy shirt into the corner of the tiny bathroom. Falstaff lined up the last of the dope and snorted it off the toilet tank top. To polish it off, he licked the bag clean.

As he waited for the effect to kick in he looked over his other few possessions. The ID badge looked official enough to work. He wondered if there were digital records to match his paper ID, or if he would get thrown in jail if someone tried to verify his job. The business cards made him laugh and mutter to himself.

"Why the fuck would you give me business cards but not a phone?"

There was a phone number on the card, and fax number as well, but Falstaff had no idea who would be on the other end of the phone.

The drugs took effect and smoothed out his jagged edges. It wouldn't last long, he could tell, but it would see him comfortably through the next little bit. He walked out of the bathroom, projecting an air of confidence to mask the signs of intoxication. Falstaff marched to the front door and started trying to open the locks. Nurse asked him to explain what he was doing.

"Gonna go see the neighbors, get the lay of the land."

"You are not wearing a shirt and you still smell like a pile of garbage. Do you know that?"

Falstaff looked down involuntarily and cursed under his breath.

"You go nowhere. Go to bed."

Feeling brave and stupid, Falstaff puffed himself up and stood toe to toe with Nurse.

"Or what?"

Falstaff had never been picked up by top of his head before. Nurse had him dangling off the ground before Falstaff could react, his meaty paws clamped on either side of Falstaff's skull. In a flash Falstaff's face was pressed against the stucco covered wall. The force that Nurse exerted so effortlessly mashed Falstaff's face into the ridges of plaster. He tried to shout for help, but only managed a weak mewling sound. The pressure intensified. Falstaff saw flashes of light behind his eyelids and started to go limp. He found his voice and pleaded to be let go, with promises of complete obedience. Nurse lowered him back to his feet and let go. He locked eyes with Falstaff to make sure the message had been clearly received. Falstaff's quivering look of terror say it was. Nurse looked satisfied by the newly negotiated relationship dynamic. He nodded his head and unlocked the front door.

"Put on a shirt, then go say hello. Stay on porch."

Falstaff scuffed his foot across the ground. "My shirt is too dirty" he said in a meek voice.

"Go into your room. There are clothes."

Following the instructions, Falstaff slinked into the tiny bedroom across from the bathroom. The ugly pink and blue children's wallpaper was peeling off the wall at the corners and the seams, revealing a second uglier layer of paper underneath. The squat window on the wall across from the single bed was crusted with multiple layers of paint. The marks in the painted frame indicated that the window could, at best, open a few inches.

The closet door had been removed. Stacked on the shelves of the closet were clothes. 3 dress shirts, grey. 3 pairs of slacks, dark grey. 3 polo shirts, grey with white stripes. 2 ties, dark blue. 5 pairs of cheap black dress socks, and 5 pairs of generic white briefs. Falstaff looked at the pile of nondescript clothing and wondered if Nurse was colorblind.

"Or maybe I'm turning into a black and white cartoon character."

He stripped out of his ruined pants and underwear and put on a new set of clothes. The sight of the clean, pressed cuffs of his slacks hovering above his torn-up running shoes made him laugh.

He walked out to the front door where Nurse was waiting for him. They walked outside, and Nurse took up a comfortable spot leaning against the porch railing where he had a clear view of the house across the street.

Falstaff shambled across the narrow road and knocked on the party house's door. A shouted response from inside told Falstaff to wait a minute, followed by some unintelligible chatter between the occupants inside.

The door opened and a rail-thin man in a plush track suit and safari hat stepped into the doorway. He looked at Falstaff with suspicion.

"Hey man, this is the wrong place. Everything's fine here. Just heading to bed."

"Jesus, I look like a narc, don't I? Sorry pal. Clothes aren't my choice. I am not one of them. I'm living across the street for a while. This place looked festive, like there's a party going on."

"Not a party, just living life, you know?"

"My name's John. Nice to meet you."

The tall thin man shook Falstaff's outstretched hand.

"JJ. Likewise."

Falstaff shot a look over his shoulder at Nurse, hoping that he was not paying attention. He still had him locked in his vision.

"Hey JJ, can you help me out? I left some stuff behind when I left for my trip here. I really need to resupply."

"Supplies? No idea what that's all about, dude."

Falstaff sighed. "I am not now, nor am I ever going to be, a cop. I am more afraid of any police interaction than you ever could be. I get caught by the cops and a whole mountain of trouble comes sliding down on me and some other poor fuckers who don't deserve it. Some do deserve it and more, but that is a whole different story. What I am trying to impress upon you is that I am just a guy looking to get high. I need supplies."

JJ mulled over the blunt confession and came to a decision.

"I like your style, man. Straight forward. Living your truth, you know? Oh yeah, I get that. And we all need our comforts. What's the stuff you're looking for? What comforts you?"

"Bunch of things. Vicodin, for starters."

JJ scratched at his erratically shaved scalp and inspected Falstaff.

"Yeah, I think you're on the level. I can help you out."

"Great."

"$5 a pop. Can get you up to 20. What else you need?"

Falstaff's mouth filled involuntarily with saliva at the prospect of scoring. His hand went for his wallet and came up empty. He groaned.

"Ah shit. I am flat broke. Sorry man. Hold on. Oh, do you handle any of the heavier opioids? Oxy? Morphine? Maybe a morphine auto-injector?"

"What the fuck, dude? That is some spaced out shit. Dial it back, yo."

"Sorry. Just curious about the other stuff. Heard some news report about high-grade morphine being sneaked out to the streets. I'll be right back."

Falstaff shambled back across the street at a reckless wobbling pace and stood in front of Nurse.

"I need some cash. That guy might have some information for us, but he has to get paid."

"No."

"Come on. A per diem, or a pay day advance. I do get a paycheck? I should have asked the Kraut about that before. I have expenses."

Nurse waited until Falstaff's begging ran out of steam, and then slowly shook his head one more time while crooking a thumb back towards the door. Knowing that he was beat, Falstaff turned around and offered an embarrassed smile and shrug to JJ across the street. JJ replied by flashing the peace sign and going back inside. Defeated and exhausted, Falstaff turned and walked back into the squat bungalow that was his temporary home.

The clatter and clacking of the locks being shut again made the house sound like a jail cell. As Falstaff slouched to his room, Nurse called after him.

"In 6 hours we will get access to the crime scene. Go rest. Drink some water before you sleep."

"I'll do what I want, you heavy-handed goon. Leave me the fuck alone until then."

Falstaff stormed off down the hallway, running completely out of steam once he entered his room. He dropped onto the bed and yanked off his drab clothes, yelping occasionally from his assortment of wounds. In the dark he stared at the ceiling, probing his bruises and aches with the tips of his fingers, until an uneasy sleep crept over him.

4

"Get up."

The sudden noise woke Falstaff out of a frustrating dream of chasing after a stray dog. He opened his eyes to the alarming sight of Nurse's face an inch away from his, shadowed from the indirect light coming in from the hallway in to the dark room. The shock made him let out a terrified little scream. He clawed at the face reflexively, but Nurse easily leaned away from the flailing attack.

"GODDAMN IT. Don't fuck with me like that. Your ugly mug is nothing to wake up to" he rasped as his heart hammered away in his chest.

"It was a reflex test."

The look on Nurse's face and the smile playing at the corners of his mouth plainly said otherwise. Falstaff untangled himself from the thin bedspread and stood up, naked as the day he was born.

"Unless you have good reason to stand there and watch me with my dick hanging out, kindly get the fuck out while I get dressed."

Nurse ignored the order and turned on the light. Shivering in the cool room, Falstaff stood as Nurse checked his vital signs and inspected his wounds. Satisfied that his patient was in no immediate danger, he taped up Falstaff's ribcage for protective support of his broken rib, and ordered him to get showered and dressed for the day. He walked out before Falstaff had a chance to respond.

The heat of the shower brought some relief to Falstaff's aches and pains but couldn't mask the more serious wounds to his torso. Falstaff moved with deliberate care, because any sudden rash jolt made his ribs scream again. He was glad that at least the stench of last night's misadventures was now washed away and gone. He let the water run and thought about the unbelievable events he had just gone through. He had been certain that he'd wake up back in the desert, having hallucinated the whole experience. The other alternative was that he was deep in a coma and amusing himself with this twisted detective fantasy.

After getting out of the shower and drying off, he threw on another set of the baggy, ill-fitting clothes, crammed the badge and the cards into his pockets, and went out to the kitchen. Nurse looked at him and said "good. We go." With a firm grip on Falstaff's elbow, Nurse steered them through the front door. He locked the door, marched Falstaff into the passenger seat of the car, and drove.

"I feel like shit" Falstaff said as the car turned the corner. "I haven't eaten in, Jesus, 12 hours or more, during which time I died. Several times. I am in agony and all of my pain meds have worn off."

"No more drugs."

"The pain is impeding my functionality, but if you don't give a shit about stopping the killer, then fuck it. I'm also as thirsty as fuck."

"Back seat, floor."

Falstaff stared at Nurse as he drove, trying to decipher the incomprehensible statement. His mouth moved wordlessly as he failed to put the pieces together. Nurse reached back behind the seat and brought back a plastic grocery bag. He placed the bag in Falstaff's lap. Inside the bag was a lunch kit packed with a meal suitable for a senior shut-in, or a middle school kid.

"A kid's meal. Delicious. And not even a cup of cold coffee to go with it. Christ."

He joylessly chewed on the soggy egg salad sandwich. Each bite sat as a gooey lump in his mouth until he washed it down with warm apple juice. He continued to the carrot sticks and apple slices. He dug around the kit for a hidden bit of more appetizing food but found nothing. He sighed and watched the streets outside pass by.

To drown out the sound of Falstaff's intermittent sighing and moaning, Nurse tuned the radio to an AM talk station. The news update spoke in low ominous tones of a grisly murder of a young man outside of town, a bright promising life cut short in a horrendous and shocking attack.

"Bodies piling up everywhere. What a miserable state this is" Falstaff commented as the update ended and a barrage of low quality ads took its place. Nurse kept driving.

They avoided the tourist traps and morning traffic and arrived at the scene of the crime. In the light of day, the menacing rough streets of Pittsburgh were just dirty and pathetic. There were police cars and forensic vans parked at the warehouse, though the activity on the street was close to non-existent, and the door guard looked bored out of his mind. They parked halfway down the block and watched the building. Falstaff rolled down his window so that he could suck in the cold morning air and clear his perpetually foggy head.

Shortly after their arrival, a host of uniformed officers and plains clothes employees with laminated badges clipped to their jackets came out of the building. They made their way to their vehicles and drove off. "Shift change" Nurse said as he pulled himself out of the car.

Falstaff closed his eyes and moaned loudly about the brightness of the light and the intensity of his injuries. Once again, he demanded pain management. Nurse leaned through the rolled down car window and put his thick thumb onto Falstaff's left eyelid. He roughly pushed the eyelid up and looked at Falstaff's pupils. His other hand went to Falstaff's throat. The sensation of the giant hand clamping around his throat made Falstaff panic. He braced himself for the tightening grip becoming a chokehold. Instead, Nurse curled back his ring and pinkie finger, and pressed gently on the side of Falstaff's neck with his index and middle fingers to take his pulse.

"You're fine. No meds. Come."

Falstaff begrudgingly opened his door and slithered out of the car. "If I keel over and pass out because you were too much of a sadistic asshole to give me aspirin, don't blame me when they arrest us for fucking with a crime scene." He punctuated his sentence by slamming the car door closed and stomping down the street towards the warehouse.

At the perimeter of the property, Nurse caught up with him. He grabbed Falstaff's elbow and dug his thumb into the crook to press on the nerves running underneath. The pain was quick and intense.

"Pain is subjective and comparative. I could continue to offer an alternative stimulus for you to contrast."

Nurse let go and the pain faded. Falstaff muttered "you're such an asshole" and held his arm close to his body to protect it. At the door, he launched into a story about his asshole boss demanding he inspect the crime scene while waving his ID at the cop guarding the door.

"It's not even my day to go do fieldwork, but he's all fucking mad that his life sucks, so here I am. And yeah, that's the boss right there. He can't fire me 'cause HR will shit down his neck for losing a 3rd staffer in 2 months. I'm the only one who can stand him. Do I gotta sign in or some shit?"

The guard looked past Falstaff and addressed Nurse directly.

"Is this your monkey?"

The bored guard put his hand square in the middle of Falstaff's chest, holding him back from entering the building. Falstaff hid his wincing reaction to the pressure on his bruised torso. Nurse stood in front of the guard and presented his ID.

"Yes, he works for me."

"Do you always let 'em talk to you like that? He's pretty uppity."

"It's nothing. Harmless. He is mostly useful. Except when he stands around doing nothing. Get inside."

The push on his back from Nurse propelled Falstaff into the guard's arm. The guard pulled his hand away suddenly, and Falstaff stumbled forward to the sound of the guard's laughter.

"Hey boss, I'll start at the back" he said is his most subservient voice, wishing for a sudden violent death to befall the dimwit guard. Falstaff hurried inside before he opened his mouth again and started trouble he couldn't finish.

The warehouse was lit by rows of filthy overhead florescent lights. The dirt tinted the blue white light with streaks of yellow and rust. The layer of dirt was a thematic motif for every surface in the massive room. Off to the left, there was a cinderblock wall with a door and a small grimy window. Farther back on the right side, another cinderblock division created a small washroom. The main area of the floor was littered with a dozen pallets of varying heights. Most of the floor space was vacant. A couple of cheap metal desks were pressed up against the back wall, and a third desk was oddly positioned a few feet away from the others towards the center of the room. In the center of the room was a rough circle of empty floor that was now annotated with evidence tags, body markers, and blood.

Throughout the room were forensic technicians and a few cops in ill-fitting suits. Falstaff steered clear of the center of the murder scene and crept along the edge of the room until he reached the desks at the back. A sleepy-eyed technician with a paunch stood at the edge of the askew desk, browsing his smartphone. Falstaff gave the other end of the desk a small kick. The startled tech looked up from his phone and immediately pulled it up to his face, pretending to take a photo.

"Hey, sorry. Didn't mean to disturb you. Just trying to get out of the way, you know? Things are tense."

Relief broke across the tech's face. He lowered the phone and leaned back against the desk.

"No worries."

"It's all bullshit anyway. I got to come down here and sniff around for a sign of misplaced federal goods, which I know for goddamned sure I'm not going to find. Waste of time."

The tech sighed. "That's what I said. Just a bunch of dead junkies. Probably a drug deal gone bad, and some angry Mexican beaner shot the white trash dealers dead. Case closed. They'll never find the killer, so why should I bust my ass gathering evidence for a trial that won't happen?"

Falstaff made a half-turn away from the tech, to look at the space surrounding him. The first notable thing he found were binders on the short steel shelf bolted to the concrete at eye level to the left and rear of the lazy tech. The binders on each end were dust-covered, but the middle two were streaked with smudges from being recently handled.

"So, I got to ask, have you seen any strange packages or items, particularly any with a marking that indicates it is property of the U.S. Government?"

The slovenly tech picked at the scabbed swollen skin under his jaw, milking pus out of the ingrown hair pustule as he pondered the question. Falstaff noticed a square corner of transparent plastic sticking out from between the recently moved binders. The plastic was irregularly cloudy, as if there was a film of off-white material coating it in patches. He kept his eyes locked on that promising piece of plastic as the tech answered him.

"I haven't seen anything like that. They told us to focus on the bodies, get the basics done, then pack up. I'm doing a perimeter sweep for any incidental evidence."

"Must be nice to get clear instructions. I get my boss yelling at me to get in the car and look for out of the ordinary things at a crime scene. First time being at a murder scene. What the fuck am I supposed to know about what is out of the ordinary? Don't even know the details of the crime. Just a bunch of murders."

"Druggies. One choked to death, others shot. There's blood all around the bodies, like you would expect. Most of the victims came from the sticks. Except for the whore. She was a local, I heard."

Falstaff watched the repulsive tech wipe pus onto his pant leg and saw in his face the truth about him and the dead prostitute. The tech was frequent client of local sex workers, maybe even the one whose death he was now barely investigating. Falstaff wondered if he could be more involved in the crime than simply gathering the evidence afterwards.

"Who drives into the city to get killed in a drug deal?"

The tech shrugged. "Hillbillies fucked up on oxy are unpredictable. We find them all over the place."

"Beside dead sex workers? It's strange. Did you find any drugs?"

Falstaff bit his lip, disappointed with the eagerness in his voice. He hoped that the tech didn't catch it.

"I found some trace on the desk here."

"What kind of stuff? Any more of it tucked away somewhere?"

The last question caught the tech's full attention and he turned to inspect Falstaff and his ID badge. The tech stayed between Falstaff and the shelf, cutting off his access to the plastic baggie.

"I don't have any information on unsecured drugs at this site. Its policy to strictly control and log any narcotics and other street drugs. I need to finish my work here, so follow me to the site supervisor who can officially answer any other questions that you have."

The tech had taken a defensive stance, pulling his arms close to his body and turning his face to hide it from his opponent, all while stepping back from Falstaff. He pointed angrily towards the woman in a set of white, disposable forensic coveralls. Falstaff looked over at the site supervisor, then back at the agitated tech.

"Thanks, I'll go right over. You've been real helpful. I'll put in a good word."

Falstaff smiled as widely as he could and hurried away from the suspicious tech. He didn't know if the tech was hostile to anyone he suspected of seeking drugs, or if he had been caught 'misplacing' drug evidence in the past and believed that Falstaff was an Internal Affairs spy trying to trick him into doing it again. Either way, the tech was now useless to him.

The eyes of the other investigators followed Falstaff on his walk across the warehouse. He cursed under his breath. The next step after being noticed is being questioned, and he knew their cover story would fall to pieces under scrutiny.

"Or maybe not" he muttered. "I have no fucking clue on how connected that fucking German is."

Pretending that he had just remembered a vital detail, Falstaff redirected himself towards Nurse and sidled up to him with projected "hey boss, I forgot to tell you" to explain his actions to the growing audience watching him. He dropped his voice and spoke quickly to Nurse.

"We're out of time. They're getting suspicious. If they check into our ID, are we going to come back clean? How solid are they? I don't want to get shit-kicked and thrown in jail."

Nurse looked around the room without a flicker of concern or emotion on his face. He nodded to Falstaff.

"We should go."

Falstaff made a production of rolling his eyes and exhaling up into the air in feigned frustration. "Yes, sir, right away" he said loudly as he marched out of the room. He didn't stop until he reached the car, with Nurse a single stride behind him. The site supervisor was just appearing in the doorway of the warehouse when Nurse sat down in the driver's seat.

"Pretend you're chewing me out."

"Pardon? Chewing?"

"You have no idiom knowledge. Interesting. Couldn't be more obvious that you're not an Anglo. Talk to me sternly, like a manager addressing a poorly preforming employee. Make it look like you're angry at me, you wall of idiot flesh."

Nurse narrowed his eyes and leaned menacingly over Falstaff.

"I do not care for insults."

"Hey hey, dial it back. That means, 'be less goddamn terrifying, not like you're about to beat and rape me for disobedience'. You're a real piece of work. The supervisor is watching us, and if she gets any more suspicious, she'll dig down into that massive plastic jumpsuit and pull out a radio. Or a gun. "

The car creaked as Nurse leaned back to his side. He pulled out a clipboard full of papers and pointed to it repeatedly.

"Is this better? I do not change my earlier statement. I do not care for insults."

"And I don't like being scared and confused and totally out of options, but here we are. But fine, I'll stop taking cheap shots at you. It's hard, because you keep hurting me. You should try hurting people less. I bet that will cut down on the verbal abuse you suffer, you poor delicate snowflake."

"Snowflake?"

"Never mind. She went back inside. Good enough."

Falstaff studied the front of the warehouse and the streetscape on either side. Movement in the shadows between the warehouse and the self-storage place beside it caught his eye.

"We go now?"

"Hold on. I want to check something out. Keep an eye on me."

At a controlled and deliberate pace, Falstaff opened the car door, got out, and walked casually towards the alley. The shadowy figure moved forward into the half-light, then drew back again into the full darkness. Falstaff stopped 10 feet away from them and said hello. The young woman moved forward and replied.

"Uh hi. Are you from the police?"

Falstaff looked at the young woman nervously shifting her weight from foot to foot. She had bright pink lipstick that became luminous when the street light caught it fully. The small black box in her right hand looked like a mid-level video camera, and her left hand had a small notepad in it.

"No, no cop. I am affiliated with the investigation, but I can't explain. Security reasons, you know? But I'd like to help you, if you need help, that is. John Falstaff, systems analyst."

"Hi, hi. I'm Amanda Viros. Reporter for SmizNews. And videographer. And photographer too. Now."

"First day?"

Amanda's shoulders drooped in relief. The high-wire tension of trying to look professional doing a job you've never done before had made her a nervous wreck, and that conflict had been easy to read on her face.

"Yeah. This is my first call on my first day as an actual reporter."

"What have you heard so far?"

Amanda scuffed the ground and looked away. "Um, nothing. I haven't gone to the door yet. The cops are intimidating."

"They'll probably tell you to leave the area and not to interfere. That might be for the best."

"No! I have to cover this story. You were just in there. Tell me what you saw."

"No Comment."

"Oh come on! COME ON! Give me something!"

Falstaff laughed at the reporter's desperation.

"Here's a tip for you-try not yelling at people you want to get inside information from."

"Sorry. Sorry. Shit. Sorry."

"You're barely out of high school. This is a dangerous neighborhood for anyone, especially young women."

Amanda reached for the satchel purse hanging on her right hip and tried unsuccessfully to retrieve an object from inside of it without letting go of the camera.

"I'm fine. I have pepper spray."

"Theoretically. Does it automatically pop out and spray the villain if your hands are full, like they are right now?"

Amanda looked up suddenly and glared at Falstaff. She dropped the notepad and whipped out the can of Pepper spray, pointing it directly at his eyes. He threw his hands up in surrender.

"Whoa there! I'm not threatening you, ma'am. Please lower the weapon. It is a crime to threaten a federal employee."

She lowered the can to chest level but kept her shooting stance. Amanda looked down the street at the cars pulling into the warehouse, and the scattered police personnel making their way in to the building.

"Is that really a crime? Sounds like bullshit."

Falstaff smiled and shrugged. "Might be, but probably not."

"Okay, let's back this up a bit. You take a step backwards, and I'll put away the spray. After that, I'll ask you a couple of questions and then I'll leave the area."

The détente came into effect. Falstaff lowered his hands.

"I really can't say anything to you ma'am. This is an official police investigation and there's a lot of scrutiny being placed on every investigator."

"You're not a cop, though."

"But the folks going in and out of the building there, are cops. And they are watching the surroundings closely. There is considerable pressure from above to follow procedure to the letter. So I say again, no comment. Please move along, ma'am."

"Pressure from the top? The police chief? The mayor? How high? You're federal, so is the FBI involved? Is this a terrorist event?"

"I cannot comment at all. This is a secure location. No media is allowed, and I cannot answer any media questions here."

The hint landed clean. "Here? Okay. How about we meet later, some place close. I have other questions, about…other subjects. I'll buy the drinks; you tell me what it's like to be a federal employee."

Falstaff made a great display of being conflicted. He sighed and rubbed his face like a man facing a dilemma. He made a few false start responses before giving in.

"Fine. Confidential. Off-the-Record, nothing about this investigation. When and where?"

Her face lit up and her voice jumped up in pitch from the excitement. "Right now! We can walk over together to some coffee shop nearby."

"You don't get how meeting in secret works, do you? First rule is don't go for a stroll together in front of the people you're trying to avoid."

"Right. Okay. Sorry."

"And I have to go file a report before I do anything else. Let's meet at happy hour."

"Great! Um…when is that?"

"5PM, most places. Christ you're green."

"Okay, 5. See you there!"

Amanda spun on her heel and started walking away quickly. Falstaff cleared his throat to get her attention.

"And where is there, exactly?"

She stopped dead in her tracks and shipped back around. "What?"

"You didn't pick a place. We're not meeting back here. No drink service, and the ambiance is shit."

Amanda flicked her phone screen with her thumb and expertly tapped in a google search. She frowned at the results."

"There aren't any coffee shops in the area. Weird."

"It's industrial storage. Not many people working during the day. And I thought we were getting a drink, not a coffee."

"What do you mean? Coffee is a drink. Oh, I get it. The map says there's a bar 3 blocks away, at the corner of Second and Elizabeth. Okay? Do you need directions?"

"I can manage. See you at 5."

Amanda smiled and practically skipped away down the alley, into the darkness. Falstaff licked his lips in anticipatory thirst as he walked back to the car and his minder.

"Get your wallet warmed up, Nursie. We're going drinking for information."

5

Five o'clock finally came. The car was parked across the street from the cheap Irish-themed bar on the corner of Second Avenue and Elizabeth street, "Paddy O's Pub". The windows of the faux-pub were blocked with painted plywood, except for a narrow foot strip at the top of each to allow a prisoner's allotment of weak sunshine and muggy river air. The square window in the door had a wire cage screwed over it, even though the glass behind it had been replaced with a block of wood sometime in the past. No one had arrived at the bar during the half-hour Falstaff and Nurse had spent waiting, so the sight of a couple of new arrivals made Falstaff sit up in rapt attention.

The first new arrival was a broken old man with a limp and a stack of worn notebooks and loose papers tucked under his arm. Falstaff anointed the man with a new name.

"That one is Fucking Hemingway. Scribbles what he hopes to god are profound revelations in those ratty dollar store notebooks, and pens rambling opinion letters to the local paper when the creative urge isn't biting. Also drinks like a fish. He walks with a limp from an accident, but he's overselling the severity. His income depends on being a permanent cripple. Result of a lawsuit."

Nurse squinted through the windshield at the hobbling man stepping through the doorway.

"How do you know all of that? It is impossible."

"The human body gives off a symphony of hidden messages and clues. I hear the music, my good man."

Nurse turned his squinting gaze to Falstaff and studied his face. Falstaff held out for half a minute before laughing out loud.

"Fuck, no I don't know that stuff for sure. Made it up. Some of it is likely to be true. He drinks enough that he's at the bar right before happy hour starts. He needs to maximize his drink-buying dollar. He has a limp, and that part about overselling it is a fact. When his concentration slips, which was every 3rd step, the limp almost disappears. Then his conscious mind jumps back in and corrects it back. I have no idea what he writes in those notebooks, but they must be important, or he would have left them at home instead of bringing them to this piss-pot. The complaint letter writing bit was pure speculation. He looks like the kind of dude who would crap all over everything."

As the door closed on Hemingway, a second new arrival popped around the corner. He stood at the door with his head swiveling around, attempting to see the entire intersection and down the block in all four directions. He was dressed in a pair of cheap, brown slacks worn shiny at the knees. The yellowing collar of his cheap dress shirt poked out of the nylon jacket emblazoned with the logo of a now defunct minor league baseball team. His thin hair was full of hair gel and combed back to try, in vain, to hide the bald spot on top. His right hand darted down to his crotch to brush the small bulge pressing out from under his paunch, then darted back up to his hair to press it into place.

"Now that is a man looking to sin. Look at the sweaty brow, the hand sent trembling by pulsing forbidden desire. Do we have a genuine Humbert, here at his local tavern to drink down the courage to abduct his Lolita? He's terrified of being caught, but too aroused to stop. He's hoping that he can drink the lust away. He knows that isn't going to happen. This is his threshold moment, by the way. He could just run back home. Or he can give in and open that door."

The sweaty man wiped his mouth repeatedly with the back of his hand, and then he pulled the door open and disappeared inside.

"Guess the decision has been made. Do you have a cop buddy in town? You should call him. That guy is going to break the law tonight, I guarantee it."

Falstaff was playing up the illegal angle in an attempt to make Nurse squirm. He was disappointed by the lack of reaction from the big man. Nurse checked his watch and pulled the door handle open.

"That is not our concern. Only the murder is. It is time."

Falstaff slowly got out of the car after Nurse, gingerly stretching the stiffness of sitting out of his joints. Nurse went to cross the street but stopped when he saw Falstaff was not following.

"I'm just saying that your boss laid a guilt trip on me about the future victims that would be on my conscience, so its hypocritical if you let this dude molest a little girl or whatever fucked up thing he's going to do."

This time he got the reaction he was looking for. Nurse turned back and walked up to Falstaff, standing nose to nose with him. He had to crouch to remove their height difference.

"Calling the police would be problematic. The man, you say he will break the law, but you have no proof. We will spend hours waiting and arguing with a police officer who will think we are full of nonsense."

"But think of the victims" Falstaff whined, and Nurse snarled at him in response.

"This is more of your guessing, is it not? Speculation. Bullshit. You make it all up."

"Me? Make it up? Never. Or maybe I did just invent it all to fuck with you. Life is complicated. Come on."

Falstaff slipped around Nurse and jogged across the street, laughing to himself while wincing at his ever-present soreness. He walked through the door and soaked up the decrepit atmosphere. The shiny paper party sign hung over the bar was missing letters, so it now announced "Happy S. add day". The fake wood panelling was smoke-stained and pitted with gouges and unidentified smeared fluids at random intervals.

Along the east side of the pub were 3 booths with dull black tables and cracked black vinyl seats. In the center of the room were a scattered collection of tables and chairs, not more than 3 chairs at a table. The bar itself had a dozen rickety stools lined up around its corner. The two men they had watched come in to the bar were perched on stools at either end. In addition to the potential molester and the failed writer were 3 other patrons keeping their heads low and trying to wait out the last few minutes until happy hour started. Nurse stepped though the door and Falstaff pulled him to the side. He pointed to the room with a sweep and welcomed Nurse to the fine Irish experience that was laid out in front of them.

"And before we go any further, I'm going to need some cash. To get some answers from the reporter and the people here, I have to get them relaxed."

"What do these degenerates know?"

Falstaff shrugged. "I don't know yet. Probably nothing of value. But the barfly lifestyle has a certain arrangement of contacts that come with it. These 'degenerates' have friends, as much as the damned can. They know other folks caught on the wrong side of success, like sex workers and dealers. Remind me, what were the occupations of the victims? Exactly. But they ain't gonna say a word for free. Get them liquored up and they might. So, give me some money."

"I will pay the bill when we leave."

"You have never been in a dive like this, have you? No bills, no tabs. Pay up front for every drink. Someday, tell me about the bubble you grew up in."

Nurse sighed and pulled out a roll of cash from a pocket, and Falstaff's eyes went wide. He moved in front of Nurse to hide the money. Nurse pulled a bill off the roll and handed it over.

"Jesus fucking Christ Nursie, you know shit about shit. A thousand-dollar bill?" he hissed. "Do you want to get thrown the fuck out of here, because trying to break a thousand is a great way to announce that we are either stupid rich or stupid counterfeiters. Try again."

The thousand-dollar bill was replaced by a small stack of 20s, which Falstaff snatched away and shoved down in a pocket.

"That's better. Now go sit at the bar and order your own drink. I'll sit at that booth there and wait for the reporter. You'll be able to hear everything we say, I promise."

He met Nurse's distrustful scowl with a wide smile full of sunshine and innocence. They locked eyes until Nurse relented and walked over to his assigned spot.

Falstaff triumphantly waved for service. From behind a newspaper and through a cloud of cigarette smoke, the waitress rose and approached. The stench of the nicotine fog clung to her and filled the air at the table. Falstaff spoke quickly to her, ordering 3 shots of vodka, a triple gin and tonic, and a pitcher of water. She stood unmoved by his requests. He reached into his pocket and pulled out the stack of 20s to peel off 3 of them.

"And a round for my new friends in the bar, how about?" Falstaff said in a voice loud enough to carry through the dim room. The waitress snatched the money from his hand and walked back to the bar. When the regulars saw her accept the payment, a ragged cheer rose up from their ranks as the promise of a free drink came closer to becoming reality. The drinks arrived at their grateful recipients and Falstaff raised his first shot to the room.

"Enjoy, fellas. Time is short, as always."

Each shot disappeared down Falstaff's greedy gullet in quick succession. His stomach rolled in response to the flood of cheap booze hitting it, and he tried to remember when he last ate a good meal. Only the grim vision of the soggy egg salad sandwich came to mind. He decided that he did not care to lose precious booze, and he pushed down his nausea. The rolling settled down as he kept his eyes closed and waited for the arrival of the glow.

The glow wasn't the full relief, but it was a start. The warmth of the glow crept outwards from the pit of his stomach. It relaxed the hidden fear, sadness and tension hidden in every part of his body. When it reached his face, Falstaff opened his eyes and smiled at a world much easier to handle.

As he sipped the gin and tonic, Falstaff watched the door slowly open to admit the reporter. She stopped at the doorstep with wide eyes studying the interior of the bar. This was an entirely new experience for her. He body language screamed 'fright' and the urge to run back out the door was tensing her muscles.

Falstaff waved and shouted hello to her. The sound broke her paralysis. Amanda walked over to the booth with purposeful steps, studying the room without making eye contact with anyone inside of it.

"Hey Amanda, hi. Sit down. It looks worse than it is. I'll get the waitress."

Amanda sat down without taking her eyes off the bar and the patrons at it. The bartender and the patrons snuck return sidewise glances that were full of curiosity and desperate loneliness. Amanda shook her head.

"No, no thanks, I'll just have a glass of water."

"Suit yourself. Cheers" Falstaff said as he raised up his glass and held it there for a moment. Amanda ignored his salute. The glass finished its trip up to his lips and Falstaff drained half of it in one continuous sip. The burning sensation down his throat was purifying. He sighed in contentment. Amanda gave up on finding something comforting at the bar and turned her gaze downwards to stare at the table.

They sat in silence for 5 minutes. Falstaff traced elliptical patterns in the condensation left by the drinks on the table, sipping his drink at the completion of every orbit around the stationary glass, pitcher and ashtray. He transitioned to chewing the ice cubes when the drink ran out.

"So, do we sit here in silent splendor, or did you mean to accomplish more than quiet reflection? Also, have a drink. You'll feel better. I'm getting another one, if that helps you. It helps me."

Falstaff laughed at his own words. The booze was loosening him up nicely. Amanda bit her lip and found her bearings. The waitress slouched up to the side of their table and Falstaff began to order when Amanda announced loudly that she would have a rum and coke. Falstaff nodded at her choice and added his order of another round of 3x G&T and a round for the house. Again, he had to give the waitress the money to get her moving.

"That's generous. Do you know the people here?"

"We're all friends, in a cosmic sense. In a more direct sense, I don't know a soul."

"Are you drunk?"

"Not yet, but the night is early."

"Tell me about the investigation."

Falstaff snorted in amusement. "Easy girl. Got to be more casual than that, not just grab for the gold ring right away. Small talk, build a rapport, then go for the big score."

The waitress returned with their drinks, followed close behind by one of the greasy barflies with a drink in his hand. He was a short thin man with a patchy beard and an obvious piss mark at the crotch of his dirty light blue jeans. His long greasy hair was pulled back into a ponytail, tied with a rubber band. He mumbled 'thanks for the drinks' to Falstaff and turned his full attention to Amanda. Greasy went to lower himself into the narrow space beside the reporter, chuckling 'hey hey' repeatedly as an opening mating call gambit. Falstaff shot his arm out straight to block Greasy and snapped his fingers in front of Greasy's eyes to get his attention. Greasy stepped back, surprised and alarmed by the sudden sound and motion.

"Fuck off Pisspants. She's leaving alone, you shit-streaked wannabe rapist. And you are going to fuck your hand at home."

The rapist accusation hit home and scared Greasy into running out of the bar, with his drink still in hand.

Falstaff leaned back into his seat and the snarling aggression vanished from his face, replaced by the easy look of a man at the start of a good bender. Amanda was angry.

"I could have handled him on my own. The foul mouth white knight routine is sexist."

"No doubt you could. But, I didn't want to waste time being assaulted by the smell coming off that guy. My way was quicker."

"Do you threaten every smelly person with false rape accusations?"

"Are you sure they were false, Amanda?"

She thought about the question for a moment. "You have no reason to suspect him, unless this is all a set-up and you know the guy."

"Nope. Like I said, never been in here or seen these folks before."

"Then what you said was fake."

"Not fake. Without proof. Big difference from my point of view. Call it a hunch. It was written all over his face. He doesn't take refusal well. And he's a small man. Been bullied his whole life, probably. Luckily he's a piece of shit so the bullying was deserved."

"What if the bullying made him the way he is?"

"No one suddenly develops into an asshole. It's who they are. Wired in deep. Pretending we can change is humanity's greatest act."

"You are nothing like what I imagined a federal agent to be."

"Shh, with the agent talk. First, it ain't true, I work for a federal agency, but I am not an agent. Agents have guns and regulations and authority. I got business cards and a terrible paycheck. Second, this is not a crowd that likes law and order types. Which you would know if you had ever been in here or a place like it. Did your drinking in cheery chain restaurants that served fun and festive beach drinks, right? If you even drink at all."

"My social life really isn't any of your business."

"Got to talk about something."

"Okay, so you are investigating the multiple murder that happened in that warehouse."

"No comment."

Amanda's jaw dropped. "What do you mean 'no comment'? Why are we here?"

"To drink?"

Amanda looked down at her untouched rum and coke and back up to Falstaff's smirking face. She dug out her wallet and opened it but stopped before pulling anything out of it. She stood up.

"I was going to pay for your drink as appreciation for meeting with me, but you already took care of that. So, I'll just stop wasting your time and leave you to your fun. Goodnight."

"Does the public know that the victims were all hooked on opiates?"

The question made Amanda put away her wallet and sit back down. She leaned forward.

"What are you talking about?"

Falstaff took a long, dramatic pause to enjoy Amanda's anxious anticipation. She was leaning halfway over the table, eager for the answer. He finally answered her.

"All of them came back positive for opiates. A mix of different things, actually."

"Who killed them?"

"Listen, scoop, if I knew that, I would not be here. They would have kept me back there until the suspect or suspects were picked up."

"Wait, suspects? Are there multiple suspects?"

Falstaff shrugged and looked down at his glass. He was nearing the bottom of it a little too quickly. He did not want to get too drunk too fast, and he wasn't sure if he would be able to squeeze in another round. He drank a mouthful of the tepid water poured from the pitcher and grimaced at the metallic aftertaste.

"Jesus, do they pull the water right from the river? I should have asked for bottled water, though god knows if they have any here."

"Are there?"

"What? Speak full English with actual sentences, please."

"Are there multiple suspects? Many shooters?"

"They don't know yet. Looks like same type of gun used for all the killing. Maybe all the same gun, maybe different guns of same model. It's early in the investigation. Are there a lot of opiate addicts in Pittsburgh and surrounding area? Do you know who the big dealers are?"

"I, um, no. I don't know anybody who does oxy, or sells it. I met a guy last week who sold his medicinal marijuana, but that's it."

"Great. No street knowledge."

Amada scowled. "But I do know the statistics. We're above average for reported addictions in a major urban center, but still within the historical trends. But the county is another story. They don't track the data very well, but from all the hospital and police reports, there's a hell of a lot of pills in Allegheny and neighboring counties. It's coming to light that the docs in small town areas would prescribe opioids to pretty much anybody. It was the easiest course of treatment for people with little to no health insurance. Pills kept them functional, in a way. Why?"

"Most of the victims were from the sticks. What about hookers? Do you know any?"

Amanda tried hard to be stoic, but Falstaff watched a deep red blush sweep over her face. He could tell that she had never met a sex worker, much less spoken to one.

"You have to get out more, Amanda."

"To meet prostitutes?" she hissed.

"Sex workers are people too. People who see a lot of stuff that no one else sees. More reliable than homeless guys sleeping rough on the streets, like Pisspants when he's down on his luck. And in this case specifically, having a sex worker source of information could prove to be…relevant."

Amanda pulled out her notebook and scribbled furiously as she peppered Falstaff with questions. He dodged most of them with a 'no comment' but gave up just enough information to keep her hooked. She moved on to him.

"Why were you there? What's the federal connection?"

The last slurp of gin, tonic and melted ice cube went sliding down Falstaff's throat. He surveyed the room and put the final touches on his improvised plan.

"There was a federally controlled substance at the site. Military grade painkillers. Powerful stuff. Should have been locked up tight. I'm supposed to find out who stole it and how it got here."

Falstaff kept his eyes locked on Amanda, but he could still see Nurse turn on his bar stool to glare at him. He leaned forward in a conspiratorial pose with Amanda, speaking in a stage whisper that was still easily heard by anyone bothering to listen in.

"Stolen military gear that no one wants to admit was taken. Big news. Explosive. The kind of big trouble that can send shockwaves all the way to the halls of Washington."

Amanda made sounds of mumbled agreement as she rapidly made notes. She wrote an illegible paragraph and then violently scribbled it out to start again.

"Don't edit as you go, Amanda. Gonna lose your train of thought. Stick to the big details. Save flavour for later."

"Who sent you, then? Is this an official cover-up?"

Falstaff made a show of nervously looking around the bar. He held the pause for as much drama as he could wring out of it before finally answering her question.

"People don't want this to go public."

"What people?"

The door of the bar swung open and Pisspants came storming back inside the bar. Pisspants had both of his hands pushed deep into the front pouch pocket of the stained grey sweatshirt he was now wearing. He paused to suck in a deep breath and began to march towards Falstaff.

"Right on time" Falstaff muttered, then in a casual voice he told Amanda that he had to head to the washroom first before he told her the full story. He slipped out of the booth as Pisspants came storming across the bar floor, trying to chase him down. Falstaff ducked out of sight down the narrow hall leading off to the washrooms.

He reached the men's washroom. The door had been removed, and the side of the toilet stall had been kicked down by a rowdy patron. Falstaff saw the would-be molester from earlier, on his knees in the remains of the stall sucking the cock of the grizzled old writer.

"Looks like I guessed wrong. It's dirty old man cock you secretly craved, not young girl trim. No no, don't bother stopping. Enjoy it."

He gave the temporary lovers a wave and continued past the washroom. His real destination was the fire exit at the end of the hall.

He stopped at the door and listened. Back in the bar there was shouting, and quickly following the shout was a crash and a high-pitched scream. Falstaff smiled and shoved at the fire door.

"That's my cue. Thanks for the distraction, Greasy Pisspants."

Falstaff got the door to open halfway before it got stuck, lodged in the garbage filling the alleyway behind the bar. He brushed the dirt from the shoulder of his jacket and squeezed through the partially open door.

He suddenly found his forward momentum completely lost, and felt an unexpected pressure circling his neck. A sharp jabbing sensation pressed into the spot behind his jaw joint on the right side. The pain was intense and immediate. Falstaff flailed his arms in a vain attempt to stop the source of the pain, or at least understand what was happening, but the pressure kept building. He gagged and tried to ask for mercy as his knees buckled. Nurse opened his hands to release the chokehold that had Falstaff immobilized.

Falstaff hit the ground hard and lay there trying to swallow. His arms were jerked back behind his back and ties together with plastic zip restraints. He managed to roll partway to the side to watch Nurse putting a pair of zip restraints on his ankles to match. With ease, Nurse lifted Falstaff onto his shoulder like a sack of potatoes and kicked the half-open fire exit door free. Falstaff's back scraped against the door frame as Nurse walked out the door and into the alleyway. He hollered in pain, finally regaining his voice.

"What the fuck, Nursie? Keep me safe, motherfucker, don't gouge my throat out. That was totally un-fucking-called for, asshole. I should shout for help until somebody calls the cops. Let me go."

Nurse walked purposefully down the alleyway, ignoring Falstaff's continual stream of curse words and demands. At the mouth of the alley, Nurse threw Falstaff casually to the ground. He pulled out a roll of duct tape and taped Falstaff's mouth closed. Nurse looked Falstaff straight in the eye and pinched his nostrils closed. When the panic of asphyxiation set in, Falstaff started to writhe on the ground. Nurse let go and watched Falstaff frantically suck air through his nose. He picked Falstaff back up and walked him over to the car. Thrown into the back seat facedown, Falstaff weakly shouted through the tape gag as Nurse put the car in gear and drove away.

6

5 minutes later, the car stopped. 2 minutes after that, Falstaff's world was upside down and swinging from side to side. The blood was rushing to Falstaff's head. There was a pool of spit building up behind the tape keeping his mouth shut, accumulating too quickly to be swallowed down. A nylon rope was now wrapped around his lower legs, a rope that had him suspended upside down hanging from a parking lot lamp post. The rope bit into his skin. Out of the corner of his eye he watched Nurse leaning against the car, looking up at the sky and breathing deeply of the cool night air.

"I have missed nights like this. Cold but with promise of spring. In the night sky you can get lost and forget about the foolish acts of people. Like you, fool. I am going to remove the tape. I do not like screaming. Do not do it. Do you understand?"

Falstaff answered with angry but unintelligible screaming from behind the tape gag. In response, Nurse reached over and gave him a gentle push to send him swinging like a pendulum. Falstaff felt his belly full of liquor roil and threaten to come barrelling up and out of his nose. He stopped screaming and tried to make a noise that sounded like agreement and surrender. Nurse accepted his surrender and held out his massive paw, instantly stopping the swing. Nurse pulled off the tape with vicious, efficient force. Falstaff yelped.

"Jesus! My lips are fucking raw. Let me down."

"No."

"Let me down, please?"

"You tried to run away. This was expected but, it is disappointing."

"I was just going to get some fresh air. Honest. Felt a little sick."

"First lie. You claimed you were going to the washroom."

"I was! But that dude, the nervous one who I thought was going to kidnap some middle school girl and try to fuck her? He was in there, licking the dick of the crusty old writer. I didn't want to interrupt their meet-up. Love's beautiful in all its forms. LET ME DOWN!"

The rise in Falstaff's voice was answered by another disorienting shove, this time with a twist to it so he was spinning and swinging at the same time. Vomit rocketed up his throat and out of his mouth and nose, running down through his hair and splattering onto the ground in a stippled stream. Falstaff choked and writhed around, trying to clear his airways of puke. Nurse stepped around the puke and stopped Falstaff's motion. He wiped off Falstaff's face with a sheet of paper towel.

"No screaming. No running away."

"Fine. But I wasn't going to run away. Things just happened."

"The angry man with the stained pants. You knew he would come back. Smart."

Despite his predicament, Falstaff smiled. "Yeah. So little pride that he can't afford to lose any to anyone.

Knew he'd stomp around outside replaying the conversation until he got mad enough to do something stupid."

"And you counted on my protection. You used it as a distraction to escape."

"Now let's not get too hasty with labels and accusations. I wasn't going to run."

"As I said, this was expected."

"So what, you're going to fucking torture me to get me to stay and work for you? How the fuck is that going to work, genius? Why would I stay? I swear to the old dark gods that I will find a way to catch you when you sleep and drink your fucking blood, to pay you back for this nonstop fuckery."

Nurse walked around to the back of the car. He raised up the unlocked trunk lid and pulled out a folder from the dark recess. Inside the folder he found the shiny white rectangular piece of paper he needed and put the rest of the folder away. He stepped directly in front of Falstaff and showed him the photo.

"Your mother. She has a new friend. They share stories."

Falstaff laughed up a trace of vomit and phlegm.

"My mother? Nice try but way off the mark, Nursie. Threatening that deluded old crone will have zero fucking effect on my willingness to put up with your torturous shenanigans. I mean, I'm not encouraging you to off an old lady in the throes of a smorgasbord of mental illnesses or anything. Leave her alive."

"You don't care for your mother."

"Add it to my list of reasons why I'm a shitty human being but yeah. Doesn't mean a thing to me."

Nurse walked a circle around Falstaff, passing out of his line of sight. Falstaff braced himself for an attack from behind. None came.

"Our employer said you pay all her bills. You keep her in a nice nursing home. Fully medicated, fully staffed. That is expensive, and you are a filthy beggar."

"Despite the sick all over my clothes I resent that label. I found some money a long time ago, and I put it all away safe so she stays out of my life in perpetuity."

Nurse returned to standing in front of Falstaff, and he sighed.

"We know why she's there."

A long pause hung in the air. A breeze full of diesel and smoke gusted down from the nearby road and into Falstaff's eyes.

"I don't know what you're-"

Nurse interrupted Falstaff's denial with another photo, then another and another. Each photo was a smiling face from the past. Distant cousins he only met once when he was 8. The neighbours who made him cookies when he was 9. Different neighbours from a different town who smiled and laughed whenever 11-year-old him told them a joke. All people who had been suckered by his dear old mom. And him.

"If you do what you are told, they will all stay safe. Your mother. Safe. Your victims. Safe. They will never find out where the returns on their investments really came from. They would all go to jail, I think. But worse, the shame. Blood money. You gave them blood money."

Falstaff sputtered a string of fragmented words that his mind could not put into any recognizable order. The guilt and shame made his head throb and his eyes burn. His empty stomach churned and spasmed again but had nothing left to expel.

Nurse laid out the photographs so Falstaff could see them all at the same time. In the center of the photos, he added one last picture of a smiling girl with blond hair and a constellation of freckles on her right cheek. The girl who had died in Falstaff's arms, cold in a cornfield in late february, 33 years ago.

"Your mother talks about her. Should we listen?"

Falstaff shut his mouth hard, biting his tongue and lower lip. Blood dribbled into the gap between his lip and his gums. He spit a bloody gob to the side away from Nurse, careful not to offend his tormentor.

"Alright."

Nurse watched in silence for a minute. Falstaff's breathing was ragged and heaving.

"I said alright, goddamn it."

"What does that mean?"

"Fuck. I will do what you tell me. Now and until the end of time, so help me christ in heaven, as long as you leave that alone. I'll find your killers, I'll bark like a good dog. I won't run, I won't bite."

It was at this point that Falstaff realized Nurse had a cellphone in his hand, held out in front. From the phone came a tinny shrill version of the German's voice.

"Very good. We have an understanding. Continue your work, Herr Falstaff."

Nurse put the phone to his ear for the last instructions from their employer, then hung up.

"Cut me down, please."

Nurse threw the folder of incriminating evidence into the trunk of the car and locked it. He walked back to the side of the inverted L-shaped lamppost and pulled on the knot holding the rope in place. With the loose end of the rope held in his left hand, he slowly let out the length of the rope to lower Falstaff to the ground. An inch above the ground, Falstaff begged him to stop.

"I'm right above my own puke, man. Don't dunk me in vomit. Please, don't be a dick."

Nurse paused with a slight smile at the corner of his mouth. Falstaff could tell he was considering intentionally dropping him into the mess.

"Remember that I'm getting back in that car with you. The smell is going to fill the air for the whole ride home."

The logic of that warning did the trick. Nurse grabbed Falstaff's bound arms and pulled him away from the vomit splash zone before dropping him onto the ground. He roughly flipped Falstaff over and untied the rope and cut the zip ties from around his ankles. He stepped back and watched Falstaff squirm.

After a few false starts, Falstaff managed to flip himself over and get into a sitting position. He panted to catch his breath.

"How about you untie my arms too? I thought we had an understanding."

"When you are standing and calm."

Falstaff scowled. "Calm? I am fucking calm."

He switched from a sitting position to a kneeling position. He weighed his options, and decided that the best chance of standing up without falling right back down was to lean against the lamppost for support. He groaned with pain and exertion as he worked himself into an upright standing position. Back on his feet, he turned to hold his tied wrists towards Nurse.

"I'm up. Cut me loose."

Nurse came close to Falstaff. He looked him in the eye and slipped the blade of his 6" navy knife in between Falstaff's wrists. Falstaff felt the cold brush of the steel graze the surface of his skin, before it suddenly jerked up and away to cut the plastic restraint. Finishing the motion, Nurse stepped back and slipped the knife back into its hidden sheath. Falstaff put his hands up in front of his face and inspected his wrists for injury.

"You are not hurt" Nurse chided.

"No thanks to you, asshole."

"You want to hit me, perhaps?"

"Is that an offer?"

"No. You said you wanted to drink my blood. That was very dramatic. I am asking if you still feel the need to attack me."

Falstaff rubbed his wrists, then wiped his mouth with his sleeve. He looked at Nurse standing at ease but ready for a fight.

"Do I want to kick your dick in? Sure. Who wouldn't? But I got a secret weakness. I can't fight. Totally useless at it. I'm only good at taking a beating, not giving one out. Might as well be a basket of newborn kittens, for all the damage I can do. But I would pay good money to have someone slap the look off your face. Lucky for you my ass is broke."

For the first time, Nurse laughed out loud. It was a sharp sound, a combination of a dog bark and a donkey bray. Falstaff's mouth dropped open at the surprising sound.

"Honesty is refreshing. Come. We go."

Falstaff kicked at the debris covering the parking lot asphalt, cigarette butts and decaying fast food bags. He stopped kicking at the garbage when the toe of his shoe found a recently used condom. He shook it off his foot and sighed in disgust.

"Go where?"

"You are the bloodhound. Find the trail."

Falstaff rolled his eyes at Nurse and stomped around the parking lot while muttering to himself. As he approached the edge of the parking lot, Nurse took 3 massive striding steps to intercept Falstaff.

"Relax, Nursie. I'm not going to run again. I meant what I said. I swear to see this through to the end."

"Why did you run before?"

"I make it a priority to get away from people using violence to coerce me. Call it a habit. Speaking of habits, I wish I had a goddamn cigarette. Should have bummed one from the perverts at the bar. Bet Pisspants would have given me the rest of his deck to get a few extra moments of alone time with the reporter. That reporter is a smart cookie. Unexperienced as fuck, but clever enough to fake her way through the early mistakes. I thought that I could hand the investigation off to her, make it legitimate. She would chase the story down and in the process the law would catch the killer. There's no way that she would do a worse job than I'm doing. That's why I told her the almost-truth. And it got you angry and distracted. With that information handed off to her, I waited for the distraction to storm into the bar. Pisspants was supposed to buy me enough time to slip out the back. That was a miscalculation."

"Our employer was very specific. The investigation must be private and discreet."

"Sure, I'll just keep failing in the dark. Or, we can let the shining beacon of journalism illuminate the dark corners and reveal justice in all her glory."

"The reporter is a nice girl. Too young to die for a story."

Falstaff staggered backwards at the thinly veiled threat. He pointed at Nurse accusingly.

"NO. Fuck no. Now you're threatening to murder reporters for knowing too much? I'm working for the bad guys. FUCK."

Nurse looked confused. It took him a moment before the full meaning of Falstaff's accusation struck him.

"That was not the meaning I intended. Apologies. We are not the villains."

"Then who are the bad guys?"

"That is not information I am authorized to possess. There are people who want these orphaned operatives to continue to act without instruction. They want the bloodshed and uncertainty to build until there is national outrage. They want to bring down your country."

"High stakes, huh? As if chasing a murderer wasn't stressful enough on its own. Fuck, alright. We stay in the dark. Let's go to the dealer's hometown and sniff around for clues. And get something to eat. My gut is on fire."

They drove through the darkened city, navigating to the green glow of the GPS on the dashboard. Falstaff argued successfully for turning the radio on.

"No death fetish AM talk radio this time, though. Good, dumb rock'n'roll to ease my weary mind" he announced as he scanned through all the options before settling on a classic rock station. The last half of Radar Love filled the car as they left Pittsburgh.

The countryside got dark in a hurry. The radio crackled occasionally as they passed under power lines and through underpasses. Falstaff peppered Nurse with questions to pass the time. He asked about family, and career, hobbies and guilty pleasures. Nothing triggered a response from Nurse's stoic face. Even probing his sexual proclivities had no effect. His composure impressed Falstaff.

"You're stone-faced. I bet that's part of your training. Military, with some special forces. Did they teach you to endure torture? That would explain part of it. I can pick up almost nothing from your facial reactions. Good job. You should be proud. Most folks broadcast every single emotion. They never shut up. I'm guessing they shout the nice things too, but I can only pick out the ugly parts. Dirty little secrets."

The space Falstaff left for Nurse to respond fell flat and unused as the miles clicked by. He gave up on using small talk to get information on his minder and captor and closed his eyes to rest. He was startled back to wakefulness by Nurse's voice.

"You endure pain well."

"Huh? Oh yeah, thanks. I am very proud of my finely-honed ability to get the ever-loving shit beat out of me without dying. Most times."

"When I immobilized you at the bar, I was surprised that you were able to resist. Most men lose consciousness in the first 10 seconds. Women in 15 seconds. Did you not feel the pain?"

|I felt the pain alright. Fuck, it hurt. You're confusing resiliency with invulnerability. I feel pain like any normal person. But the effects of the pain don't kick in for me until the pain gets to a much higher level. You made my knees buckle and I could not see straight."

"If I did the same to a regular person, they may have died. I was concerned that you were going to die from it. Your pain resistance is a useful trait."

"Once again, you are a shitty nurse. And its not all its cracked up to be. Halfway through being beaten with a hammer, it would have been a relief to go unconscious. Lucky me gets to stay awake until the end when I'm close to death. Whee. So, you have done that hold to enough people that you can gauge their different pain reactions, eh? That is definitely some black ops dirty deeds shit. Not American, because of the obvious language issues. Mossad? Is that what Israeli special forces are called?"

A single small twitch ran from Nurse's right eye to the base of his right ear, confirming that Falstaff had guessed correctly. He then noticed Nurse's hands grip the wheel tightly, curling his fingers around the steering wheel until they made fists around the bar of the outer circle.

"Huh. Never mind. Just fucking around. Ignore me. Hey, there's the sign for the town. New Bethel. Bound to be a roaring good time in a place with a biblical name. Hope you brought your fancy cross and American Jesus bible."

Nurse pulled the car to a stop in front of the town hall. The main street was deserted, with every store closed for the night. He turned the engine off and asked for clarification.

"I have never heard this phrase, the American Jesus. Explain?"

"I made it up. American Jesus likes shooting his way out of trouble, and thinks poor people are poor because they're lazy. Wealth is sacred, government is wicked, and American Jesus will be coming back in the next few years to kick some infidel ass. Mix in free flowing pain pills and an economic dead-end for uneducated white America, and you got a recipe for…. well, I don't know. A big fucking mess."

They stepped out of the car and stood on the steps of the New Bethel town hall. The yellow streetlights were sparse and spaced out, casting their weak light over the cracked concrete sidewalk and the rough asphalt road. The main intersection to their left had a continuously blinking red traffic light. Falstaff turned towards the town hall front doors and looked through the glass window in the door. He could only see the faint glow of an emergency exit sign from down the hallway running alongside the narrow staircase to the second floor. He looked at the index board mounted to the side of the entrance, reading the list of offices and scheduled meetings held in the building. The primary function of their town hall was as a venue: for job search support groups, narcotics anonymous meetings, and couples counselling couples. The mention of a monthly council meeting was tacked onto the bottom of the list like an afterthought.

"Not big on local governance around here."

"Town runs well. Can I help you gentlemen?"

The arrival of an unknown voice made Falstaff spin around to see the source. At the base of the stairs stood a squat, muscular man with a badge. His hand sat on his gun, and he glared at Falstaff and Nurse. Carefully groomed sideburns framed his face, a shade lighter than the hair on the man's head. The cop's clothes were clean and properly pressed, but the top 3 buttons of the shirt had been left undone to show off the thick gold chain and cross hanging tight against his neck. Falstaff saw the hunger for violence hiding just beneath the civility of the cop's words. He smiled and walked slowly down the steps.

"Good evening, officer. We're just on a drive through the countryside, on our way up to Cleveland. We stopped here for a quick stretch of our legs and then we'll be back on our way."

The cop glowered at Falstaff and sized Nurse up. His doubt at being able to physically overwhelm Nurse was making the cop nervous. Falstaff couldn't blame him for being unsure: Nurse was a good 6 inches taller and thick with muscle. The cop didn't even know that Nurse was capable of startling violence. Falstaff thought about egging the cop on, to see how the conflict would turn out. That would get him the revenge he wanted to inflict on Nurse. Revenge for being strung up, humiliated, and threatened into cooperating.

"Listen, this is a nice quiet town. We don't need party boys from the city coming in here and corrupting us."

"Really? Corrupting? Is this 1950? I know the buildings were last painted around that time, but are you really going to chase us out of town for being tourists? Small town police get the reputation they deserve, apparently."

The cop's gun hand twitched, and a rage pulled his lips tight against his teeth.

"I am the goddamn Sheriff of this county, you prissy little faggot. You can take your search for cheap drugs and cocksucking back to Pittsburgh or whatever hellhole you squirmed out of. Or I will throw you in jail and you can bugger each other raw until I remember to call the judge in to hear your sentence."

The conversation was hurtling towards an ugly conclusion a little too quickly for Falstaff's liking. Falstaff put on his most contrite face and tried to de-escalate.

"Hey, Sheriff, sorry. We're not from this part of the country. We don't want to make any trouble for you, sir. And we are certainly not looking for drugs of any kind. Like I said, we're just passing through. If it's okay with you, we would like to buy a drink before we leave. If you can tell us where the nearest Gas'n'Gulp is, we'll be on our way."

Falstaff watched the reaction as his words landed. The Sheriff remained enraged and dangerous, but the immediate violence threatened in his face began to recede. Nurse, on the other hand, was relaxed and amused by the whole exchange. Falstaff wondered if Nurse was overconfident, or if the Sheriff was less of a threat than he had feared.

The Sheriff drew a mouthful of saliva with a loud and grotesque slurping sound. He let a massive wad of spit fly, aiming it directly at Falstaff's feet. Falstaff pretended the spittle that now coated his left toe did not exist and kept smiling stupidly. Satisfied that he had asserted his dominance, the Sheriff raised his arm and pointed down the street.

"Down there, 'round the corner is the Buy and Sell. Only place open at this time of night. Go there, grab your sparkling water, and get out of my town. Understand?"

"Oh yes sir. Thanks, Sheriff. Have a nice day."

Falstaff walked briskly down the street to escape the gaze of the Sheriff, with Nurse keeping pace at his shoulder. They turned the corner and saw the Buy and Sell.

"An Army Surplus general store? That's a little messed up. Well, it is the only open place I've seen."

They walked through the slow-opening automatic door and into the fluorescent glow of the store. The army surplus was arranged on the left side of the store, but it bled into the convenience store items as you reached the middle shelves. A rack of condoms and adult diapers was sitting beside a pile of gas masks.

"Now there's the gear for a fun Saturday night, eh Nursie? Who says small towns can't get freaky?"

"I do not understand."

"Never mind, it was a joke."

Falstaff browsed the aisles at a leisurely pace, noting the high quality of the military equipment for sale. He picked up a canvas ammunition satchel and inspected the interior of it.

"Good stuff, it looks like. But I'm no expert. This look like top of the line gear to you, former or current military operative?"

Nurse scowled in response.

"Okay, be that way. Did you notice that the Sheriff suspected us of being drug tourists? Cheap drugs. Now he either made that up because he watches too many bad cop dramas, or people have come here before to buy cheap drugs. And drug seekers don't take shots in the dark. If they came here, then there's dope to be bought."

They passed a stick-thin girl barely out of her teens, standing in front of a jerky display rack and staring intently at the package in her hand. In slow motion, she opened the package and took a bite of it without breaking her stare. One hand kept holding the open package while the other slipped 2 additional packages into her pocket. Falstaff confirmed that the sleepy looking woman at the counter could easily see the girl shoplifting but was choosing to do nothing about it. He walked through the narrow space between the shoplifting girl and the display, brushing past her elbow on the way. The girl didn't react at all.

"Yeah, no drugs in this town. That girl is profoundly stoned on jerky, not pills. Sure thing, Mr. Sheriff. What do you want to drink, Nurse?"

"Water."

"You really know how to live it up, Nursie. Water it is. I will be enjoying a big bottle of high caffeine, high sugar garbage to wash down the handfuls of greasy chips I'm going to shovel into my face on the way back. And I'll wash it down with this 40oz bottle of malt liquor. God Bless America, land of the chemically dependant."

"No booze" Nurse corrected him, putting his hand on the door to the beer cooler to keep Falstaff from opening it.

"Fucking spoilsport."

Falstaff slouched his way up to the front of the store, put the drinks and chips on the counter and stepped back to force Nurse to pay for it. Over Nurse's shoulder, Falstaff tried to make small talk with the tired clerk, but she was uninterested in anything not related to the transaction.

Back outside with his plastic bag of junk food clutched in his hand, Falstaff looked at the dark stores and buildings surrounding the Buy and Sell. 3 blocks in either direction the town ran out and became brown farm fields.

"I get why the small-town kids go off to the city for fun. This place is dead. We're 30 minutes away from Pittsburgh, but it feels like we're 50 years in the past. Their town motto should be "New Bethel-what's the fucking point of this place?" Do you think we can go back to the crime scene tonight? The cops looked like the were going to wrap up their investigation when we dropped by last time."

"We can stop there."

"Well great. Look at that, our friendly local law enforcement officer was waiting out here for us."

A spotless, highly polished Jeep Cherokee sat across the street around the corner. The driver started the engine and slowly pulled onto the street, displaying the Sheriff's office logo on the side. Falstaff resisted the urge to wave at the Sheriff and walked back to the car. The Jeep crept along behind them as they walked.

"When you turn around to head back, make sure to follow each and every road rule. We're not in his good books."

Nurse looked in the rear view at the Sheriff idling behind them.

"You made him mad."

"Ah, whatever. He was already mad. Wonder why?"

Nurse cautiously signalled and did a U-turn to point back towards the city. They passed the Sheriff and waited for the sirens and lights to come alive. He let them leave unmolested but followed them until they reached the edge of town. As they crossed the town boundary, the Sheriff gunned the engine and did a controlled fishtail turn down the side road, spitting up clouds of dust and sending a shower of gravel spattering against the pathetic squat houses on the side of the road.

"Glad that asshole is gone. I want to stop to grab some food on the way back. I'm famished" Falstaff said, in between mouthfuls of salt and vinegar chips. Nurse rolled his eyes and drove off into the night.

7

Nurse had given in to the whining demands of his prisoner patient and stopped at a greasy drive-thru on the way back to the crime scene. Falstaff had eaten with reckless enthusiasm, ignoring the last few blocks of the drive and the grumbling of Nurse as he parked down the street.

The parked car was suddenly filled with a loud, noxious-smelling belch that rattled the loose change in the cup holder. Falstaff paused to admire his performance, then went back to devouring his second cheesesteak sandwich. The fast food sack was wedged between his knees. He alternated bites of the sandwich with handfuls of soggy French fries from the bag. His eyes were focused on the seemingly deserted warehouse crime scene.

"You are a pig and a glutton. Stop dropping your food on the seat. This is not your garbage pile."

"It's a rental, isn't it? They'll clean it."

"Stop eating like a slob or I will stop you."

"We went several hours without a threat to my personal wellbeing. That's a new record for us."

"If you listened when I made a request, these situations would not happen."

"Alright, alright."

Nurse watched Falstaff eat.

"Why are you not fat? You eat like a fat person."

Falstaff crumpled up the now-empty cheesesteak wrapper and went to throw it on the floor. The disapproving stare from Nurse reminded him to put it in the bag instead. He thought about the premise of obesity for a moment.

"I don't know why I'm not fat. Metabolism, maybe. Part of my particular genetic assets. My body burns more calories than ordinary folks do, as it repairs itself from the damage people like you keep inflicting on it. I don't eat very regularly either. Binge when I can, go hungry when I can't afford food. Plus, I did get drunk earlier. That always makes me hungry, vomit notwithstanding."

The windows of the warehouse showed a minimal amount of light inside the building. The bright yellow tape warning people of the site being an off-limits crime scene was strung across the employee's entrance where the guard had been posted earlier.

"They sent the racist guard home. That makes me think the building is empty."

Falstaff got out of the car with the fast food bag full of garbage clutched in his hand. He ducked into the side alley and threw the bag onto the mountain of discarded broken office furniture and bags of rotting garbage. The pile moved as hungry rats came burrowing up through the old trash towards the new source of food. Falstaff grimaced and wiped his hands on his pants at the idea of being so closed to filthy rat vermin. He did not care for rats.

"You said he was a racist? How did you know?" Nurse asked as they walked to the building.

"Called me a monkey. Hold this" he instructed as he pulled the crime tape up and out towards Nurse. Falstaff worked under the tape to get to the door itself.

"Monkey is racist for sure?"

"Yes, Mr. ESL. My skin tone makes 'monkey' a racial slur."

"Are you black?"

"Black enough for bigots like him."

"I did not think you were."

"I pass for a lot of different groups. Mostly, I'd appreciate being seen as a goddamn human being instead of a pile of stereotypes. But people are shit, so that doesn't happen. Fuck. The door is locked. You got lock picking skills?"

Nurse shook his head, and Falstaff slipped back around the tape. He surveyed the building.

"We have to find another way in, then. Gotta say, I am surprised the cops closed up the investigation so quickly."

"It is a bunch of dead junkies. No one cares."

Falstaff stared at Nurse as he thought about his response. He licked his lips and spoke in a low, measured tone.

"They don't stop being people when they get hooked on drugs. They had lives, and those lives were taken from them by a killer. Their lives were probably shit, true. That's why they chased dope in the first place. But they deserve some basic human dignity, like giving a shit that they were murdered. Let's try the roof. There might be a way in there."

They walked to the back of the building where a fire escape ladder was mounted to the cinderblock wall. Falstaff stepped into Nurse's cupped hand and reached up to grab the release latch on the ladder. The latch had rusted shut and refused to move.

"Shit. No ladder. Boost me up higher and I'll climb up."

"What if there is no entrance on the roof?"

"Then I end up jumping back down and falling flat on my ass when I land. Sound good?"

Nurse laughed and agreed to the plan. He easily pressed Falstaff into the air to bring him level with the fire escape. Falstaff vaulted over the railing and continued up the stairs to the roof. He walked the edge of the roof in a stooped hunch to keep from drawing more attention to himself, checking the distance between the warehouse and the adjacent buildings. The 3 neighboring buildings were all too far away to safely jump to, so his theoretical escape options were nonexistent.

Falstaff moved to the middle of the roof and found his entry point. The roof access hatch was closed but unlocked. Falstaff struggled to raise the heavy hatch. He managed to get the hatch high enough to allow him to slip in, but he stopped himself from going in. The moment he let his grip slip, the hatch would come slamming down, pinning him in place. He lowered the hatch instead and searched the roof for something to prop the hatch open.

Behind a rusty air vent stack, Falstaff discovered the remains of a shipping crate. He sorted the wooden lengths to find a usable piece. At the bottom of the disassembled crate was a partially destroyed DVD case with a smiling, naked, large breasted woman holding a bucket on the cover. The woman was surrounded by naked men wearing rubber Halloween masks. Falstaff tossed the DVD case to the side while muttering about the depravity of the human species.

Using the crate board, Falstaff wedged the roof hatch open. He popped his head over the side of the building to tell Nurse that he was headed inside.

"Found an entrance. Going in."

Nurse waved Falstaff away and went back to watching the street for activity. Falstaff shrugged, went back to the center of the flat roof, and lowered himself through the hatch. His feet touched the steel ladder leading into the inky darkness of the warehouse, and he climbed down the ladder to the scaffolding below.

The reality of his situation hit him. He was on a catwalk above the floor of the warehouse in almost complete darkness. He had no idea where the stairs leading down were, or where the light switch was. He swore loudly at the empty room, cursing the German for not giving him a smartphone.

"Could have used the flashlight feature right now to keep from breaking my fucking neck in an avoidable fall, but mean German daddy doesn't trust me enough to give me a goddamned phone."

Falstaff dropped to his knees and started tentatively crawling away from the ladder. Every few feet he fought off the sensation of imminent danger. His imagination painted a picture of a missing section of catwalk grating just in front of him, where his hand would find only empty air and he would crash down to the concrete floor.

When his hand did find nothing but air, he flattened himself against the catwalk and held on for dear life. The pressure of the metal against his torso aggravated his wounds. The panic sent his heart thumping against his battered ribs. Falstaff wondered if his heart could handle scares like this anymore, or if the resuscitation in the ambulance had permanently weakened him.

His heart hammered away but didn't explode. He forced a slow deep breath through his lips repeatedly until the panic passed. Carefully probing again, he realized he was at the stairs leading down to the warehouse floor.

Falstaff slithered down the stairs. At the base of the staircase he pulled himself fully upright. His eyes had adjusted as much as they could to the weak light. He looked around in the dim gloom, trying to reorient himself using his memory of the room's layout. Falstaff navigated slowly through the room with his hand running along the surfaces at hip level to guide his path. He could see the beam of light coming through the narrow window above the entrance, and he used it as his guiding star. Overconfident, he stepped away from the desk his hand was touching and walked into a shin-high obstruction.

Falstaff barked a surprised 'FUCK!' and fell to his knees. His hands splayed out to keep his face from smashing into the floor, and they landed in a pool of thick, sticky liquid. Falstaff made a sound of disgust and wiped the tacky fluid onto his pants as he stood back up. He returned to his cautious pathfinding, slowly making his way from desk to boxes to chairs until he reached the door. He turned the lock and pulled the door open.

"Hey, Nursie. Door's open. Don't grab the handle, I accidentally wiped something sticky on it."

As he waited for Nurse to come inside, Falstaff ran his hands up and down the wall in search of the light switch. He found the panel and flicked the lights on as Nurse stepped through the doorway. He wondered why Nurse was giving him a confused and alarmed look, until he looked down at his hands.

Blood. He had crawled through blood. It coated his hands and pants. And the trail that he had followed from the blood pool to the door was marked in bloody smears. The light switch and the wall around it looked like a painting, a murderer's confessional cry for help.

"You have spoiled the crime scene."

"This is fucking disgusting! And all your fault for not giving me a phone. Goddamn this is gross. I gotta wash this shit off."

"And the walls?"

"I'm not a fucking maid. The walls are staying dirty" Falstaff yelled as he marched off towards the washroom in the back-right corner.

He washed as much of the coagulated blood off as he could and used the coarse brown paper towels to wipe off his pants and the cuffs of his shirt and jacket. It didn't do much good. Falstaff did a quick search of the tiny bathroom for any kind of chemical relief, but all he found was an empty bottle of generic ibuprofen. He gave up and walked out of the washroom.

"You look like a horror show."

"Yeah, well, luckily, I stink like puke and congealing blood and that distracts from my appearance. Great night I'm having. Here it is."

Falstaff stood in front of the binder shelf and pulled out the plastic baggie wedged between the two blue binders. He flipped the baggie around to inspect it and found a logo stamped in ink on it. It was a line drawing of a chess knight in profile. Through the clear space in the center of the drawing, Falstaff saw traces of white powder covering the interior of the bag.

"A knight? Chess references seem a bit too pretentious for your average dealer. The powder inside is chalky and there's a lot of it. Most commercially available pain pills have 'tamper-proof' coatings to keep you from grinding them up. But people are resourceful bastards, and they find a way."

"You are very familiar with narcotic users?"

It was a question and an accusation. Falstaff dodged.

"This baggie was left behind by someone involved in the murder."

Nurse was skeptical. He challenged Falstaff to prove proof.

"Proof? None. But follow this train of thought. The dust here was recently disturbed. The other binders haven't been touched for years. The smeared dust trail runs from the binders to the shelf and down to the top of the file cabinet underneath the shelf. There's even a palm print in the dust, which would mean something if we had a real forensic team at our beck and call."

"There are no palm records."

Falstaff was surprised to hear this. "Really?"

"Only on television shows. Palm prints are not unique."

"What the fuck do I know-I'm a college dropout with a vivid imagination. Anyway, the same dust that was on the top of the cabinet is now on the floor, tracing the outline of a second desk-shaped thing that used to sit beside this desk. The person who moved the furniture found this baggie laying on the ground and tucked it onto the shelf to get it out of the way, or maybe saving it for later as a secret stash, and then they forgot about it. Plausible enough for you, killjoy?"

"The bag was left by the killer?"

"Or a victim. But they got it here."

Falstaff opened the bag and licked the tip of his left pinky finger. He swabbed the inside of the bag until his fingertip was coated in the white powder. He sucked on the tip of his finger, eagerly licking off the drug paste. There was something pornographic about the intensity of his actions. He went back again to recover more of the powder but came up with almost nothing. He frowned and sighed.

"Only a bit of trace left in there. Opiate. Strong one, too. That tiny bit made my whole tongue and the inside of my cheeks go numb. This shit is high-octane pain management."

Nurse took the bag from Falstaff, gingerly holding it with the tips of his fingers.

"It is coated in your saliva. You are contaminating everything."

"Oh now you care about physical evidence? Fuck off."

"What does this chess piece picture mean?"

"It's a brand. The dealer wants people to know that this is their stuff. "Accept no substitutes, buy knight brand morphine". Or Oxy. No, not oxy. Tasted like a mix. Maybe fentanyl too? Ha, I just figured it out. It's a White Knight."

Falstaff paced around the room, looking in every nook and cranny. While he walked, he swallowed down the mouthful of saliva that had pooled in his mouth at the first taste of dope. He wanted more, and he hoped that he would find another forgotten baggie, this time full of pills.

His scattered search was rewarded by the discovery of a canvas ammunition bag crammed behind a stack of metal chairs by the office door. He brought the bag to the nearby desk and brought out the contents. First came out a fat roll of worn 20s, rolled up and bound by a thick elastic band. Then a scale, and a stack of clean unused baggies.

"It's the dealer's prep kit" he said to Nurse as he joined him at the desk. Falstaff rooted around the inside of the satchel but didn't find anything else. He flipped the satchel around and located a seller's tag.

"Well look at that-this genuine military surplus ammunition bag came from the Buy and Sell in New Bethel, Pennsylvania. The very store that we visited a couple of hours ago."

"And so? These bags are popular with young people. We already knew that one victim lived in that town. This tells us nothing new."

"It's a connection between the crime scene and the home town of a victim. Someone here was a local reseller of the White Knight brand or was going to become one. This looks like a sales kit."

"Sales kit?"

"Yeah, used for dividing up and repackaging bulk shipments into individually sold packets. Like a variety store buying its pop from Costco, then selling it by the can at their store. Maybe the wholesaler bought this bag and had it ready for our small-town guy. If so, it puts our drug supplier, and possibly our murderer, in the small town at some point."

"Or it belongs only to a victim and tells us nothing. How does this guessing help you find the killer?"

"Christ, you're a bringdown."

Falstaff marched away from the desk and studied the victim outlines on the floor. He forced himself to ignore the blotchy smear in the middle of the blood stain, the spot he had fallen into. Falstaff looked at the alignment of the bodies and the area surrounding them and frowned.

He crossed the length of the warehouse and looked back at the crime scene. He repeated this process for each corner of the warehouse as he mapped out the design of the placed bodies. He returned to the center of the room, where a long steel desk sat just outside of the circle of victim outlines.

"Hey Nurse, you still have the preliminary coroner reports for the victims?"

Nurse retrieved a leather attaché case that hung from a shoulder strap underneath his coat and pulled the report out of it.

"Have you had that thing under your coat all this time? Is there anything else you have tucked under there?"

"I have reports."

"You're no fun, you know that? Does the report say that there was evidence of recent sexual activity?"

Nurse stared at Falstaff, his surprise at the question plainly displayed on his face. He looked down and scanned the report until he found the answer. "Yes. Why?"

"The layout of the room is odd. Why did they move the furniture around and make a clear space in the middle of the floor, with this big old desk in the center of the space? Did I mention that I found an old crate on the roof that used to contain bootleg porn? What if this was staged to be filmed? Four male victims and one female victim is enough for an amateur gangbang. Imagine one camera down there, between the two short pallet stacks, and another camera over by the office door."

"Sex movie?"

"Jesus, yes, that's what porn is. I wonder if you're just pretending to be barely understand English. Porn is an international term. You'd have to grow up feral to avoid it."

Falstaff struggled to push the large desk back to the exact center of the clearing. With a sigh, Nurse came to his aid. Once the desk was in place, Falstaff hopped up on it. He laid on his back and looked off to the theoretical camera locations. He switched over to his hands and knees, jutting his ass up into the air. He wagged his ass back and forth and leered suggestively at Nurse.

"This getting your fired up, big guy? You like?"

"Stop the foolishness."

Falstaff pouted and hunched down to get a better look at the desk surface. He rolled off the desk.

"That steel is cold. And far too clean to have been recently fucked on."

He scanned the room again and noticed a trash bin in a chain-link enclosure at the back. Falstaff went to the enclosure and dug into the trash bin.

"Did they rape the woman?"

Falstaff replied while he pulled a powder blue pile of fabric from the garbage bin. "It's possible, I guess. But this comforter makes me think it wasn't rape."

He walked back to the desk and threw the blue comforter over the top. He reached under the desk and tied the ends of the comforter together to pull it taut and fix it in place. He leaned close to the soft fabric to inspect its surface.

"There we go, a nice soft fuck sheet. Coated in jizz, vag juice, and assorted other fluids. This was a planned event. It still could have been coercive and, depending on the amount of dope they all did, consent would be problematic. Except they all ended up dead, which was probably non-consensual. Did the men have signs of penetration too?"

Nurse looked at the file again. "They did not check for that."

Falstaff rolled his eyes. "Typical. What a thorough investigation these jokers are running."

He went back to the hypothetical location of the first camera and held his hands up to make a frame around the sex stage.

"They set the shot up like they meant to keep the footage. Maybe it's a snuff film? Weird way to go about it."

"Does the sex matter to why the murders happened?"

"It took place right before the victims were killed, so it matters. I just don't know why."

"And you suspect they filmed the murders too?"

"They could have kept rolling. But that would have been hard to pull off. First, they all get high. Then they get naked and fuck. Then the killer doses four of the victims with the elephant shot of morphine."

"Elephant shot?"

"Enough to knock out an elephant. Try to keep up, Mr. ESL. The killer manages to inject 4 of the victims and choke the 5th victim to death without any of them realizing what's going on and running for the door. That doesn't make sense. Where was the morphine injector found?"

"The report says it was found on the supervisor's desk in the office."

Falstaff made his way to the office door and tried to peer through the greasy window beside it. He couldn't make out anything through the dirty glass.

"Here's a theory: The office was the doping station. The killer brought each victim in to the room and shot them with the morphine. Then they called the last guy in and choked him out. Couldn't kill him first, in case the other victims saw the body. The doped-up victims would lay down and look like they were just sleeping. If there's enough room in here."

Falstaff went into the office and paced the rectangular space. He crouched down and examined the floor along the walls, tracing out the faint outlines of disturbed dust. He clapped the dust off his hands and returned to the main warehouse space.

"There's room, and there were blankets or sleeping bags placed on the floor to make it more comfortable. Those are probably in the alley with the rats. There were two deliberately staged scenes. The first was a porno shoot. After they finished the movie, the participants were drugged in the office, except for the New Bethel dealer who was choked instead of being sedated. The victims were then relocated in this space and arranged into the murder tableau. The killer shot each of the doped victims, cleaned up and left."

"Was the sex film the lure to bring them in?"

Falstaff considered this and shrugged in response.

"Maybe. It enticed the dudes, probably, but I would guess the free dope would have done that. Assuming they were all high on the same stuff, the same stuff that was in the baggie I found. The sex scene was important for the killer too. The whole thing is about fucking, though isn't it always?"

Nurse stood at the edge of the steel desk and looked at the cum-stained comforter covering it.

"And you are certain she wanted to be part of this? They could have held her down and taken turns."

Falstaff turned to face Nurse, and he caught a glimpse of a dark and ugly impulse playing across Nurse's face. A flush of blood at the periphery of his cheeks, a slight hitch to his breath. Falstaff wanted to ignore the message but couldn't manage it. Nurse was aroused at the idea of a gang rape. Falstaff cocked his head towards the street.

"Did you hear that? Sirens, I think. We gotta go. Nothing else to learn here, anyway."

He walked out the door without looking back at his jailor. The urge to bolt was singing through every muscle of Falstaff's body, but pushed it down and walked calmly to the car. Like it or not, he was bound to the investigation until its end.

8

Falstaff spent the ride back to safe house with his fists balled up and pressed hard against his eye sockets. He desperately wished for the whole situation to magically resolve itself. He would settle for a temporary chemical reprieve from the wretchedness of the human race.

The car pulled into the safe house driveway and Falstaff jumped out before the engine was off. He stood at the end of the driveway, staring up into the cloudy night sky, praying for a meteor to end it all. Nurse made it to the front door before noticing Falstaff lagging.

"Come in. It is late."

Fighting back the bile and disgust rising from his gut, Falstaff put on a relaxed tone of voice and pointed across the street.

"I'm going to go check in on our neighbors. They like to party. One of their guests might have seen this dealer brand before. Plus, I want to bum a smoke off the dude."

He finished his sentence and looked back at Nurse to read the response. The big thug didn't trust him.

"I do not believe you."

"Aw Christ, come on. I said I was in. Until the bitter end, no more running away. We can't go through this bullshit every time I want to follow a lead. I will be back in, fuck if I know when. Because YOU DIDN'T GIVE ME A FUCKING PHONE AND I DON'T HAVE A WATCH. Sorry. Sorry. That leaked out. I'm tired and sick of the world. Look, I will go over, spend a while there to get them relaxed, ask a few questions, and then I'll come back. Promise. I can't get into any trouble."

His hand twitched and moved towards the roll of twenties he had stolen from the crime scene. Nurse knew about the first roll of cash. It was the second roll, tucked into Falstaff's pocket, that Nurse didn't know about. It was going to help him forget for a while. Agonizing seconds ticked by in silence. Finally, Nurse nodded curtly and waved him off before walking inside. Falstaff clapped his hands in gleeful delight and pranced across the street to JJ's house.

JJ opened the door after the third round of knocking, bleary-eyed and nervous. Falstaff apologized profusely and invited himself inside.

"I freed up a little cash and I am looking to party. Can you help me out?"

"Oh hey man, sure. Come inside."

They navigated the cluttered hallway filled with planters holding half-dead houseplants, and second-hand bookcases displaying collectible toys. The living room was crowded with 3 oversized couches lining the walls. An old refrigerator with its door removed served as an entertainment center in the corner of the room. The television mounted to the upper edge of it was showing the movie "Bladerunner". Through the mismatched speakers snaked around the room blared the jagged sound of a dubstep track building up to a bass drop. The audio assault knocked Falstaff off-balance, but he did not mind.

"Nice décor, JJ. Very personal."

JJ beamed at the compliment. "Thanks! Every piece in here was hand-picked by me, mostly. My bro added some stuff here and there. So, what can I do you for?"

He rattled off his wish list like a Catholic reciting the Rosary. "Vicodin, ecstasy, valium, pot, coke if you got it."

JJ shuffled back and forth on his feet. "That's a bunch of stuff, man. You good to pay?"

Falstaff casually threw the roll of cash he had stolen from the crime scene on the table. JJ saluted the money and the man, before zipping out of the room. He returned carrying a plastic ice cube tray that rattled with each step. The tray was placed on the coffee table in the middle of the room, and JJ beckoned Falstaff to take a seat on the couch with him.

"I can get you 5 vikkies, 10 x, 5 valiums for now. 100 bucks for that. Cool?"

"What about the pot?"

JJ grinned from ear to ear, revealing a rotting front tooth.

"Easy, tiger. I'm getting to that part. I like to break up big package deals, to keep track of everything."

"Yeah, yeah, fine. Hundred bucks for the pills."

"Nice."

With the speed of an expert dealer, JJ plucked the pills out of their individual spots and slid them into a grimy sandwich baggie that he pulled from a recess in the coffee table. The pill bag was zipped closed and placed on the table, near Falstaff but not directly into his hands. He knew he had to wait for the whole transaction to be finished before getting into the pills. He was already drooling for them. He hated the automatic physiological response. JJ popped his hand under the table again and came back with a large freezer baggie full of pot.

"Roll your own, man?"

"No time these days. Got some pre-rolled?"

"Anything for a friend, man. Here."

The large bag of pot vanished back to the nether realm of the coffee table and was replaced by a small mint tin. JJ flicked it open with one hand to reveal the 5 joints inside.

"20 bucks for these. High quality shit, guaranteed."

"Deal. Here's the cash."

The money and drugs changed hands and the deal was done. As he fished two Vicodin out of the bag, Falstaff asked JJ if he had a beer laying around the place.

"Going for everything at the same time? You're a real renaissance man, man. Be careful you don't go too fast and get too hot, okay?"

Falstaff shot JJ a dirty look. "I know what I'm doing. Can I crush and chop on your table?"

"Hold on. Here, use this. It's dishwasher safe. I wash it after every use. Precautions" JJ said in a low, conspiratorial voice as he handed a square granite tile to Falstaff. He brought a bottle of cheap Mexican beer back from the kitchen and placed it on the table. Falstaff took the bottle and used it as a pestle to grind the Vicodin to powder. He laughed to himself as he pulled out one of his new business cards and used it to move the powder into two thin lines.

Using a rolled up 20 as a straw, Falstaff snorted the Vicodin in two quick blasts. The bitter, acrid taste filled his throat and mouth. He popped a valium and an ecstasy tab into his mouth and washed the whole mess down with a long pull from the beer bottle.

"Can I hang out here for a while?" he asked as he wiped his nose and mouth.

"Sure dude. Hey, I never seen anyone rail vike before. Not really much point, eh?"

Falstaff leaned against the plush back of the couch and let it engulf him. The first creeping effects of the Vicodin took hold of his body.

"It's just an onramp. The Vicodin gets the process kick-started, and passes the time until the valium and x kicks in."

"But it burns when you snort it, right?"

Falstaff smiled. "Like a motherfucker. A just punishment from a righteous god. A toll to be paid."

They kept exchanging dealer's den small talk as they shared 2 joints. Falstaff spent the last of his found money on a second purchase of a 5 gram bag of cocaine. JJ eyed the coke with lazy lust, but Falstaff tucked it away.

"That's not for fun, that's for emergencies. When I'm under, and I am nicely under now, I get slow to react. If I need to speed back up, the coke is my accelerant."

"Cool, cool. I dig it."

Falstaff closed his eyes until they were slits, only letting in a blurred warped version of the movie crawling across the television screen. Time had become flexible. The people in the room were now far away and muted. Falstaff sighed in contentment. He dug his hands deep into the pockets of his pants and discovered the forgotten crime scene baggie. He pulled the empty baggie out and rolled it around the palm of his hand.

"Can I say something, dude? I don't want to offend you."

Falstaff looked up at JJ. His eyes took a moment to refocus, leaving JJ hovering as an indistinct blur in the meanwhile. Then the world snapped back into focus.

"Ask away, neighbor. I am an open book."

"You kind of smell terrible. I'm not judging, yo, but the aroma is pungent. Like sweat and something worse. Spoiled meat or sumptin."

"It's been a hell of a night. I'm going to shower when I head home. Sorry for the stench."

"Is it the shit all over your clothes? Oh man, is that blood?"

"No, probably not. Truth be told, I don't really know. But I appreciate your honesty, JJ. That takes integrity."

JJ smiled and blushed at the praise. Falstaff held the empty baggie up to the light of the ugly brass floor lamp beside the end of the couch, letting the yellow light diffuse through the vinyl.

"Have you ever seen this brand before, JJ? I came across it in my adventures tonight."

He threw the baggie at JJ. It fluttered erratically and fell to the carpet halfway between JJ and Falstaff. JJ scooped it up and examined it.

"It looks kinda familiar, but I can't tell ya where I seen it before. Most dealers around here don't do their own marks like this. We know who sells what. Do you want me to show it to the other dudes?"

Falstaff waved his hand in approval, enjoying the sensation of cutting through the viscous air. He was on a good mixture.

JJ took the baggie on a tiny pilgrimage to the other occupants of the house. The red-eyed high school kid in the Austrian soccer jersey didn't recognize it. The muscle-head in the cowboy hat, rocking out with a pair of outdated headphones plugged in to the ancient component stereo system, shot JJ the finger when he presented the baggie. The girl with the long greasy hair and bad teeth in the corner giggled incessantly as she shook her head.

"Sorry man. The other chick is asleep in back, and there are two other dudes passed out in the spare room, but they probably wouldn't know either."

"No problem. Thanks anyway."

Falstaff took the evidence back from JJ and shoved it back into his pocket. He exhaled and wondered how long he had been sitting on the couch. His sense of passing time was fully adulterated by the chemical cocktail working its magic on his mind. Falstaff went to check the time and found himself staring at the blank spot on his wrist where a watch would normally rest. He said "right" is a slow, slurred voice that tailed off into a deep, drunk belly laugh. When he caught his breath again, he winked at JJ.

"That, my friend, is a sign that it is time for beddy-by. I'm going to grab a smoke for the road, if this is a communal box on the table here."

JJ nodded in the direction of the assorted cookie tin that now held a variety of loose cigarettes.

"Help yourself, man. It's like a take a penny, leave a penny thing."

Falstaff scooped up a Dunhill Special Reserve from the bin and lit it. He hadn't tasted a Dunhill since high school. Relishing the flavour while assiduously avoiding the associated memories, Falstaff sauntered out the front door with JJ following him closely behind.

On the porch, JJ put his hand on Falstaff's arm and spoke softly in accordance with the deep dark of the late hour.

"Like I said, I'm sorry I didn't remember anything about that dealer mark. It's going to bug me for days, man. I know I've seen it but no idea where. But thanks for coming over."

Falstaff stepped clear of the porch overhang and exhaled a massive plume of cigarette smoke into the night sky. The night air her drew back in exchange tasted cool and moist with the promise of rain.

Thanks for the hospitality, and don't sweat it. You know what you know, you know?"

Falstaff walked down the steps as JJ laughed at that profound stoner wisdom. Falstaff was on the street when JJ snapped his fingers and said to hold on.

"I got it. I have seen that logo before, I think. I never bought or sold anything in a bag like that, but some dude who hung out at the house had one. He was a strange guy, only came around once."

"Strange? How?"

"Showed up in a uniform. An army dude! That was who it was. Didn't get along with anybody except the chick who brought him. She threw the baggie across the room to him when he shouted at her to give it to him. It hit Lars in there and I picked it up. Saw it for a second before army dude ripped it out of my hands. If you want to find that dealer, go talk to some army dudes. But be careful, okay, because they are rough characters. Feral, man. Feral."

"And where would I even find a soldier in Pittsburgh, much less one who was willing to talk about his dope connection?"

JJ laughed. "You're definitely a tourist, man. There's always army dudes in town. There's a training base less than an hour from here, out in the Pennsylvania Rust

Belt, and they all come into town to party. Nothing to do out there."

"Yeah, I visited one of those rust belt towns earlier. Shitty place to find yourself."

"Dude, things are shitty everywhere. It's those one percent motherfuckers killing the economy that normal people depend on. Everywhere is going to be rust belt soon. We need a revolution."

"You going to start one JJ?"

"Naw, man. I got flat feet and a sore back."

"Ha."

"Those army dudes have the only jobs left in those towns, pretty much. Military complex is the biggest employer in the whole area. And that job ain't free, right? It breaks you inside, being a killing machine. That's why they take dope, I bet."

"If they have a connection to this mystery dealer, I should go chat with them."

"I'm telling you, that base has a bad reputation. Be careful. It's where the military dumps the defectives."

"That is a harsh warning that I will take into serious consideration. Thanks again for a good night."

"I'm all about a good time, all the time. Take 'er easy!"

Falstaff waved goodbye to JJ as he crossed the street, thinking about the baggie and the soldier. Another tenuous connection that might mean nothing at all. He stopped at the steps of the safe house porch and took one final drag of the Dunhill. He exhaled as he dropped the butt and ground it into the cracked cement with the heel of his shoe.

Falstaff gathered himself together and walked carefully through the front door while doing his impression of a completely sober man. He continued through the front hall, past the living room where Nurse was sitting.

"Got a lead. It's a thin one, but it's better than nothing. The recreational dealer across the street has seen the dealer mark before, in the possession of a military man. There is a training base in the area, so we should go poke around there."

"And if this is not connected?"

"Then we're no farther back than we are right now. Now, I'm beat up and dead tired, so I'm heading off to bed. Goodnight, my dear nursemaid. We'll hit the base tomorrow afternoon."

"Morning. We leave at 8."

Falstaff groaned.

"I need to catch up on my sleep. Tired people make mistakes."

"8AM. Go sleep now."

Tired of the conversation, Falstaff gave in and slinked back to his room. He stripped his noxious clothing off and threw them down the hallway towards the second bedroom. He padded naked across the hall to the bathroom and brushed the film of filth from his teeth. He came close to passing out as he sat on the toilet, caught in the confluence of physical trauma, fatigue, and narcotics. Falstaff gulped down a mouthful of metallic-tasting tap water to wash down one more valium for the night and crept back to his room. Laying on top of the comforter he let the sensation of cool air on his exposed skin overwhelm his senses until sleep finally shut everything off.

9

Despite his best efforts to sleep late into the morning to spite his keeper, Falstaff woke up at the crack of dawn. The weak sunlight sneaking through the one narrow window fell across his face. He squinted and crawled out of the way of the light. His eyes were caked with sleep rheum that had crusted around the edges of his lids. He sluggishly pulled himself to a standing position and left the room.

Moving like the recently risen undead, Falstaff stumbled to the bathroom to void himself. After, he started the water running for a shower hot enough to fill the tiny bathroom with steam almost instantly. As the mirror fogged up, Falstaff charted the color change in the cartographic bruises covering his entire torso. The darkening stippled contusions looked foul and rotten, completing his zombie appearance. He scrubbed the layers of mess from the previous day's misadventures and let the nearly scalding hot water pumice away the feeling of disgust and hopelessness.

"Hell of a way to start the day" he mumbled under his breath, with a sob half-hidden in his throat. He had started a lot of days just like this one, just not to this extreme. The caked blood from a multiple murder scene that was now running down his legs to the drain was a new twist, but the dull hangover and returning shame of past deeds was all too familiar. And the knowledge that he would do it all again as soon as he got the chance sat like a millstone on his chest.

For the moment, though, he could tolerate the world and the wretched people within it. A night of full excess bought Falstaff peace of mind for a period of time, a neurological buffer that would be persistently eroded away by each interaction. To buy himself a little more time, he swallowed down a Vicodin and a valium as a breakfast prelude.

He towelled off and looked again at the darkest bruises on his ribcage. The black in the center of them was inky and ominous. Falstaff pulled on his clothes but left his shirt unbuttoned. He walked into the kitchen and presented the bruise to his sadistic medical care professional.

"Hey Nursie, is this bad? Am I going to die? Are they massive embolisms preparing to break free and blow out a major section of my brain?"

Nurse looked up from the newspaper he was reading and put down his cup of coffee. He examined the bruises with a few sudden and coarse jabs from his wide fingers. Falstaff tried to keep a stoic appearance, but the final set of jabs dug deep into the very tender flesh above his heart.

"Goddamn it! You don't have to hurt me to prove you're in charge."

"It is bruises. You will be fine."

Nurse picked his paper back up and took a satisfied slurp of his coffee. Falstaff buttoned up his shirt and searched for breakfast.

"Your pain tolerance is not so dependable after all" Nurse said with a smirk. Falstaff gave him a glare over his shoulder then went back to searching the pathetic contents of the fridge for food.

"You just don't fucking listen. I never said I don't feel pain. It still hurts. I would like to avoid it, like any other sane person. But my body seems to tolerate the abuse more than most people, which is shitty. I can push past the obvious warning signals that my poor flesh sends to me. I already told you this. Where the fuck is my breakfast?"

Nurse pointed to the cheery yellow plastic bowl sitting on the faux-granite laminate counter beside the sink. Falstaff peered into the bowl to discover cold, congealing oatmeal. His stomach flipped and growled, unsure if it was repulsed or starving.

He poured himself a cup of lukewarm, gritty coffee from the cheap coffeemaker. The first sip made him grimace. He powered through the cup and refilled it. This time adding 2 heaping tablespoons of sugar to it. He added double the amount of sugar to the oatmeal and took his place opposite Nurse at the kitchenette table. Over the top of the World News section Nurse watched Falstaff shovel the gooey, over-sweetened slop into his mouth.

"That's disgusting."

"Ya eat what's available" Falstaff mumbled through his full mouth. He took a gulp of the coffee and continued shovelling.

"I can eat pretty much anything. It's another of my high tolerances. That is the bright side of my messed-up physiology: an iron stomach. Food is fuel."

Nurse turned away and tidied up the kitchen to avoid watching. He wondered aloud about the potential for adult-onset diabetes, based on the amount of sugar Falstaff was ingesting.

"Honestly, that is the least of my worries. If I live long enough that diabetes is the problem, I'll have dodged a host of worse fates."

Scraping the bottom of the cheap bowl, Falstaff finished the oatmeal. Nurse took the bowl and coffee cup from him and ordered him to finish getting ready.

"We leave in 5 minutes for the base."

Falstaff saluted and dashed off to his room. He weighed the pros and cons of bringing his little stash of drugs on the road trip but decided against the convenience of it. He made a mental note to grab a pack of smokes when the opportunity arose, grabbed his business cards and ID badge, and left the house.

The GPS led them on a winding and indirect route down the rural roads of the Pennsylvania countryside. A repeating montage of decrepit farmhouses, tiny hamlets, rusted cars in front yards, and brown barren fields. As they passed the sporadic road signs, Falstaff matched them to the county map unfolded in his lap. He studied the map and came to a realization.

"The base is surrounded by a ring of tiny towns. And guess what those towns have in common? Our 4 local victims each came from a different tiny town in that ring."

"And this means what?"

Falstaff shrugged. "Means the base is worth checking out. We got the eye witness report of a soldier in possession of the same type of narcotic bag that we found at the crime scene."

"And that witness, what is his profession? Remind me."

"Why does that matter?"

"It matters."

"Fine. Our witness is a casual entrepreneur specializing in reselling non-traditional product."

"Drug dealer. You work so hard at hiding the obvious things."

"Thought it would work. You barely speak English. Yeah he deals, which is how he knows about the dope."

"Or he lies, like all drug dealers and junkies lie."

"We also have the army surplus satchel with the baggies in it. And the eyewitness saying that the army personnel here are less than reputable."

"Hearsay from druggie is proof?"

"It's enough to warrant checking the base out. Christ. Shut up and drive, unless you have some great revelation to share."

Falstaff stared out the window until the boredom forced him to close his eyes and drift off. He woke up when they stopped at the guardhouse of the military base. On the opposite side of the road was a sign with cracked black painted letters, announcing that they were about to enter "Camp Penn, U.S. Army training and integration centre.". The landscape was empty except for the squat buildings past the guardhouse. Nurse turned the engine off and spoke to Falstaff.

"We are here."

"Uh, yeah, kinda. But the actual base is on the other side of this guardhouse. We can't do anything from here."

"Then you should find a way to go inside, yes?"

Falstaff rolled his eyes. "Oh, I see. You are just going to sit here and watch me try to get inside. Dick. You couldn't get us in?"

Nurse refused to respond. Through the window Falstaff could see that the guard in the booth was getting curious. Nervous would follow curious, and then escalate to hostile. Falstaff opened the door and walked over to the plexiglass window in the side of the booth, aware that the sleepy-eyed guard had his hand resting on the pistol holster on his belt.

"Good morning. I'm here to take a quick look at the supply situation. John Falstaff, department of defense, logistic division."

The guard with a couple of day's worth of stubble and bleary red eyes took the offered ID badge and looked it over. Falstaff looked at the mess of garbage and paperwork on the guardhouse desk, and the general dishevelled state of the guard himself.

"My partner and I are doing a routine check of the logistic supply chain in the Armed Forces facilities in this region. We'll do a quick walkaround, make a few notes, and be on our way."

The guard flipped the badge over and studied the other side of it, despite the lack of real information on it. He leaned to the left and looked around Falstaff, so that he could squint at Nurse as he sat in the car. Nurse held up his own ID badge in response. The guard scratched his face with a slow and prolonged effort. Falstaff knew the guard was going to punt the responsibility of their entrance to someone else, but he was debating if he should arrest them first.

"So where is the commanding officer, anyway? I have to check in with them first, before I look at anything. Regulations, you know?"

The guard mulled the question over as he flipped the ID badge end over end repeatedly. To keep himself from staring nervously, Falstaff looked past the booth to the interior of the base. The cracked asphalt road split at a T-junction, forming a large square of mud and scrub grass in the center. Black spray-painted letters identified the closest buildings as the commissary and the Post Exchange. A small, pathetic-looking group of soldiers jogged lethargically down the road towards the long building marked 'canteen'.

Falstaff was knocked out of his study of the base by the sudden impact of his badge hitting his face. The guard leaned heavily against his desk as he planted his elbows on the top of it and rested his sagging face on his fists.

"Go down past the PX, turn right at barracks 4, and go all the way to the end to the CO's office."

Realizing his window of escape had arrived, Falstaff smiled and nodded at the guard.

"Thank you for all your help sir."

The guard turned his head and spit out of the narrow open slot in the opposite window, leaving traces of spittle running down the edge of the glass.

"I ain't no fancy officer. Save the 'sirs' for the tightasses, civvie."

Falstaff resisted the urge to salute, knowing that it would only get him further into trouble. He had no idea of what military etiquette was, other than what he had seen in old war movies. Instead, he walked back to the car and got back in.

"Drive before he shoots me" he muttered to Nurse. Nurse laughed and drove the car past the guardhouse.

The rest of the base was rundown and faded, as were the soldiers they passed on the way to the CO's office. They pulled into the single empty parking space at the end of the lane. Beside their car was a late model jeep that was covered in mud and an engine still ticking as it cooled down. Past the parking spots was a roughly circular dirt patch where a soldier in fatigue pants and a tank top stood. They got out of the car as the soldier dropped flat to the ground, then sprung back up to his feet before jumping straight up into the air.

Falstaff went up the three rough wooden steps to the door of the CO's office and knocked. He waited for a response and knocked again. On the third unsuccessful attempt, Nurse gestured towards the exercising man and pushed Falstaff towards him.

"That is the Commanding Officer."

"Are you sure? He probably doesn't want to be interrupted, in any case."

The soldier repeated his exercise again, landing on his feet with a growl.

"State your business, unauthorized civilians, before I call the MPs."

Putting on his best corporate toady persona, Falstaff walked forward with his hand outstretched.

"Good morning! John Falstaff from the Department of Defense. I'm here to take a quick:"

His words were cut off by the sudden grab and jerk of his hand by the CO. Falstaff was sent tumbling onto the dirt without a warning.

"Morning combat training. Mandatory for all on base. Why are you interrupting me?"

Falstaff rolled up to his knees and brushed the dirt off his arms and chest.

"I'm not a military person, really, so I had no idea. This is just a misunderstanding, officer."

He scanned the soldier and the green jacket laying a few feet away from him. He found a nametag on the jacket.

"Listen, Col-that's Colonel, right? Listen, Colonel Grizz...oh Jesus. Really? Colonel Grizzley? Is this a prank? How is that possibly your actual name? Big, hairy guy with hands like bear paws? Ridiculous."

The CO squared his shoulders to Falstaff and pointed at him.

"Get up. Light sparring to start the day. I'll go easy on you. Then we talk. Offense, now."

Falstaff slowly stood up as he examined the CO's face. The man was tired. The lack of sleep was tattooed onto his sagging eyelids. His face was covered in a thick, dark stubble that would manifest into a full beard in less than a week if left untended. The tight pull of his lips against his teeth revealed a man at war with himself and the world. The sudden random eye movements told Falstaff that the CO was close to coming apart. He tried one last time to get out of sparring.

"Really, sir, I am no good as a sparring partner. I can't fight. I'm a pencil pusher from Washington."

"You attack, or I do."

Picturing the CO charging full-force into him, Falstaff decided his chances of survival were marginally better if he went on the offensive. He shot a dirty look at Nurse who was standing impassively and letting the scenario unfold.

"This is bullshit, for the record."

Falstaff crossed himself, in lieu of any real protection from what was about to occur and charged with arms wildly flailing. The CO put his hairy hands on Falstaff's shoulders and twisted at the hip. The redirection of Falstaff's momentum sent him crashing face-down to the muddy ground. To add unnecessary certainty, the CO mounted Falstaff and pressed him flat against the earth.

"Okay, you win" he wheezed through the dirt clumped around his mouth. The CO jumped up and pulled Falstaff to a standing position.

"Again. Attempt to injure me."

"Like that's going so fucking well so far."

"ATTACK."

Wondering what mad hell he was now trapped in, Falstaff approached the CO with his balled fists frantically punching out erratically. The left fist was caught in mid-swing and pulled low. The right fist was trapped in the crook of the CO's left arm. The CO yanked on both of Falstaff's arms to pull him close, and he welcomed him with a head butt. As soon as his arms were freed, Falstaff returned to his native state of being flat on the ground and dazed. The CO sighed with disappointment and disgust.

"I told you I couldn't fight, but you wouldn't believe me. Why don't you square off with my boss here? He'll give you the challenge you're looking for. Go to it, sir."

Falstaff waved in Nurse's direction.

"Go on, boss. Show off your skills."

Falstaff brought his hand back to his face and tenderly probed the growing welt above his nose and between his eyes, the spot where the soldier's forehead had made contact. Nurse seemed completely uninterested in engaging the CO, so Falstaff gave him a push.

"I get it. Fake military meets real military, gets scared of being outed. Should have known. You're only tough to weaklings and defenceless mothers. Kind of a coward is what it all comes down to."

The taunt worked. The flush of blood to his cheeks and the clenching of his fists at the word 'coward' meant Nurse was ready to fight. He stepped towards Falstaff with murderous intent on his face. The soldier intercepted him.

"I will go easy on you, civilian. You look like you can handle yourself."

Nurse set down his attaché case and neatly folded his blazer to place it on top of the case. He fully extended his thick arms and stretched in preparation.

"Do not go easy. Test me."

The two large men circled each other for a moment before slamming into each other with a terrifying amount of force. Nurse stood a head taller than the CO, but the soldier carried more muscle. They locked arms and struggled for control. It was a violent dance punctuated with quick elbow strikes that were narrowly avoided. Short brutal kicks aimed low to buckle the opponent's knees were absorbed by shins raised to block the attack.

Back and forth across the bare patch of earth the two massive men fought to a stalemate. Falstaff sat back on his heels and relished the battle. A surprising uppercut came rocketing up from the clinch and caught Nurse on the mouth. The bloom of blood on his lip made Falstaff cheer.

Nurse responded with a knee to the soldier's groin. To his credit, the CO groaned and swore but refused to fall to the ground. He pulled Nurse close to negate a follow-up attack as he recovered from the ball shot.

They fought within inches of each other, foreheads pressed together as their limbs searched for an opening to exploit. The soldier brought the fight to the ground and attempted to wrench Nurse's arm out of the socket. With astounding dexterity, Nurse spun out of the arm bar and trapped the soldier's neck in the crook of his arm. With increasing desperation, the soldier sent elbows back towards the bulk pinning him to the ground, trying to dislodge the chokehold tightening around his neck. Nurse shifted his weight away from the brunt of the elbow strikes but kept the pressure on the arteries supplying blood to the soldier's brain. A wavering hand signaled the imminent arrival of mandatory sleep for the soldier. He made one last effort to escape the hold, by jamming his stiff fingers into the nerve bundle in Nurse's armpit. Nurse grunted in pain and the chokehold loosened for a moment, but not long enough for the soldier to escape. Defeated, the soldier tapped Nurse's arm repeatedly in a signal of submission.

Falstaff was impressed at the display he had just watched. He was also disappointed that his captor had won the match. If it hadn't been clear before, it was now perfectly plain to him that Nurse was not a man he could fuck with in any way.

The two combatants disengaged from their martial embrace and stood up. Both were coated in mud and sweat. Nurse had two thin trails of blood drying at the corners of his mouth, making him look like a cheap horror film vampire. The soldier held his hand out to

Nurse, smiling and panting. Falstaff saw joy and a hint of arousal on the CO's face, and he felt creeped out. The CO slapped Nurse on the arm with his other hand and congratulated him.

"Helluva fight, son. God, what a work out. Now, what can I do you for?"

"We have a few questions about the base and the supply process. Totally routine" Falstaff said. The soldier completely ignored Falstaff and kept shaking Nurse's hand until it got awkward.

"Just fucking kiss and get it over with, for fuck's sake" Falstaff muttered under his breath.

Nurse pulled his hand away and repeated the cover story about supply process review. Grizzley nodded and walked briskly towards his office, picking up his jacket on the way. Nurse matched the soldier stride for stride, while Falstaff scrambled to follow along. The CO gave them a brief introduction to the facility.

"Camp Penn is a specialized training facility for combatants returning to active duty from medical leave. We strive to engage each service person to the best of their ability until they are ready for full duty once again. You will find that our supply administration follows the regulations and procedures as closely as is possible. Any variances are corrected as soon as identified."

"What about loss prevention? How many pieces of equipment go missing each week?" Falstaff asked.

They entered the main room of the office and Grizzley directed Nurse and Falstaff to the cheap folding chairs placed in front of a rough wooden desk. Grizzley remained standing and stripped off his tank top. He pulled a pale green towel from a gym bag tucked under the desk and continued to speak as he toweled off the sweat and applied deodorant.

"We take very good care of Uncle Sam's equipment, and our misplacement rates are consistent with most facilities. But you have that information, do you not?"

"Uh, yeah, of course we do. But what ends up on the inventory list and what is actually sitting in storage can be vastly different."

"Not in this base, son."

"And have you seen this type of bag before? Is it from your base?"

Falstaff lay the army surplus satchel on the desk. The contents of the satchel were stored safely in a tote box in the trunk of the car. Grizzley stopped in the middle of pulling his dress shirt on to examine the bag.

"It is a surplus item. Clearly marked as such in the interior label. Standard protocol to sell excess materials."

The soldier tossed the bag effortlessly back to Falstaff. The casual effort didn't hide Grizzley's newly arrived nervousness at the topic of conversation.

"Well that is a relief. You know, the boss here said the same thing, but I was watching T.V., and they said there are all these pill junkies out here in the Northwest, so I worried that these bags were getting lifted by some addict and resold to feed their habit."

The mention of pills and theft shifted Grizzley's nervousness into full-blown defensive panic. The big man suddenly appeared small and trapped in the corner of his own office. Falstaff smiled at the military man.

"This has been a very informative discussion. And more exercise than I was planning on, but that's never a bad thing. Thank you for your time."

"Is that it?"

"Yes, Colonel. We might have to come back and do a quick count of a few items from the inventory, but that won't be for a few days. I don't think we'll find anything to note. When we come back, should we stop here first, or just pop over to your inventory control official?"

"He refers to your quartermaster officer. He is new on the job, and forgetful" Nurse interjected with a warning glare to Falstaff.

"Yes, that is what I meant. Sorry, I'm very new, as he said. I should have brought the manual. Anyway, thank you, you've been very helpful."

"Once again Grizzley looked right past Falstaff and spoke directly to Nurse.

"Pleasure's all mine. Haven't sparred like that since Fort Bragg in 2007. Dark-skinned Brazilian almost broke both my arms. That's where I learned that arm bar I put on you."

Nurse rubbed his shoulder. "It is a good hold."

"Here's my card. When you come back this way, give me a call and I'll get the gate to expedite your entrance."

Another long handshake kept Nurse on the doorstep while Falstaff slipped around and out to the car. When they were both in the car, Nurse filled his hands with gel disinfectant and rubbed it thoroughly into every inch of his hands.

"That is a joke of an officer. The whole base is comical. Where is security? I brought an unsecured firearm onto the base. No record of entrance. Easy access to commanding officer. 5 minutes. In 5 minutes I could take control of facility"

"The lack of professionalism is pissing you off."

"There are rules to be followed. In live combat operation, these soldiers would die."

"And here I thought you were grumpy because the Colonel enjoyed your wrestling in a mildly inappropriate way."

Nurse pursed his lips together and gunned the ignition while mashing the gas pedal. The engine roared in protest, as loud as an economy sedan engine could.

"Shut up. You are a pervert."

They drove back towards the gate. Falstaff wanted to goad Nurse further, so he could explore how deeply the man's homophobia ran, but the possibility that he would provoke another beating out of him kept Falstaff's mouth shut.

There was a soldier walking slowly and erratically behind the PX as they drove past. The soldier held her hands out to keep her balance, weaving side to side with each footstep.

"Hey slow down, Nursie. That kid might need help."

As the car slowed to a crawl, the soldier caught her toe on the corner of a wooden crate. It was enough to compromise her fragile balance, and she stumbled forward until she crashed into a pile of empty boxes and garbage. Falstaff rolled down the window to ask if she needed help. He heard the woman laughing hysterically at the top of her lungs, as she struggled to find her way out of the pile.

"Oh, she's all fucked up. That seems out of place on a military base at ten in the morning. They got some problems here."

The car accelerated away, and Falstaff rolled the window back up to block out the sound of the drug-addled soldier. Her laugh haunted him on repeat until the base was out of sight. The worst part was he recognized that kind of laugh, but he usually heard it coming from his own mouth.

10

"Let's get lunch."

"It is 11AM. Too early."

Falstaff sighed in exasperation at his dull warden. Every suggestion was met with resistance and refusal, and it was becoming tiresome. He dug down for additional self control and politely made his case.

"That base was a mess, eh? I have no idea how a base commander is supposed to act, specifically, but I have a hunch that the Grizz was doing everything wrong."

"Yes. He was making a mockery of real military leaders. Undisciplined."

Falstaff nodded enthusiastically and urged Nurse to further explain. "Go on." With the prompt, the floodgates opened and Nurse's anger came rushing out.

"When you wear the uniform of your country, you represent the best ideas and beliefs of your nation. His insignia of rank sat in the dirt like forgotten children's toy jewelry. Leadership is earned with blood and sacrifice. It must be respected by the people blessed with it. He did not care about order, so his subordinates did not either. The security was compromised. There was an intoxicated soldier walking freely. In my country, she would have been jailed immediately and then sent to re-education."

The phrase 're-education' made Falstaff curious and very nervous. He wanted to keep moving towards his goal, however, so he put the disturbing phrase aside and pressed on.

"So, my thinking is that the base is sufficiently dysfunctional to be a great place to steal from. Maybe the mysterious morphine injectors came from there? In a base full of drug users, it would be a high priority target. The connections to our case are circumstantial so far, sure, but it's the best lead we have so far."

"Full of junkies and failed soldiers. Weaklings" Nurse seethed.

"Which is why we should pop in to the nearest town to check out the local scene for any additional connections. The base staff would be regular visitors to the town. Maybe the next part of the stolen goods chain is there."

"That may be true."

Falstaff leaned back and stretched his entire body. He had convinced Nurse to make the stop.

"Plus, I'm famished. The local diner seems like the best place to look around."

They entered the town of Freiburg. The little town seemed to appear out of nowhere, a trick of the depressed elevation leading down to the river that ran through the town and the thick forest that blocked sightlines from the road. The car filled with skunk scent as they drove down main street. The flattened skunk corpse by the side of the road at the intersection was the source of the smell, and the wait at the red light was a test of physical endurance. They drove off in a rush to escape the smell.

At the end of the next block Falstaff spied the local restaurant. The unlit neon sign with peeling paint sloughing off in patches proclaimed that the restaurant was 'The International', serving 'steaks, sandwiches, and all-day breakfast!'. He pointed at the sign.

"That's our place. Pull in, please."

Nurse parked the car downwind around the corner. The stink was fading but still pervasive, sticking to their clothes even after they sat in a booth inside the restaurant.

"Whenever I smell a skunk in the future, I will think fondly of this wonderful town. Get a load of these seats. Cracked red vinyl seats. Classic. Half-empty refrigerator at the counter, containing tiny glasses of juice and long-forgotten bowls of rice pudding. And manning the till, a surly old Greek who doesn't like anyone who sets foot in here. Bet the gravy is a powder from a generic package."

"You complain too much. This is not a luxury vacation."

Falstaff rubbed his hands together. "Am I complaining? I don't think I am. This kind of place is a classic piece of small town Americana. Either a Greek shop like this, or a Chinese place. Prosperous towns had both."

The old Greek man with the permanent scowl and one errant eye came begrudgingly over to the table and threw two menus onto the table with a wordless grunt. Falstaff ordered a coffee, a pack of smokes, and a

Jeungling Premium beer. "Here's hoping they have it" he said, mostly to himself.

The Greek was walking away from the table when Nurse added his request for a coffee. It wasn't apparent that the Greek heard him or cared. Falstaff flipped open the discolored menu in its protective plastic sleeve and perused the choices. He chuckled as he went down the list.

"Like I said, classic. Hot hamburger sandwiches. Full turkey dinner for lunch. Every side vegetable comes out of the freezer and has the shit boiled out of it."

While Falstaff gleefully weighed his options, Nurse went to the counter and picked up a copy of the local weekly newspaper, The Allegheny Standard. He brought it back to his seat and carefully laid the first section out in preparation.

"You're a deliberate reader. Very organized."

Nurse answered with a single raised eyebrow, then held the paper up as a divider between him and the world. The drinks arrived. Falstaff put in an order for the farmer's special full breakfast, with a second beer to come with it. The Greek left again without acknowledging the order in any way. Falstaff alternated between the beer and the coffee, after loading the coffee with sugar and cream until it came close to overflowing. The hot, sweet diner coffee mixed with the cool golden beer to make a perplexing flavor combination that he savored. He gulped it down and smacked his lips.

"Disgusting pig."

"Joie de vivre, motherfucker. I'll be back in a minute. Going to wash the mud off before the food gets here."

He was aware that Nurse was watching every step that he took, to make sure that he wasn't going to run off. Falstaff scanned the room to get a sense of the occupants, as he meandered towards the rest rooms at the back. The booth immediately behind theirs had the only lively diners. Two young men in their twenties were scraping at the last bits of their meals while preparing to get into the meat of their conversation. The man sitting with his back against the divider between his booth and Falstaff's was a lily-white hick. The grubby t-shirt proclaiming 'American Pride' was riding up on his paunch. His dirt-encrusted blue jeans were frayed at the cuffs, where they had caught on his heels as his pants rode too low. The John Deere hat perched on his greasy hair was the fitting complement to his country costume. Falstaff wondered if the man was an actual farmer.

Across from the hick sat a man with skin dark enough to cause him no end of trouble in rural America. The man had a tight pile of curls on top of his head that transitioned to a buzzcut from the crown of his head down to his neck. His jeans were clean and fit properly, and his t-shirt advertised a cutting-edge band from parts unknown. A short-sleeved, checkered dress shirt was layered on top of the t-shirt. The young man had leather bands, thin copper bangles, and multicolored woven bracelets adorning each wrist. The two men were exchanging bland opening pleasantries as Falstaff passed by. He guessed that their conversation wouldn't become interesting for a few minutes, unless one of them stormed off before that happened.

The washroom was tiny but relatively clean. Falstaff realized how muddy he was and made a silent apology to the hick for judging his slovenliness. "Glass houses" he said to himself as he scrubbed his hands and face clean. He finished by brushing the dried clumps of dirt from his pant legs and straightening his shirt to attempt to look presentable. He decided that it would be a good idea to bring a change of clothes with him whenever they went investigating, since he always ended up covered in dirt, blood or shit.

Back at the booth, his food was waiting for him and the guys next door were arguing. Falstaff tucked in to his meal and eavesdropped enthusiastically.

"You got all that city crap on you now, like you're too good for your home town."

"My home town is full of assholes who used to shout 'nigger' at me as they drove by at night. You're damn right I'm too good for them."

"I never did that to you, Kyle. Nobody we hung out with did."

"But you knew the guys who did. They were on your football team. You picked crops with them too during the harvest. Don't tell me you never heard them say shit like that. But you said nothing."

"Wouldn't do no good anyway. People around here think a certain way."

"Which is why I had to leave."

"The whole place has fallen to shit since you left for college. The papers say that kid who got killed over in the city, he was from New Bethel. They said they got killed after a big sex orgy. It was probably Satanic."

The earnest fear captured in the way the hick whispered 'Satanic' made Falstaff laugh under his breath. The college kid laughed out loud.

"Man, you are naïve. Bunch of people having sex isn't automatically devil worship. Probably a party that went bad."

"Decent folk don't have sex with multiple partners. The paper called the murderer 'the gangbang killer'. I thought gangbangs only happened in porn."

"Because you live in a shit town where nobody is good-looking enough to fuck, that's why. The things that happen downtown on a Saturday night would blow your mind."

Falstaff rolled his eyes at college boy's pretentiousness. He was doubtful that the college kid had seen any more action in Pittsburgh than he had in Freiburg.

"I don't know about any of that, and I'm proud of that" the hick said defensively.

"Gotta learn how the world works, or it leaves you behind, stuck in this place."

"That's your big problem. You think the city is the whole world. This is real America out here, where things are going bad for people. That gangbang killer gets all the attention, but nobody talks about the other guys who are getting gutted and left in the fields around the county. Regular guys like me and you, or like how you used to be before you went off to your fancy college. They found, shit, 3 of the guys so far, butchered like hogs, but no one cares because it happened out here. No one done nothing to stop it. If your life is in danger in the Rust Belt, you are on your own. Washington don't care, reporters don't care, no one cares about the poor folks left behind. The jobs were all stolen away, and those rich politicians did nothing. Now we got this devil of the Rust Belt, murdering anybody they want and leaving the bodies carved up into piles of meat. Jesus help the poor folks of the Rust Belt."

"MAN, FUCK THE RUST BELT" yelled the college kid. A clattering of cheap silverware hitting the kitchen floor was the only reply. The silence settled, and after a tense moment, the college kid continued at a normal volume.

"You should take a look at the voting records of the last few years. Every time these white, pill-popping idiots had a chance to vote, they chose the assholes who campaigned on cutting spending and getting tough with criminals. The programs they want to cut are the only ones helping folks around here. The extra cops mean more guys like you having their lives ruined by jail time. Unless you happen to have dark skin like me, in which case there's a good chance y'all don't even survive a traffic stop. And why do your people choose leaders like these? Because you cannot admit that even good people can be poor. You are so convinced that poverty is a sign of moral failing that you have to blame someone else for your financial woes. And that person is invariably a person of color."

"We ain't all racists. You and me are friends."

"That doesn't mean anything. You've turned a blind eye to the shit happening every day all around you. I cannot wait to get enough money to move out and leave this town behind me forever."

There was a surprising amount of hurt in the hick's voice. "It means something to me. I never been racist to you or anyone. I thought we were good."

The college kid let out a sigh as his anger deflated. Falstaff waited for the next line to come out. He was betting on a peace treaty of a sorts.

"Look, Chad, we are good. You have done the best you can in these circumstances. Our friendship is probably the only good thing I got from this town. I gotta go to work now. We'll meet up for beers this weekend, okay?"

"Yeah, sure. Later Kyle."

Falstaff pushed the salt and pepper shaker around the table in lazy ellipses, thinking about the conversation behind him and the state of the murder investigation. He heard the college kid dig out a pocketful of cash and drop the money onto the table, with a feeble attempt at protest rising from the hick. The matter was settled, and the college kid left in a hurry. The hick left as soon as the college kid was out of sight. Falstaff nudged Nurse's elbow to get his attention.

"Devil of the rust belt."

"What are you speaking of?"

"Those two dudes who were behind us were talking about murders. About ours, and about some other murders that have been happening in the area. Maybe that was the one the creepy news radio nerd was talking about. 3 killings is the start of a little spree. Not that it competes with our own murderer's score. Any reports of those murders in that paper?"

Nurse put the paper down and sneered down at it.

"It is a weekly paper for the bumpkins. It has livestock sales and bale sale advertisements. This is not where you find any real news."

"No mention of our killer, then? Ah well. The word on the street will have to do, if I can find the street."

Falstaff scanned the room's occupants again, studying each person for whatever secrets they had. He also waved at the surly Greek to get his attention for a repeat order of beer and coffee. The fresh bottle and cup arrived as Falstaff watched the nervous busboy check his watch 3 times consecutively.

"That's the best bet in here. That kid is eagerly awaiting a scheduled appointment."

Nurse craned his neck to look at the busboy. When the busboy noticed that Nurse was staring at him, he jumped and slipped into the kitchen to unload the bin of dirty dishes he had on his hip.

"You made him skittish, that poor lamb. If that kid isn't waiting for a dope connection, I'll eat my hat."

"What about a sex rendezvous?"

"I'm amazed your accent doesn't show back up when you butcher English like that. A sex rendezvous? What kind of mishmash is that? Oh good, the kid didn't run out of the place. He's checking his watch again. Don't glare at him this time, okay? Back to your question. Here's my response: Who would fuck that skinny bag of nerves? He's too scared to be ready to fuck, anyway. He wants the meeting to happen, but he's also dreading it. That's what meeting with a dealer feels like.

Here's the plan. The twitchy kid is going to slip out the back in a minute or two. He keeps looking back there. I'm going to follow him out to see who he's meeting with. Give me 5 minutes, and then come out looking for me. The kid is already tweaking on meth. Hands are picking at his clothes and his skin. There he goes."

The busboy wiped his hands on his apron and checked his watch for a final time to confirm that the hour had arrived. He shouted into the kitchen that he was going on break, and then scurried out of sight. Falstaff raised his beer in a salute and drained it in one long sip.

"To the chase, Watson. Let us see who the mysterious visitor in the alley will turn out to be."

Falstaff stood up and made his way back to the washrooms. Past them, as he expected, was a propped open back door. It was held open by a menu wedged near the top hinge, leaving a 6-inch gap between the door and the frame. Falstaff eased himself through the gap without moving the door, emerging into the wide alley running behind the diner.

The stench of old grease and rotting vegetables hit his nose instantly. The grease trap to his right was coated inside and out by old fryer grease and clouded by a perpetually circling cloud of flies. The dumpster on his left was also filthy and vermin-infested. Falstaff blinked away the tears in his eyes brought on by the smell. He looked down the alley to the right but saw nothing but the trash accumulated in the back corner where the alley made a 90 degree turn to the north. From behind the other end of the dumpster, Falstaff heard a wet smack that was immediately followed by a cry.

"That was for the rules you chose to ignore, Walt. Business gets done a particular way. Now what did you call me for?"

"Ya didn't have ta hit me. I need something to get me through."

Falstaff crouched down and peeked under the wheeled dumpster. He could see two sets of feet standing in the approximate source of the two voices, and there didn't seem to be anyone else in the alley. Falstaff sauntered around the corner of the dumpster to push his way into the conversation.

"We could all use a little something. I'm fresh out of- Oh shit."

Falstaff's clever opening line fell flat as he realized what he was walking into. The busboy had been on the receiving end of that loud smack, a slap to his face that had been hard enough to stagger him. Lording above him, ready to strike again, was the Sheriff Falstaff had met the evening before, the same Sheriff that had threatened them to leave town. The smug look on the Sheriff's face turned to startled embarrassment in the presence of a surprise witness.

He lowered his slapping hand, and hurriedly tucked the small package in his other hand into his jacket pocket.

"This is official police business."

"Sure looks like it. Young, vulnerable man cowering before a big strong police man standing erect above him, in a secretive back alley."

The Sheriff's face twisted into a knot of narrowed eyes, flared nostrils and bared teeth. He was on the edge of losing his temper and all control of his actions. Falstaff was amazed that a man could be so unhinged by a simple insinuation of homosexuality, even though he had seen it happen time and time again. The American Man myth tolerated no deviance from the expected sexual norms.

"You looking for a stay in the jail, vagrant? I'm going to arrest you for suspected lewd public conduct. You came out here looking for this youth, planning to force yourself on him. You're a goddamn rapist."

"Easy now, Sheriff. Let's take a few steps back. First, I apologise for interrupting your policework here, and for making a badly worded joke. It's all a simple mistake."

The busboy chimed in. "I don't know him, honest Sheriff. You know I need some help. Can you help me out?"

The Sheriff kicked the busboy in the side, knocking the wind out of him and sending him to the ground. He lay on the ground wheezing as the Sheriff stared Falstaff down.

"Get up, faggot, and go back inside. This no longer concerns you."

"B...but Sheriff, I need it."

"Get going or so help me…" The Sheriff punctuated his undefined threat with another kick, this time aimed at the busboy's thigh. The kick made the busboy squeal in pain, and he scrambled away from the confrontation to slip back inside. Now the center of the Sheriff's undivided attention, Falstaff wondered how many more minutes had to go by before Nurse showed up. He suspected the big thug was watching and enjoying the situation as it unraveled. Falstaff tried to deescalate the standoff and escape.

"So yeah, I followed the busboy out here, thinking he was going to the storage room to get a new jar of salsa. Love salsa with my eggs, but they ran out. Turns out he was going to the alley, not the store room. I'll just go back inside and use ketchup instead."

He turned on his heel and stepped towards the back door. The Sheriff grabbed his collar and pinned him against the dumpster. The Sheriff's forearm pressed into Falstaff's throat, forcing his head to turn. His cheek was pressed firmly against the dumpster and the tip of his nose was forced in to the crack between the lid and the metal body of the dumpster. The stench was tens times worse, and it filled his nose and mouth with a foul taste.

"That is the stupidest excuse I have ever been provided, son. You are staying right here until I get an understanding of what your purpose in this vicinity happened to be."

"Can you let up on the chokehold, Sheriff? The garbage is ripe and I'm going to hurl if you keep my face in it."

The Sheriff ignored his plea and stared intently at him. The wind shifted, and Falstaff caught the overwhelming wave of cheap cologne coming from the Sheriff. The cloud of perfume was giving the Sheriff limited immunity to the odors rising from the decomposing trash heap.

"Seriously, Sheriff. I'm not going anywhere. Just ease up a bit, huh?"

Falstaff regretted winding the Sheriff up so thoroughly at the start of their encounter. The anger he had stoked was still burning bright and was looking for an outlet. A look of confusion crossed the Sheriff's face.

"Do I know you, boy? There's a familiar aspect to your face."

"Uh, no sir. Just passing through."

The Sheriff smiled and leaned in to put pressure on Falstaff's windpipe. He gagged in response.

"Oh I do know you, asshole. We had words in New Bethel just yesterday. And now you are in my home town, and intruding into official police business. I think that there's more going on here than you have been forthcoming about. We are going to have a little chat."

True to his habit, the Sheriff punctuated his sentence with an act of violence. He drove his knee up into Falstaff's groin, smashing both of his testicles. Falstaff went weak in the knees and slipped down the side of the dumpster, stopped in his descent by the forearm now blocking off his oxygen. He had a bad feeling that this chat was going to end with his body in the noxious dumpster behind him.

11

"Are you still full of smart answers, or are you prepared to be honest with this representative of the law?"

The Sheriff grunted the words at Falstaff through his clenched teeth. Falstaff's only response was a panicked, wide-eyed, wordless plea to be freed from the chokehold cutting off his air. There were a multitude of personal indignities and physical threats Falstaff could endure without flinching, but suffocating was not one of them. He was about to lash out with his useless fists and feet, knowing that any hit scored on the Sheriff would lead to an even worse situation. The Sheriff suddenly stepped back and took his forearm off Falstaff's throat. He carefully brushed the dirt from his hands and smoothed his well-greased hair back into place as he spoke down to Falstaff.

"Christ, son. You are a mess. Look at the state you've put yourself in. Covered in dirt and stinking to high heaven. We are going to re-start this conversation, and this time you are going to answer my questions honestly. I hate to see anyone in this kind of sorry condition. The use of force to protect myself and the local citizens is regrettable, and I do not want to resort to that again."

That was the biggest lie the Sheriff had said to Falstaff yet. He loved hurting people. It was what got him out of bed in the morning. Now that he knew the depth of the Sheriff's love of violence, Falstaff changed his tactics and tried to get on the Sheriff's good side.

"Sorry, Sheriff. I say stuff without thinking about the consequences, sometimes. Can I light a smoke? The stress is getting to me."

The Sheriff sighed and shook his head mournfully. "Addiction is weakness of character, son. Clean body is necessary for a strong mind, and vice versa."

"You're right, Sheriff. I'm weak."

Falstaff slumped against the dumpster and looked up through his tangled hair in an appeal for pity from the law man. The Sheriff bought the beta act and gave his permission to light up. As Falstaff breathed in the fragrant cigarette smoke, the Sheriff began his line of questioning.

"You said you were tourists last night, is that correct?"

"Yes sir."

"But that was not a factual statement, now was it?"

"No sir."

"Now we are getting somewhere. What is your business in my county, boy?"

"Work. I'm a logistics systems analyst, on contract to a subsidiary division of the Department of Defense. I'm trying to identify any loss prevention opportunities for Uncle Sam."

"Bullshit. Don't lie, boy. You're down here, sniffing around for illicit narcotics. For all I know, you are a narcotics dealer attempting to prey on the innocent children of our fair county."

The rage crept back up the Sheriff's neck, turning it red. The man had a hair trigger.

"No lie, Sheriff. Do you want my ID?"

Falstaff held his open hands out towards the Sheriff to make it very clear that he was unarmed and nonthreatening. The cigarette bobbed erratically in Falstaff's clenched teeth. The Sheriff gave him permission to retrieve his ID. Slowly, without breaking eye contact, Falstaff reached into the inside breast pocket of his jacket and pulled out the ID badge. The Sheriff snatched it from his hand and examined it. He scowled first at the picture on the badge, then at the real-life version of the image. Falstaff launched into a more detailed fabrication to explain his presence and diffuse the Sheriff's suspicion.

"The focus of my trip is the military base outside of town here. Really, the towns in your county aren't involved directly in this at all. The Army Surplus may have some of the missing supplies, but that's a long shot. We weren't even properly introduced before. I'm John Falstaff. I can't quite make out your name on your badge there, Sheriff."

"Sheriff Dunner."

"Nice to meet you, Sheriff."

Falstaff stood with his left hand outstretched in hopeful anticipation of a friendly handshake. The Sheriff looked at the offered hand like it was covered in shit, then started tapping the ID badge against the gun holstered on his hip. Falstaff silently cursed the man's dedication to bullying the defenseless and lowered his hand down to wipe some of the perceived filth from it.

"I'm going to have to confiscate this identification until I can verify its authenticity with the appropriate authorities."

"Come on, Sheriff. I need that to do my job. Do you think I can just wander onto the army base and poke around in any room I want?" he said with a straight face, though he was certain he could do exactly that at the poorly run and disorganized army facility.

"Your job is not my concern. I have to keep the people safe, boy, not keep your public service paychecks rolling in. Living a soft life on the taxpayer's dime, like all the government leeches."

"But aren't you paid by tax money too, Sheriff?"

The question was an honest one. Falstaff wasn't trying to antagonize the lawman. But what he wanted and what had happened were two different things. Dunner lunged at Falstaff and threw him against the opposite wall with enough force to make Falstaff's teeth ache. His broken rib and multitude of bruises screamed in a chorus of pain. He slid down to the ground as the Sheriff stood hunched over him, panting like a bull preparing to charge again.

"Listen you piece of mongrel shit, I am done with your fucking around, do you understand? I am going to throw you in a deep dark hole and keep you there until I am good and satisfied that you are harmless. And if you look at me funny or open that shithole of a mouth of yours again to be a smartass, I am going to take you out to a special place that I have reserved for problems that need to go away. Stop being so goddamned clever."

Falstaff looked at either end of the alley and weighed the odds of reaching the street or vanishing around the corner. He braced himself for his flight attempt. The Sheriff was comfortable with threatening violence to a complete stranger. He was going to kill him eventually.

"There you are. Lunch break is over, Falstaff. Time for work."

Nurse's voice was an angelic reprieve floating across the alley from the back door of the restaurant. The Sheriff whipped his head around violently to see who had dared to interrupt his duties. He saw the phone in Nurse's hand, held at chest height and pointed at their conflict. A new emotion washed over the Sheriff's face: fear. Falstaff was glad to know the Sheriff had some sense of how out of line he was.

"Why are you filming this? That's illegal."

"It is a home movie of a public place. Do you need assistance in standing up, Mr. Falstaff?"

Nurse's dismissive tone was eating away at the Sheriff, but he was frozen in a moment of indecision. It helped that Nurse was twice the size of the Sheriff. Dunner stepped back away from both men and tossed the ID badge at Falstaff. Falstaff smiled and slipped the ID back into his pocket.

"I'm good, boss. Just had a slip and fall back here, after I took a wrong turn on the way to the john. You know how bad my sense of direction is. The good Sheriff

Dunner here was giving me a hand to get pointed in the right direction."

Slowly Falstaff pushed against the wall and brought himself to a standing position. He ignored the throbbing pain radiating up from his groin and his chest as he smiled at the Sheriff.

"I was going to ask, Sheriff, if you had any ideas about how materials are being removed from the army base without permission."

"That is outside of my jurisdiction. You will have to contact the appropriate resources at the base."

Falstaff walked over to Nurse's side to seek shelter behind the massive man. The irony of hiding behind one violent bully to escape another was not lost on him. He had to give Dunner credit for quickly shifting to a more professional demeanor. There was almost no trace of the raging psychopath who had been hunched over Falstaff a moment ago, ready to kick his heart into his throat.

"I think it's time we get back to work."

"Is your associate also a federal agent?"

"Does he work for the same division? Yes, he does. He's my field supervisor. If we have any questions about the area, can we contact you?"

"Let me walk you fellas back to your car so you can be on your way" the Sheriff said as he gestured towards the diner's back door. Falstaff and Nurse exchanged a look, followed by a quick nod of Falstaff's head. They walked ahead of the unanswered question on their way back to their table.

The surly Greek was brooding at the side of the table, ready to shout at them.

"You pay! Sheriff, they are cheats."

"Now now, Stan. They are ready to settle up their bill right now and head back out of town."

"I haven't finished my food, though."

The Sheriff frowned and lost a bit of his affected composure. He barked an order at the Greek, telling him to bring a takeout container. When the container arrived, the Sheriff grabbed it and threw it on the table.

"Pack it up and get going. Please."

Falstaff was tempted to prolong this odd scene and test the limits of the Sheriff's public persona. A nudge from Nurse pushed that idea from his head. He shovelled the last half of his breakfast platter into the foam container and sucked down the last of his cooling coffee. He smacked his lips and handed the container to the Sheriff.

"Hold this for a moment, would you? Got to tie my shoe."

"Tie it outside, son" the Sheriff snarled, but still took hold of the food container. He pushed Falstaff forward with enough force to make him stumble into the next booth. Falstaff looked back for his protector, but Nurse was happily paying the bill while ignoring the resuming confrontation. Falstaff regained his balance and walked out the front door of the restaurant.

Dunner followed close behind with one hand firmly locked onto Falstaff's right elbow.

At the car, Falstaff went to open the door but was stopped by the door lock. Nurse sauntered across the street with the car keys in hand, able to unlock it remotely at any time, but choosing not to. He was enjoying the uncomfortable torment Falstaff was caught in. Finally, the tinny beep of the car key fob rang out. Falstaff pulled open the door and jumped into the seat to escape the cop.

As Nurse lowered himself into the driver's seat, the cop knocked on Falstaff's window and pointed downwards. Falstaff was tired of this fight and this whole situation, so he did as he was told and lowered the window.

"I want to be clear with you two. Stay out of my towns. The army base, that is outside of the county, so you have no need to be in my county business. Understand?"

"You're a busy man with business all over the place, eh Sheriff?"

The look that crossed the Sheriff's face told Falstaff that the Sheriff did indeed have business interests across the whole county, and that those interests were not something he wanted publicly talked about. He filed the info away in the back of his mind and put on a grateful smile.

"Thanks for your help, Sheriff Dunner. We're heading directly back to the city now. You won't see us again."

The Sheriff leaned down and carelessly dropped the takeout container into Falstaff's lap. It popped open and a handful of greasy hash browns fell out. Dunner stepped back and pointed down the road.

"Safe drive, boys. Get."

The Sheriff stood with one foot on the curb and watched their car pull a U-turn and drive out of town. Falstaff watched the man recede in the side mirror as they drove away.

"Amazing that a turd like him can keep a job like this, or maybe the job naturally attracts guys like him. That was, what, 3 assaults and multiple threats in the span of 20 minutes? The townsfolk must be terrified of that shitheel. He's the local drug distributor, by the way."

Nurse's jaw dropped open. "What?"

Falstaff picked a handful of the piled hash browns up from his lap and popped them in his mouth. He sucked the dirt off them first before chewing them.

"The reaction he gave me when I mentioned his business around the county. And the fact that he was selling to that poor tweaker busboy when I came out to the alley. He keeps accusing us of bringing drugs into the county. That's because he has unidentified competition in the drug trade and it is killing his profits. Our mysterious distributor/murder suspect is trying to take over this market."

"You seem to be very sure of this, with no proof."

"That's how I do things. It's a hallmark of my terrible detective style. Besides, bad guesses are better than no guesses. Let's sniff this trail and follow it until we find the end of it. Could be a dead end, who knows? In any case, the angry spray-tan Sheriff Dunner is going to be involved in this investigation whether we want him to be or not. The 4 victims came from towns in his control. When the full tox report comes back, and I hope our boss sends it along to you on your fancy telephone, we're going to discover that all the victims had the identical painkiller in their bloodstream."

"The morphine. We know that."

Falstaff batted away Nurse's interruption with an irritated wave of his hand.

"Let me finish. Jesus. In addition to the final knockout dose of morphine, each victim will have ample traces of a different opioid in their blood. That is the drug that the new distributor is selling in those baggies. So, if all the victims were high on the same drug, it is a link we need to chase down. The challenge right now, dear Nursie, is to find a place that potential customers would gather to pass the afternoon away. In a place that the Sheriff would avoid while on duty. I got an idea. Pull in to that gas station we passed on the way here."

Driven by curiosity, Nurse steered the car into the weed-choked parking lot of Earl's Hi-Test gas station. Falstaff hopped out of the car and walked to the long-neglected payphone booth that stood forlornly under a drooping light standard. He flipped through the book and laughed as he found the page he was looking for. He ripped it out of the book and skipped back to the car. He leaned over and plugged a new address into the

GPS. The nondescript rural route designation gave no clue as to their new destination, and Falstaff refused to let Nurse in on the plan.

"I will give you one hint, oh nosey one. We're heading to a cultured place of leisurely decline. Or is it recline? Hard to say."

He chuckled at his own joke and popped the last of the hash browns from the container into his mouth. He wiped the last bit of grease from his hands onto the cuffs of his pant legs.

They continued to drive down cracked blacktop roads that passed by a ramshackle trailer park, a boarded-up motel, and a handful of farmhouses in the distance down their long gravel driveways. The final turn brought a grey, featureless building into view.

"Before we get any closer, I gotta warn you. This could get weird."

The car slowed as Nurse pulled his foot up from the accelerator with growing trepidation. The grey building ahead was nestled into the base of an off-ramp from route 99, and the paired on-ramp was across the 2-lane road they were on. They came even with the gaudy sign attached to the grey building's façade as the car edged into the parking lot. The sign proudly announced that they had arrived at "Rude Licks, the Dirtiest place in the State!" and Nurse groaned loudly in disgust while shaking his head in disbelief.

"No better place to find the underbelly of an area than the local nudie bar. If a peeler ain't seen it, it ain't happening. Get out of the car, Nurse, and get ready for a real American experience. Word of advice, play it safe and take a piss in the parking lot if you gotta go. The bathrooms tend to be a real horror show in places like this."

12

Nurse dug in his heels and shook his head with a look of disgust on his face. He couldn't take his eyes away from the cheap 'Rude Licks' sign, and he held his arms outstretched to ward off the imagined lurid horrors lurking inside the club. Falstaff laughed at the sight.

"A trained military combat killer can't bring himself to get near a little 3rd rate U.S.A. trim? You must have been inside a strip club before. You didn't serve your country from the comforts of a monastery."

"This place is disgusting."

"Such is life, Nursie. The gross places are where humanity gets real. Relax, I'll keep things running smoothly. Nice and casual, nothing uncomfortable. We'll buy a few drinks for the couple of loyal perverts hanging around near the stage, give the least ugly dancers a few compliments, and then get some information from them. We'll be out of here in less than an hour. Promise. Do you want to pay the waitress?"

"Yes. I will keep the money."

"Okay. For your information, they expect tips, and you are supposed to tuck it between her tits. You cool with that?"

Nurse looked at the waitress leaning against the bar, pushing her cleavage together in the halter top straining to contain the majesty of her breasts. Despite the heroic efforts of the elastic fabric, her cleavage sat midway between her collarbone and her navel, her nipples pointed downwards.

"I change my mind. You pay" Nurse muttered as he handed a stack of bills to Falstaff.

A round of drinks for the house followed quickly, with an extra gin and tonic for Falstaff. They picked out a table near the private dance lounge and watched the disinterested dancer onstage. The drinks arrived, and the club denizens gathered around their new benefactor. One of the dancers, a big girl wearing a naughty school girl outfit and towering platform shoes made her way to Falstaff's side with a leer on her face. She leaned over him to give him a good view down her top and spoke into his ear in a husky smoker's voice.

"Hey darlin'. You look lonely."

Falstaff smiled politely at the woman as she teetered on her impossibly high shoes. He turned his head to reply into her ear.

"I'm doing okay, but my friend is a little uptight. He's never had a lap dance before, and I want to get him one as a surprise. You up for it?"

"If you're paying, I'm grinding."

Falstaff pulled out 100 bucks and displayed it for her.

"Deal. 25 right now, to get the show started. Another 75 if you can get him too turned on to stand up. Do it right here, so I can watch his reaction."

The 25 bucks disappeared into the big girl's shiny gold purse, and she got to work. The look of surprise, discomfort and shame on Nurse's face brought joy to Falstaff's petty heart. The thick-legged woman was grinding her pelvis into his lap with a fearsome determination brought on by the 75 bucks promised to her.

Nurse was trapped under her for the entire length of the song, afraid to reach up and remove her. At the end of the song, she stood up and reached down to grab his erect dick through his pant leg.

"75 bucks! Mission accomplished."

Falstaff waved her back over before Nurse overcame the shock of being groped. He handed her the cash and congratulated her on a job well done.

"You better give us some space though, honey. He might have a bad reaction to the whole scene and I don't want you to get any trouble from him."

She shrugged, tucked the second installment of cash into her purse and stilt-walked away to a door marked 'employees only'. Flanked on either side by gap-toothed locals, and with an older stripper sitting across from him batting her heavily made up eyelids at him, Falstaff asked the group for party advice.

"What do you folks do for fun around here? Other than hanging out in this fine establishment."

The response from the backwoods strip club denizens was a mess of barely enunciated suggestions. The two perverts who had been right up front when Falstaff had come in took up the lion's share of the conversation. Falstaff ignored their introductions and labeled them internally as Blacktooth and Dogbreath. Blacktooth was both underweight and flabby simultaneously. His red-rimmed eyes blinked compulsively every few seconds, and he snorted back the ever-present phlegm in his throat at regular disgusting intervals. Two teeth up top and three on the bottom were stained with tobacco juice and rotting out of his head.

Dogbreath was in better shape than his buddy. His teeth were yellow but healthy. The scars on his knuckles spoke to a long history of fist fighting. The sour smell of his breath made speaking directly to him impossible. It was the foul odor of a dog's mouth after it has eaten a dead skunk and a pound of shit. There was a terrible medical condition eating its way out of Dogbreath, and the smell was its calling card.

The two men went back and forth in a meaningless patter. Falstaff got a snapshot of the pathetic lives these two lived. And as they were in front of the 2 strippers roaming the audience for lap dance customers, the sad stories Dogbreath and Blacktooth told were exaggerations meant to impress the ladies.

They had to shout over the booming dancehall song currently providing the soundtrack for the unenthusiastic lady on stage with a million things on her mind and little faith that she was going to get a big tip this afternoon. Falstaff looked back to the darkened square off to the side of the private lounge, a box made from plywood that had been spray-painted black and gold. He gave it a nod and lowered his flat hand held out at eye level. After a moment, the music dropped to a more conversational level, drawing foul stares from the gyrating woman. Falstaff gave a 'thumbs up' to the presumed DJ booth, then ordered another pair of drinks for himself.

They circled around the topic of illicit substances until Falstaff blurted it right out. He asked who had a good connection to oxy. The small crowd hesitantly played dumb. Blacktooth thought there was an opportunity to make some cash, so he offered to sell Falstaff a couple of pills from his personal supply.

"I got 'em on account of my chronic pain issues" he slurred.

"Sounds like selling those could get you in trouble, pal. The law seems pretty testy about drugs in this county. From what I have seen, the Sheriff is a war on drugs kind of guy."

The circle of people squirmed. Falstaff scanned their faces and laughed at the secret they were all desperate to share. They may as well have shouted "I buy my dope from the Sheriff!". The mention of the law man had chilled the prospect of a continual free ride good time, and the denizens crept back to their accustomed locations with a bashful 'thanks' mumbled over their shoulders.

Nurse continued to shiver with repulsion and stare at his lap and hands as if they had been covered in rotting, liquefied flesh. His head shook slowly from side to side in half-time synchronization with the last few beats of the song.

"That was pointless. You put that whore on me."

"Easy, tiger. She's a dancer, and a good one, all things considered. You'll be fine-nothing in here is that contagious."

"This accomplished nothing" Nurse growled, slamming his fist onto the uneven table. Falstaff raised his glass to finish off his 3rd drink in 10 minutes. The warm glow of a fast, good buzz settled into his bones.

"Depends on your perspective."

"To get drunk? That was the point? You are a worthless shit."

The song finished, and the DJ blared out a command for the room to thank Mystery for her performance. The scattered sparse applause was fitting for the way Mystery stormed off stage without one look back.

"Day strippers have a rough go of things. Poor girl."

The DJ announced that there would be a short break before the next dancer, Bella, took the stage. The music came back on, returned to the full raucous volume. The door to the booth opened and the DJ walked out towards the bar. Falstaff watched him walk and was surprised to recognize him.

"Hey, hey DJ. Thanks for turning the tunes down earlier. Can I get you a drink?"

The DJ stopped and looked Falstaff over. The DJ was suspicious but willing to approach him.

"Naw, I don't drink when I'm working. Don't worry about it."

"Got a tip jar, then?"

The DJ looked more uncomfortable with every passing moment. Falstaff smiled and pointed at him.

"Did I see you in town earlier? At the diner? I think I was sitting right behind you."

"Yeah. Listen, man, I gotta go."

"That was some debate you were having with your friend. He was really worried about the poor folks of the Rust Belt."

That was enough bait to draw College Boy the DJ into sitting down with them. He leaned back in his chair and yawned.

"He's one of my best friends, but he's a fool, yo. All these chickenshit white bread dirt farmers and pill poppers are moaning about the state of the world. There have been people on the barricades screaming a warning about the collapse of western manufacturing and middle-class lives, but these folks paid no attention. When it was young black men out of work and desperate, the media called them thugs and sent in the brute squad police. But now, whitey white is trapped in a prison of his own making and it's a big fucking problem."

"The people in this club seemed scared to talk about any of that. Especially the drugs."

"You a narc? You sure look like one."

Falstaff laughed, and a belch snuck out in the middle.

"Look closer, DJ. I am covered in dirt, grease, and honestly I don't know what the fuck else. Oh, and I am well on my way to good and drunk. I'm a, what do you call it, a private investigator. Close enough. I can't arrest shit, If I go to the cops, I go to jail first. If I'm lucky."

College boy shifted his weight forward and inspected Falstaff.

"Then what about your gorilla buddy right there?"

"Him? Not a cop, either. He's my guard."

"Keeping you safe, or locking you down?"

Falstaff held his hands up on either side of his shoulders in a tipsy approximation of a scale.

"Little bit of both."

"Alright, this is a fucked-up scene, but I believe you. Everybody in here is terrified to tell you anything because they think the gangbang killer will make them regret it. The talk is, the murders were a reprisal over territory, or a deal gone real wrong."

"Could be. Does anyone think the Sheriff was involved?"

College Boy was rocked back into his seat by the suggestion. He rubbed the stubble dusting his jawline and considered the idea.

"Shit. Maybe. Dunner is a man with a bad reputation. Hypothetically. But spreading rumors like that gets a nigga like me lynched, so leave me out of your speculating."

Falstaff caught motion from the corner of his eye, and assumed it was the waitress coming to collect the empties. He turned to order another drink, and realized it was the bartender who had approached the table. She was a tall woman in her 40s, dressed in a long sleeve ringer t-shirt and faded blue jeans with sequins along the pocket seams. The pock marks on her cheeks were expertly camouflaged with makeup, but the momentary flash of light from the stage betrayed the uneven landscape. She folded her arms and addressed the table.

"Excuse me, gentlemen, but my employee here needs to get off his lazy ass and go back to work."

College boy squirmed in his seat. Falstaff watched the struggle between his fierce independence and his obligation to respect his boss play out on College Boy's face. The paycheck won. College Boy mumbled an apology and hurried off to the bar.

"He pours drinks when the girls are on break. Now why are you two fellows sniffing around my club, getting my people all riled up and nervous?"

"Your club? You manager or owner?"

"Owner, not that its your business."

"You used to dance too. You're comfortable here."

"Listen, I need you to answer why you have come into my club, asking dangerous questions like a couple of badly trained cops."

"Are there any other kind of cops?"

The owner smirked. "Not that I've met."

"We're not trying to get anyone here in trouble. Just looking into some stuff in the county."

"Well I believe your visit is all done. Hope you fellows enjoyed yourself. It's time to settle up."

The owner locked eyes with Falstaff, then stepped back and beckoned Falstaff to follow her to the till. Nurse started to follow behind Falstaff, but he waved him off.

"Go out and wait in the car. 5 minutes. She wants to talk to me alone."

"Why?"

"Fuck who knows. Your face is upsetting her. Now fuck off."

Nurse was too happy with the chance to escape the club to take issue with the order. He left as Falstaff met with the owner at the cash.

"Name's John Falstaff. I have an ID badge that you can look at, if you want."

"Don't wave a badge around in here, for Christ's sake. It's probably fake anyway. I'm Doreen. Call me Dot."

"How Midwest."

"So John, why are you disrupting my place of business?"

"There was a murder. Bunch of guys and one woman. The guys came from around here. I'm trying to figure out who killed them."

"But you're not a cop."

"Points to you for good observational skills. Nope. Like I told College Boy, I am a private investigator."

"Really?"

"More or less, sure. Do you know anything about the gangbang killer? The one victim was a small-time dealer in the area. Maybe he came in here."

"I don't tag each dope dealer who crawls in here to sell. I just throw 'em out when I catch them. Goddamn leeches."

The subtle motion of Dot's left hand gently rubbing her right forearm gave Falstaff a clue about where she had picked up her intense dislike of drug dealers.

"Do you know where he got his dope from? Before recently, that is. I have a hunch he started buying bulk from a new player in the last month."

"No idea. None of the girls here will know either. The more you ask about a dealer's source, the worse the prices get."

Falstaff sighed and nodded his head. He pulled out one of his business cards and slipped it forward, hidden under a 20-dollar bill.

"One more drink for the road. Double rum and coke, for a change. If you remember anything about the victims, get a hold of me."

Dot took the money and the card and mixed Falstaff's drink. She placed it in front of him and he smiled a pure and simple smile at the full glass. He took a long, slow sip and let the sweet fluid wash around his whole mouth.

"Careful you ain't too fond of that drink."

"I have many loves in my life. I'm a man of variety."

Dot watched him methodically sip and swish the drink until the glass was empty.

"The girl, she was a working girl, right?" Dot asked with an uncertain waver in her voice.

"That's right. Sex worker, with a long list of minor criminal charges."

"What was her name?"

"To be honest, I don't know their names yet. My partner has the files with the details."

"You don't know the names of the victims?"

Falstaff raised his glass to her in agreement. "I'm a shitty detective."

"This is so typical. No one cares about a murdered woman. She means nothing to you."

Falstaff hated to see that much hurt and sadness come over a person. Dot was reliving a lifetime of being mistreated and devalued.

"Look, I'm sorry. I know she meant something, and she did not deserve what happened to her. I'm going to do my best to catch her killer, I promise."

"What about her face? Can you remember if she had a trail of stars tattooed at the corner of her right eye?"

Falstaff remembered lifting the sheet at the morgue and seeing the destroyed face of the sex worker. If there had been a tattoo there beforehand, the bullet erased it along with the rest of her features. His mind wandered to thinking about the kind of bullet that could do that to a human being. He would have expected a single hole with some damage around it, not a swath of ruined, jagged flesh. He noticed that Dot had said something he had missed and was waiting for a response.

"Uh, no, I don't know if she had a tattoo. That area was…damaged in the attack."

Dot sighed, and her shoulders sagged.

"I wish that made me believe it isn't her. But that's not how things turn out. The rumors say it was a girl I used to know. Rumors are probably right. She danced here, couple years back. Then she went to the city to make more money. You can't make much dancing here. The motivated ones leave as quick as they can. But we keep in touch, the girls who leave and me. An informal support group to keep everybody safe. That's how I know Val went missing."

"How reliable is the group? Maybe she took a few days off or went on vacation."

"She would have told the group. That's what we do, so we don't worry."

"Is it dangerous every night?"

Dot shrugged one more time.

"Sometimes. Girls take risky jobs."

13

"Who's ready to fuck?"

4 nervous men backed away from the man speaking from the center of the room, and from each other. The speaker clapped his hands and brayed out a long, loud laugh that echoed around the warehouse.

"You should see the looks on your faces. Priceless. Relax fellas, that was just a joke. You're all nervous and I get that. My name is Looey. I am the producer of this little amateur film. My goal is to get the best performance from you, and that means loosening up and having fun."

Looey gave them a smile that showcased every long, yellow tooth in his head. The thick black stubble covering most of the bottom half of his face and his deep-set eyes completed the allusion that he was a rat made human. He held up 4 baggies with matching numbers of chalk white pills inside of them.

"When you start a party, you got to have party favors. One for each of you. I highly recommend taking exactly one pill. Even if you have a tolerance of steel, these little beauties will knock you on your ass. But who am talking to? Of course you guys know how good this dope is. Catch!"

He tossed a bag to each man. The first three opened them up and dry swallowed 2 pills apiece. The fourth man shifted from foot to foot as he looked around the room nervously. Looey watched him build up the courage to finally ask his question.

"Is there a bathroom where I can shoot?"

Looey took a step forward and put his arm around the nervous man, like an older brother offering safe advice.

"For the good of the movie, I want you to swallow the pills. No injecting. All the actors have to be at the same level, if you know what I mean. If you shoot up with this stuff here, you'll be snoozing in the corner for the evening."

Still unsure, the nervous man leaned away from Looey and started to stammer a protest. Looey squeezed the junkie's shoulder as he pulled him close.

"Listen buddy, just keep your cool and stick to the plan. After we finish the scene, you will have so much dope you'll run out of places to put it. You can go home and shoot up until you're high as a fucking kite. In fact, I'll throw in an extra dose because you're such a cool guy. Alright?"

The nervous man reluctantly accepted the instruction and swallowed the pills. Looey brought out his own baggie and joined in to the fun. He washed a half-dose down with a swig of his bottle of Bud.

"While we wait for the magic little pills to do their work, you can all chill out in the green room over there. Yeah, it's just a desk with chips and beer. Grab a chair and hang out until I call you back over. We are going to have some fun tonight!"

Looey laughed again and left the 4 men to amuse themselves. He walked to the camera at the east end of the stage and squinted through the viewfinder to ensure that the action would all be in frame. Satisfied with the camera's alignment, he went to its partner camera on the west side and repeated the process. He turned to walk over to the snack table when a quiet voice spoke from the dark doorway of the adjoining office.

"You should check the coversheet. It slipped last time."

Looey faced the direction of the voice. The dark, darting eyes of the uneasy woman standing in the doorway seemed to swallow all the available light.

"Hey, here's an idea. Why don't you check it yourself?"

The woman held her arms tightly bound around her chest, as if letting go would cause her body to completely fall apart. She rocked on her heels, fading in and out of the light like a vanishing ghost. Looey gave up waiting for an answer.

"Fine. I'll do it. The glamour of show business."

He crouched down at the side of the desk positioned in the center of a roughly circular clearing in the middle of the warehouse floor. He wiggled the new metal clips that held the edges of a thick floral-patterned duvet fast to the surface of the desk. He hopped up and lay back on the table, throwing his legs up in the air and pantomiming the gyrations of frenetic coupling. He stopped and got off the desk, pointing to the duvet still in place. The woman in the doorway bit her nail and nodded.

"We are operational" Looey stated to the west camera. "Ok fellas, come on over here. You should all be feeling more relaxed by now. I know I am."

The 4 men shuffled over in a clump, each standing an arm's length away from each other. One of them stood a step ahead of the other three. He had slicked back hair cresting a wave of acne raging across the young man's forehead. He made occasional slurping noises as he vacuumed the excess saliva that pooled around the jeweled grill covering his top teeth. His matching black velour track suit had shiny patches where the fabric had been worn down. Mismatched rings and bracelets covered his fingers and both wrists. The other 3 men willingly fell in line behind him, to hide in his shadow.

"Here's the deal. We are going to shoot a porno today. It's in the genre of amateur gangbang, where 4 regular guys have sex with one hot girl. The goal is to make it authentic, and fun for everybody. And fuck as much as possible, of course."

Looey laughed until the men joined in. The nervous IV user was the last to add his thin, high-pitched giggle to the mix. The laughter died back down and Looey continued to the specifics.

"Rule number one is: stop when she says stop. This is always in effect. If you are not sure that she wants you to stop, stop. We can always reshoot parts of the scene. And guys, if you feel like something is not right and you want to stop, say so. The camera amplifies your discomfort. If you have fun, the audience will see it and they will have a good time too. No rough stuff: Spanking, slapping and anything like that is out. If you're the primary partner, fuck her energetically but stay in control. If you fuck her so hard you both fall off the desk, the shot will be worthless. Remember where the cameras are, but do not look directly at them. You will notice that they are at opposite ends of the room. As long as you are looking in the other two directions where there are no cameras, you'll be fine. Best case scenario is that you're watching the hot girl getting fucked in front of you instead of staring at the filing cabinet over there.

And this is most important instruction I have for you: when you're going to cum, let me know. Don't shout out 'Looey I'm going to cum' because that would sound stupid and creepy but announce the fact that you're going to cum with enough warning for me to line up the shot. Cum on her face, her tits, her hand her hair, I don't care. Just make sure I get it on film. So, who's ready to meet their leading lady?"

A sad, disorganized whoop rose from the 4 men, supplemented by Grill's overly enthusiastic clapping. Looey nodded to the woman in the shadows and she ducked out of sight. Moments later, she stepped back into view leading another woman into the room.

The new woman was tall, nearly 6 feet, with an extra few inches added by an impressively tall hairdo of styled blond curls. She had a robe partially tied up to cover her starting outfit. The men saw glimpses of bright pink neon and black fishnet stockings. The woman had well applied makeup heavily covering her face, muddying her features instead of bringing definition to them. She smiled with a wink and waved her fingers at the men watching her.

"Hi boys, I'm Ginger Bangs. Are you ready for a good time?" she said with a slight slur of her words that revealed she was on the same meds that the men had been given. She walked forward, dropping the robe en route to display a collection of bad tattoo art covering most of her arms and legs. She stood in the middle of the group and slipped her arms around Grill and IV. Looey continued his address.

"This is a professional film shoot, everybody. We are going to keep you safe and sound. At the end of filming, you will each be given a medical injection of a powerful anti-viral vaccine. It prevents every major sexually transmitted infection for a period of 24 hours. This vaccine is not cheap, because it is incredibly effective, but we are committed to keeping all of you disease-free. This shot will kill every last nasty bug that can affect your naughty bits, so don't worry."

The actors considered Looey's words and muttered amongst themselves. The drug-assisted consensus accepted that the shot was exactly what Looey said it was, and they all agreed to get dosed after the filming.

"Great. Any questions?"

"We still got payments to settle" Grill said with a false bravado.

"Patience, my man. All accounts will be settled before you leave, including your additional finder's fee. I appreciate the effort you put in to this event. You are going to be a great part of the team."

"Cool. Let's get to it."

Looey smiled wide again and shook the hands of each of the actors. He scuttled back to the west camera and worked on the high-powered laptop that sat on the small desk beside it.

"Cocks out, cameras are rolling!"

The men disrobed to various states of undress. Grill was the first one to get fully nude, proudly displaying his chest covered in gang tattoos. The matching White Supremacist tattoos adorning each of his shoulders proudly announced his White Purity, bracketed by poorly inked 'SS' insignias. He stepped up to be the first to encounter Ginger, with his arms outstretched to keep the others back. He looked straight at the camera and loudly asked 'you want this fucking huge dick, ho?' as he brandished his half-erect, average sized penis at Ginger. Ginger told him she wanted it bad, in a candy sweet voice that brought him to full attention. She lowered her mouth onto the tip of his cock.

IV was in the back of the group. Like the other two men, he had his cock in hand, stroking it aggressively to achieve some kind of erection. He was the most endowed one of the group, but the lack of response from his frantic masturbation boded ill for his ability to participate.

Grill moved around to the side of the desk and told Ginger to get on all fours. He started to fuck her doggie style, and Looey waved at the waiting men to join in.

The man on the left stepped up. He was naked from the waist down, but still wearing his grimy flannel shirt fully buttoned up. When he pulled his arms up, the shirt rode up to show the underhang of his belly. There was very little distance between the end of his erect cock and the lower part of his fat gut. He took the spot in front of Ginger and made awkward eye contact with Grill as they spit roasted her.

The guy on the right got a panicked look in his eye. He ran forward and blurted out 'I'm coming'. He made it to the edge of the improvised fuck station before ejaculating in a single explosive shot. The blob of jizz missed Ginger entirely and spattered on his own foot. He looked over to Looey with red-faced shame, but Looey just smiled and gestured for the man to step back and return to stroking.

Eventually, IV managed a workable erection, and the three men tried for simultaneous penetration. Grill switched spots with Ginger and she mounted him as he lay with his legs hanging off the end of the desk. She leaned forward to let the fat guy press his cock coated in lubricant into her ass, as she navigated IV's cock into her mouth. The 3 men began to pump and thrust in different rhythms while Ginger fought to keep her balance. Fat Guy was overcome with enthusiasm and pulled back too far. His short cock popped out, and on the forward thrust it deflected downwards, past Ginger's vulva and Grill's testicles, to slip neatly between Grill's ass cheeks. Grill let out a surprised and offended yelp. He tried to kick Fat Guy away from him, but only managed to writhe and rub against the unwelcome erection in his crack. Fat Guy called out an ejaculation warning and grill bellowed a curse. It was a photo finish, but Fat Guy was at the last second able to pull his dick back up above the two people below him. He sent a thin stream of semen shooting up Ginger's back while he mumbled 'sorry'. Grill ordered Ginger to get off him and when he was standing again, he looked to be caught in a dilemma. His glare at Fat Guy spoke to his desire to kick the shit out of him, but his raging hard-on said he wanted to finish. He turned back to Ginger and told her he was going to cum on her dirty whore face. IV said he was going to cum too, so Ginger brought them around to either side of her face and told them to coat her with their spunk. The guy with the hair trigger laughed at the word 'spunk', triggering a fierce snarl from Grill.

The two men lined up and stared intently at Ginger's face, trying to avoid the sight of the man opposite stroking his cock to climax. Grill came first with a paltry amount of ejaculate leaking down the end of his dick to connect with Ginger's chin. IV compensated for his difficulty in joining the party by blowing a massive load onto Ginger's mouth, cheeks and left eye. Looey called cut as IV apologized empathically to Ginger. She looked up at him with her one eye clamped shut to keep his cum out.

"Don't worry about it, sweetie. Can you get me a towel?"

Looey walked over with a set of towels for all the participants, with an additional warm damp towel for Ginger. She did a preliminary clean-up of her face and a quick pass of her genital area. The men did a hurried wipe down and quickly pulled their clothes back on. Even Grill had a temporary bout of humility and a need to cover up.

"Congratulations folks, that was a great shoot. Plenty of passion, and a real authenticity. That is money."

Fat Guy raised his hand and confessed that he thought he looked at the camera.

"Naw, you didn't. It was all great. Now, here's the order for the post-filming process. One at a time, you will go back to the office over there with my assistant. She'll give you your vaccine shot and give you a few minutes to rest and let the shot kick in. It may make you a little tired at first, so go ahead and lie down until you feel reenergized."

Looey pointed at Fat Guy. "You are the first one to go."

The other woman emerged from the office doorway again, looking nervous and preoccupied. She meekly came over and directed Fat Guy towards the office without coming into direct physical contact with him. The two of them vanished into the dark of the doorway and the door closed behind them.

The next fifteen minutes passed in awkward semi-silence. The other woman returned to retrieve another participant every few minutes. Ginger was the only one who she talked to on the way, with a hand gently placed on Ginger's arm to guide her to the back. The other woman asked if Ginger was okay and if she needed anything at all. Ginger laughed and said it was an easy paycheck, better than the majority of her dates.

The last actor left in the warehouse was Grill. Looey brought a canvass ammunition bag over to the smaller desk near the snacks and flipped it open.

"Good job, boss. You got a good group of guys together. As promised, your payment is right here. A full week's worth of product to divide up and sell as you see fit. Future shipments will be sold for cash, you understand. This was a one-time deal. But you will make a fucking mint from this dope."

Grill looked in the bag and gleamed with greedy joy. He lifted out the large double-bagged sac of pills and held it close to his cheek, like he was cradling a baby.

"And you have to keep using the branded bags, so people know they are getting the good shit, not the garbage that other shithead sells."

"The heat's gonna get hot, yo."

"Then you have to keep cool, right? I have faith in you. Remember this is an exclusive deal. You didn't tell anybody about tonight, correct?"

"Only the fools who came with me. And they is lonely motherfuckers with no family or bitches so they got nobody to tell. Hush hush, motherfucker."

"Great. Looks like it's your turn for the shot. Head back to the office."

Looey pointed at the other woman, who had just re-emerged from the office. Grill swaggered towards her with the dope bag tossed over his shoulder. He stood toe to toe with the nervous woman and towered over her by a good foot. She looked up at him with those deep, dark eyes that seemed to drink in the available light. She stared with such an intensity that Grill wilted away and averted his eyes. She pointed at the office door and he hurried past her.

Grill was halfway through the door when the loop of wire slipped around his neck and pulled tight. He tried to turn around, but the sudden weight of the nervous woman on his back sent him stumbling into the office. The garrote bit deeply into his neck, breaking the skin stretched over his larynx. He looked around frantically for help as he batted uselessly at the woman hanging suspended from the handles of the garrote.

Grill walked into the plain metal desk in the room and fell on top of it. The woman put her feet onto the desktop on either side of him and used the leverage to pull the wire even tighter. He saw the bodies of the other participants laying on sleeping bags lining the walls of the office, arranged head to toe like corpses in a makeshift morgue.

Grill's hands drummed the top of the desk with a rapidly weakening tempo until his life ran out. The woman kept choking him for a full minute after his hands stopped tapping on the desk, letting the blood leaking from the gash in his neck spread across the desk.

Looey scooted around the desk to examine Grill. The open bloodshot eyes and protruding purple tongue were enough to convince Looey that Grill was dead. He gave the woman a 'thumbs up'. She let the garrote go slack and removed it from the victim's neck in an efficient single gesture. She stepped off the desk and wiped the blood residue that was on her nitrile gloves onto the back of Grill's denim jacket.

Looey slipped his arms under Grill's armpits and hefted him from the desk.

"I'll get this one into position. Are the others ready?"

The woman, nervous and agitated moments ago, was now sedate. She tilted Grill's head back to inspect the garrote wound. She probed the edge of the broken skin with her index finger.

"The blood surprises me each time."

Looey laughed as he started dragging Grill's corpse into the main room.

"It's because you pull so hard, back and forth. Someday you're going to saw some guy's head clean off. What a mess that'll be."

14

Lost deep in the dreams that only the profoundly drunk can enter, Falstaff felt waves of unrest running through his body. The dreams went twisted and sideways as the sensation intensified, until he rose out of deep sleep and approached wakefulness. The waves of unrest were caused by someone crouched by his bed, shaking him awake.

For a moment, Falstaff forgot where he was. The last clear memory he had was drinking a final boilermaker at the strip club, and his first guess was that the hands shaking him belonged to whatever stripper had decided to come home with him. He scrambled back from the hands and tried to find his voice.

"Hey, hey man, sorry for waking you but something is wrong" whispered the dark shape at his bedside. The male voice surprised Falstaff. He squinted in the dark and tried to identify the man.

"I snuck in the window to avoid your narc roommate and this house arrest scene you are stuck in. I would normally not invade a dude's privacy like this, but I need help."

"JJ? What the fuck?"

"Shh! Keep it down, man, or that hulk in the other room is going to kick my ass."

JJ clamped his scrawny hand over Falstaff's mouth and gave him a pleading look. Falstaff nodded, and JJ removed his hand.

"Why are you in my room, JJ? I was having a perfectly good drunk dream that you have now interrupted. All I have now is a slight case of the spins and a smelly hippie breathing in my face."

JJ pulled back and covered his mouth with his hand.

"Sorry, sorry man. I really regret waking you up, but you gotta understand, I got no choice. I need help and I can't turn to nobody else."

Falstaff sat up and rubbed his face. He picked a spot on the wall to stare at and kept staring until the world stopped wobbling around his field of vision.

"Why me, JJ? You've known me for, what 2 days? Maybe less than that. We are not exactly best friends. I bought dope off you once."

"I'm fucking desperate, that's why. You are a guy who knows things about things. And you will take chances and do risky shit, especially if it gets you free dope, am I right?"

"Hah. The risky part is way off, but the free dope part isn't. Tell me what the fuck is going on and maybe I'll consider it."

"It's my brother, man. He's missing."

"Call the cops."

"He left 5 hours ago and never called or came back."

Falstaff yawned and belched. "5 hours? That's not missing, that's a good night. Speaking of which, good night, JJ. Fuck off."

Falstaff closed his eyes and tried to go back to sleep, but JJ resumed shaking him until he opened his eyes again.

"Jesus you're persistent."

"He went to make a deal. A big buy from a new source. He was light on the details, but he said it was some new, high-powered stuff from a brand-new distributor. The distributor was going to sell the big payload to a local dealer, and my brother was going to buy a generous amount of that dope for us to sell. The new guy wants to aggressively expand his territory, so the deals are insanely good. My bro said it would take a little while, maybe an hour and a half, but he swore he would call when the deal was done."

"So call him."

"Shit, man, that was what I did first. I been hitting up his phone every 10 minutes, but nothing. Not even voicemail now."

"Are you sure he would come back? He could have left to get high, or to go resell the dope."

JJ shook his head in growing frustration.

"No no no, he only gets fucked up at my place. He's paranoid somebody's gonna fuck with him anywhere else. He will smoke a joint or pop a pill when he's out to be social, you know, but he would come right back here if he really wanted to party. And we got buyers in the house right now. That's another reason why this is an emergency. They are getting agitated. I can't stall them much longer."

"So send them home, JJ. You got bigger problems than their happiness."

"I will, if this goes on any longer, but come on dude. You gotta go look for my brother. Please."

"Why, again, am I going to do this risky endeavor?"

"I'll take care of later. Full night of good times."

"Pay up front, JJ. You know how it is. Never trust a dealer."

JJ grumbled and dug into his pockets. He reluctantly brought out a baggie and showed it to Falstaff.

"Could just have a heart and go look for my brother. That's an option too, man. Don't have to squeeze me for dope."

"I'm a professional. Pay me. What's in the bag?"

"It's all I had around the house. Busy couple of nights, and you bought most of the good stuff I had left already. Some valium, some Adderall, a block of hash, and a few other pills that I grabbed and stuffed in there. I don't remember what they were."

"Eh, doesn't matter. I'll adapt" he said as he reached for the bag. JJ pulled it back and stuck his face forward so Falstaff could see his eyes clearly.

"Find him. I gotta know where he is. The address is 101 Apex Avenue. It's a warehouse."

"Okay, I'll check it out." His eyes were locked on the baggie of free dope that was about to come into his possession. Everything else in the room was indistinct and unimportant.

JJ dropped the bag of miscellaneous drugs into Falstaff's lap and turned to the window. A dog barked in the next street over, scaring JJ into a strangled scream.

"I can't handle this stress, man. Bring my brother back safe, okay?"

"I never promised that, JJ. Going to take a look around. If I see nothing, I come back. I see something, I call you. Then I am done."

"He's my only blood. He has red hair and one of his front teeth is tilted out on an angle. His name is Archie. Try, okay? Please?"

Falstaff felt the waves of pitiful but completely sincere worry radiating from JJ, and he sighed.

"I'll try. Get out of here, JJ."

JJ slinked through the narrow window while Falstaff fished a couple of pills out of the baggie and popped them into his mouth. He ground each into paste, trying to guess the compounds now dissolving in his saliva. One was a valium. He was pretty sure of that. The second was too difficult to pin down. "A little surprise for later" he said to himself as he pulled a new pair of pants from the shelf.

He left his room for the kitchen. With a full tumbler of water in his hand, Falstaff sauntered out of the kitchen and into the living room. He leaned against the archway separating the kitchenette from the living room and watched Nurse as he slept in the recliner. The water washed down the mysterious pill combination, with Falstaff's tongue exploring the back crevices of his molars for any last pill bits straggling behind. Nurse opened one eye slowly.

"Why are you here?"

"Why are any of us here, my man? On second thought, forget I asked. I have a lead we should follow."

"Where did you get this lead? A dream? Or is your lead another attempt to get more drunk?"

"I am sober now. Mostly. Not the point. Did I wake you up when I went to the bathroom?"

"The light in your room woke me."

"Really? Light sleeper." Falstaff was impressed that JJ had been stealthy enough to avoid waking Nurse, and he also noted that it wasn't the sound that woke him. Could be his hearing was not as sharp as his vision, Falstaff supposed.

"Go back to bed, drunk. You need sleep."

"There's a deal going down that we need to check out. It sounds like our mystery supplier."

Nurse sat up and gave Falstaff a harsh apprising stare.

"You are lying to me."

"Not at all."

"Why wait until this late hour to tell me?"

"I put the pieces together in a dream."

Nurse laughed with a snort and lay back into the recliner again. He waved Falstaff back to his room.

"Enough with your foolishness. Go to bed."

"Fine, the dealer across the street snuck through my window and told me about the deal. His brother is there, and he was supposed to be back hours ago. It's a shady drug deal in a warehouse. We need to go check it out."

Groaning, Nurse pulled himself out of the chair. He stretched his arms wide and breathed deeply, exhaling twice as slowly as he inhaled. He shook the last bits of fatigue from his fingers as he walked to the coat hooks by the door. Falstaff watched him walk, aware for the first time that there was a pistol in a holster tucked neatly into the small of Nurse's back.

"Come. No screwing around. No drinks, no drugs. Understand?"

Falstaff swore off any additional substances for their trip to the suspected drug deal, carefully avoiding a discussion of what he may have recently put into his system. They grabbed their coats and left the safehouse. Falstaff gave a wave and a point across the street, to signal JJ that he was on his way to find his brother. JJ waved back from his dark front porch before disappearing back inside.

The car navigated the dead streets easily, sailing through the calm of a cold, damp night devoid of human activity. The address led them to an industrial and commercial mini-park surrounded by an electricity substation and a junkyard.

The car slowed as they came within sight of the building. Nurse scanned the block for any signs of activity. He continued past the warehouse and circled back twice to confirm that no one was watching. He parked the car at the junkyard gates. Falstaff hopped out of his seat and walked down the middle of the road towards the warehouse. The absence of cars and people made the block seem abandoned to the ravages of time.

"If I had to lure people to a trap, this is the place they would end up. This is the kind of neighborhood that is beyond god's vision. Even she wouldn't know what happens here. I have a bad feeling."

Nurse ignored Falstaff's musing. He walked along the curb, sticking to the shadowed pools hiding on the other side of the sporadic flickering street lamps. At the corner of the warehouse, a gust of wind blew through the open window in the wall and carried a scent to Nurse's nose. He held up his fist in a signal to stop moving.

"Burned gunpowder. There has been a firearm discharge inside the building. Several times."

"Shit. Door's half-open too."

Falstaff stood at the partially open steel door and peered through the gap. His sightline of the dim interior was blocked by a stack of boxes. The wind dropped off, and in the sudden silence Falstaff heard a gurgling moan from the warehouse. He shot a wide-eyed look at Nurse before barrelling through the door. Nurse hissed at him to stop, but Falstaff was propelled forward by panicked sense of impending death. He was sure that JJ's brother was hurt and needed to be found as soon as possible.

The hallway leading into the main part of the warehouse was narrow and partially blocked by columns of stacked boxes pressed to either wall. Falstaff pressed himself between the stacks while trying to keep them from toppling over. Behind him, he could hear the bulky mass of Nurse's body pushing indelicately through the stacks. He was too wide to gracefully slip through, so Nurse had opted for the charging bull method.

Falstaff emerged into the open space a second before Nurse bashed a massive stack of boxes down to the ground. The top box tore open and spilled its contents across the floor, making a rug of cheap surgical gloves and diabetic socks. Nurse took up a defensive position, with his pistol held ready in his hand.

The light from the windows and the doorway was too dim to reach the deep interior of the warehouse. Despite his straining, Falstaff couldn't see anything further on, except for undefined shapes filling the darkness.

"Got a flashlight? Or use your phone. It should have a flashlight app."

Nurse complied and used his phone to light the area. Falstaff gestured towards the wall, and the light followed. He found the light switch panel and rested his hand on it. He held his breath and turned on all the warehouse lights.

The bodies were arranged in their appointed spots in the bloody tableau. This time, the blood was flowing freely and pooling across the floor. It would be hours before it was thick and congealed like it was the last time.

"Oh fuck, no. One of these poor bastards is JJ's brother."

Falstaff moved from victim to victim, skirting the blood and trying desperately to avoid looking at the entirety of their wounds. The female victim had been shot in the face, sending brain and viscera spattering the ground around her head like a foul halo. He felt his gorge rise fast and strong, but he forced it back down.

The 5th victim was the source of the moan. The sound rose again from the man with no strength left in it. The pool of blood around him was as large, if not larger, than the others.

"He's still alive. HE'S STILL ALIVE. Get over here, Nurse!"

Nurse moved to Falstaff's side and bent down to examine the man on the ground. He felt for the man's pulse on his neck. The wounded man's mouth moved in a vain attempt to say something, but the only sound he could make was the same low, weak moan. He locked eyes with Falstaff and moaned again. He wanted a last-minute reprieve from the doom circling him, and he reached out to Falstaff to pull him into his fight for life. The bloody man's arm jerked up to grab at Falstaff, sending a thin line of blood spattering up his shirt and face. Fear locked Falstaff into a paralyzed stillness, leaving the diagonal slash of blood to ooze slowly down his face. Nurse stood up suddenly and grabbed Falstaff by the arm.

"We are leaving. Now."

Nurse charged back through the hallway with Falstaff in tow behind him. On the street Nurse accelerated the pace until Falstaff's numb feet were stumbling and catching on every uneven stretch of ground. When he came close to falling, the iron grip on his arm tightened even further as Nurse easily carried Falstaff's body weight with one hand. A strange staccato hitch in Falstaff's breathing was the only noise in the empty streetscape. They reached the car and Nurse shoved Falstaff into his seat. He scanned the street for any sign of witnesses, then sat down in the driver's seat and jammed the key in the ignition.

When the car engine roared to life, a terrified scream finally escaped from Falstaff's temporary catatonia. The scream was cut short by Nurse's massive hand slamming into his mouth and pressing his whole head against the window.

The car raced down the street and around the corner, then around two more before slowed down to a stop in the parking lot of an abandoned gas station. Nurse fished his phone out of his pocket with his weaker hand as Falstaff flailed uselessly against the arm pinning him in place. He dug his fingernails as deeply as he could into the thin skin over the wrist until there was a slight hiss of pain from Nurse. He leaned over to Falstaff and pressed him hard against the window. Falstaff's lower jaw was jammed back far enough that when Falstaff moved his tongue, it gagged him. He gave in and stopped struggling.

"No more screaming, or you are going to sleep."

Falstaff nodded and held his hands clear to signal his surrender. Nurse pulled back and released his grip.

"We gotta go back. Why didn't you do some medical shit on him? He was fucked up. Call 911."

"No. Be quiet."

"No? Be quiet? Fuck you, you goddamned monster. If you are too fucking evil to do the right thing, I'll take that phone from your paw and call them myself. You piece of human trash, you waste of life, I would fucking kick the shit out of you if I could-"

Falstaff's shrieking tirade was cut off by the return of the hand gag. This time, the force of the hand slammed his head into the window, making Falstaff see stars. Nurse dialed a number and waited for it to answer.

Falstaff tried to find his bearings. He heard a click from the phone receiver as the party on the other end answered. Nurse spoke a short phrase into the phone, paused, then repeated it and disconnected. A minute passed. Falstaff probed the side of the door for the latch, hoping that his captor wasn't watching very closely. He found it and pulled. His plan was to fall through the suddenly open door and roll away to the sidewalk. Free of the car, he would find his feet and run top speed in the direction of the sound of traffic in the distance.

The plan was ruined by the door's refusal to open. It occurred to him that the power locks were engaged, but even that should have been able to be overridden by physically activating the handle. He pulled frantically on the handle, giving up on the idea of subterfuge. By the fifth pull Nurse was laughing at his efforts. "child lock, idiot" he said as the phone buzzed. He answered it and recited a short string of numbers and letters. After a pause, he gave a detailed description of what they had just encountered. A short back and forth followed as the person on the other end asked for additional details. Nurse answered as best he could, then asked for instructions. He listened with rapt attention. Falstaff tried to eavesdrop or read the reaction to the instructions as Nurse heard them, but he managed neither. The call ended with a terse "understood" from Nurse. He put the phone away and turned his full attention back to Falstaff.

"You are upset. It is a normal reaction to seeing what you have seen. Battlefield shock is what I have heard it called. The man you saw was already dead. The blood loss and trauma were terminal. No medical effort could save a man in that state. I am going to take my hand from your mouth. Please breathe deeply until you feel calmer. I will unlock the door, so you can open it. Many people vomit when they experience this shock."

There was a calm and compassionate tone to Nurse's words that took Falstaff by surprise. It weakened his resolve to attack him, or to run off into the night. Falstaff nodded again, wincing as his bruised scalp rubbed against the window. Nurse released him and waited for his reaction.

"You could still call 911."

"It has already been done by a third party. No connection to trace to us."

"Jesus my head aches. You broke the window with my head, Nursie."

"I am…sorry. The stress of the situation made me overreact when I became angry."

Nurse put the car back into gear and drove out of the neighborhood. In the distance, the sound of sirens was building to a crescendo as a myriad of emergency vehicles sped towards the carnage they were running from. The sound made Falstaff's head pound. He closed his eyes and wished that he had died in the desert. It wasn't the last time he would wish for that.

15

He kept his cool for 10 blocks. Waiting at a red light, Falstaff scratched at the odd sticky patch above the right corner of his mouth. He sent the tip of his tongue out to investigate the substance glued to his skin. The animal part of his brain instantly recognized the taste of dried blood. He gingerly touched his scalp and his forehead in search of the source of the blood, but only found the rest of the blood trail. His defensive amnesia collapsed, and he remembered the dying man's gesture with a flash of vivid imagery. His heart hammered in his chest.

"We left him to die. Fuck. I am going to hell for this."

"He was already dead, I told you."

"I know you said that, and it makes sense. But it does not make it better. Until that second, this was all just a ridiculous game. I look for a killer, I sneak booze and pills into my body, you beat me up, fun times are had by all. But this, this is the guy's blood. Real and up close. Shit, the murderers could have been nearby."

"That is why I told you to stop."

"But it didn't occur to me that they could still be there. None of this was real. Now that poor bastard is dead, along with the other three dudes and that poor hooker without a face. No fucking face, what a horrible way to leave this world. Her friends can't look at her one last time. If she had friends. Fuck."

He had started crying and rocking himself in his seat without realizing it. He reached blindly into the back seat in search of the first aid kit. He found a package of wet wipes and scrubbed his face clean. He stared at the soiled wet wipe in his hand and cursed again.

"Jesus, what evidence did we leave behind? You knocked a bunch of shit over. Did I touch anything? Are my prints at the murder scene? They are going to find them and put out an arrest warrant for me. And you, if you even officially exist. What about cameras? We could be on video. Shit, shit, SHIT."

"We will not be arrested. Calm, remember?"

"I can't calm down, you asshole. I left all sorts of evidence at the scene of a multiple murder that I was supposed to prevent somehow, and when they find those prints, they'll check the first scene again and find, you guessed it, my prints again. Are you going to hide me from the police? Not fucking likely. You and that fat FUCK German will turn me over at the first sign of trouble and I will go to jail. I'm going to die in prison and the killer will just keep merrily traipsing across the rust belt killing groups of post-coital drug users. It's all coming apart."

The hysteria took full control of Falstaff's faculties. His words were a screeching confession of his sins and his failures. He was beet red and gasping for air in between his babbling sentences. Nurse offered a pre-emptive apology before slapping Falstaff hard across the cheek. He explained and apologized again.

"I told you to calm down. I am sorry for slapping you. I want you to think about the detectives at the first scene. They were sloppy, no? They found nothing. They will find nothing now. Police are not like the ones on television. They need confessions to win trials. Forensics are bullshit."

"Fine, maybe that's true. But they'll be looking a hell of a lot more closely now that the gangbang killer has struck again. That's serial murder."

Nurse navigated into a bland subdivision full of identical homes with tiny yards and long driveways. The dark streets felt safe, for the moment.

"If they look for you, they will find nothing. Your records are gone. No fingerprints on file, no convictions in the databases."

"You erased me?"

"Not me. The management."

"The German?"

"No, he is employee too."

"Are you erased from the official records as well?"

"Yes."

"So I don't exist, as far as the government is concerned?"

Nurse slowly drove down the long bend of a crescent and crept past a public park. A handful of tiny orange lights blinked in and out of existence from the top of the jungle gym. The lights were fading out of sight when Falstaff identified them as the lit ends of cigarettes. He pulled out his own smokes in commiseration and lit one up.

"I should clarify. You are not erased, simply misplaced for now. If the situation demands it, your records will be found again."

"I don't know if that's supposed to comfort me or threaten me. Knowing you, it's both."

Falstaff rolled the window down to feel the cold night air rush over his skin. He blew a plume of cigarette smoke out the window and watched it stream behind them as they drove on. He thought about the pills hidden in his sock and how he could slip one into his mouth. Then he remembered JJ.

"Aw, no. I forgot that JJ's brother was supposed to be there. He was probably one of the dead guys."

"You do not know? Did he give you a description?"

"I don't remember. He caught me in the middle of a deep dream. I didn't know he was really in my room for the first bit of the conversation. Hold on, he did tell me right before he snuck out. I was thinking about how to get you to go look for the guy. He said his brother had red hair and a crooked front tooth."

The two men sat in silence, idling at a 4 way stop. The sound of an approaching car broke the silence. Nurse went through the intersection and pulled the car to a stop by the side of the road.

"It was him. The dying man."

"Yeah, looks like. Fuck, I have to tell JJ his brother is dead. Fuck. Give me your phone, please."

Nurse turned the phone over after unlocking it and flicking to the phone app. Falstaff took it and stared at the digital keypad. He let out a short, pathetic bark of a laugh and tossed the phone back.

"I don't know his fucking number. Jesus, I am on the ball."

Tears filled his eyes again and his throat felt like it was swelling closed. The car pressed in from every direction. Falstaff felt like the world was slowly crushing him into nothingness. The level of panic consuming his every thought was more than he had ever felt before, and that set off a warning buzzer. His life had been worse. His reaction was being amplified artificially. The pills. If it had been a valium, he would be farther away from the edge of complete terror. He had been wrong about the valium. The anxiety and impulsiveness were the opposite of what he had expected to happen.

"Double addys. That's it. Grab bag fucked me" he muttered under his breath without meaning to speak out loud. He shot a nervous glance at Nurse, hoping that he had gone unheard. There was no reaction from the driver's side of the car, and Falstaff felt a tiny swell of relief.

"About that slap, not that I'm arguing I didn't need it, could it have been a little less tooth-rattling? The odds are good that I'm racking up a string of concussions. And I'm not assigning blame, but you have been the one handing them to me."

"The sudden pain interrupts compulsive thinking, forces the patient to redirect their focus."

"But so hard? A light slap would have worked."

"We need to move further away from this area. Where do we go? Back to the house?"

Falstaff thought about the worried drug dealer, pacing his porch and watching anxiously down the street for the brother that would never come home. He did not want to tell JJ that his brother had bled out on the floor of a dirty, faceless warehouse.

"We need to move forward, keep looking for the killer."

"I must ask again, where do we go? We have no new clues."

"That's because you ran us away from the scene."

"To avoid the police."

"Oh fuck the police. They can't find their asses with both hands and a team of helper monkeys. You said so."

"Monkeys?"

"Figure of speech. The police are incompetent."

"When they find you standing over a dead body, they are very good at arresting you. In jail, you cannot find the killer."

Falstaff let the argument lay and turned his gaze inward.

"Give me a minute. I'm going to see if I can remember anything from the scene that might help us."

"You did not mention any new details. What is this you do now?"

Falstaff flicked the dying cigarette out the window, replacing it instantly with a fresh one. He blew a cloud of smoke from his nostrils and adjusted himself into a more comfortable sitting position.

"My conscious brain didn't see shit. Completely true. It saw the dead bodies and heard the moan of that poor fuck and it freaked out. But, the mind is a spectacular data collection machine. A sensory catchall bucket that sifts through the noise to present selected facts to the rest of your consciousness. I'm going to close my eyes, relax, and walk through my memory of the scene. If I am very lucky, I will find a bit of information that was filtered out during my initial panic, and that piece of info will point us in a direction. While I do this, drive to the edge of the city. The odds are likely that our destination will be in one of the shithole towns."

Nurse didn't look like he believed Falstaff's explanation, but he went along with the plan regardless. They drove slowly down by the river and followed the northern branch as it wound its way to the outskirts. Falstaff closed his eyes and went back to the scene of the crime.

He walked into the door this time, instead of running blindly into the warehouse. The lights were already on. The stacks of boxes were intangible, and he passed easily into the center of the room. He stopped at the first body and studied it. The male victim was grey and pudgy, wearing a buttoned-up shirt and jeans. The front of the shirt was obscured by the bloom of blood that soaked through it.

Falstaff moved to the next victim, the woman. He forced himself to remember the horror of her destroyed face. The craters of missing flesh and bone. The one intact eyeball staring at the wall. He saw the bits of her hairdo that were not marred by the mix of blood and brain, bottle blonde and full of hairspray. Her arm had a tattoo portrait of Snow White being tempted by a red apple. He filed the detail away and moved on to the next victim.

As he stepped past the female victim, he caught sight of a canvass bag left underneath the large metal desk pushed to the side of the clearing. The bag was Army Surplus, matching the one from the first crime scene. The hunger in his gut urged him to move to the bag, to order Nurse to drive back to the scene so he could look inside the bag for forgotten pills. Falstaff ignored the mad hunger and continued his recollection.

The third victim was near the edge of the clearing. The moan from the dying man had drawn Falstaff quickly past this victim during the actual visit, so his memory of the dead man was a smudged blur at the periphery of his vision. There was a glint of light reflecting from something around the dead man's neck. Falstaff stepped back and forth in that memory moment, trying to decipher more detail from that momentary flash. Silver in color and rectangular in shape. He opened his eyes and sat up straight.

"Dog tags. Victim 4 had dog tags. Army base. Go."

The car picked up speed and rushed into the last hours of the dark night. Nurse pushed the car to the speed limit and far past.

"There was another surplus bag there, too. The distribution premise holds up. And they want the drug dealing to be the focus of the investigation. Leaving one bag behind would be a significant accident, but two? A dealer leaving a kit like that behind would be furious with themselves."

"Why?"

"Because any asshole could take those baggies and sell shitty dope under your brand. This dealer doesn't care about their long-term retail success. The drugs are a cover story, an easy way to lure these poor fuckers to their death."

"You need to be calm when we arrive at the military installation. It will be unusual to have civilians arriving at this time."

"Fine. Fine. I'll be cool. Like a cucumber. Ice cold. I only want to talk to the C.O. again. Grizzley. Jesus, what a name. What a world. I want to rattle his cage, but only verbally. The shock of one of his boys being killed should upset him enough to get his secrets out. He knows more about the dope on base. If he can point us to the local source, we can follow the trail of pills to someone with a real connection. I hope."

The drive progressed in silence through the back stretch of the county. Nurse spoke up as they saw the few lights from Freiburg on the horizon.

"Your plan is harsh. A commanding officer is most wounded by the death of one of his soldiers. It will hurt him deeply."

"That's probably true. Unfortunately for him, I am an asshole at the end of his wits. Everybody's going to end up hurt, anyway. It's the way of the world."

At the end of the camp's driveway the guard was slouched over the desk, fast asleep. A neat stack of empty beer cans was piled on the floor beside him, high enough that the top of the pile was visible through the window. Nurse swore and stopped the car at the barrier. He got out and leaned through the window to hit the barrier control switch. The yellow bar rose slowly with a grinding sound that resonated through the guard hut.

Inside the car, Falstaff took the opportunity that had presented itself, to retrieve the baggie stuffed in his sock and find a little chemical help to smooth out the evening. He shook the pills into the palm of his hand and fought the urge to scream in rage. Most of the pills were over the counter muscle relaxants and anti-inflammatories. A few were more Adderall, the last thing he wanted, and the final pair of pills were premsyns. He lowered his forehead onto the dashboard and gently knocked against it in rhythmic frustration.

The irritating drone from the gate motor rattled the windows and knocked the top can of beer from its perch, but the guard continued to sleep undisturbed. The barrier reached the apex of its journey and Nurse turned back towards the car. He stopped in midstride and instead went into the guard hut. When he re-emerged, he had a small triangular package in his hand. He tossed it to Falstaff and started the car again.

Falstaff looked at the package in his hand and flipped the leather cover from the top of it.

"Jesus Christ, did you take his gun and holster?"

"A soldier who is negligent in his duty does not deserve the honor of carrying a weapon. If there are any rules left in this circus of fools, he will be punished severely for losing his weapon."

"And in the meantime, I have a stolen army gun in my possession? How is that a good idea?"

"No one will notice."

"What if I lose my shit and blast you? Thought about that? I'm a desperate man with repeated head trauma."

"If you can pull the weapon from the holster on the first attempt, I will give you 1000 dollars."

Falstaff yanked the butt of the gun. It stayed firmly contained in the holster, and the force of his pull sent the holster and gun flying into the back of the car. Nurse laughed and did not stop laughing until the car pulled into the C.O.'s office parking spot. He took the forlorn holster and easily slipped the gun from it. With another practiced gesture, he removed the magazine and checked for a chambered round. He gave a disapproving cluck when he found that the weapon had been loaded with a live round in the chamber. He ejected it and put the now unloaded gun back into the holster. The ammunition disappeared into his coat pocket.

"Storing a weapon with a live round in the firing mechanism is against basic weapon safety. He should feel lucky that he has been saved from shooting his manhood off."

There was a wealth of rage and disgust playing out across Nurse's face. Falstaff was amused by the seriousness that Nurse assigned to military protocol. If there was any doubt before that Nurse was a soldier, it was now completely erased. Falstaff gave the front door a perfunctory pair of knocks before twisting the handle and stepping through the open door. He wasn't prepared for the sight that was on display in the waiting room of the office.

Sitting in a tank top and baggy boxers with a large wet stain on them, Grizzley had his head in his hands as he sobbed steadily. The recliner he sat in had been dragged in to the office waiting room from Grizzley's adjoining living quarters. In between his knees he held a bottle of Jim Beam Black Label Bourbon that was almost empty. In his right hand was a revolver. Falstaff coughed politely to get the Colonel's attention. The sobbing continued unabated.

"Is there a little bit to drink for a couple of thirsty visitors, Colonel? It's a shame to drink alone."

Grizzley looked up with bloodshot bleary eyes. He had forgotten about the gun in his hand, and it sank down to his lap. His other hand searched for the bottle. He held it up to the light and sloshed the liquid around.

"It's gone. There's another bottle somewhere. Find it for me."

"Any chance you could put the gun away first? Safe storage is everyone's responsibility."

Nurse rolled his eyes at the sanctimonious attempt to disarm the drunken man, but the words worked. The gun was shoved deep into the crevice of the chair.

"Great. Where should I look for the booze, boss?"

Grizzley drank the last swallow of bourbon before pointing erratically in the direction of the office. Falstaff nudged Nurse and pointed him in the same direction.

"I'll keep him company while you get the bottle and glasses, if you can find it. Can I sit down, Colonel?"

The drunken man sat in miserable silence. Falstaff sat on the end of the short bench beside the armchair and watched Nurse warily leave the room. When he was alone with the distraught army officer, Falstaff lowered his voice and spoke calmly but quickly.

"I know its hard. This time of night is the darkest stretch. Can you tell me what's the matter?"

"I'm haunted."

"Haunted? By what? Ghosts in this room?"

"Decisions. The weight of command is unbearable. I have done my best to save these men and women from themselves. But I am weak."

Falstaff edged closer. "How are you weak?"

"They show up hooked on narcotics. This camp is a haven for drug addicted soldiers. I have failed to protect them. We do a search and secure for all illicit substances one day, and by the morning the drugs are back."

"Was it always this bad, Colonel? That's a hell of a situation to take command of."

The drunken man shook his head vigorously, weaving back and forth in his seat with each pass.

"It was always here, but there was a change in the last month. The base is drowning in pills. Everyone is high."

"Everyone, Colonel? Do you have something you need to get off your chest? I have seen this before, a man carrying a heavy secret, trying to make it through the night, just one night, without giving in to a temptation. Is that you right now?"

The intermittent sobbing turned into a high-pitched, wailing cry. Nurse rushed back into the room carrying a decanter of clear liquor. Falstaff took the decanter from him, took a deep drink from it, then gently offered it to Grizzley. Grizzley put the glass bottle to his lips like a tired child searching for their soother. He suckled on the bottle with tears running freely down his cheeks until the bottle was half-empty.

"I have a problem" he croaked out.

"Let it out, buddy. It's the only way to be free."

"I stayed up all night, to demonstrate to myself that I have the ability to abstain for one night. One lousy night."

"It's not easy. Keep talking."

"But I want one. I need one. I'm addicted to painkillers."

Falstaff gave Grizzley ample time and space to cry loudly after finally confessing his addiction. The way that Grizzley leaned to the right, where a briefcase sat beside the chair, made Falstaff curious.

"The temptation is powerful. You're not weak. The drugs are too strong to fight on your own. Do you have them near you now?"

Grizzley didn't answer, but his eyes darted to the briefcase. With his suspicions confirmed, Falstaff crept closer.

"I'm going to take the temptation away from you, okay, Colonel? Just for a moment, so you can have a rest. You are in charge."

The drunken man moved to guard the case from Falstaff's reaching hand, but after a moment of internal conflict, he relented. The cheap briefcase popped open easily to reveal its sparse contents. Other than a handful of old invoices and a magazine about boating, the only thing of note was a full plastic baggie stamped with the White Knight logo. Falstaff discreetly showed the bag of pills to Nurse.

"Who did you get this poison from, Colonel?"

"It started when I got shot in Anbar province. The medics pumped me full of painkillers, and the field hospital kept pumping. When I got stateside they put me into that hospital, the same one most of these kids came from. They got me hooked through the balls on my meds, just like the rest of the bastards here, then they kicked me down the road to this hellhole. A base full of goddamned junkies."

"That's understandable. Now where did these pills come from?"

Caught in his memories and his confession, Grizzley ignored the question again and kept talking.

"This is the first night in 2 years that I have been clean. At 9PM I began drinking, because the itch was under my skin and the time was dragging by in agony. By midnight the whispers of doubt started. 3AM I found my personal sidearm and loaded it. I brought my chair out here to get away from the blank walls in my bedroom. I need help."

Falstaff wanted to slap the drunk, but he could still see the butt of the gun poking up from the space between the cushion and chair of the arm.

"But you made it, buddy. You stayed clean through the whole night. Out there, the first traces of sunlight are glinting off the frozen dew on the grass. The day is coming. Help is on the way. But the first step you need to keep taking so that you can get help is being honest. You're doing a good job. Now who did you get these pills from?"

Grizzley finished the gin in the decanter and absent-mindedly tossed it into the corner. It smashed into splinters and shards at the base of the fake plant placed there. He shook his head with his eyes closed, as a funny short wheeze rose from his chest. He opened his eyes again and glared at Falstaff with bewildered rage.

"What in the name of the Lord are you doing in my office, civilian? Get the hell off my base, pronto."

"Did you think I was a ghost before? A drunken hallucination? You must do a whole lot of junk if this is the effect of one night of sobriety. Where did those pills come from?"

"I ordered you to get out, maggot" Grizzley shouted as he pulled himself up to an unsteady standing position straddling the chair.

"Easy, easy. I'm going. But tell me who gave you the pills, so I can keep him from killing some poor addicted kid on base. It'll happen again, because it happened tonight. I'm here because one of your men is dead. The drugs are to blame."

Grizzley staggered backwards as if hit with a brick. He sat down heavily on the arm of the chair and braced himself to keep from falling to the floor.

"You're a goddamned liar."

"The call is going to come soon, Colonel. Found dead in a warehouse. Tell me where the pills come from."

"The Private at the gate. Polonz. He buys from a local kid, and I buy from him."

"Did he describe the local dealer?" Falstaff said as his pulse quickened. If Grizzley refused to help, they could make a stop at the gate and ask Private Polonz directly. A real lead to follow.

"I seen him. Stupid greasy punk, with slicked back hair. Wears those fake dentures covered in imitation gems."

The memory of the crime scene flashed to the forefront of his mind again, this time focused on the man with the deep gouge in his neck. As if his own memory was mocking him, the gem-encrusted mouthpiece in the dead man's mouth now sparkled in the light of the warehouse. Falstaff tilted his head back and swore long and loud to the heavens above. The promise of an actual lead to follow had vanished into nothingness.

"Well isn't that fucking wonderful? And egalitarian! The Commanding officer buying his dope from his subordinate, all of it helping pump money into the local economy. What a leader you are."

Grizzley lurched forward with the revolver back in his hand. He swung the butt of the gun at Falstaff's face, a wide sloppy swing that Falstaff slipped under easily. The momentum spun Grizzley around and sent him sprawling over the metal and glass coffee table. His weight crushed the table around his body. His head ended up wedged beneath the bench against the wall, and he struggled to find enough coordination to pull himself out. Falstaff took that as his cue to leave and he slipped out the door, followed by Nurse. He closed the door on the crying and swearing Army officer in crisis.

"Well isn't that a shitshow of epic proportions. Getting clean is an ugly process. Good luck to him. Did you catch that description of the local dealer? It was the dead one we just found. So, goodbye to that lead."

Falstaff spoke quickly as he walked down the steps and hustled towards the car. A stride away from the car, Nurse put his massive hand on Falstaff's shoulder and brought him to a stop. Another pull turned him around so that they were face to face.

"Pills. Give to me. Now."

Falstaff rolled his eyes dramatically and sighed with exaggerated exasperation.

"Oh come on. It's evidence. Relax, it's totally safe with me."

Nurse's thumb found the bony ridge of Falstaff's collarbone and pressed hard as he closed his hand into a vice. The pain was tolerable but escalating at an alarming rate.

"Only takes 7 pounds of pressure to break this bone. Give me the pills."

Falstaff fumbled with the bag tucked into his coat pocket, trying to extricate it while pulling away from the painful grip on his collar. He brought the bag out and waved it in Nurse's face.

"Here, take it. For fuck's sake, is hurting me your only method of persuasion? Fuck. Let me go so we can leave."

The grip on his collar relaxed, allowing him to squirm free. He rubbed the tender spot where the thug's thumb had dug in deep.

"Asshole. I wasn't even going to take any of the pills now."

Nurse laughed as he got into the car. "Never trust a junkie."

"On the contrary, my asshole friend, drug enthusiasts can be incredibly dependable if they are properly motivated. Speaking of which, I have a variety of aches, pains and wounds inflicted by you. Can I get a little relief for the drive home?"

Nurse shook his head in response. Falstaff groaned.

"Great. At least let me drive for a while. Give me some illusion of control in my life. Everything else is out of my hands and spinning into a horrifying mess."

16

Despite the fatigue and pain and defeat that currently defined his life, Falstaff was happy for a moment. He drove the car with joyful abandon down the narrow gravel roads that fanned out and threaded through the corn fields and creek beds. The temporary freedom was enough to make him smile from ear to ear.

Nurse sat wedged into the passenger seat with the phone up to his ear. He had gone through the two-stage contact protocol again, first calling the message service, then waiting for the return call from head office. Falstaff mused aloud as he sped.

"I've been replaying the good Colonel's tearful confession, picking through the self-pity for anything usable. That bit about the hospital was interesting. Do you think he was literal about it? Like, is there an actual hospital down the road from the camp? Screw it, I say there is. Would you mind googling it for me?"

Nurse shot him a dirty look and kept the phone in place. Falstaff was undaunted by the obstacle.

"Fine by me. A pit stop is called for, anyway. Get some directions, grab a snack, then head off on yet another wild goose chase. Failing is fun!"

The steady stream of high-pitched laughing that followed Falstaff's sarcastic comment filled the car. He was punch drunk from the accumulated stresses and traumas of the last 2 days. He wondered if he would just keep laughing until he passed out and drove them into a tree. He calmed down and took his foot off the accelerator so that the car could drop back down to a reasonable speed.

Following the barely legible road signs, Falstaff navigated to the intersection where two of the county's biggest roads crossed. The gas station by the side of the road was the first sign of human activity he had seen in the last half hour. He pulled the car in to the lot and went inside.

He toured the aisles of convenience in the gas station, leisurely examining the greasy sugar and salt bombs that made up the American Diet. He picked a bag of spicy pork rinds, a package of chewy cookies filled with birthday cake frosting, and a 6 pack of malt liquor tallboys. At the fresh food counter beside the checkout, he poured himself the largest cup of coffee they offered and filled it with sugar and cream. He plunked the items onto the counter and smiled at the dozy clerk who kept his mouth hanging open in perpetuity.

"Hey buddy. Slow night?"

"Whut" the clerk slurred.

"Yeah. So, we need directions to the vet hospital?"

"Vets? Cat hospital?"

"Uh, no. For soldiers. There's an army base nearby, correct? Well, that base has a hospital associated with it, and we need to find that hospital. Fuck, are you retarded or something?"

"Hospital's in Pittsburgh. They charge you get an ambulance, so I didn't go."

"Hey that's a great story. Must go over like fucking gangbusters at the Mensa meetings."

The clerk slowly scanned the items without responding to Falstaff's insult. Falstaff wondered how slow the clerk would have to be to get fired. The slow movement of the kid's right eye did not match the motion of the left. As the kid passed the bag of pork rinds by the barcode scanner repeatedly without success, Falstaff caught sight of the long, undulating scar running along the side of the clerk's head. The clerk had been on the wrong end of a collision, a fall or a car crash, and it had left him with a significant brain injury.

"Christ, I really am an asshole. Hell has a special spot for me set aside" Falstaff muttered, following it up with a cough to cover the sound of his pathetic realization. The clerk didn't notice. Falstaff held out a 20 to the clerk.

"Here ya go. Keep the change."

"Whut?"

"The change. You keep it as a tip. You did a good job. Did you remember if there was a veteran's hospital nearby? I can pay you for directions to the veteran's hospital."

The clerk was focused on the money in his hand. Falstaff waited for an answer patiently until the clerk turned away and laboriously made change. He placed the change from the transaction on the counter, still unclear on the offer of a tip. Falstaff went to explain it again when Nurse reached over and pulled him towards the door.

"Time to leave."

Falstaff managed to grab the bag before Nurse forced him away from the counter. With an iron grip on his upper arm, Nurse propelled Falstaff through the front door, across the lot and into the passenger seat of the car. In the blink of an eye, he was in the driver's seat with the key in the ignition. The quick exit had caught Falstaff off-guard, and he only found his voice again as the car hurried out of the lot.

"What the hell? Where's the fire, Nursie?"

Nurse pulled the car down the street until it was hidden by the gas station, then came to a stop. He pointed back towards the gas station's front door.

"Sheriff."

Falstaff's head whipped around to look at the front door, and sure enough, the Sheriff was strutting towards the entrance.

"I hate to build you up, but that was a good call. The last thing this night needs is a confrontation with that small-dicked cop. How did you know he was coming?"

"The window on the wall behind the counter, it faces the other part of the parking lot. I saw the Sheriff's jeep pull in."

"The unfortunate part is that I didn't get directions from the zombie clerk in there. Shit, I hope that kid has a helper or therapy or something. His brain has been severely scrambled. Any chance you can look up the hospital now that you're off the phone?"

"I have directions."

"You do? Alright, let's get the show on the road."

As the car drove off, Falstaff began eating. He ripped open the pork rinds and crammed a handful into his mouth. He took a long sip of the hot, sweet coffee, mixing it with the pork rinds until the two combined into a wet slop. He mashed two of the sickeningly gooey and sweet cookies into his mouth in between sips. He switched the cup of coffee for a can of beer and added the amber liquid to the paste. He swallowed the mouthful forcefully, pushing the wad of unsettling texture and flavor down. The mess hit his stomach and Falstaff gasped.

"I do not recommend that combination."

Despite the initial revulsion, Falstaff continued to eat and drink the mix until he was bloated. He intermittently offered the bag of pork rinds to Nurse, delighting in the look of disgust that filled his face each time. The bag was almost empty when Falstaff noticed their overall direction.

"I don't want to second guess your sense of direction, Nursie, but where the fuck are we going? This is the onramp to the southbound interstate, per that spiffy sign up there. The base and all the towns encircling it are to the north east of Pittsburgh. Is the vet's hospital in a whole other state? The C.O. said it was down the road. Seems like an awfully long road."

He drank from his can of beer and watched Nurse's reaction. It was subdued and barely broke the surface of his demeanor, but that was enough to confirm it. They were heading somewhere else.

"I think it is unlikely, but it is a possibility that you've completely given up on me and decided that I am nothing but a liability. And because of that, you are taking me to a secret government slaughterhouse to kill me and dump my body into a bottomless pit underneath the Lincoln memorial. Or hey, maybe you're that devil of the rust belt, and you're going to carve me up like a butcher with severe tremors and dump my body in a corn field. Whatever. I'm easy. In celebration of my impending doom, I am going to get nice and drunk on cheap malt liquor as I enjoy the last car ride of my life."

He knew Nurse wasn't going to kill him, but that wasn't going to stop him from guzzling beer until the car stopped. He cracked the next can open and returned to his verbal harassment.

"It's not like we had any urgent business, of course. We all the fucking time in the world to drive across the country and see all the sights along the way. Just another pile of dead bodies looming on the horizon. Just junkies, right? Who care about dead drug users anyway? It's not like they're people."

Nurse didn't rise to Falstaff's bait, other than accelerating down the interstate. 20 minutes later the car left the interstate and made its way down a narrow gravel road. The thick stands of trees on either side of the road blocked all peripheral lines of sight, leaving only a tunnel in front and behind them. Every few miles there was a stenciled sign warning that they were on federal land with restricted access. The road they were on ran out, and they turned to follow a set of tire ruts dug into the soft mud that ran perpendicular to the gravel road. 5 minutes later the ruts met an asphalt laneway leading off in an arc to the left and to the right. Above the trees in front of them, the top of a building broke the sightline. Nurse gritted his teeth and exhaled with a growl. He was tense and did not want to be heading towards their destination.

"We have been requested by the director. He wishes to speak with each of us. He has concerns."

They came around the left bend of the laneway and the hidden building was revealed. The 3-storey red brick building sat proudly in the middle of a manicured greenspace, with an oval driveway leading past the front doors. The laneway they were on ran from behind the building to meet the driveway. Nurse brought the car to the front of the building and killed the engine.

"Still alive, cheers to me" Falstaff said as he finished off the beer in his hand. He belched and wiped his mouth with his sleeve. They left the car and stood looking up at the front door.

The ornate columns decorating the second and third floor balconies made the building appear to be a stately manor from a long-dead age of American largesse. Falstaff felt dirty and small in comparison, and he tried to straighten his clothes and brush the crumbs free.

Nurse walked purposefully up the wide stone steps. Falstaff followed, but stopped short to read the plaque fastened to the right side of the stairs.

"The Everett Memorial Psychiatric Hospital was built in 1897. Originally named the Allegheny Lunatic Asylum, it served as the first mental health facility for eastern Pennsylvania. It became an administrative hub for the state in 1952, serving in that capacity until 2006. After decommissioning, the facility and surrounding affiliated property were purchased by a private health provider, and the facility now offers specialized mental health services under the Safe Respite brand."

Falstaff read the last sentence a second time aloud and ended it with a laugh. He hopped up the last 3 steps and passed through the door being held open by Nurse.

"A looney bin is this crazy operation's HQ. How goddamned appropriate. I should get a quick electro-shock treatment while I'm here. Do I have to order that myself, or did you already have a plan to fry my brain?"

"Follow me."

Nurse walked him past the unoccupied front desk. The soft hum of the heating system blowing warm moist air over everything filled the room. The steady stream of air blew down from the vents to move the leaves of the well-maintained plants along the walls. They walked up spiral marble staircase to arrive in the second floor's foyer. The hall in front of them had a small desk to the right, staffed with a prim secretary. The older man gave them instructions to sit down before picking up the phone receiver and speaking softly through it. The secretary primly put the phone down.

"Mr. Jakob, the director will speak with you now. Mr. Falstaff, please stay in the waiting area outside of the office until being called for."

Nurse cleared his throat and marched reluctantly down the hall, with Falstaff shuffling along behind him. The end of the hall had a wide set of double wooden doors, marked with a placard that identified the room as the chief psychiatrist's office. On the wall to the right of the doors was a smaller single door with a plate that said 'director'. It struck Falstaff as funny that his boss had the smaller office here.

Across from the director's office was a trio of plain, plastic chairs that were standard waiting room issue. He sat down and watched Nurse knock curtly on the director's door. The response from the other side of the door was one simple word, but the tone of that pronounced "Enter" carried a threat of stern judgement. Nurse shrunk visibly at the sound, and his shoulders drooped down as he entered the room and closed the door behind him.

Falstaff hoped to catch some of the conversation from his spot, but the low sounds didn't reach him. He stood up and walked around the small waiting area, creeping closer to the director's door. He caught snippets of sound as he stood by the door, but to get a clear sense of what was being said, he would have to be in the room itself. He wondered if he should try the classic 'glass on the door' or 'peering through the keyhole' routines. The images made him giggle until he belched a foul cloud of malt liquor vapor, which only made him laugh harder.

His amusement ended when the door opened and he was escorted inside by Nurse. He stepped into the director's office and came face to face with the scowl of the German. It was the very first time that he had seen him angry, and that anger promised to manifest painful outcomes.

"Leave us" the German said curtly to Nurse. Falstaff caught the rush of relief on the big man's face as he turned and hurried to leave the room. The door clicked closed behind him.

The German marched the perimeter of the room with short strides punctuated regularly with a grumbled grunt. Falstaff's head spun as he tried to track the march of the irritated Kraut. The world seemed to shift its balance randomly, sending Falstaff listing from side to side. A greasy belch rocketed up from his gullet and was barely contained in his inflated cheeks. The flavor of cheap malt liquor, pork rinds and burned coffee coated his taste buds and revealed why the room was listing.

"You are drunk."

Falstaff opened his lips and vented the mouthful of stink that he had trapped there, out of the side of his mouth.

"I'm just tired."

"You weave from side to side as if you are standing on the deck of a storm swept ship. You smell like a beggar's nest. Are you going to be sick, Herr Falstaff?"

Falstaff shook his head, sending him farther to the right than he intended.

"I'm fine. Yes, I drank some beer on the way here. It's been a stressful day. Why does that even matter?"

The German stopped his walk around the room to stand in front of the glass and copper display case that covered the entirety of the west wall. The green tinted glass matched the color of the oxidized copper. The pottery on display filled all three levels of the case, creating an exhibition that spoke more of one man's fixation on local artisanal crockery than the pots themselves.

"You sure like your clay pots, boss."

"These are not mine."

"And the green of the shelves and the glass makes me think of Emerald city. Does that make you the Wizard?"

The German pulled his arms tightly around his chest and glared at Falstaff. It sucked the fun out of Falstaff's roaring buzz.

"So many jokes. The dead will be glad that you are having such fun at their expense. Like Matthew."

"Who's Matthew? Is this a biblical reference?"

The German pressed a button on the tiny remote he had hidden in his right hand. Above the display case, the monitor suspended there came to life. A picture filled the screen, a smiling man in a camouflage ball cap, with a smiling pair of girls sitting on his lap.

"Matthew and his two daughters. Emily, 6 and Baryssa, 4. Photo taken 15 days ago. That would be 13 days before he was given a lethal dose of morphine and shot through the heart twice. Are they not having such fun in this photo? Perhaps we should let you continue to investigate in your fashion, to satisfy your indulgences as the priority. Do not hurry. What does it matter if another father dies, or another vulnerable young woman? And the young men who have no warm family connections, they have no value, is that not correct? As long as you remain entertained, their lives have no impact on you."

Falstaff felt lost in the picture. The warmth of his drunk fatigue seeped away and left a sick feeling of cold regret and helplessness. He waved at the picture to make it go away.

"Not interested in Matthew? I see. What about Evelyn? Yes, Evelyn you would not recognize. She had no face when you met her the first time. This is what she looked like before she lost her way. She may have found her way back to being happy, but the killer you refuse to stop took that choice away from Evelyn."

The picture had changed to a slideshow of all the victims. Each image floated on the screen for 10 seconds, an eternity to Falstaff. There were 2 pictures of Evelyn. In the first she was a nervous teenager, hugging a small, furry dog close to her chest and smiling a hurt smile at the camera. The second photo was displayed beside the first, a mugshot picture where a fully-grown Evelyn was looking away from the camera. At the corner of her eye was a trailing line of tattooed stars.

"Fuck. That's her, the one Dot was worried about. Fuck fuck FUCK. I get it. They are dead and I am an asshole. I fucked around and self-medicated instead of magically developing superpowers to go back in time to save them. My bad. Though the side trip back here was your idea, for the record. Just turn the screen off. Please."

"So soon? I want you to remember these faces. The dead. We do not have the pictures of the newest victims yet, but they will come. How many more will we add to the slideshow, Herr Falstaff? When will you put an end to this?"

"What the fuck am I supposed to do?" Falstaff shouted.

"Your job. Find the killer."

The German left the slideshow running at its agonizingly slow pace as he walked to his desk and sat down. The guilt and anger filling Falstaff hit his breaking point. He walked to the display case, picked up the ornate vase in the middle of the shelf, and threw it with all his strength at the monitor above. The clay vase hit the screen and bounced to the left, falling safely onto the carpeted floor. The Monitor flickered momentarily but otherwise showed no sign of the attack. Falstaff lowered his head and laughed at his own futility.

"Sums up the whole investigation so far."

"You have another location to investigate, is this correct? Please explain."

Falstaff turned away from the display and looked for a chair to sit in. The only chair in the entire office was the one the German now occupied.

"There's a veteran's hospital near the victim's home towns, affiliated with the Army retraining facility."

"I do not understand why this is relevant. I would like an explanation of your investigation so far."

"The victims were looking for cheap drugs. The small-town dealers were in the process of becoming local distributors for a new source, one that uses the White Knight logo. The dealers agreed to find participants for an amateur sex video. They offered the participants free drugs as payment. After the scene gets filmed, the actors are given powerful sedatives. The small-town dealer gets choked to death, then the other actors are shot to death. At both crime scenes, I found the new distributor kit, full of the branded baggies and the gear you need to divide up a wholesale supply of dope into consumer packages. I know the first kit had that stuff in it, but I didn't get a chance to look in the second one. Tell the cops to look, if you need to confirm. That's the first common factor: drugs. High-powered opiates, from the trace amounts found at the first scene. That's in addition to the morphine auto-injectors being used to prep the victims for death."

"You are well versed in narcotics, Herr Falstaff, but how certain are you that the substance is an opiate?"

"Certain enough for now. I tracked down a dealer in Pittsburgh, conveniently located across the street from our luxurious safe house. He said the army guys and gals show up with those branded baggies from time to time, so we ran over to the base. The base is a shambolic mess, FYI. Nursie pitched a fit over the lack of military rigor. Once a soldier, always a soldier. The commanding officer is an addict too, of the very same pills that we're chasing. I would show you those pills, but my minder confiscated them. We caught the C.O. in the process of hitting bottom for the first time, and his rambling confession pointed us in the direction of the hospital. The drugged soldiers get their dependencies at the hospital, so I'm going to go sniff around there."

"What is 'hitting the bottom for the first time'? Is this an American idiom?"

"Kind of. Every addict hits bottom a bunch of times before they actually try to quit for real. Every other time they hit, they bounce back up. The C.O. is going to bounce. Then he's going to go get more pills. Maybe he'll shoot himself next time. Hard to read how that will pan out."

"I see. And what are you looking for, when you get to the hospital?"

"Specifically? A clue to the identity of the new drug kingpin. The dealer is the killer, or is working with the killers. Get Nursie to give you the pills he took from the C.O. and have them tested. They didn't look like regular pharma. I assume they were stolen from the military too."

The German leafed through a sheaf of papers covering his desk, making notes on the pad of white paper at his right hand. He left Falstaff standing in awkward silence for 5 minutes. Each attempt to restart the conversation was met with a distracted 'hush' from the German.

With his need to avoid watching the montage of murder victims presumably still playing out on the monitor behind him, and a lack of windows to stare out of, Falstaff was forced to study the uninteresting watercolor print that dominated the west wall. The weak colors and meaningless lines said nothing at all to Falstaff. He couldn't imagine the level of delusion necessary to create that painting and be proud of it. He assumed it was churned out by a factory artist somewhere in southeast Asia, a bland painting in a series of thousands. The German completed his note making and cleared his throat.

"I have one last video to show you, Falstaff. Please turn around."

He didn't want to look, but he wanted to end the meeting, so he turned to face the monitor again. One last glimpse of Evelyn filled his vision before the image switched. Now the screen was filled with a grainy video. He felt a cold sweat immediately cover his forehead and his palms as he recognized his mother as the subject of the video. The video began to play, and the warbling sleepy voice of his mom filled the room.

"Is this good?" she asked, and a voice off-camera assured her it was. The off-screen man handed his mother a plain beige folder and asked her to look inside of it. She looked confused but went along with the request. Her brow furrowed as she tried to make sense of what she was reading. The off-screen voice told her that it was a conviction report for a young man, a person that she had met many years ago. She agreed that the name was familiar, but she could not place it.

"He was a friend of your son, in high school. They got into some trouble."

Falstaff muttered 'no, don't' under his breath. On screen, his mother frowned. She studied the paper in the folder with renewed effort. The voice urged her to read the summary of the charges that the man was sentenced for.

"A terrible crime, isn't it?"

She looked up with wide eyes full of tears. She could not speak, but simply shook her head back and forth in vehement denial of the facts written on the paper. The voice from off-camera took on a soothing tone and reassured her that it was in the past.

"This sounds so familiar, but I can't remember it. My mind is not what it used to be. I don't remember exactly what happened. Have you spoken to my son? He went away, and I need to speak with him."

The video froze on a close-up shot of his mother's worried face. Falstaff felt everything start to slip away into the black hole hidden in the pit of his stomach.

"She was quite upset, but she was relieved to know you had no connection to that man anymore, or any hand in the terrible deeds he did. She believed the lie, for now. Are you motivated?"

The German stood up and walked briskly past Falstaff and out into the hallway. He summoned Falstaff to

follow him as he trotted down the stairs, sprightly for a
man of his size. Falstaff's steps plodded one after
another in an autonomous march down the stairs. He
was numb and shut down. The rational parts of his
mind were feverishly trying to talk him down, to lessen
the fear that grabbed his heart. He told himself it was
ridiculous that a grown man was so threatened by the
sight of an old, confused woman but the words had no
effect. In his heart, he was 10 years old and terrified.
He would do whatever necessary to keep her forgetful
and forgotten.

Every room they passed on the journey into the depths
of the building was completely deserted. Falstaff
expected to see a basic complement of staff for a well-
maintained facility, but it was silent and empty. At the
distant intersections of hallways they had ignored when
they passed, there were hushed whispers that Falstaff
tried to make into words. The more effort he put into
deciphering the sounds, the more they became
gossamer background noise. The hiss of recirculated
air was an ever-present ghost haunting their trip.

They walked down a narrow hallway with doors set in
pairs on both walls. The brass name plates on the
outside of the rooms were all blank, except for the final
one. It simply read 'John'. The German held out his
hand and grasped the wide brass door handle. After a
moment, they heard the mechanical click of a lock
disengaging. The German smiled and held the door
open for Falstaff.

"After you, Herr Falstaff. This is your private room.
Your temporary home for the duration of our working
relationship."

Falstaff stepped into the room. It was bland and sterile, full of soft tones and inoffensive design like a chain hotel trying to be an upscale boutique. The space was dominated by the king-sized bed in the centre of the room. To his left was a sliding door that led into the chrome and ceramic bathroom. Other than the bed, a simple three drawer dresser with a chair beside it furnished the room. There was a television mounted to the wall across from the bed, and a small floating shelf holding a modified telephone was attached to the wall on the right side of the bed.

"Nice, I guess. I live here, huh?"

He picked up the phone and examined the base. There were no numbers to press or a rotary dial. Through the receiver came the sedate sound of a woman asking how she could help him. He mumbled 'never mind, thanks' and hung up.

"No long-distance calls for me. No contact with the outside at all it seems. Very reassuring."

"This will be your home between investigations, and you will have access to all the services here. For official purposes, you will be recorded as a patient. But this is a good thing for you. The counselling services here are of the highest quality. They can address many of the concerns and challenges you have ben facing in your life. Someday, you can begin to work through the mother-son issues you have."

"Motherfucker you do not even know. Sure, sure. You'll fix it so I don't worry about what she might do, thereby making it harder to control me. I totally believe that."

"I assure you, John, that we want you to be an enthusiastic and willing member of the team. This current situation is unfortunate but necessary. You have not had time yet to see why this is all so very important. You want to run away. This is normal. Soon, you will want to stay. Lives will be saved. No more photos for the memorial."

"Don't fucking lie to me about the victims. You don't give a good goddamn about any of them. You're good at this performance, but that fact was blaring across your porky demeanor. This is not about saving lives to you."

"If that is true, then it makes it most critical for you to do your best. No one else will save them. Does that feel more acceptable to you?"

Falstaff went to the door. He moved the handle and watched the mechanism slide in and out of the frame.

"No lock control on the inside of the door. I'm not a guest, I'm a prisoner. Or an involuntarily committed patient. Which is it?"

The German smiled. "You are mine, and you have work to do. That is all."

17

Like spirits summoned from the dark beyond, a pair of orderlies soundlessly appeared at the door of Falstaff's room . They flanked Falstaff and marched him back through the building. Falstaff didn't have the heart to cause trouble or escape, so he slogged along as he was directed to do. He wondered how many other patients there might be hidden away here in Safe Respite. It would be an expensive solution to keeping one man hostage. He also lamented that he hadn't chugged down the entire 6 pack of malt liquor before coming inside. That would have made him drunk enough to totally tune out his surroundings and arm him with the ability to projectile vomit down the ornate staircase in a shower of brown and black sick protest.

The orderlies walked him to the threshold of the front doors and gently pushed him through. As the large doors closed quickly behind him, he squinted up at the early morning sunlight now beaming down through the skeletal tree limbs above. The new day was underway, and he was still far behind and failing. There was nowhere to go but blindly forward to the next calamity.

Sitting on the front of the car with his right foot on the bumper, Nurse was taking measured bites of the sandwich in his hands, savouring the flavor of the sandwich with sensual determination. After a particularly large and satisfying bite, he sighed and threw the remaining crust into the grass. He lifted a plastic cup filled with a deep red liquid to his lips and sipped it until it was empty.

"That was a fancy looking sandwich. Where did you get it, and did you get one for me? And is that red wine?"

Nurse brushed the crumbs from his hands and stood up.

"From the kitchen. The cook is very skilled. Yes, it was wine. You ate on the trip here."

"Well, fuck you then."

Falstaff stormed to the car and sulked into his seat. He fished around under the seat for the remaining cans of beer but came up empty. He gave an accusatory glare at Nurse.

"Where's my fucking beer?"

"In the trash. Director's orders."

"That's a shitty way to build trust. I'm thirsty and tired."

Nurse started the engine and cruised down the driveway, exiting the property from the front approach. The trees engulfed the building once again, hiding it and the outlying support buildings from sight. Nurse threw a half-full bottle of warm water into Falstaff's lap.

"Drink that. You need to be sober."

Falstaff muttered and thought about throwing the bottle at Nurse's face. He had a vivid daydream of the bottle momentarily blinding Nurse, who then panics and loses control of the car. They carom from the road, becoming airborne and flipping end over end until they crash into the wide Oak tree at the end of the lane. Fire explodes in every direction. As Falstaff crawls away, he sees Nurse's melting face trapped in the car and pleading for help. The vision ends with Falstaff toasting the burning man with the can of beer he has found lying beside the wreck. In the end, Falstaff decided that the whole scene would be too much hassle, so he drank the water and closed his eyes.

"I am hungry, you know. It is morning of a brand new shitty day and I need to eat."

"That garbage you ate before filled you up."

"Doesn't count as food. If I'm going to give up sleeping more than 2 hours a night, I need to eat more food."

"Eat the granola bar in the back seat."

"You eat it. And I gotta take a shit too. Do you want me to do that in here, or can we stop for a coffee and a cheap sandwich for me? Real coffee, not gas station gut rot. Give me some human dignity, Nursie."

"If we stop, you shut up. No more complaining."

"Done and done."

Nurse made a sharp left turn and followed it up by 2 quick right turns. 5 minutes down the road, the edge of another small town became visible. Past the large farm equipment dealership and the municipal road salt storage facility was a coffee shop rehabilitated from an old chain store. The previous branding had been painted over with layer after layer of black paint and finished off with the new shop's name: Lovie's Donuts.

The shape of the building was so familiar that it was odd to see a different name on it.

They parked by the broken front door with the crack in the glass taped over to keep it from falling out. Falstaff worried about the condition of the food inside, but that was secondary to his main goal. He dashed past Nurse to get inside the building.

"What way to the can?" he asked the woman with a blank stare who was standing near the iced coffee machine. She pointed to the left at the narrow door that was opposite the door leading into the seating area of the shop. He gave her a 'thumbs up' and went through the door.

The door opened into another seating area, this one smaller and covered in dust. At some point in the past, this had been a fast food counter, put in by the same conglomerate that also owned the previous coffee shop. Now it was storage for Lovie's Donuts, and the indirect route to the washrooms. He walked through the strange dusty room and turned down the narrow hallway at the other end of the room. He took one wrong turn that led him to a storage closet full of cleaning supplies, then turned around and arrived at the men's washroom. He hurried to the toilet, closed the rusty stall door, and dug into his pocket. He found the three stolen pills tucked into a fold of fabric in the bottom of the pocket, covered in lint but intact.

"Nice search and seizure skills, asshole" Falstaff gloated.

Despite his sharp eyes and suspicious ways, Nurse had missed Falstaff's sleight of hand at the Army base, where he had worked the baggie open with his index finger and thumb as he argued with the C.O. Right before Nurse had demanded the baggie, Falstaff had tipped it over to spill its precious contents into his pocket. He had hoped for half a dozen, maybe more, but three would do for now. Falstaff put the pills into his mouth and bit down hard. He wedged the pills between his molars and ground them into a chalky bitter paste. He swallowed the paste and licked the inside of his mouth for the remnants left behind.

After using the toilet, he came out and bent down at the sink to drink from the tap. The water had a strange sulfurous odor to it, but it did the trick to clean the last of the pills from his teeth. He was certain that the pills were opiates, even more so than he had been. The early onset of the first wave of relief was telling him that they had a powerful punch. He rubbed his face as he stared in the bathroom mirror, watching the rubbery motion of his skin. His lips felt numb and a warmth was creeping up from the tips of his fingers and toes to the rest of his body. The pills were stronger than he anticipated.

As the drug settled in and took hold, Falstaff regretted taking all three pills. His fear that one or two would do nothing had pushed him to triple the dose, but the wave was too strong.

It felt like an hour had gone by while he had been staring in the mirror. He lurched to the washroom door, missing the handle on the first two tries. In the hallway, a shaft of sunlight reflected into his eyes by an old aluminum sign decorating the wall overwhelmed his senses. He closed his eyes and pushed ahead.

Thrown off-balance by his lack of sight, Falstaff tilted forward and hit his head on the opposite wall. His redirected momentum sent him stumbling down the hallway, groping the walls for direction, until he fell spinning into the storage closet.

A cacophonous racket filled his ears. Mops and brooms, boxes of napkins, and empty plastic buckets clattered together into a pile. He landed on his side, on top of a wide mop bucket filled with dirty cold water. His left hand was under water, and he flailed like a drowning man. Falstaff was trapped in the pile of cleaning supplies and unable to plot an escape path in his severely incapacitated state. He stopped struggling, his eyes still screwed shut, and went limp.

A repeated tapping on his knee barely got his attention. He cracked his left eye open and squinted cautiously in the direction of the door. The blurry shape standing there had a long probe that was repeatedly being jabbed into his chest. The next jab was more forceful, and it hit one of his many deep bruises. Things were going to get painful if he let the blob continue to poke him. Falstaff opened his other eye and concentrated on focusing the blur into a defined shape. Once he could see it clearly, he could decide if it was a hallucination. Reality felt very fluid and treacherous at that moment.

His left eye agreed to work in concert with his right, and the blob transformed into the coffee girl who had directed him to the bathroom. She had a long, metal spatula that she was using to prod him. Her face was as blank as a sheet of ice. The woman stared down at him, and he smiled a wobbly, drool-covered smile up at her. Falstaff could hear each breath he took rushing into his body like a gust of hurricane-force wind howling through a canyon. His dilated pupils filled his eyes to the edges.

"Hi there. I got lost and fell. Took a wrong turn leaving the toilet room. Bathroom. I'm fine" he said to her. His numb tongue and lips made the words lose their corners and sound more like a continual hum than a sentence. The coffee shop hostess kept staring. Falstaff tried to put together a better explanation, but each attempt failed in a pile of misplaced words and sentence fragments. He switched to a charm offensive to distract from his predicament.

"Are you Lovie? Is this your place? It's a nice place."

She stood still and continued to stare into his eyes.

"Lovie's dead."

"Aw, man, that's, you know, bad. Sorry you had her die." He lost the ability to join his words together in any semblance of coherence, and he trailed off to a low continual 'uhhhhhh'.

"You're high" she said with shotgun bluntness. He moved his mouth and made random sounds that failed to become actual language. He forced his limited attention to focus on her face, to search for a clue of what she wanted to hear. He saw nothing hidden in her demeanor. It was like staring at the wall.

"Yeah."

Falstaff said his one-word confession reluctantly. It crept out of his mouth like tar, stretching languidly out through the air for an eternity. When it was over, the woman who was not Lovie asked him a question.

"Are you tired of it yet?"

Falstaff lost sight of her as his eyes swam in and out of focus. She was like a desert mirage, vanishing and reappearing as the heat waves shimmered up from the sand. The question swirled around his brain, but he refused to let it land. He took a deep, heaving breath, and spoke in a slow and measured voice.

"That is an odd question to ask a stranger. You don't even know me."

The woman shrugged. "This is familiar."

With herculean effort, Falstaff regained a fraction of his spatial awareness and physical coordination and brought himself to an unsteady standing position.

"See? I'm fine. Told you, Lovie. No, you're not Lovie. She died. Fine."

He smiled at her again, trying to casually wipe off the thin string of drool running from the corner of his mouth without her noticing. She watched the whole performance with an absolute lack of reaction. She said "okay" and walked away.

Alone again in the back hall, Falstaff maneuvered towards the entrance with the care and caution of a mountaineer climbing a treacherous iced approach. He pushed gulps of air deep into his lungs, and forced the air back out in long, slow exhalations. He saw the world through the tunnel vision of the over-medicated. His peripheral vision was gone, but the rest of his sight had stabilized. He thought his chance of avoiding an overdose were good.

He managed to crack open the door leading back into the coffee shop, and he slipped his body through the narrow gap. Triumphantly, he stood in the shop and attempted to affect the mannerisms of a stone cold sober person. Nurse took one look at him and swore in a language Falstaff couldn't identify. Nurse put a 10-dollar bill on the coffee counter, picked up the tray of drinks, and wrapped his arm around Falstaff. The arrival of physical support allowed Falstaff's legs to buckle as they had wanted to do with each step.

Nurse carried him like a rag doll at his side. He poured Falstaff into his seat and buckled him in. The interrogation was underway before Falstaff could say anything.

"What did you take?" Nurse barked as he leaned over hold Falstaff's eyelids open to examine his eyes.

"Pills, Nursie. Fucking powerful pills. That army boss has a rocking addiction if this is the shit he's normally on. It's definitely opiates. I don't know what kind. Oxy isn't this powerful. What was the dose of a single pill? I didn't look before I took it."

Nurse retrieved the baggie from his satchel and fished a pill from inside it. He flipped it over and read out the mark on the pill.

"AMX100. So 100mg. But I am unfamiliar with the 'AMX' designation."

"You and me both. But 100s? Fuck me. Should have only taken one."

"Damn you. How many did you take? You should take zero."

"Just a few, Nursie. One, two, three. Barely having an effect on me."

Nurse pulled Falstaff's eyelids open again.

"Hey, leave my face alone."

"You closed your eyes. I thought you had gone comatose."

"I'm just tired from lack of sleep and an excess of stress. And yeah, maybe I'm a little high too."

Nurse proceeded to search every pocket and fold in Falstaff's clothing. From the outside of the car, it looked like the big man was stripping Falstaff down roughly with ill intent. He ran his hand between each finger and toe, and in the creases of Falstaff's groin and ass.

"That's pretty friendly, Nursie. Ask next time before you molest me. I could scream for help. Maybe the weird girl inside would rescue me."

"Do you have more pills?"

"No, as you have discovered. I am fresh out. I only had three."

Nurse accepted this answer and started the car. As they drove away from the coffee shop, Falstaff re-dressed and sat like a puddle, pooled against the door. He slurred his words into the window glass.

"That girl was hella strange, yo. I couldn't read her. Not, like, at all."

"You can not read me. Plus, you are intoxicated."

"It's different. You hide your shit well, but it's still there under the surface. I can't read it but I know the dirt is there. When you get distracted or excited it sneaks through. She was broadcasting an aggressive silence. It was like a detuned radio hissing noise without pattern or meaning. Being high usually mutes most of the noise of the world, making it easy to not see the bits I want to avoid. But that girl's empty noise was loud and unavoidable. I don't even know if she's a girl. I mean, she presents as female, that's not what I mean. Though she might be packing a cock under the frock. But is she 17? 25? 40? Her face was blank."

"You find this woman too interesting. She is a dullard working in a decrepit coffee shop."

"You suck the fun out of life's mysteries, Nursie. I have never seen a person giving off that particular anti-signal. It's note-worthy. And fuck you for being judgemental. Oh, hold on."

A wave of disconnection rolled through Falstaff's senses, sending his world spinning haphazardly around him. His heart fluttered in a worrying staccato rhythm and his lungs stopped inflating. He held onto the seat for dear life until his body stopped its rebellion.

"The poor bastards hooked on this stuff are fucking doomed. It is too strong. I can handle almost any dope and this shit is trying to kick my heart out. Definitely not for casual users. I am going to take a nap. I should be okay, but if my heart stops, give it a punch, will you?"

"You should remain awake. Do not go to sleep."

Nurse's order fell onto deaf ears, as Falstaff had already slipped into the warm embrace of a deep opioid dream.

18

A nightmare unfolded. Falstaff's dream self was lying naked on a giant, overstuffed bed. His wrists and ankles were immobilized by massive concrete blocks. The obscenely cushioned mattress enveloped his body and pressed in from all sides. He felt like he was slowly sinking into the plush blue fabric, and it was increasingly difficult to breath. An angry wasp, ten times the size it should be, sat perched on Falstaff's naked foot. The wasp was drilling its stinger deep into the sole of his foot. It burned with a building intensity, but he was paralyzed and could not swat it away. The pain bloomed throughout his foot and leg until his whole body twitched in agony.

He woke up and the pain retreated to his foot but entrenched there. Falstaff drew in a lungful of air to scream but a sudden series of open-handed slaps to his cheek interrupted his yell. His limbs refused to respond to his panicked orders to move and escape. They were still lost in the fading narcotic fog. Falstaff's mouth felt like it was lined with rough wool. He found his words again.

"Stop hitting me! What the fuck!"

Nurse stood straddled above Falstaff, bent at the waist with his right arm pulled back in preparation of another slap. Falstaff grabbed at the ground underneath his hands and wondered how he had moved from his car seat to his current location. He managed to sit up and look around.

Falstaff was 5 feet from the car, sitting on the muddy ground beside the rutted dirt track that led back to the road. Farther down, the track was flanked by recently turned fields that stretched off to the horizon. At the edge of his sight, Falstaff could make out a squat brown building surrounded by a security fence. He rubbed his cheeks and scowled at Nurse.

"Slapping me awake is a bit over the top."

"You had overdosed. I needed to rouse you."

The shocking pain in his face was fading away, and in its absence, the localized agony on the sole of his foot came roaring back. The new pain joined his ever-present companion pain from his broken rib. A throbbing ache had settled into the sole of his right foot, and it was worsening with every second that went by. He stared at his one socked foot with confusion.

"Why is my shoe off, and why does my foot hurt so fucking much?"

The pain was escalating as he became more alert. He pulled his foot up and gingerly massaged it. Even a slight touch made the pain flare.

"To counteract the opioids in your system, I administered an emergency opioid blocker. It was injected through the first available site, the sole of your foot."

"That's not the first site you found and you know it. Goddamn this hurts. Could have shot me in the arm or the ass. Or just let me sleep it off, because I wasn't overdosing."

"I need you clearheaded to continue investigation."

"So you admit that I wasn't Od'ing? Nice, very nice. Barely any sleep, lack of food, and regular physical abuse are not, by definition, how you make people clearheaded. Now on top of all that other shit, I am totally sober. Even my shitty beer buzz is gone. Fuck this, and fuck you, you fat-handed sadist."

Nurse reached down and grabbed Falstaff by the shoulders. He jerked him upwards and stood him up, forcing him to stand on his feet. The pressure on the injection site made the pain flare up and he let out a little shriek. Nurse growled at him.

"You are expected to do your job, not take drugs. There is no more time for your addictions."

Nurse leaned on Falstaff's shoulders, pressing him down deeper into the mud. It made his chest hurt.

"Okay, okay. Clean living for the rest of the investigation. I'm not an addict, I'm an enthusiast. I can quit whenever I want. Let me go."

The hands clamped on his shoulders were removed, and Falstaff hopped to his uninjured foot to relieve the pain from the other one. His clothes were covered in mud, and his head was throbbing.

"I can't walk in to a hospital looking like this, or they'll try to lock me up. They sure as shit won't believe I'm a logistics systems analyst, or consultant, or whatever I'm pretending to be. Where are we, anyway?"

"I do not know. When you convulsed I drove away from the road to find a place to revive you. That building in the distance, it is the hospital I think. Here."

Nurse took a nylon gym bag from the trunk and threw it at Falstaff's feet. Inside was a full change of clothes.

"Aw, you packed me an overnight bag. How sweet."

He shimmied out of the dirty clothes, shivering from the cold wet air. Falstaff threw the dirty clothes back in the bag and put on the clean ones. He found his missing shoe wedged under the front tire. With a little work, he cleaned the inside of the shoe well enough to slip it back on.

"As pretty as a picture, I am. Do you have any aspirin for my thundering headache?"

Nurse glared in response.

"Yeah yeah, I know. No pills at all for the bad little boy. If my attitude is perpetually terrible, that is your fault."

The adrenaline faded from Falstaff's system. He was now bone-tired and nauseous, beat-up and lost. But in that moment, standing in the quiet of a fallow field as the sunlight warmed the cold air around him on an early Spring day, Falstaff felt a brief touch of serenity brush past him.

The only other living things he could see, other than himself and his jailor, was a trio of pitch black crows hopping from clump to clump in a depression in the field. They were picking at the dirt and chattering to each other. Falstaff meandered towards the birds, stretching his legs and prolonging this brief interlude of calm. He carefully picked his way through the uneven terrain, noticing that there were deep and irregular furrows that formed arcs from the rutted road. Where the furrows met, he saw a muddle of footprints pressed into the sloppy mud.

"Huh, you brought us to a popular field. There were a group of cars and people here recently. Bet they left something that caught the crows interest."

As if he had called it by name, the fattest crow looked at him, with a pale cylinder trapped in its beak. The crow tilted its head back and forth, causing the pale pink tube to wiggle in a manner that struck Falstaff as mildly obscene.

Falstaff hopped over the last car tire furrow and shouted at the crows. The two accomplices took off for the safety of the nearby trees, but the fat one simply hopped back. Falstaff took another step, and the crow matched him. They repeated their strange dance in a semi-circle. The crow led them around the spot where he had first landed.

Falstaff stopped pursuing the crow to search the ground instead. He wanted to know what the fat crow refused to leave behind. He kicked at the dirt pile that was ringed by crow footprints. It broke off in a mass and fell to the side. Stuck into the remaining mud base was another pink cylinder, this one sticking straight up. Falstaff leaned over and realized he was looking at a human finger.

"Fuck! Hey Nurse, I found something you should see."

"What? Is it the bird or the mud that I am supposed to be tricked into seeing?"

"I'm not fucking with you, Nursie. I found a goddamn human finger."

He looked at the fat crow again and corrected his sentence.

"Two fingers so far. One is in the bird's beak."

Nurse sighed and walked over to stand beside Falstaff.

"See?"

"Yes, its finger."

"And the bird's mouth."

"Another finger. Very good. May we go now?"

"Don't you find it a little bit curious that there are human body parts strewn around a field? Most normal people would be concerned."

"You are too sensitive. You imagine this is a safe happy world where bad things rarely happen."

Falstaff watched the fat crow watching them, mesmerized by the bird's shiny black eyes and the flopping finger in its beak.

"So in your reality, it is perfectly normal to find a severed finger or two in the course of a day."

"People die."

"In gruesome dismemberments at random locations across the country?"

"Life is cheap. Leave this for the crows to eat."

The bird agreed with Nurse's idea. It tossed the pale pink bit of flesh upwards and gobbled it down. The finger disappeared down the bird's gullet. The fat crow gave out a triumphant squawk and flew off to the closest tree. Falstaff backed away from the finger left on the ground.

"Should we tell the police about this? It could be the remains of another victim of that Devil of the Rust Belt murderer. Unless it's part of our investigation, but that doesn't seem likely. Doesn't fit the usual pattern."

Nurse had his back to Falstaff and was walking back to the car.

"Leave it alone. This is not your business."

They were back in the car and driving back down the road when Falstaff pushed the issue. He thought there was some moral prerogative to report the body pieces, and he repeatedly said so to the unconcerned man driving the car. Nurse refused to contact the police, but after being pestered for a steady 5 minutes, he agreed to have a 3rd party make an anonymous tip. This failed to put Falstaff at ease, and he pressed for more. There was a note of growing frustration in Nurse's voice as he responded.

"What would you like? We go back and have a little funeral for the finger? You give an emotional eulogy, then we have the bird come vomit the rest of the finger into the tiny grave. Stop being a child and focus on the problem you are responsible for solving."

The conversation stopped with that sarcastic reply, and the last mile to the hospital was full of bitter silence.

The hospital building was a squat 4 storey square with no redeeming visual features. It had been built in the age of institutional ugliness, where the passive loathing for government that ran through the American psyche manifested in repugnant design esthetics for all public buildings. They parked in the tiny visitor's lot and walked to the front door. Falstaff finished the last of the now cold Lovie's coffee and spit a thick wad of phlegm neat Nurse's feet.

"What's the story here? I'm at a loss. This is a fishing expedition and I don't even have bait."

"I thought aimlessly sniffing around other's people's business was your talent. Bother them for drugs until they throw you out."

"I hate you, you snide motherfucker. Put that in the official report." Falstaff spit the words at Nurse and stormed inside with an unsteady wobble in his steps.

The reception desk of the veteran's hospital was in the center of the room, with doorways on either side leading into the reception area. The desk was staffed by a slope-shouldered scrawny man with flushed cheeks and a pungent body odor. Falstaff launched into a song and dance about supply line disruptions and military procurement, speaking so quickly that the words blurred into a single continuous sentence. The clerk was flustered by the barrage, and looked like he wanted to run for the doors. Falstaff noticed the tablet in the man's right hand was playing a video of two women kissing each other as a thick uncut cock slid between their lips. He refused to search for the location of the clerk's other hand. The clerk fumbled with the tablet to stop the porn, mashing the screen repeatedly until the scene was frozen in mid-lick. He hid the tablet beneath the folders stacked on the side of the desk.

"As I said, we're here to investigate the supply lines and any disruptions to them, so if you can direct us to the place where we could do that which we are here to do, we can begin and leave you to get back to work."

It took a lot of restraint to avoid putting air quotes around the word "work". Falstaff watched the horny little toad as he squirmed in his seat. The toad was confused and embarrassed, unsure of how to comply with Falstaff's garbled request but desperate to get him to go away. They stood locked in a battle of indecision, Falstaff with his foul coffee and stomach acid breath and the clerk with his flagging erection pulling at the crotch of his cheap blue scrubs. The standoff was broken by Nurse's laughter. He stepped in front of Falstaff and flashed his badge at the toad. With ease and efficiency, Nurse spoke the language of military procedure and restored order to the chaos at the desk. The clerk understood authority and direct instruction. He snapped to full attention when Nurse dropped Colonel Grizzley's name. Nurse explained that this was a routine inspection that was no cause for concern.

"As long as protocol is followed. You will lead us to the location of your laundry services and the delivery point for your linens."

"Linens?"

"Yes. Linens. Towels, specifically. Is there another on-duty clerk who can accompany us?"

"The rest is all orderlies. They gotta stay with their charges."

"Very well. You have 2 minutes to organize yourself to escort us."

"Yessir."

Nurse nodded and turned away from the awkward toad at the desk. Falstaff went to the opposite doorway and looked through to the reception room and the patient lounge past it. There were less than a dozen patients and staff sitting in the lounge, at least as far as Falstaff could see. He tried to pick out more detail from the patients inside but was interrupted by Nurse calling him to attention. The clerk had put a handwritten note on the desk, saying 'back in 5, and he was now standing meekly in front of Nurse, avoiding eye contact. Falstaff glanced down and was relieved to see that the Toad's arousal had subsided enough to be unnoticeable.

The tour through the hospital was rushed and erratically planned, jinking down hallways that seemed to double back on themselves and heading into dead-end rooms that connected to hidden service hallways. The persistent layer of dust and dirt over everything made Falstaff feel bad for the patients in the place. The staff obviously did not make cleanliness a virtue or a priority. The few patients they passed appeared to be totally unattended in silent rooms. Falstaff mentioned that things were a little dirty and the patients could use some company. The clerk shrugged and said "not my job."

They were crossing a large room full of couches and tables, with flickering televisions in each corner, when Falstaff watched a woman in a wheelchair drop her paperback book. It bounced in the empty spot where her left leg was supposed to be and fell to the floor. The few staff members in the room steadfastly ignored the woman as she feebly reached for the dropped book. He scooped the book from the ground and handed it to the woman.

"Fuck those guys, amiright?" he said with a wink. Her hand closed slowly on the book as her eyes tried to focus on his face. She was heavily sedated. Falstaff knew the feeling and he envied her disconnection from the real world. He patted the back of her hand and left her to her drug-induced stupor. At the exit of the recreation room, Falstaff mentioned the sedated woman to the clerk.

"She was pretty out of it. Is that normal for patients who are unsupervised?"

"They all on meds here. Keeps them safe and calm."

"All of them? All the time? That's unhealthy."

Nurse shot Falstaff a warning look and he dropped the line of inquiry. At least this confirmed Grizzley's story that the patients were addicted before they left the hospital. The question he couldn't get out of his mind was why they would sedate the entire population of recovering vets. He also wondered if he might be able to borrow a few doses from them to get him by. The clerk finally offered a weak explanation for the constant sedation.

"Everyone of them has "profound catastrophic injuries" so they need continual pain relief."

The next turn took them past a dimly lit hallway that ended in a wall of windows. Beyond the windows were empty planters and stunted trees, with a hedge wall defining the outer boundaries. The hallway had 2 doors set into either wall, halfway down its length. An anonymous low moan rose and fell from one of the side rooms.

"What's down the spooky hall?"

"Long-term care ward. The LTW."

"Aren't most folks here for the long haul?"

"These ones ain't gonna recover."

"We should head down there, give them a visit."

The clerk scowled at Falstaff. "There ain't no towels down there. Laundry is this way."

"Right, right. Lead on."

Nurse looked at Falstaff inquisitively, and Falstaff responded with a shrug, followed by a pantomime of casting a lure. They continued into the guts of the building.

"Yeah, that LTW must be the most boring place to go. Not a lot of conversationalists down there."

"They're all vegetables or head case freaks. A couple of them just scream bloody murder when you get close to 'em. Crazies." The clerk laughed.

"That must be upsetting. Do they get any visitors?"

"Why you asking so many questions about them?"

"No reason. Just shooting the shit, pal. Place must be full of stories. Being trapped in a room full of crazies sounds dire. And lonely. Which is why I wondered about visitors."

"Hospital policy is to limit visitors to that particular ward. Visitors upset the population."

Falstaff was entranced by the clerk's compulsion to over-pronounce every syllable in words with 4 or more of them. He guessed that Toad the Clerk didn't have a large supply of multi-syllabic words, so he put considerable effort into saying the few he did know. The clerk had stretched 'particular' into a drawled 'par-tic-eee-you-lair'. A strange verbal affectation.

Like cresting the summit of an uninspiring hill, they reached the dank cubby that served as the linen supply closet for the hospital. A couple of tall, dark-skinned men folded towels in the corner, and they gave the clerk a perfunctory nod of greeting before returning to their work.

"This is our laundry room, such as it is. Them two are the laundry guys. Somalis, I think. They been here longer than me. They don't say much."

"Hey, is there a place I can pop out for a quick smoke? The boss here can spare me for a couple of minutes."

"There is no smoking allowed on the property of the hospital. You would have to leave."

Falstaff was certain there was a little tucked away place out in the untended garden where the staff snuck out for their smoke breaks, but he wasn't going to push clerk to reveal its location. He accepted the answer and stood beside Nurse.

Nurse proceeded to ask a series of mundane questions about delivery times, storage procedures, and unexpected disruptions. The two Somalis answered each question with terse short sentences. They looked to Falstaff when they answered, not the massive man asking the questions. Falstaff smiled and nodded to them in an attempt to make them feel more comfortable. Nurse continued with due officious pomp, inspecting delivery logs, sign in sheets, and examining the stacks of towels and linens for orderly arrangement. The clerk stood at the doorway until they were done asking questions, shooting dirty looks at Falstaff. He did not trust Falstaff at all. Nurse ran out of details to question, and announced to the room that the inspection was satisfactory. He gave the men thanks and instructed the clerk to direct them towards the exit.

The horny toad clerk led them back towards the front desk and right to the front doors. Falstaff was tired of the clerk's attitude and suspicious looks.

"Yeah, thanks for the great tour. Informative and fun! Sorry we interrupted your self-pleasure time. You can go back to jerking it under the table while earning your minimum wage."

The clerk went red with shame and rage. Falstaff saw the fist balled up and pulled back, waiting to swing forward. Nurse put his body in between the two of them. He bumped Falstaff through the door with a hip check while addressing the clerk.

"I apologize for my assistant. He is on probation and has an attitude problem. I will report him for this unprofessional behaviour. Good day. You! To the car!"

The door closed behind Nurse as he sent a kick aimed at Falstaff's ass. Falstaff maneuvered out of its trajectory and scurried to the bottom of the stairs. He turned back in triumph and wagged his middle fingers at Nurse.

"Time for a celebratory smoke."

Falstaff pulled out a cigarette and slipped it between his lips. A quick scan of the ground confirmed that no one was smoking directly outside the front door, because there was a complete lack of cigarette butts. He paced forward while continuing to search the dirt.

At the end of the sidewalk, there was a pile of cigarette butts to either side. For all their other lapses, the hospital staff was diligent in enforcing the smoking ban publicly. Falstaff lit up and took a deep drag. He looked down the long line of the perimeter hedge that ran perpendicular to the building. Worn into the thin grass cover at the base of the hedge was a narrow footpath. Curious, he walked along the path to see where it led. Nurse stayed a few paces behind him, following along the wandering trail.

Through the gaps between the branches of the hedge, Falstaff could see the tightly spaced links of a security fence hidden. The hedge gave it the illusion of not being a fenced off compound, but the simple addition of a gate at the end of the sidewalk would turn the hospital into a makeshift prison. He paused and commented to Nurse.

"They could lock them up here. Maybe they already do. It's not a great barrier. A healthy person could hop this fence with a little effort. But they aren't healthy whole people in there. Should have checked for automated door locks when we were getting the royal tour from Sir Pulls-his-Pud."

He continued down the path towards the corner of the hedge fence. The gentle incline of the ground below led to a small hill past the back edge of fence. On the top of the hill was a small copse of birch trees circled around a tall pitch pine.

As he crested the hill he looked back to the hospital. From where he was standing, Falstaff could see over the top of the hedge, but the sharp angle made it difficult to see anything clearly. He knew he was looking down at the garden, but he wanted a better look. He looked upwards instead, inspecting the limbs of the pitch pine above him. Amid the thick nest of pine needles, he found a long sturdy branch 6 feet off the ground that was free of smaller offshoots. Below the branch there were the stubs of broken branches that served as adequate footholds.

He clambered onto the branch. The branches and needles that obscured his perch from below did not do the same from that height. He could see through the cover, peering down at the garden and the back wall of the long-term ward. Falstaff could also see glimpses of the interiors of the rooms on the second floor above the large common room. A low mean wind blew up from nowhere and shook the branches around him. His right hand brushed the bark of the tree as he steadied himself, and he felt an odd regularity in the rough skin. Carved into the bark were a set of 10 horizontal lines that were spaced evenly along a vertical line. He alternately studied the view into the ward, and the lines that had been carved with care into the bark.

Falstaff lowered himself back to the ground and did a quick search of the dirt at the base of the tree. He found no other trace of someone spending time there.

"Interesting. A curious person has been watching the lifers in the LTW from this perch. They are keeping a tally on the bark."

"What does this mean?" Nurse asked as he peered up at the perch.

Falstaff looked at the tree and the hill and the flat fields and the ugly square hospital.

"Wish I knew."

19

They marched back to the car as Falstaff complained about his lot in life and its inherent unfairness.

"Honestly, I would love to have even one clear answer. The peeping tom in the tree might have fuck all to do with any of this. Christ, even the drug dealer could be innocent of the murders. It's all a bunch of puzzle pieces that don't fit together. Puzzle pieces and a stack of corpses. Goddamn it. I knew I would suck as a detective, but no one believed me. What a colossal waste of time."

"Did this trip tell you nothing?" Nurse asked.

"You actually sound disappointed, Nursie. Did this tell me something? No. Yes. Maybe, I don't know. Like I said, it's a jumbled mess of pieces. Are they even from the same puzzle? Like that perch up there. Its occupant could be a coma fetishist who gets off on watching the non-responsive patients, and they hack a mark into the tree each time they jerk off to a vegetative state pin-up model. Whoever uses it, they don't leave much behind. If it was just kids fucking around, there would be garbage and shit strewn all around the tree. Looked clean to me."

They got into the car and sat staring off into the distance. Falstaff had no plan for the next step. The only thing commanding his attention at that moment was the relentless pounding of a headache fueled by the numerous abuses heaped upon his body. He was exhausted.

"Let's go back to the safe house and get some sleep. When it's dark, we'll troll the streets for drug info. It's the only common thread we can keep chasing after."

Nurse started the engine and drove out to the road.

"It is always about the drugs for you."

"Pills make the world go 'round, Nursie. Human consciousness is an unfair burden for the regular guy or gal. Too much thinking, no good answers. A little self-medication gets people through the day."

"I do not self-medicate."

"Not with dope, sure, but you got something that takes away the edge. I can't be bothered to drill down to find out what it is. Probably something monstrous and perverse. Wake me when we get home, Nursie."

The car rumbled to a stop in their driveway 40 minutes later. Falstaff's eyes flew open as soon as the engine died, as an unpleasant realization hit him. True to his fear, he looked across the street to see JJ running towards the car.

"That poor fucking guy. He's going to want to know about his brother."

"Do not tell him we saw the body."

"Of course fucking not. I'm not voluntarily putting myself at the crime scene. Shit I have to give him a bullshit story that explains why I didn't save his brother. You go in so he doesn't escalate and freak out. He doesn't trust you."

"He should not. I dislike junkies and dope pedlars."

"Good for you, upstanding citizen. Now fuck off."

Nurse obliged and went quickly inside. Falstaff stepped out of the car and met JJ at the end of the driveway.

"My brother, man. He's dead. Dead! I guy I know called an hour ago to tell me. I thought you got killed too."

The unexpected concern for his wellbeing made Falstaff feel sick about lying, but he was committed to staying out of the reports or rumors.

"I got there as things were going wrong. There were gunshots, a lot of gunshots, and I freaked out. I hid around the corner and waited until the shooting stopped. But then I heard sirens coming and I ran off. I had to stay clear of the whole scene until the cops calmed down. I am so sorry your brother didn't make it, JJ."

JJ flipped between anger and sadness, crying and shouting incoherently as his grief took over. Falstaff stood awkwardly watching the breakdown. He couldn't do anything to help JJ. The outburst trailed off to sobbing and looking up at sky, and Falstaff saw a few of the other neighbors peering through their curtains to watch the uncomfortable scene. He needed to get JJ out of his driveway and away from prying eyes. It was a miserable affair to stand and watch a grown man weeping with such intensity that two trails of snot and tears ran continuously from his nostrils.

"Dude, you need to go chill out inside. Get yourself together so you can go handle the morgue and the cops."

"Fuck, man. Cops. The cops, man. They're going to come looking for me when they officially ID Archie. I gotta clean the house."

JJ ran across the street, still blubbering, to remove any illegal materials before the police arrived. Falstaff limped inside as quickly as he could, wincing when his right foot came down too hard on the tender injection spot. He walked directly past the living room where Nurse was settled into the easy chair, eyes closed with a half-smirk on his face.

"Foot still hurts like a motherfucker, so thanks for that. Did you break the goddamned needle off and leave it in? Have a nice nap, asshole."

Falstaff continued to his room without waiting for a response from Nurse, trailing his defiant middle finger flying high behind him. Back in his room, he sat on the edge of his bed and gingerly peeled off his sock to inspect the injection site. A bloom of red skin radiated from the pinprick blood spot on his heel. The skin felt warm to the touch and swollen. Too tired to do anything more about it, he laid back on the bed and let his mind wander. He thought about infections and festering wounds and amputations, until a restless sleep took him over.

Falstaff woke up startled and dug through his room to count his stash of pills. His supply was running low. He dry swallowed one valium and hid the rest of his meager stash in his sock. Falstaff lay back and drifted in and out of sleep for another couple of hours.

He emerged from his bedroom when the sun had set again, to find Nurse sitting at the dinette table. Spread out on the table was joyless but nutritionally adequate meal: overcooked chicken breasts, limp green beans, flavorless mashed potatoes, congealing gravy, and a syrupy fruit cup for desert. Parked beside Falstaff's plate was a tall plastic tumbler of milk. The 1950s domesticity of the dinner arrangement was a jarring mismatch to the brooding provider of the meal. Nurse pointed at the plate and grunted at Falstaff. He followed the wordless instruction and sat down to eat the meal.

They sat in silence and ate the unappetizing food. Falstaff ate until he was packed full, washing it all down with an additional tumbler of milk. He belched long an loud, defiantly aiming it at Nurse's face. The big man stared blankly.

"Thanks, Nursie. That was super. I have a well-balanced meal to give me the energy to succeed in my everyday life. It was obviously ordered from the finest geriatric restaurant in the city. You're the best jailor and torturer a guy could hope for. So thoughtful."

"I am glad you enjoyed it. You will clean the dishes."

Falstaff was halfway out of his seat before he realized Nurse was serious. He froze in that half-standing position as he weighed his options. The thought of rebellion faded when Nurse casually pulled a syringe from his pocket and placed in on the table in front of him.

"Is that a good shot or a bad shot?"

Nurse held his hands in front of his body and turned the palms to face the roof. He wanted Falstaff to know that it was a mystery for him to solve, and he would not like the answer.

"At least you're getting creative. Always being intimidated by brutal physical violence was getting stale. Now we have chemical threats in the mix. Fun!"

Falstaff washed the dishes as he dreamed of jabbing that needle into Nurse's eardrum, spraying whatever toxic and pain-inducing concoction it contained into the depths of his ear canal. It made the time go by more quickly.

After the cleaning was done, Falstaff went outside to have a cigarette. He stood on the porch, watching the parked cop car across the street and smoking. JJ had a cop inside of his house, the worst-case scenario for any dealer. Even a violent home invasion was preferable to the cops coming in. Broken limbs heal, but more importantly, you can keep living your life while the wounds heal. When the cops get you, your life is interrupted, sometimes permanently.

Nurse came out and nudged Falstaff towards the car. He made a great show of the slow, painful walk to the passenger side. As he sat down, Falstaff moaned with the pretence of deep, aching pain.

"My foot, there's something wrong with it."

The car pulled out of the driveway and they made their way out of the neighborhood.

"Your pain tolerance claims are mostly bullshit, I think. One little needle."

"We went over this twice already, so stop being a dick about this. Head down to that shitty Irish bar where we met the reporter. We'll troll the streets from that point out towards the edges of downtown."

The next few hours were lost to repetitive scenes of fruitless investigation. Bumping over countless bridges as they circled through the rundown streets on one river bank or the other, they stopped at every clump of night people gathering for the evenings festivities. Every junkie, dealer, pimp and whore said the same things in different words. They all knew the new pills were on the street, but they couldn't point Falstaff in the direction of the seller. The new pills arrived sporadically, brought in to town by a small-time dealer who vanishes shortly after. The people on the street hadn't figured out what was happening to those dealers afterwards, and Falstaff neglected to mention their bloody end.

A few of the people he spoke to offered to sell their personal supply to Falstaff, as well as different sex acts and some stolen property they had on hand, but each time, Nurse pulled him away from the transaction before it could commence in earnest. After the third failed buy, they sat in the car and Falstaff hissed a tantrum across the front seat.

"You have to let me buy from someone. They don't trust us for shit when we drive up and ask for information without spending some money. It makes us look like cops and that means they shut up and keep secrets."

"No buying."

"What do you mean no? I need to buy, just one pill. You won't give me anything for the pounding headache or the fucking stabbing wound in my foot or the general shitty experience of living this life, so let me buy one tiny pill to get us some goodwill and relax my tension. I'm fucking high strung, if you had not noticed."

"Director has instructed that you have no more access to narcotics."

"I get that, I do, but Christ, it's hard. Each one of these people we been talking to tonight, they have ugly secrets pouring out of their souls. I want to stop looking, but I can't. It's easy, relatively when I'm around real shit heels, the people who embrace their awfulness. They don't try to hide the evil in their hearts. But these folks on the street are almost the worst to deal with. They all see themselves as good people on a temporary bad streak. It's a lie for most of them, but it gets them through. The pills, the booze, the whatever, it all numbs me enough to ignore the self-directed human tragedy they are caught up in."

"Who is worst?"

"Excuse me?"

"You said these people are almost the worst. Who are worst?"

Falstaff went limp with complete spiritual defeat.

"Decent people are the worst. No one is actually good, you know. All people are shit. Decent people are convinced they are not shit, but they can't hide their shitty secrets from me. Can we just go back to the safehouse now? No one has a lead."

"But this was your only plan. The investigation has to continue."

"I know, I know. I'll think of something. Put a pot of coffee on, do a visioning exercise, make a diagram of the investigation, hold a fucking séance. I'll try everything until something clicks. Or we end up dead in a warehouse like all the victims. The other option is you give up on pushing me to figure this mess out and take me to a bar to watch me get cataclysmically drunk."

Nurse thought about the situation, then started the car and headed back to their temporary home. Falstaff kept his eyes closed for the trip, tired of looking at the rundown city and the haunted faces that occupied it. When Nurse parked the car again, Falstaff sat upright and slapped the dashboard.

"My brain is so fogged up with the swirling chaos and bullshit of the last 2 days that I'm missing clear leads. JJ's brother connected with the mystery dealer. I need to find out how that happened."

As if on cue, JJ stormed through his front door and marched up to the passenger side window of their car. He knocked angrily on the glass repeatedly. Nurse got out of his seat and moved to intercept JJ. Falstaff grabbed Nurse's arm before he was out of reach and told him to stay cool. He gestured to JJ to take a step back so that he could open the door and stepped out to stand face to face with the scrawny man.

"They shot his heart out, man. That's cartel-level aggression. I want to get revenge on these assholes."

"Shit. Shot his heart clean out? That is terrible. I want to help you find the killers, I do. Tell me how he got in contact with them."

"I will, but we need some privacy. The cops just left but there are still unfriendly ears around."

JJ glared at Nurse with hate in his eyes. Falstaff gently suggested Nurse head inside and leave this up to him.

"I will talk with our neighbor here and help him sort things out. No partying, no messing around. I promise."

Nurse cautiously backed away from the conversation, keeping his eyes locked on Falstaff. The threat of new violence as a reprisal for taking anything stronger than an aspirin was clearly conveyed to Falstaff. JJ waited until Nurse disappeared behind the closed door before speaking again.

"It was a rival dealer. It had to be, man. Killing poor Archie in a bloody display, on the same night where I was supposed to make a bunch of deals."

"Do you think his new source set him up?"

JJ's eyes lit up at the suggestion. "A set-up! Definitely!"

"The new dealer rolled into town and was planning to get rid of the competition. So, we need to know how Archie met the new dealer and set up the meeting."

"It was over the phone, but I don't have Archie's phone."

"Who gave the new dealer Archie's number? One of your customers?"

"No, it didn't go down like that. Archie gave the guy his number. Over the internet."

"A lot of people connect on that internet, that sure is true."

"Hey, don't fuck with me, man. You know what I mean. Archie uses this underground website that he said was on the 'deep web'. Hard to access but safer to talk about complicated things. He found a post looking for new entrepreneurs and contacted the poster. They exchanged messages and Arch gave the guy his number."

"Do you have his log-in info for the site?"

JJ scowled and paced down the driveway to the curb, and back.

"No, he didn't give it to me. He did all the electronic stuff. But, he used my laptop, the one in my room."

Falstaff slapped JJ on the shoulder and smiled.

"Then all is not lost, pal. Take me to the laptop and let me sniff around for the sweet sweet data. I bet he's got the log-in info saved. If not, it might get complicated."

JJ stopped still and looked at Falstaff with revulsion. He was full of rage in search of an outlet.

"My brother's dead, man. Don't joke around like this is fun."

The scrawny drug dealer puffed up his chest and made bony little fists that shook in anticipation of being thrown. Falstaff switched gears to console JJ.

"JJ, I'm sorry. My stupid ass has been up pretty much for days and I was excited about tracking down the bitches who killed Archie. But I won't forget again that this is about your brother. He didn't deserve this, and we need to make it right."

"But it was still not something to laugh about."

The anger locked into his fists was preventing JJ from moving pat the perceived slight. There were several ways to deescalate the situation without violence, but those answers swirled around in the ether out of reach to Falstaff's tired mind. Instead, he catalyzed the violence. He gave JJ a light push backwards.

"Back the fuck off, JJ. I didn't send him off to get killed. That was you."

Buttons pressed, JJ exploded with a flurry of unskilled punches. Most missed their mark. One landed in the middle of Falstaff's right cheek and glanced off without inflicting any damage. Falstaff cupped his hands around his nose and cried out as he voluntarily fell to the ground. His landed on his hands and knees with his face turned back to his front door. The door cracked open and he held up his left hand as a signal to Nurse to stay inside. The door closed again.

"Oh shit, JJ. That hurt. My nose is burning. Sorry. I'm sorry. Just don't hit me again."

JJ wheezed and stumbled around the driveway. He was exhausted by the unfamiliar exertions of combat. He could barely muster enough breath to accept Falstaff's apology. JJ offered a helping hand to get Falstaff to his feet, but Falstaff pushed it away. Arm in arm like old drunk friends they crossed the street and entered JJ's house.

The hallway had been cleared out in a hurry, stripping it of the cluttered shoes and plants that had lined the space hours before. The living room had been likewise sanitized. All the posters and memorabilia that had any drug reference to it had been removed and hidden away. JJ had tried to make the house look as law-abiding as possible, though it was a symbolic effort. Falstaff guessed that there was already a lengthy file on the house as a drug den, and if the police had wanted to arrest the brother of a murder victim, they could have easily done so. He hoped JJ hadn't dumped all his product, but the likelihood was that it had all gone down the drain.

JJ told Falstaff to sit down and wait for minute. He ran off before Falstaff could ask for a drink, so he lit up a smoke and waited patiently. JJ returned with a laptop covered in novelty stickers and beer labels. He plugged it in to the power adapter held together with electrical tape, placed it on the table in front of Falstaff, and flipped the screen up. The computer woke up from its suspended state to show a browser window filled with a still image of one trans woman fucking another as she jerked her cock. JJ's eyes went wide and he dove over the couch to reach the laptop. He mashed buttons until the window closed.

"That was nothing. Virus, man."

"Never mind that, JJ. Humans are curious. Let's get looking for the killer."

Falstaff launched the browser, readying himself for a return of the previous pornographic picture, but a simple Google search page was displayed instead. He opened the list of previously visited sites, but the long list of various porno searches from the last 24 hours gave him no useful information. He shot JJ a mildly disapproving look for compulsively browsing for porn, but JJ could not become any more embarrassed than he already was.

"Did you guys share this laptop every day? When did your brother last use it?"

"He mostly used it. I, uh, borrowed it when he went out yesterday morning."

"Yesterday morning? All this dirty shit happened since yesterday morning? Come on, JJ. You need to cool it with the porn."

"Hey man, I did not ask you about that. Shut up."

JJ pinched Falstaff and tilted his head towards the large wicker chair with the immense pink velvet cushion as the seat padding. What Falstaff had assumed as being a pile of laundry or old coats was in fact the same nervous girl with greasy hair that had been in the house last time, curled up and passed out. Falstaff let the subject drop and instead opened the browser history from 2 days ago. There were repeated visits to alternative "news" sites that catered to every conspiracy theory under the sun, various clothing and footwear brand sites, and a string of comedic YouTube videos in the list. JJ jabbed his bony finger at the screen as he pointed out an inconspicuous entry for 'desjeb.org'.

"That's it, man. Desjeb! Its in the deep web."

Falstaff typed the address into the search window. It was the top search result, and had its own ad displayed on the results screen. If this was a deep web site, it was doing a terrible job at staying hidden from prying eyes. He went to the site and browsed through the multitude of sub-topics. It wasn't, as he had been led to believe, a secret and secure communication nexus for illicit trade. It was an anonymous message board that was easily accessed by any 10-year-old with a computer and a lack of supervision, judging by the average content and maturity level of the posts. The username and password fields were auto populated with saved information, so Falstaff clicked on the login button and became ArchiBomb69.

The site allowed private messages between users, and that was where Falstaff looked first for the identity of the killer. There was only one message in his inbox. Archibomb69 had been in a conversation with another user named 'WhiteKnightRides', and the final message directed Archibomb69 to download a secure messaging app on his phone to wait for a message. Without Archie's phone, it was a dead end.

"No luck there, unless the cops dropped off his phone."

"No, man. They are keeping his stuff as 'evidence' in the investigation. Fucking pigs, man."

Falstaff switched to looking at Archibomb69's comment history. Archie made a few comments on various unrelated posts, but nothing older than 2 weeks. Falstaff popped open a second window and asked google 'how often does Desjeb delete posts?'. The answer was that all posts were automatically deleted after 2 weeks.

"That cuts in to our available information. At least it doesn't flush itself clean every 24 hours or we would be shit out of luck."

He scanned the list of links to Archie's comments, looking for the post where he came into contact with WhiteKnightRides. Most of Archibomb69's comments were praising the hotness of nude selfies from other users, or noting the design flaws of various strange bong designs. A page down, Falstaff found the post where Archie had replied to the white knight. He clicked through and read the entire post.

It was a simple post that implied more than stated the intention to sell drugs. Someone from outside of the dope economy would skip past it without a further thought. The poster, WhiteKnightRides, was looking for reps in a new area, top grade material with good supply potential. A few other users had jumped in to the conversation, but only Archibomb69 had known how to continue the negotiation properly. The final message from the knight told Archie to check his private messages for the next step. There was no additional information in the post. Falstaff sighed and stubbed out the cigarette that had burned down to a nub while clenched between his teeth. He lit another one and blew smoke at the ceiling.

"JJ, get me a drink. Nothing over the top. One of those beers."

"I threw them out, man."

"Jesus. There is such a thing as being too cautious JJ. Get me a coke."

JJ brought back a lukewarm can of coke, and Falstaff sipped the sweet caramel-colored fizz while fuming over his cigarette. He dove back in to his electronic investigation, this time walking through the conversations of the White Knight themselves. There were several posts that all fit the same format as the one with Archie: looking for sellers in your area. Each one that Falstaff read ended one of two ways, either silence or an invitation to a private message. The last post had a variation. The other user in the post, shapelessghost, had repeatedly demanded to know why the Knight had cancelled the deal in progress. From the sounds of their argument, the two had met to begin a business relationship, but knight had called a stop to it suddenly and left without any explanation. This had left Ghost high and dry. Despite their increasingly plaintive pleas for another chance, there had been no response at all from knight. The final message from Ghost had been sent the day before at noon, and contained only curse words and wishes for revenge to be thundered down upon the Knight.

"Looks like we have a potential local dealer who was left unsatisfied by the suspected killer. We're going to make friends with the kid."

Falstaff clicked on the user name and sent a private message to shapelessghost.

"Saw your messages to that asshole WhiteKnightRides. I got the same proposal they did, but I won't fuck you around. Meeting?"

The message rushed off to the recipient with a quiet ring of an electronic bell. Falstaff worked on the can of soda in his hand, the syrupy sweetness becoming increasingly unappetizing. A nauseating belch announced the end of the can. He ground his cigarette butt into the ashtray and stood up.

"I'm going to go chill out at the house for a while. Leave the computer running and keep an ear out for a reply notification. When the disgruntled dealer replies, come get me."

"How long will that take?"

"Dunno. Could be days. The dude was enraged and desperate for dope, though, so it could be sooner."

The computer chimed as if in response, surprising both Falstaff and JJ. Falstaff clapped his hands loudly together. The noise startled the sleeping girl in the chair enough that she grunted, rolled over, and farted a long single whistling note. Falstaff fell into a laughing fit that was interrupted with repeated apologies to JJ. He wiped tears of amusement from his eyes as he read the message reply.

"Tomorrow. 5PM. AG County gravel pit, ravine road entrance."

Falstaff walked to the door, with JJ following close at his heels.

"We gonna rough that kid up, to get the info on the killer?"

"We're not doing anything, JJ. You couldn't rough up a sack of French pastry. I'm going to meet with the kid and ask some questions. It would help if I actually had something to sell to him, but you flushed your whole stash. Doesn't matter, I'll bullshit him into telling me where to find the killer. You are going to chill the fuck out here, get your house in order, and wait for further details. Give me your cellphone number, JJ. I'll call you when I know anything."

JJ scribbled down his number on the back of a half-empty pack of zig zag rolling papers. He handed the pack to Falstaff with an apology for not having any dope to sell to the informant.

"You should also apologize for pawning muscle relaxants and menstrual pain pills off on me as actual drugs, but I am in a forgiving mood. Goodnight, JJ. Don't crawl through my window again."

20

The layers of plywood nailed to the window frame blocked the dying light from outside and kept the bright lights inside from being revealed to anyone outside the abandoned triplex. It was an old house that had been mutilated and subdivided into 3 uneven apartment spaces. When years of neglect and abuse from tenants and owners had taken their toll, the bathroom on the 3rd floor had collapsed onto a family of 5, killing the father. The state had condemned the building after that. Then the squatters moved in.

The drywall that had divided the original living room into two separate rooms had been kicked down by a punk high on angel dust, returning the space to a rough approximation of its original state. Looey and the woman arranged the camera lights to illuminate the room and the only piece of furniture in it, the padded fuck table.

The trash had been cleared from this room and the adjoining rooms to make it more professional, but the drooping support beams poking through the water-damaged plaster were impossible to ignore. Anyone concerned with their long-term wellbeing would have looked at the dilapidated building and turned around. But when you're chasing the next high, the future is already dead to you.

Looey scratched at the soot-covered east wall and rubbed the black grime between his finger tips.

"Hell of a strange new location. A collapsing house in an abandoned neighborhood on the edge of the city limits. The warehouses were luxury compared to this.

Going to take some work to explain this location convincingly to the actors."

The woman worked on the computer connected to the cameras, ignoring Looey's monologue.

He walked around the room touching every surface. He looked at the scene from each corner, squatting down at some points to get a different view from that elevation. He looked over to the woman, and the light caught his fully dilated pupils. He wiped at his nose and giggled.

"It's post-apocalyptic porn. End of the world, collapsing civilization shit. The actors are fucking to repopulate the world."

"You did too much coke."

It was less a question than a statement from the woman. Looey shrugged and smiled. The woman continued making sure that the equipment was properly adjusted, and all the supplies were in their appointed locations. Looey kept talking.

"Hey, I got to say that this is pretty far off the game plan. I don't got a problem with that, so long as there's nothing else I need to know about. I can't do my job if I am out of the loop."

"You're doing great, Looey. Check the washroom, make sure it's ready."

Looey shambled out of the main room, through the narrow kitchen to the south, and into the tiny first floor bathroom between the spots for the stove and the sink. The stack of old doors and wood that had been piled in front of the bathroom were now on the floor of the kitchen. The stack had kept the bathroom hidden from the squatters, leaving it in relatively pristine condition. By some miracle of bureaucratic amnesia, the water was still running to the house.

Looey made sure the basics were in place while he took a long wobbling piss. The mix of cocaine and ketamine he was on had him feeling rubbery and energized.

He crossed the kitchen to the long hallway that led from the front of the house to the back door. Across the hall were two rooms, both swept clean and prepared for the evening's event. The green room would be the relaxation area for the actors. Next door to it was their temporary mortuary. Looey swaggered back into the main room with his eyes fixed on the table. He laughed.

"Hey, do you think I could join in this time? I'm feeling pumped up. The gangbang looks like fun, and we got this whole procedure under control. Besides, what is it going to matter anyway?"

The woman stood up from her hunched over position at the lap top and considered the request. Her eyes went all sorts of far away, and she spoke in a soft low voice to herself more than to Looey.

"In the end, there are no bystanders."

"Uh, say again, please. I don't understand the message."

She snapped out of her distant thoughts and returned to the here and now. A smile too wide for her narrow face spread out from the corners of her mouth. Her dark, shining eyes darted from Looey's face to the table and back again.

"Sure, if you want to. Like you said, in the end it won't make any difference."

The words hit Looey at a strange angle, full of a hidden echo that made him shiver. He nervously laughed to chase away the ghost.

"Spooky. Fucking spooky. Must be the room messing with my mind."

The crunching of gravel in the driveway signalled the arrival of the next victims. Looey slipped out the side door and ushered the group inside, closing the door shut tight behind them and locking it with a pair of padlocks.

Looey gave the introduction speech and the initial instructions in a rush, sometimes letting one word blur into the next. The woman intervened to prompt him to slow down and speak clearly. Looey buckled down and made it through the rest of the spiel without issue, save for his hands compulsively clenching and unclenching from his chemically agitated state. He led the men into the green room to dose and relax, while the woman led the sex worker into the second room to prepare herself.

Looey led the actors back into the main room, and the scene began. There was a frantic and out-of-control edge to the fucking. The initial interactions were confused and timid thrusts by reluctant participants. The hooker was tuned out as she stared up at the ceiling and made robotic moaning noises that were disconnected from the actions around her.

It got worse when Looey disrobed and waded into the action. He barked instructions to the nervous men, slapping the most reluctant one as he shouted at him to 'man up'. Looey's drug-fueled bravado crossed back and forth into aggressive territory as he maneuvered himself from position to position, fucking the hooker in every spot possible. The other men came quickly, choosing to jerk themselves off to completion over the chest of the inattentive star instead of jockeying for position with Looey. They backed away and nervously watched as Looey continued to fuck with reckless abandon despite his flagging coke dick erection.

The woman watched the scene with a steady, impassive gaze. The cameras kept rolling as Looey looked over to her. Time and time again they locked eyes as he checked for permission to continue. She gave him no indication that he should stop.

Looey crossed the line from enthusiastic to violent, slapping the star hard across her tits. She yelled in pain and surprise and told him to stop. Looey's hips pistoned back in preparation for another thrust, and the rest of the watchers held their breath in dread anticipation of his breaking the main rule. He struggled against his urge to keep fucking, but the scared looks of the 4 men watching him, combined with the steady stare from the woman at the computer returned him to his senses.

The video was paused, the star had a moment to gather herself while Looey managed an insincere apology for being too 'into it'. The star accepted his apology, along with 3 good rails of coke, and they finished the scene with Looey shooting his load onto her face while staring at the woman across the room. He moaned and grunted in triumph and he jerked the last drops of cum from his partially limp cock.

"Fuck, that was good. Good work, everyone. Especially you, baby. That was fucking hot. Alright, guy number one, the tall one. Head into the office with the producer there and she'll get you all medicated and paid up."

The woman ignored Looey and moved to the star's side and quietly asked if she was okay. The sex worker nodded yes. The other woman led the sex worker towards the second room. Looey noticed the change in routine and spoke up.

"Is she going first? That's not the way things usually are."

The woman continued without replying to Looey. Alone in the back room, the woman used a small damp towel to clean the ejaculate away from the sex worker's face.

"You did a good job, but you did not deserve any of this. I'll take care of you."

She presented a big bag of pills and a wad of cash to the hooker who beamed with the complete and temporary happiness of a well-supplied addict. The other woman gently stroked the star's hair away from her neck and administered the sedative shot. She caught the sex worker in her arms as she fell unconscious and laid her safely on the floor.

The parade of victims to the sedation lounge proceeded without any additional deviations. Looey sat on the fuck table with a beer in his hand and his grey bathrobe partially open, exposing his flabby belly over the wall of muscle underneath and his grey little limp dick laying meekly on the cushioned surface. As each victim left for his doom, Looey raised his beer and toasted the man's future.

The woman returned to the main room after the 4th man was choked to death, left bleeding in a pool at the doorway of the sedation room. Looey still sat on the table, now smoking a joint and absentmindedly fondling his genitalia. He kept touching himself as the woman walked into view.

"How did it look? Was it hot, because it felt hot. Did you like it?"

He leered at her as his dick twitched once in a hint of arousal. She smiled with dead eyes and a complete lack of interest and told Looey to finish up so that they could move on to the next stage. The woman made herself busy with packing up the laptop and disconnecting the cameras.

Without an audience, Looey lost interest in jerking off. He hopped off the table and pulled on his jogging pants and sweat shirt. He asked over his shoulder if the dealer was first, as normal. It surprised him when the woman's voice replied from a few inches behind him.

"Same as always, Lieutenant."

He straightened up at the mention of his rank, and for a moment he rediscovered his old military discipline. He hustled the dead body of the dealer into the main room and placed him in the first position. He felt the woman shadow his every step, just behind him and out of his peripheral vision. He started talking to ease the sudden tension.

"I am glad that you let me jump in to the shot, boss. Fuck, I haven't had fun like that in years. Forgot how coke gives me limp dick, though. Took some work to get it up an keep it up."

"Move him to the left. He's too far from the center of the stage."

Looey lifted the corpse, sending a new gush of blood from the deep cut around his neck. He dragged the body to the spot that the woman was pointing at and laid it back down.

"That is a lot of blood. You took the saw to his neck this time. Real deep. Must have hurt like a son of a bitch."

"Life is pain. Turn around baby."

The seductive tone in the woman's voice caught Looey off-guard. He had never heard her speak like that. He spun around to see if it was indeed the same woman he had been working with for the last few months. His confusion was matched by his excitement, and he faced her with smile on his lips that lasted until he felt the jab of the revolver's barrel stab into the left side of his torso, angled up under his rib cage.

She shot him six times, all straight shots up through the heart. Looey's body locked up in total system shock as buckets of blood cascaded from the gaping wound. He lost consciousness and dropped to the floor where he died seconds later.

The woman watched the last second of life run out for Looey. She sent him off to the afterlife with one final hard kick to the groin and a short sharp laugh.

"Choices have consequences, Lieutenant."

The woman crouched down to begin preparing Looey's body for the scene. She started with his eyes.

21

Falstaff threw a flat grey stone at the 'no trespassing' sign and missed it by a country mile. It skipped off the crest of the gravel pile to his far left and crashed into the brush beyond. Nurse huffed a soundless laugh and threw his own rock. It hit the sign true in the centre, ringing out like a bell.

"Your aim makes me worried for your vision, John."

"Yeah fuck you. I can't aim, or throw, for shit. Another arrow in my sports ineptitude quiver. That's irony, you see, because I suck at archery too."

He went back to throwing rocks near the sign to pass the time until their connection arrived. Finding the ravine entrance to the county gravel pit had taken an hour of frustrating navigation down a multitude of identical country roads. They had left the safe house early to make sure they didn't miss the meeting, but it had been close. Now it was 5:05 and there was no sign of the buyer. Falstaff had argued successfully for a cash float for any needed transactions, and the roll of cash was burning a hole in his pocket.

"Not that it matters at all, but this isn't actually a publicly owned gravel pit. The name made me assume it was owned by the county, but nope, some private citizen owns this hole filled with rocks."

The sign rang out again with Nurse's next toss. The new dent from his rock blended in with the countless historical marks left by scores of bored teens come before.

"That is a stupid fact. It means nothing."

"Making small talk to pass the time, you giant pile of shit. I am going to demand the ability to fire you as soon as I talk to the boss again. You are of no use to me."

The rapid growl of a small gas engine rose from beyond the scrub brush. A dirt bike broke through the cover and skidded to a stop by the base of the hill. The driver killed the engine and hopped off the seat while pulling their helmet off in one fluid movement. The driver stayed standing beside the bike, with one hand on the handle in preparation of a quick exit.

Falstaff studied the driver from their position 30 feet away. The driver was thin with delicate facial features. A mop of ginger blond hair swept down over their right eye. The trailing end of a tattooed line of calligraphed text was visible running along their collarbone. The multiple layers of loose-fitting clothing hid all the curves and bulges of the driver's body. Their face held an equal mix of ever-present fear and motivating desperation.

"You shapeless ghost?"

"Archibomb99?"

"Close. Archibomb69. Actually, his representative. He was unable to come himself. I can speak for him."

The macabre truth of the statement amused Falstaff. Archie was in no state to speak for himself. There was an incredible amount of latitude available for a person willing to negotiate on behalf of the dead.

"Who is the other guy? He looks like a cop."

"I get that a lot. No, he's not a cop. He's a bodyguard. He won't be involved with our deal. You don't look like a dangerous person, or a drug dealer."

The driver nervously picked at the rubber grip of the handle and hid behind their hair.

"I'm not a dealer. They are vultures who force you to pay double if they don't like you, and they love to pick on people different than them. This is how I'm going to skip dealing with them and help my friends get what they need safely. I'm only going to sell to the kids who don't fit in."

"Sure. For the record, this shit is too powerful to be associated with the word 'safety'. Your friends better know how to deal with heavy stuff."

"I know how heavy the stuff is. I'll take care of my people."

"How compassionate. The drug dealer who worries about the feelings of their junkie clients" Nurse sneered.

Simultaneously, Falstaff and the driver turned to Nurse and told him to fuck off. The awkward pause they shared afterwards lasted until Falstaff moved things along.

"The last guy who was selling to you, he backed out of the deal. He's been a fucking pain in my ass and a bad businessman. Tell me what happened."

Ghost kicked at the dirt repeatedly, until the half-buried rock came loose and shot across the clearing. Falstaff encouraged the Ghost to speak up by tossing a roll of bills at their feet. Ghost scooped the roll up and examined it.

"Why are you giving me money? That's not how this was going to work."

"Relax, its just a fee for information."

"I don't need money. Well I do, but I need the pills too."

"Money creates all manner of solutions, kid. Trust me, we'll do the deal. This is a bonus. And there's more where that came from."

Falstaff hoped the kid didn't unroll the wad of bills on the spot. It was a 20 wrapped outside a stack of one dollar bills. If there was more than 40 bucks in total, he'd be astonished. Lucky for Falstaff, Ghost accepted the offer and tucked the roll into their front hoodie pocket.

"I don't know why the deal went wrong. It was all good at first. I had the cash, he had the dope, and he was asking about my customers. He wanted to know if I could find a few who would go to a party that was a little fun and weird in exchange for some free pills. I said I could, probably. Then, all of a sudden, he gets a text and he reads it and then he says the deal is cancelled. Gave me a handful of pills as a consolation prize, and said I wouldn't have enjoyed the party anyway, and took off."

"What did he look like?"

"Greasy as fuck and dangerous looking. Like a man-sized rat. I almost took off when he got out of his car."

"Describe the car."

"Grey, 4 door. Ford maybe?"

"Bet you didn't get the license plate."

"Can we skip to the deal, please?"

"Who sent him the text?"

"I can't read minds! He got a fucking message and he called the deal off."

"What about the pills? Have any of them left? Did the baggie have a logo on it of a chess knight?"

"Yeah, that was on the bag. That logo's been turning up all over the place around here. The pills are all gone now. That's why I'm here, remember?"

Falstaff racked his brain for a better question that could lead to a great revelation but came up dry. It was approaching the moment where he would have to admit that he did not have any dope to sell to the kid, which would bring their conversation to a screaming halt. Before he had a chance to ask another question, a white Jeep Cherokee came tearing up the driveway. It slammed into the front wheel of the dirt bike, forcing Ghost to jump in a panic to the side. The jeep came to a stop and the Sheriff came barrelling out of the driver's side door to kick Ghost down to the ground.

"Goddamn it, Rennie. This is a shit poor example of following the rules. You have been told repeatedly that dealing with strangers is not allowed. I own you, Rennie. You buy anything in this county, it comes from me. You try to double-cross me, and I find out. Nothing happens in my yard without me knowing."

A pair of quick kicks hammered the Sheriff's point home onto Rennie's torso. Rennie curled up in a protective pose and rolled away. The passenger in the Sheriff's jeep exited the vehicle and stood snickering at the kid lying on the ground. The Sheriff continued his tirade.

"You been conspiring with the prick who has been undercutting my business, Rennie?"

"No Sheriff, no. I swear."

"Is it this asshole?" the sheriff growled as he turned his fury towards Falstaff. "That story you spun for me in the diner alley, about missing army supplies was simple horseshit. Deputy, cover these men. Shoot em if they try anything funny."

The snickering dimwit pulled his pistol from the holster and aimed it between Nurse and Falstaff. Falstaff caught a slight eye roll from Nurse in response to the Deputy's sloppy firearm handling. He wasn't impressed. Falstaff chose the cautious approach and put his hands up high, nudging Nurse to do the same.

The Sheriff gave Rennie another kick as he turned away to confront Falstaff. Rennie moaned and tried to roll away, but Sheriff Dunner planted his right foot onto Rennie's hip to prevent escape.

"You come into my county and steal my business. You arrange clandestine meetings and murder the townsfolk who are lured there. And all the while, you two are skulking around under my nose. That takes some giant-sized balls, son. Do you think I can just look away and let you walk away? These people respect me. They fear me. I let two jerkoffs get away with undermining me, I lose authority. This is a bad situation for you."

"Whoa there, Sheriff. Take about a dozen steps back from the ugly edge you're leaning over right now. Nobody here is undercutting you. I don't have any dope. I am looking for the same dealer that you are."

"But the army supplies story was a total fabrication."

"Well, 'total' sounds over the top. But it may not have been, you know, the whole truth."

The deputy chuckled under his breath and raised the gun to point directly at Falstaff's face.

"Hold on! I can explain."

"You better get to it then, boy."

"I will, I will! It's just that being held at gunpoint makes me fucking nervous. Most regular people are like that. Your man there looks like he wants to start shooting."

"I do what the Sheriff tells me to do" the deputy said in a thick, slow voice. Falstaff didn't get the sense that the deputy was one of God's smartest creatures.

"I get that, I do. Let's all calm down just a tiny fucking bit so we can sort this out. I don't care about your business. I want you to sell boatloads of every type of goodtime dope to the fine upstanding citizens of rural Pennsylvania, to keep them in a blissfully fucked up state in perpetuity. High as fucking angels. Forever and ever, amen. What I have to do is stop the goddamned murders the other dealer is involved with. I don't know if they are the actual killers, or just in some bloody partnership with the killers. I need to stop them, and so do you. We have a shared enemy, Sheriff. I solve my problem, yours goes away. No blood on your hands."

The talk about murder was exciting the dimwit deputy in the worst way possible. He was agitated and twitching, causing the barrel of the gun to sway erratically between the two targets. Falstaff shot a panicked look at Nurse, who purposefully ignored the plea within it.

"Sheriff, listen. Your man here is riled up and there might be an accident. Accidents make life more difficult than they need to be. We can't figure out a good deal if one side of the negotiation is terrified for their lives. He's going to sneeze or fart and accidentally pull the trigger. Come on, come on, COME ON."

Falstaff's rising terror only encouraged the dimwit deputy. He suddenly pushed the barrel of the gun forward, and Falstaff let out a tiny shriek. The deputy laughed and went to feint again. His finger was so tight around the trigger that it was inevitable that the gun would go off.

Nurse gave a quiet whistle through his teeth and casually threw his set of keys through the air in a high arc towards the deputy. The deputy's eyes tracked the keys and he lifted both hands up in preparation to catch the flying set. In the time it took for the keys to reach the dimwit, Nurse crossed the space and struck the distracted deputy. He grabbed the gun hand wrist and wrenched it so forcefully that one of the small bones inside snapped, forcing the deputy to drop the gun. At the same time, Nurse sent a short powerful jab into the bridge of the deputy's nose, shattering the bone. The deputy cried out and fell to his knees, both hands cupped around the bloody mess in the center of his face. Nurse crouched briefly to retrieve the deputy's gun and was back to a standing position with the gun ready at his side before the Sheriff had a chance to react.

The Sheriff twitched as his arm locked up in the process of reaching for his own gun. A casual flick of Nurse's gun was enough encouragement to send Sheriff Dunner's hands up in the air to hang beside his shoulders.

"Now, now. This is a big misunderstanding. Rennie, would you kindly fuck off so that we can discuss this and sort out the confusion?"

The Sheriff spoke with a greasy laugh in his voice and a shit-eating smile on his face. His eyes, however, shot daggers at the kid on the ground. Rennie rolled away from kicking range, then scrambled onto the dirt bike. The small gas engine of the bike roared to life and Rennie sped out of sight with a shower of gravel spraying from the back wheel.

The deputy continued to wail and moan. His current fear was that he was going to bleed to death. Falstaff laughed.

"Your man's stupid, Sheriff. Unless Deputy Fuckstick is a haemophiliac, its just a broken nose and the blood will clot up if he stops fucking with it."

"He's loyal but very emotional. Buck up son. You'll be fine. Don't interrupt the negotiations."

"That's better, Sheriff. Friendly negotiations, not ugly threats, will save the day here. Like I wanted to say before: we have the same enemy. The new dealer in town is a part of the multiple murders that have happened in Pittsburgh. Murders that I am trying to stop from repeating. It's not an easy job, let me tell you. So, we both need to find the new dealer. We can spend all of our time wagging our guns at each other and kicking each other in the balls, or we can call a truce and solve this motherfucker."

The Sheriff hated being at the mercy of anyone, and something about Falstaff was making that hate even stronger. He watched the struggle to keep composure play out across the law man's face. Falstaff decided to help him accept the deal. He put on his most contrite face and pleaded for clemency.

"I know I've been a real piece of shit to you. Sneaking around your town and lying to you. Sorry. I should have come clean with you at the start. But here is where we are, and the clock is running out. One mass murder is a problem, two is a worrying trend, but three would be a serial killer crisis. That brings attention. Federal attention."

"But the two of you purport to be federal employees. Is that the truth?"

"In an extremely roundabout way, yeah it is. But we want to keep things quiet. More than anything, we need to put this to bed."

The Sheriff scratched at the finely shaped sideburn outlining the left side of his jaw as he considered the situation. His finger traced the well-defined edge of the neatly trimmed facial hair with such slow care that there was something uncomfortably erotic about it. The Sheriff's vanity was robust.

"You help me find the alleged perpetrator, then we go our separate ways."

"After I get a chance to ask the dealer a couple of questions, you can arrest them and throw away the key."

The Sheriff flinched at the word 'arrest' and Falstaff had a bad feeling about the final resolution to the new dealer's storyline. Forced to dig their own shallow grave while the Sheriff and deputy Fuckstick watched was the plan Dunner had in mind.

The radio in the Sheriff's truck crackled to life with an agitated voice calling for Dunner specifically. He looked at his car and back to Falstaff. The radio squawked again, and Falstaff nodded.

"It's cool. Answer the radio. Things are non-hostile here, now."

The Sheriff walked to the car and reached through the window to get the radio handset. He cut off the caller and shouted his displeasure at being interrupted.

"Good god in heaven, Martin, I left clear instructions to not be interrupted. I am on a stakeout, and this is compromising my cover. You better have a damned good reason for breaking radio silence."

The tinny voice of Martin carried across the clearing.

"Sorry Sheriff but it's an emergency. Real emergency. Real bad. There's been a murder. A bunch of them. We have a situation, Sheriff."

"Say again?"

"Murders, Sheriff. 6 bodies. Out past the closed oil change place on Redgree avenue."

Falstaff looked at Nurse and mouthed the word 'six'. He didn't know what the addition of another victim to the scene meant, but it wasn't anything good.

The Sheriff let loose with a continual string of curse words and bigoted insults aimed at the unknown murderer, and at the bad luck of having the murders occur in his own jurisdiction. He finished his rambling hate crime of a sentence and told the dispatcher that he was en route. He kicked Fuckstick and told him to get in the car.

"Make sure you don't bleed all over the goddamned place, idiot."

"Hey Sheriff, we'll follow you to the location."

"Non-police persons at a murder scene? Absolutely not."

"Not our first scene, Dunner. We've seen the other bodies. I need to see this new atrocity to find out what's the same and what's different. There's already one big question."

The engine of the jeep roared to life and the Sheriff mashed the accelerator to the floor while keeping the car in park, to make the engine scream. The roar died down and the Sheriff snarled through the open window.

"Then hurry the fuck up and get to your vehicle. I want that site secure ASAP."

Falstaff shrugged, and they jogged back to their car, with the Sheriff's jeep crawling along behind them every step of the way. He sat in the car and the jeep sped by.

"Lucky he didn't just gun us down. That fellow is wound too tight."

Nurse pulled around to follow the speeding jeep. The deputy's gun was tucked into the plastic storage space on the bottom of the driver's door, and it slid from one side of the compartment to the other whenever they turned a corner.

"That seems a little unsafe, Nursie."

"No bullets. I unloaded it on the way back to the car."

"Clever. Not like that Sheriff. Some investigator he is. Didn't even ask what my big question was."

22

"Why are there 6 bodies? Who is the new guy?"

The room of pale, shaken small town medics and cops looked up in astonishment in response to Falstaff's question, like he was laughing at a funeral. These first responders had never responded to a grim collection of purposefully arranged corpses on display for an audience. The Sheriff crossed the room, stepping over the five bodies on the floor and past the sixth on the side, to stand nose to nose with Falstaff.

"What the hell are you talking about? This is a murder scene and we don't need a smartass making light of the situation" he hissed. The stress weighing on him was reaching his breaking point.

"That's the big question I had. I mentioned it at the gravel pit. You didn't ask what it was, so I'm telling you now. That body over there, the sixth one, is brand new to the tableau. That's the staged presentation, if you're not familiar with the word. It's French."

"I am aware of the word 'tableau'. Now get to the fucking point."

"Easy now. Just trying to inform."

Dunner led Falstaff by the elbow into the room that held a folding table covered with half-consumed drinks and snacks. He squared up with Falstaff and talked quietly but forcefully at him.

"Those people out there are frightened by what they have to deal with today, and you need to show some respect. Keep quiet and out of the way, or our deal will be finished, and you will spend the next month in jail."

Falstaff snapped a quick salute and gave a wink over Dunner's shoulder to Nurse. Nurse stepped away from the doorway, leaving the Sheriff and Falstaff alone together.

"Yes sir, quiet as a mouse, sir. We'll keep to ourselves. Who called the murder in? Where's the witness?"

"No witness. Anonymous call."

"Did you trace it?"

"No. That is beyond our normal capabilities."

"Figures. Would have been nice to have the call, to hear the killer's voice. Or the accomplice with second thoughts, though that is unlikely by now."

"You can look around but, by god, if you send my people running out of the room with your pinhead retard antics, there will be hell to pay." The Sheriff left before Falstaff could reply.

Alone in the room, Falstaff rooted around beneath the draped vinyl tablecloth. His hand closed on a cold glass cylinder and he pulled it out. He wanted to shout in triumph when he confirmed that he now had in his possession one unopened bottle of cold beer. He held it close to his chest and cautiously eased the cap off the top, letting the carbonation hiss out in tiny, controlled bursts. He put the bottle to his lips and guzzled the amber liquid until it was all gone. He let out a contented sigh followed by a barely contained belch. A quick scan under the table revealed the unfortunate reality that he had polished off the last bottle.

"Ah well, it was nice for a second. Have to remember 'pinhead retard'. Never been called that before."

Falstaff stepped back into the main room where the bodies were arranged. He skirted the shocked first responders as they stood scattered around the room, frozen with uncertainty, and scanned the five bodies for anything that deviated from the first two scenes. The standard five bodies were arranged as they had been at the other scenes, with the same horrific wounds inflicted on them. There were small details that were different, like the visible trail of blood from where the small-town dealer was garrotted to the spot where he was deposited, but the big details were all the same. And so, he moved to the new addition.

To the side of the cleared space in the middle of the room was a wheelchair holding a dead man taped in place to remain upright and stationary. A solitary light stand on the other side of the bodies was a spot light aimed at the dead man in the wheelchair.

"Whoever this dude is, he's the new star of the show. But who are you, buddy?"

Falstaff crouched down to examine the man. He had thick black stubble covering his jaw. His long yellow teeth poked through his dead slack lips. There was something strange about the dead man's eyes, and it confused Falstaff until he leaned close to understand what he was seeing. To be sure, he called Nurse over for a second opinion.

"Tell me what's in his eyes, Nursie."

Nurse leaned close to the corpse and inspected the open eyes.

"Is gunpowder."

"That's what I thought. Huh. The killer murdered him with a fuck load of bullets to the gut."

Nurse took his gloved finger and poked into the large wound. One of the cops fainted.

"Heart. Not gut. He was killed by multiple gunshots to the heart. Weapon was in contact with the victim when discharged."

"Point blank murder."

Nurse shot Falstaff a withering glare and corrected him at a volume sufficient to let the whole room participate.

"Point blank is misused term from movies and cheap detective books. Only means the distance that the bullet flies straight. After that range, gravity pulls bullet down, curving trajectory."

"But it applies, right? The bullets, in this case, were fired from the gun when it was within point blank range."

"Technically, but it is a less accurate description."

"It's right, so shut your fucking gob with the overly literal correction. Fuck, like that's the biggest problem in the room. Everybody, pack the fuck up, we've solved the case of the pedantic asshole who corrects people to make himself feel like a big man."

Falstaff was giddy with glee as he watched Nurse tremble with rage, unable to beat Falstaff in a room full of witnesses. But that rage could abide until a time more private, and he needed to diffuse it while he could. He walked back his insult with a profuse apology and an admittance that Nurse was correct. He had to resort to full blown grovelling before Nurse calmed down. Luckily Falstaff had little pride left to speak of. He changed the topic back to the murder scene investigation.

"The new victim is put in this spot, as if he had watched the murder of the others. He is a witness, but not a participant of the scene. He was put in the wheelchair after death, taped into place, with gunpowder filling his eyes. And, there's additional decorative tape work on his left wrist and his shoulders. Any ideas on why, boss?"

The public deference to Nurse bought Falstaff the reprieve he was hoping for. Nurse liked violence, but he was less satisfied when beating a beta with his throat bared. Nurse examined the duct tape bracelet around the left wrist of the corpse. It was folded onto itself so that it didn't stick to the skin underneath. The tape on the shoulders was identical on either side and placed with care in their locations.

"The tape on the shoulders is a simulation of rank insignia, the shoulder boards on uniforms. Two bars like on a U.S. Army uniform like that mean Captain, I think."

Falstaff stepped away from the dead man in the chair and observed the stage in its entirety. The murders had always been about sending a message, but now the message had changed. He said as much aloud to Nurse and to the Sheriff hovering around them in agitation. Then he stepped back another 3 feet and saw the bigger picture.

"It's a zoom out of the shot. Now we can see the message and, more importantly, the intended audience. The new dead guy is the subject of this blood-soaked communique. The shoulder tape tells us he's a military man. Would be nice to know if the victim was also military. Did you find any ID on him?"

Dunner shouted at one of the deputies scurrying around the room trying to avoid the bodies, and the deputy brought a black wallet to him. He pulled out a laminated card from inside the wallet and handed it to Falstaff.

"Well well well, our friend here is a former military man. The ID is expired. I would love to know what his record says."

Nurse took the hint and stepped outside to make a call. Falstaff continued putting the pieces together.

"The wheelchair tells us he's damaged somehow, injured in combat possibly."

"He could be a regular cripple" the Sheriff said with a total lack of tact.

"There's not a lot of room in the Army for wheelchair-bound soldiers, Sheriff, as far as I know. That would mean he was injured and that put him in the chair. Recently injured."

"Why?"

"Because the wrist tape is a hospital ID bracelet. This body is a proxy for an injured captain who isn't listening to the message being sent to him. And that is a gigantic fucking problem."

"Why?"

"Because the sender is getting frustrated with the lack of response. The addition of a 6th victim is a massive deviation from the pattern. The lack of clean-up after the fact means the murderer has stopped worrying about being caught. That table in the other room, as an example, was forgotten about. Is the man in the wheelchair a local resident?"

"Not in our records, no. He is not known to the officers on scene."

Falstaff went back to the body in the wheelchair and looked closely at the man.

"Then you are not one of the local yokel dope buyers. Your haircut is shaggy but used to be military issue. There's a good layer of muscle under a bit of fat, so you still had physical strength and fitness until someone blew your heart into pieces."

He stared at the grey paste caked around and over the dead man's eyes. The murderer had no concern for the dignity of human remains, that much was abundantly clear. Falstaff walked to the door towards the car, with the Sheriff walking hurriedly behind him.

"Where in the hell do you think you're going without clearing it with me first?"

"Come on, Sheriff. Put a little effort into your sleuthing. The answer is right there. Injured soldier in medical care. The vet hospital. Christ, its barely 10 minutes away on the other side of Freiburg. We need to get there now, just in case the killer has spun completely out of control. It's going to happen, by the way. The self-imposed rules about the murders kept the broken parts of the killer's mind from unravelling. Now they're breaking the rules, and each broken rule weakens the others. Wherever that leads to, it is ugly and bloody."

The Sheriff considered Falstaff's words and nervously looked from the house behind them to his jeep as he decided. He shouted back into the house to delegate authority at the crime scene to one of his other deputies.

"You follow close to my jeep. Don't get yourselves shot."

23

They were caught in the exhilarating rush of speeding behind a cop on official business, blowing through stop signs as the Sheriff's siren blared. Nurse drove their car with the expert ease of someone trained in high speed pursuits. Falstaff watched the man calmly swerve around a rusty pick-up truck that crossed between their car and the jeep.

"I got to ask you something. Is my head regular-sized?"

"What?"

The car skittered to the right as the wheels on that side hit a patch of loose gravel on the shoulder of the road. Nurse wrestled it back to the asphalt.

"It's a simple question. Is my head the same general size as the average person?"

"It is a stupid question and it is distracting me from driving."

"You looked comfortable driving at high speed like this, so I thought it was safe to ask."

"You are an idiot with a regularly sized head."

"See that's what I thought. But the Sheriff called me a pinhead and that made me wonder about relative head sizes. I don't usually compare the size of my head to others."

"I cannot believe that this is the topic of discussion right now."

"You're a man of meager imagination. Fine. Back to the case at hand. What did you find out about our new victim during your top-secret hush hush phone call to Herr Overlord?"

"He was a military man. He enlisted in U.S. army 3 years ago, dishonorably discharged 1 year ago. Was in the process of being court martialed when he disappeared."

"Does that mean he broke out of jail and ran away, or did he get erased? What was his crime?"

"He was discharged for impersonating an officer. He was a private, but he told civilians that he was a lieutenant. Then evidence was presented that he was also stealing supplies and selling them. He was injured in arrest and was in the field hospital until his trial. The field hospital is the last location that he was recorded at. He disappeared from there."

"Stealing supplies. Bet they were sedatives and painkillers. If this poor dead private is the source of the killer's drugs, then he has been an accomplice to everything up to the point that the killer decided to cut him loose. Hey, be careful."

Nurse frowned at Falstaff, then checked his speed and scanned the road ahead.

"My driving is safe. Do not worry."

"Sure, that's great, but its not what I meant. The Sheriff and his Deputy Fuckstick are two very angry and fragile men. This situation is beyond their capacity to control, and they get violent when they feel powerless. Fuckstick was giving you the evil eye before you cracked his nose, so you can imagine how much he wants to get you now. And the Sheriff is the biggest potential threat. He's got a lot of dirty laundry to hide, laundry that we know about. It would be easier to get rid of us than clean all of his mess."

"You speak like the man that you are, a timid coward afraid of the world. I will keep both of us safe, little scared bunny. I did not realize you cared about my wellbeing. It is heartwarming."

Nurse reached over and patted Falstaff on the cheek and laughed long and loud when Falstaff wriggled away in embarrassment.

"I don't like you, asshole. It's a matter of survival. Once you go down, there's nothing stopping them from taking me apart."

"You worry too much."

"Fine. Don't say I didn't warn you."

They pulled to a stop beside the Sheriff's jeep at the front doors of the vet hospital. Dunner got out of the jeep and stormed up the steps. Falstaff and Nurse were a couple of steps behind, and they entered the building as the Sheriff was bellowing orders at the desk clerk.

"Put down that tablet son and bring the on-duty administrator down to this desk on the double. And so help me if you take your time."

The clerk was the same horny toad pervert who they had caught watching porn while at work on their last visit, and by the sweat on his brow and the nervous look in his eyes, he had been back at his self-touching hobby. He bolted into action at the sound of the Sheriff's shouted instructions, and in the process of leaving his seat, he knocked the tablet to the ground. As it fell, the earphone came unplugged and the sound of exaggerated moaning filled the room. The Sheriff took the moaning tablet and threw it like a Frisbee through the closing front door, narrowly missing Falstaff's head. The clerk ran out of the room, bent at the waist to conceal the bulge in his crotch.

Nurse pointed down the hall that the clerk had run down. "He is a pervert. You said the group sex was an important element of the killer's plan."

"That clerk is a dedicated masturbator, but that's all. He couldn't organize a gangbang or bring himself to perform in one. In front of an audience he goes limp. But yeah, the sex is important. The funny thing is, the sex is an integral part of the killer's script, but they don't enjoy it. Not that I think the murderer enjoys the killing part either. Or at least they tell themselves they hate having to kill anyone. It's all to serve the greater purpose of sending a message. In other news, I smell something fucking delicious."

Falstaff sniffed at the air to get another sample of the fragrance wafting in from the rooms and hallways beyond the front desk. A warm blend of spices mingled together with the savoury smell of fire-roasted meat. It brought a gush of saliva into Falstaff's mouth, reminding him that he hadn't eaten anything truly enjoyable for days. The Sheriff watched the performance of a dishevelled man in a baggy dirty suit sniffing at the air and licking his lips.

"Is he an idiot?" he asked Nurse, pointing a thumb in Falstaff's direction.

"I have my suspicions."

Falstaff wandered the room from doorway to doorway. The smell was pervasive and unavoidable.

"There's no way a shithole like this place has a cafeteria or food service staff that can make something that smells this good. They'd just boil a fucking shoe and call it beef stew. We should just head in and look around."

"Absolutely not. Chain of command is the only thing that has any authority here. I am going to impress upon the current supervisor that I am in charge and not one to be fucked with. He will then lead us to, well shit, what are we exactly looking for?"

"We'll search by rank. Find all the captains and see if they know anything. Can't be that many."

The horny clerk returned briefly, to point in the Sheriff's direction and whisper to the tall man behind him before vanishing back down the hall. The tall man walked in and shook the Sheriff's hand.

"Good afternoon, I'm Doctor Wellins, the day administrator. How can I help you?"

"Sheriff Dunner, Allegheny Sheriff's department. I am investigating a multiple homicide in the area and there is a possibility of a connection to a patient in this facility. You need to show us to every patient with the current rank of Captain in this hospital."

The Doctor ran his hand repeatedly over the lacquered veneer of his dyed black hair. It was a practiced gesture born from years of precisely maintaining the same hairstyle. The thin moustache under the doctor's large nose was also dyed the same deep black color.

"That's a terrible thing to hear. Murders nearby. Terrible. There are only 2 captains currently being treated right now, if my memory serves me."

"Are either of them in the Long-term ward?" Falstaff asked.

"I'm sorry, who are you?"

"Part of the crime solving team. Are they there or not?"

"They're both in the Long-Term ward."

"Ha, I called it. See, the poor sods in the LTW don't get visitors from the outside world, so anyone looking to communicate with them would have a lot of trouble doing so. They might go to extraordinary lengths."

"I resent your implication that we do not allow visitors. All patients are free to have visitors that will help them recover and bring them comfort, but we must, of course, maintain a level of security for their safety and ours."

"Functionally, that's a ban. A nice, soft and squishy ban. If you don't want to give your name and ID, or you don't have ID anymore, then you can't get in. Right?"

"I'm sorry but I don't understand."

"Never mind doc. Just musing."

"Very well. Follow me please."

They trailed behind the doctor as he led them back through the hospital towards the long-term ward. In the large visiting room, Falstaff went wide of the group and paused at the side of the sedated woman in the wheelchair, once again high as a kite and staring at nothing in particular. On the small table to her left was a red and white checkered paper tube containing the source of the delicious smell.

On the side of the wrapper was the name of the restaurant that had provided the food, a place called 'Shawarma Deelite'. He bent down to get a nose full of the scent straight from the source and was about to grab the shawarma when the Sheriff barked his name. He rejoined the group and lamented his lost opportunity.

They passed the medication dispensary and the doctor stopped to quietly confer with the staff member inside. Another orderly moved through the hallway with one of the same shawarma sandwiches jammed in his mouth. Falstaff intercepted him.

"Hey dude, where did you get that? Is there more? It smells fucking fantastic."

The orderly chewed noisily with an open mouth as he replied.

"Naw, they is all gone. Come from that place in town. It's the real deal, so the patients tell me. The owner or the cook is from Iraq or Iran or Turkey, I don't know. But he knows his shit."

The group had started to move again, and they were about to turn down the hall to the long-term ward. The

Sheriff let out a piercing whistle to call Falstaff back to the group, and the noise upset everyone within earshot. Various cries of alarm and distress rose from the patients in every direction. The doctor shot a disapproving look at Dunner but turned away and coughed nervously when the look was returned. The doctor was not one for direct confrontation.

At the entrance to the LTW they stopped. The doctor sent the nurse at the nurse's station into the ward to prepare the patients for an unexpected influx of strangers. She nodded while looking at the motley crew behind the doctor with her bulging wet eyes. She scurried down the ward towards the first bed on the left. As they waited for her to return, Falstaff made nice with the doctor.

"Boy, that shawarma smells great. It must taste even better."

"Oh, it is very well done. Authentic. Like most of the patients here, I developed a taste for the cuisine when I was stationed over there. We're hooked on it."

"Not the only thing you're all hooked on" Falstaff muttered to himself.

"Pardon me?"

"Sorry doc, I mutter sometimes. I was asking if everyone here likes the food. That's a lot of shawarma to order."

"Yes, they do. We have it delivered once a week as a special treat. The owner himself brings it in and chats with the patients as he hands the food to them. It's funny, really. They love it. Even the men who were grievously wounded in combat, the ones who curse the 'sand niggers' at every opportunity for their injuries. Oh."

The realization that he had let a racial slur slip out in casual conversation struck the doctor and made him break out in a sweat. He was studying Falstaff for an indication of being offended. The doctor was assuming that Falstaff was partly Arabic. Falstaff looked away and waited for the awkward moment to pass by. Nurse didn't even notice that anything offensive had been said. The doctor cleared his throat and stammered through a poor apology.

"I am sorry for being…inappropriate. I continue having difficulty transitioning to civilian life and the expectations that come with it. The language spoken amongst servicemen can be rough."

"Yeah, rough. Sure. Don't worry about it. Slip of the tongue" Falstaff replied.

The racial slur was a completely honest statement of belief from the doctor, a truth he would never actively acknowledge, but there was no point in berating him on the spot. He wouldn't care what a "mixed-blood" like Falstaff said, anyway. Forgiving the doctor of his hateful slight made Falstaff grind his teeth together, but he swallowed his dislike and smiled like nothing was wrong.

The ward was arranged with a row of 5 beds on either side. They were the fully maneuverable and adjustable hospital beds designed to accommodate a lifetime spent laying down. Each bed was flanked with machines to support the basic functions of life, and to monitor for the looming mortal disasters that haunted most of these wounded vets.

The doctor led them to the first captain. Falstaff took a quick look at the withered old man sinking into the padded sheets and decided that it was unlikely that this was the target of the killer's message.

"Strike one, doc. Let's see the other one."

They walked down to the end of the right-hand row. The doctor stopped short and cautioned the group to lower their expectations.

"This patient is non-responsive. Has been from the moment he arrived. He will not be able to communicate with you in any way."

Falstaff slipped around the doctor and walked up to the bedside of the last captain. He stared into the deep grey eyes of the young man in the elevated bed. The mobile table parked over the man's lap held one of the wrapped shawarmas, and a comic book adaptation of the story of Lancelot.

"So, tell me about our man here. The food on his table confuses me."

"He has some automatic physical responses. If we place the food in his mouth, he will reflexively chew and swallow. Usually. The inconsistent non-responsiveness is part of the mystery of his condition. We have no medical history for him, unfortunately. He arrived here at the end of an emergency evacuation from an overseas installation. He had no identification or records, and every search for matching records has returned no results. We guess that he is a captain, because he had captain's bars clutched in his left hand when he was found."

"And this comic. That seems out of place for a comatose dude."

"He's not comatose, he's catatonic. The cause is most likely psychological, but we've made very little progress in identifying it."

The doctor picked up the comic and flipped through the pages. Falstaff kept eye contact with the non-responsive grey eyes and thought about stealing the food from his table on his way out.

"I have no idea where this came from. Perhaps one of the orderlies left it here. Yes, that's the most reasonable explanation."

"Fans of classic tales of English chivalry working in this hospital would surprise the hell out of me."

"Reading to our patients is one of the many ways we reach out to them, even the non-responsive ones."

Falstaff took the comic from the doctor and closed it. The heroic Lancelot stood bravely on a hill, pining for his Guinevere off in the distance.

"Of course the dashing heroic knight is as white as they come. An Aryan dreamboat" Falstaff mused to himself. He looked back at the catatonic patient and repeated the sentence until the words 'white knight' tumbled into place. Falstaff turned and spoke to the others of his group.

"He's fine. He's safe, and so is everyone here. We have what we need from here. Thanks doc, we can find our way back out."

He tossed the comic back to the table and gave the patient a wave goodbye. A faint tremor ran through the man's upper torso and vanished a moment after it appeared. Falstaff caught it and smiled. He turned from the bed, gave Nurse a nudge, and marched out of the room.

The doctor sputtered and protested as they made their way back to the entrance, but Falstaff had no interest in further conversation with the man. He left the burden of explanation with the Sheriff and walked out to the car with Nurse at his side. The Sheriff emerged a moment later.

"What was that horseshit, son? A false alarm? You were convinced that there were lives in danger here."

Falstaff lit a cigarette and grinned up through the cloud of smoke and his tangled hair hanging over his left eye. "Unrelated fun fact: the good Captain in there is not catatonic. He wants to be, and his act is an incredibly sincere one, but he's aware and alert. I have to commend him for commitment to the act. I don't know if I could voluntarily wear a piss bag or diaper or whatever, just to avoid the real world. Anyway, I did think he was in danger. And he might be, eventually, but he's at the end of the line for the killer. By the time that happens, the murders would be so far out of hand that martial law would be declared. Now that I've seen the man, I can confidently tell you that the killer isn't coming for him."

The Sheriff's temperature was rising, and he was edging towards his boiling point. He paced from vehicle to vehicle, making a growling noise deep in his throat. He stopped to bring up a wad of phlegm that he rinsed around his mouth like mouthwash before letting it fly. The impressive knot of sticky goo landed on the windshield like a fat dead splattered bug.

"I have reached the limit of the shit I will tolerate from you, boy. You fast-talk me into leaving a crime scene, to come here on a wild goose chase that accomplishes nothing."

"We eliminated a potential victim, Sheriff. That's not nothing."

"And what next, smart ass?"

Falstaff shrugged and said "I dunno-dinner? That shawarma smelled good, and the place is nearby. I'll treat."

Sheriff Dunner was barely able to restrain himself from drawing his gun and shooting Falstaff as he stood there grinning. When he saw how enraged the Sheriff was, Falstaff took a half-step to the side to hide behind the Nurse's bulky frame. Nurse matched the motion and left Falstaff exposed at the mercy of the Sheriff's displeasure. The dangerous moment lingered until Nurse opened the car door and retrieved the deputy's firearm.

"Sheriff, this should be returned to you. Please apologize to your subordinate. His injury was unfortunate."

Dunner snatched the empty gun away from Nurse and glared at the two men antagonizing him. He turned without a further word and drove away at top speed. Falstaff shook his head and sighed.

"That could have ended better. Bet he's hungry. Should have joined us for dinner."

24

Falstaff waited for a few minutes, until he was sure that there was ample distance between him and the Sheriff. He dusted off his hands and sat in the car.

"Glad that asshole is gone. We gotta get a move on. I have a hunch."

Nurse lowered himself into the driver's seat, laughed and shook his head.

"Another pretend emergency to get lunch. Or you found drugs in the hospital and now you want to get high."

"Jesus Christ I'm not fucking around this time. I know I've been a dick. Sorry. I mean, it will happen again, but for now I am being honest. Contrary to your cynical assumption, I am terrified that another murder is about to happen. The catatonic captain is safe for now, but the killer is unravelling. They left the last scene partially cleaned up. Maybe next time they don't even bother with the elaborate trap and instead just shoot a room full of high school kids. Or a garage sale. Or yeah, a hospital. There's going to be a rapid increase in body count. But we can stop it if you just do what I say. So, indulge me one more time and drive to that restaurant so I can ask the owner about the hospital and what he's overheard."

The car started, and Nurse pulled away from the hospital.

"Why would the cook know anything about the murders?"

"I don't think he knows anything about that. But he might have noticed anyone else who has been hanging around the hospital, regularly watching through the window that is conveniently a couple of feet from the captain's bed. And the good folks inside that hospital are racists who pay very little attention to the brown people around them. They say whatever crosses their mind without considering that the guy delivering their food is listening to their chat. The doctor used a racial slur and he's a well-educated professional. The rest of them are bound to be worse. But that hostile environment means our delivery man is going to be in a heightened state of vigilance when he's on-site, to keep his ass safe. Or he's a drug mule himself, slipping forbidden dope to the patients for a little extra cash. Fuck, it could be a dead end, is that what you wanted me to say? It's still worth a shot."

They arrived in town at Shawarma Deelite five minutes later. Falstaff opened his door and told Nurse to give him 5 minutes alone with the owner.

"On account of your menacing presence, it would be best if I went in solo. I'll be back as quick as possible, on the straight and narrow. Honest."

"Go."

Falstaff jumped out of the car as soon as Nurse gave him permission. He walked through the front door of the tiny restaurant and rang the bell on the counter. From the kitchen, a tall thin man with crooked teeth emerged and greeted him. Falstaff started replying before the man's greeting was finished.

"Hey give me a shawarma plate and a falafel plate to go with 2 bottles of water and a side of extra hummus. Where's your bathroom?"

Falstaff finished his order by putting a 20-dollar bill on the counter. Convinced that Falstaff was a paying customer, the thin man pointed to the narrow door behind the pop cooler. Falstaff dashed into the bathroom and locked the door. He quickly pulled his foot out of his shoe and retrieved the emergency baggie hidden in his sock. It had the last of the dope he had bought from JJ. He swallowed the pills, washing them down with tap water, and snorted the 3 lines of coke off the back of the toilet. He flushed the empty bag away, washed underneath his nose to remove any trace of powder, and returned to the counter. He was ready to get back in the fight.

The thin man was busy gathering the items for Falstaff's order into the takeaway containers. The smell was ten times more delicious than it had been at the hospital, and Falstaff said so.

"Thank you. They like the food very much there."

"No shit, my friend. Everyone was raving about it. Not that the food put the manager in a mood to buy my product. Talk about a terrible sales call. Whole bunch of racists up there. The only thing that got me through the call was the thought of coming here for some of this food. Is this your place, pal?"

"Yes, my place. Very small. That's okay."

"It's a strange town to open an exotic restaurant. The locals don't strike me as the type to enjoy anything foreign."

"The people, maybe. But the soldiers like the food. Every day, they come and buy from me. I know them now."

"From the hospital?"

"No, not usually. Sometimes. But mostly from the army base."

"I drove by that base the other day. Passed a few soldiers who looked pretty rough. And the news said there are a lot of drug addicts in the area. You see any of those folks in here, high on oxycontin?"

The owner shook his head from side to side with an alternating tilt on each pass, signalling his proposed unfamiliarity with the entire subject. It was a mostly sincere gesture.

"The drugs are terrible everywhere. Here in this country and at home."

"Where is home? Hold on, I am being very rude. My name is John."

The owner smiled and nodded cautiously.

"You can call me Sam."

"Shawarma Sam. Great. Love it. So where is home, Sam?"

"My home was a small village near the Afghanistan border but it does not exist anymore."

"Was it annexed into a city?"

"It was blown up."

"Oh. Shit. Sorry."

"I left my village and moved many times to avoid the fighting. Then I get chance to come to U.S."

"It must be terrible to have no hometown left. I feel bad for you."

Sam shrugged. "It happens. I am here now."

"Is that the area where all the opium poppies are grown? I bet a person from there would know how to get some good drugs."

Falstaff looked at Sam with pathetic longing. Sam didn't understand the ask that was barely hidden in the question, so Falstaff asked him a second time.

"I want to buy drugs. Do you have some?"

Sam's mouth dropped open, and a loud laugh like the bray of a donkey emerged.

"Is this the real life? I do not sell drugs. Do you think every Afghani is an opium smuggler? You are racist against my people."

"No, no I didn't mean that. Christ, no."

"Then this is a trick. You are trying to get me deported. No, I do not have any drugs to sell. I do not know where to get drugs. I have enough trouble staying in your country. All racists shouting at me, your lawmakers trying to ban me. Why would I take such big risk to make a few more dollars? No one in this town needs help from me to get drugs. They get their pills from the army."

The mention of the army snapped Falstaff out of his shameful hunt for dope and back into the actual investigation.

"Hold on, tell me more about the army stuff. The Army veteran's hospital, is that what you're talking about?"

Sam turned away and made himself busy with the food order. He delayed answering the question until the bags were ready and on the counter. Falstaff prompted him again to answer, and he did.

"The hospital patients, yes, but all the other soldiers too. All of them are on drugs, most of the time. When I met them in my country they were all taking pills. It made them very dangerous."

"You saw this in person? Most drug users don't show off their habits to local civilians."

Sam suddenly got busy with cleaning the counter to avoid the conversation.

"You worked with them, didn't you Sam?"

Without looking up, Sam replied. "Yes. Interpreting for a task force."

The abrupt defensiveness showing through every motion of Sam's body set off alarm bells for Falstaff. There was a deep dark secret attached to the restaurateur's time as a military liaison, and he wanted to know what it was. He shifted his attitude to a mix of awe and inoffensive appreciation and hoped that a little over-the-top flattery would get Sam ready to open up.

"Wow, and you keep that information hidden away. You should talk proudly of your service, Sam. Thank you for working with our military. It's exciting to meet such a brave person. You are everything that's great about this glorious country."

Sam snorted in derision at Falstaff's blatant attempt at sucking up, but the change in his posture said that the words had worked.

"You talk like a man who wants free food. It was a job, not more than that. Almost every day it was boring. We went to the same places and talked to the same people. 2 years of working to get the chance to come here."

"If it was so boring, why not talk about it?"

"The end was bad. Very bad. No one wants to talk about. No one is allowed to talk about it. When they try, I say no."

"Who tries to talk about the end?"

"The wounded soldiers. They sometimes want to talk about the things that should be forgotten."

"You know patients at the hospital."

"Yes. For many months."

"Oh shit, you were over there with them."

The nervous shrug and smile returned. "Maybe, maybe not." From the parking lot the horn rang out as Nurse began to lose his patience.

"I'm running out of time here, Sam, so let me get down to the essentials. I'm not a cop, or immigration, or an army investigator, or a news reporter. I am just a man with a sister who is worried to death about her injured fiancé. He's in the long-term ward up at the hospital, gunpowder gray eyes. There's no information about what caused his injury. If you know anything about it, it could be really helpful."

"What is fiancé? This word is not familiar."

"Promised to be married. Betrothed. Future husband."

"Oh! That is surprising."

"Do you know the guy or not? And hurry it up. Here, take this to speed your memory."

Falstaff shoved a wad of bills into Sam's hand, the last of the money he had slipped out of the car when Nurse wasn't looking. Sam's greed overwhelmed his caution.

"No one else will hear this?"

"No."

"I met Captain in Zaranj, after the second trouble."

"What troubles? Stop fucking around...please. Sorry, I meant, please continue with some speed. I'm going to get dragged out of here if I take any longer."

"I don't know nothing about the first one, except that it was something that Captain was moved away from. Some bad thing with local military, I don't know. Second one injured him, and we meet in the army doctor tent."

The memory of the meeting was shaking Sam's composure, reducing his English fluency as he became more and more rattled. He looked around the room repeatedly until he was sure there was no one else in listening range, then leaned forward and hissed into Falstaff's ear.

"A bomb in a suitcase went off. Nuclear bomb. It destroyed the place where the Captain's first trouble happened. He almost got blown up by it. Small, thank god. After explosion, the whole task force base evacuated. I was in hospital with knife wound to my back from angry local politician. I rode in same helicopter that Captain did. He did not say full words, only make sounds. They closed the door on his girlfriend, telling her there was no more room and he did not react at all."

Falstaff grabbed the food as the horn blared again. He went to leave but stopped and looked back at Sam with a confused look on his face.

"Did you say girlfriend?"

"Yes, very dedicated. She cried and threw herself at his stretcher, but the guards kept her away. She called to him over and over, but he did nothing."

"Why were the guards there?"

"They were arrested. Captain and his girlfriend did something bad, I think."

"Thanks Sam. I gotta go."

25

Somehow Falstaff managed to get through the door and into the car while unwrapping and taking a massive bite of the hot beef shawarma sandwich. The smear of garlic sauce, hot sauce and hummus now circling around his mouth gave him a passing resemblance to a clown. Nurse laughed derisively at the sight of him as he put the sack full of food onto his lap.

"You're a pig. Did you buy some dope too? You spend all that time in there and have nothing to show for it."

"Just shut your fucking mouth and call the Sheriff. I got a plan" he replied through a mouthful of food.

"What? You have plan?"

"How much clearer do I need to be, Nursie? Christ on a crutch and his 12 doddering idiot apostles. Call the fucking Sheriff and give me the phone when he answers!"

Nurse obviously disliked being bossed about by a twitchy dope fiend, but he complied and handed the phone over when the click came through from the other end. The Sheriff answered with a lack of identifier or any politeness. It seemed like the handwritten number on his card was for a private phone.

"Who's this? You better have a good goddamned reason for calling me right now."

"Well hello to you too, Sheriff. I have some good news for you, but you sound super busy. I'll just go take care of it without you. Bye bye."

"No, you will not hang up on me. What could you have discovered in the last 20 minutes? And clear the shit out of your mouth, son. If I wanted to hear that kind of chewing, I'd spend my days at a pig pen."

Falstaff swallowed his mouthful and continued. "A way to catch our killer, that's what I found out. I got a suspect in mind, and a plan to lure them out. We're on our way to your office to set up the details, so put on the coffee Martha."

Falstaff smacked his lips and made gross, wet chewing noises into the phone before hanging up and tossing the phone back to Nurse. He waved his hand at the man and settled into his seat to eat his food in earnest. Nurse gunned the engine and sped to the Sheriff's office.

Parked at an angle in the handicap spot was the Sheriff's jeep, another testament to his 'fuck you I do what I want' attitude. At the trash can positioned on the edge of the small parking lot, Nurse dumped most of his falafel platter into the garbage. Falstaff clucked in disapproval.

"That is wasteful sir. Your dear mother would be horrified."

"It was covered in parsley. I fucking hate parsley."

"Oh my, enough to swear at it. That is true hate."

"Shut up, John."

In the reception area of the tiny Sheriff's office, a bored looking secretary dominated the tired pastel room that served neither form nor function particularly well. Her over-applied perfume choked the air with its cloying sweetness. She asked 'can I help you?' in a voice that clearly said she had no intention of being helpful.

Falstaff went through the dance of the bureaucratic delay with her, running around the need to see the Sheriff without actually achieving it. Through the half-drawn blinds on the inside glass wall of a meeting room, Deputy Fuckstick glared at Nurse through his two black eyes. A wide white bandage covered most of the man's nose.

The pointless argument between Falstaff and the receptionist continued until the Sheriff came storming out of his office. He told the woman to find something useful to do and bellowed at his injured deputy.

"Stop hanging around your office like a beat dog and go process the evidence from the crime scene, Dwayne. For the love of god, I am surrounded by simpletons. You two, follow me. Brenda, make some coffee."

They walked dutifully behind the Sheriff as he marched back into his office and slammed the door closed after them.

"Here's the good news for you, Sheriff Dunner. The dealer has a personal connection to the catatonic captain, and I think we can use that connection to set a trap. I will reach out to the dealer using the website where the dealer has connected with and arrange a meeting at the hospital with the captain. I'll pretend that the captain is ready to chat, and that should get the dealer very interested in stopping by. We watch, and we wait, and when the dealer rolls in, we swoop in."

"What's your proof?"

"Circumstantial but more than what you have. The pills were stolen from a military shipment. Lots of pills."

"How many?" the Sheriff asked with a look of avarice in his eyes.

"Dunno. It was meant for a field hospital in a region with active combat, so it would need to have a good supply. And the army doesn't do things by ones and twos. As a guess, a few thousand pills to supply them through the entire engagement."

"Thousands of those pills. Good god almighty. Each one could be cut by a quarter and still kick a horse's ass."

"Yeah, it's a big haul. Definitely kick-start any dealer's career. But that's not the only military connection. The army base commander said that there was a new seller on the block. And that seller has been trying to connect with an old buddy trapped in the hospital. Huh, maybe that comic book came from the dealer somehow. Doesn't matter. Anyway, you do what needs to happen to do a stakeout-do they actually call them stakeouts? Whatever."

The Sheriff stared out through the blinds of his picture window overlooking the front parking lot. He popped piece after piece of gum into his mouth and chewed the wad ferociously as he deliberated. Falstaff sidled up to him and watched the Sheriff from the corner of his eye.

"It'll work. It's the only plan we have. The faster I go put this into motion, the sooner we can close the trap and be done with each other. That would be great, right? Never seeing me or my lumbering friend over there again."

"I am considering the logistics of your plan, but I have some concerns about it, and about you. Why should I believe this is a reasonable course of action?"

"Up to you to believe or not, chief. But I want this all to be done, just like you do. Right now, we are spinning our wheels and getting nowhere. By the time the next murders happen, and they will happen, the FBI will get looped in to the investigation and you will lose control. It is a simple fact."

"Threatening me with the FBI is a risky play, son. There are problems waiting to come home to roost that you don't even know about. And another thing-oh Hellfire and shitting brimstone. The news whores are here."

Falstaff caught sight of two news vans from competing Pittsburgh network stations speeding into the parking lot. The Sheriff grabbed him by the elbow and steered him out of the office and down the back hallway.

"Get it done and do it quiet for god's sake. Call me as soon as its set up. Now get out of here and do not talk to the press."

Falstaff and Nurse were pushed out the back door of the station, into the narrow alleyway between the station and the old building behind it. They made their way to the west end of the alleyway to witness the arrival of another wave of reporters rushing into the front doors. In the middle of the pack was Amanda the intrepid internet reporter, elbowing her way towards the front.

The reporters met a rebuffing force just inside the doors and were forced back outside to pool on the steps. They were marshalling for another push inside as Falstaff and Nurse crossed the parking lot. They skirted the building chaos and drove off.

"You could practically see the saliva pooling in the Sheriff's mouth when I told him there were thousands of pills. He wants that stash so badly that it makes him ache."

"He likes drugs more than you? Impossible!"

"To sell, you turd, not to take. The Sheriff isn't into sedation. He likes to get pumped up. Cocaine, or amphetamines. He's running too many shifty side ventures to delve deep into the chemical relaxants."

"You are very excited. Not tired or whiny like earlier."

"We have a lead! A real, genuine lead that will get us closer to solving the case. But we have to take some safety precautions with our law-enforcement friend back there. Did you call the boss yet, to give him an update on the new murders?"

"I have not. He will not be pleased."

"No shit he'll be unhappy. Dial him and gimme the phone so I can tell him. I don't give a rat's ass if he gets angry with me anymore. He's hit the limit of how much he can threaten me. I can't get more worried. Anyway, I'm currently feeling bold."

Nurse pulled the phone out and dialed a number while keeping half an eye on the road in front of them. As it started to ring he handed it over.

"It will go to voicemail automatically. Leave detailed message. If a response is required, there will be a text later."

"Seems like some slap-dash security measures, but it's your show. Ok, it just picked up. John here, with a message for the boss. First of all, there's been another incident. Same general format except for a major deviation of an additional victim. The extra body was ex-military, possibly working with the killer. Following connections from the crime scene and the victims, I figured out a possible method of communicating with the killer. En route to the safe house to attempt to set up the meeting. Major complicating factor in the investigation is the tremendously crooked Sheriff of Allegheny county, Sheriff Dunner. He has been selling narcotics through a distribution network all over the county and has used violence and threats to manipulate the citizens into silence. He believes the killer is trying to take his drug business. If he catches the killer first, he's likely to make them disappear in an unmarked grave. For optimum resolution, I'd advise removing the Sheriff from the equation. He's only going to make everything complicated."

He hung up and watched the phone. 5 minutes later it buzzed with an incoming text from a blocked number.

It had no identifying name to it, simply a short line of words.

"Focus on objective. Ignore distraction. Time is short."

"That's not much help to me. Guess we're on our own with the Sheriff. Keep an eye on him, Nursie."

Back at the safe house, Falstaff ran across the street and knocked on JJ's door. When the door opened, he pushed his way inside and headed to the bedroom where the laptop had come from last time. JJ barred the door and protested the sudden intrusion."

"Dude, I am a friendly guy, but you can't just barge in here and go into my personal space."

"Ha, shit. Sorry. I'm moving a little fast and I am fired up. I think I know how to catch the fucker who killed your brother. I gotta use your laptop though."

"What are you talking about?"

"Plans, man. Plans! Get the laptop, shut down whatever you were jerking off to, I don't care what it was, we all have different kinks, and bring the computer out so I can get things moving. Can I grab a beer while I wait?"

He was halfway to the kitchen before JJ gave him permission to look for one. He found a Bud Light hidden behind a wide hot sauce bottle near the back of the fridge and cracked it open. JJ returned as Falstaff finished the bottle and put the empty down with authority.

"Take it easy, man. I don't need broken glass everywhere."

"I don't know my own strength."

"You're riding something, so tone it all down a couple notches. Don't tweak out in my living room."

Without realizing it, Falstaff brushed at his nose reflexively. It had been a while since he'd done any cocaine, and it was affecting him more than he expected. The lack of sleep and stress was strengthening his twitchy demeanor. He took a deep breath and calmed his mind as he smoked a cigarette. When he reached the end of the smoke, he stubbed it out and flipped open the laptop. He was relieved to find an empty desktop devoid of any digital perversity.

Falstaff went back to Desjeb and looked for the post that had connected him with Rennie, the would-be dealer. He found it and went back through it, looking for signs of new activity. As he reached the end of the message thread, the countdown timer at the top of the post hit zero. The window refreshed automatically and the post was gone, a victim of the timed auto-delete policy. He swore under his breath, lit another smoke, and trolled through the other message posts in the 'buyers and sellers' sub-section.

Near the bottom of the page he found a new post, barely 2 hours old. It was a short message offering an opportunity for new distributors, posted by WhiteKnightRides. Falstaff's pulse quickened as he typed, deleted, and retyped his response multiple times. His mind raced with countless variations of the words all tumbling into each other, forming garbage sentences that meant nothing. He closed his eyes and counted to 10 to give his brain a moment to calm down. The words he wanted to use finally stopped writhing around each other and lined up into a coherent string.

"Guinevere, Lancelot is awake and he needs to speak to you. He will be in the garden of Hotel Dieu, 9PM tonight. Will you be there?"

He posted the message, hoping to god that he wasn't being too clever for his own good. It was entirely possible that he had imagined connections, clues and meanings where there were none, and this message was meaningless. He drummed his fingers with frantic intensity on the coffee table. With a little cajoling, he convinced JJ to light up a generously sized joint, and he focused on drawing and holding as much smoke as he could. The edge to his manic energy ebbed as the pot slowed things down. He was still perched on the edge of the couch, watching the page refresh each time he hit f5.

5 minutes later a reply was posted to the message. It was one word: yes. Falstaff clapped his hands in triumph, but JJ was unconvinced.

"It could be anybody writing that, man. What if it's, like, a trap?"

"Could be, I suppose, but I like my odds. It's the only road forward, JJ. Hold tight here and keep things cool. If I get any news, I'll find a way to get it back to you. Cool?"

"Yeah, yeah, Cool."

"Got some vikkies for the road? Maybe the whole feel good package?"

"I got nothing. I told you, it all got gone when the cops were on the way. You're lucky I scored some pot earlier today. And shouldn't you be clearheaded for this meeting?"

Falstaff hopped up from the couch and moved through the hallway to the exit. He tipped his imaginary hat at JJ and gave him a wink.

"I'm at my best when I'm properly medicated. See you later, JJ."

Falstaff rushed back to the safe house and apprised Nurse of the progress. Nurse relayed the information in a phone call to the Sheriff, with Falstaff shouting in the background that Dunner needed to keep things low-key or the killer would bolt. They agreed to meet 30 minutes before the set time to coordinate their trap, and the Sheriff hung up.

Falstaff paced around the kitchen, drinking from a tumbler of cold water. Nurse made another quiet phone call, leaving a hurried message for their employer. Falstaff was at his side as he finished his call.

"Did you get that commanding officer's contact information, or did I? Grizzley. What a fucking name. I want to give him a call."

"Why?"

"To shake things up, mostly. And to hedge my bet. I should have asked the Sheriff for the name of that private who pretended to be a lieutenant and ended up murdered, because there's a chance he was connected to the rehab base here. Longshot? Fucking yes, but that hasn't stopped me yet. Anyway, I am going to rattle

Grizzley's cage, which will cause him, in turn, to rattle the cages of the dope-peddling private and anyone else connected to the drug deals. And there is a possibility that the noise will reach the killer dealer and put some stress into their life. It will get the bees buzzing all over the hive."

Nurse stared at him like a doctor humouring a lunatic. He dug out the contact information for the army base commander and handed it and the phone over to Falstaff. He dialed the number and waited patiently through a dozen rings before the phone was answered.

"Good afternoon, scratch that, good evening Colonel. Where has the day gone?"

"Who is this?" the army man replied in a raspy voice.

"The crumpled-up scarecrow man you manhandled the other day, for the audacity of coming to ask you questions. Or if you like, you can remember me fondly as the guy who talked you out of blowing your brains out during a late-night bender. Didn't follow through with the dark thoughts. Good for you. If you're back on the pills, I don't need to know. What I do need to know is if this sounds familiar: there's a private, caught impersonating an officer to get some pussy or whatnot, and after he's booted they also find out he's been stealing supplies from the medical dispensary. A load of powerful narcotics goes missing at the same time that the base is flooded with very similar pills. Pills that everyone and their mothers are hooked on. Even those in charge. Incentive to turn a blind eye and let the guy keep stealing after he slips out of custody."

The only response was the ragged heaving breath of a frightened and enraged man. After a minute of near silence, the army officer let loose a string of epithets and hung up by throwing his phone against the wall with enough force to make it shatter. Falstaff caught the sound of plastic and glass splintering before the electronics inside the smashed phone cut out.

"That got him riled up. Buzz buzz buzz."

26

Falstaff sat on the hood of their car and looked up at the rolling cloudbank passing overhead. The minutes remaining until the meeting time with the dealer were crawling by. They had driven to the hospital immediately after the plan had been put into motion, since Falstaff couldn't bear to sit and wait at the safe house. During the drive, the bulk of the drugs in his system had petered out, leaving him dried out and irritated. He had cajoled the night clerk inside the hospital to get him a large cup of coffee, and he sipped it while smoking a continual string of cigarettes.

"Your lungs are black and useless now" Nurse commented.

"I value the concern and opinion of my medical professional, but my lung condition is literally the last thing on my mind. This isn't my normal habit, by the way. I barely smoke most days. One or two on a fun night, sure, but other than that not much at all. But it turns out that being in the center of a rapidly devolving situation is more stressful than I can cope with. So, I'm going to smoke like a motherfucker, unless you want to give me a little something to calm me down."

Nurse ignored the request for medication. Falstaff looked around the space surrounding them and at the darkness settling in to cover everything.

"This is the last chance to walk away. Pick up our shit, get in the car, and drive in the opposite direction of this whole shitshow. Change our names, go our separate ways, and hope it all just fixes itself."

Nurse moved to step in front of Falstaff but he waved him away.

"Don't worry, that's not what I'm going to do. It's not what I want to do, not really. This just feels like a good spot to recognize that there was a choice made to face the music. I want to see this all through. But it won't end nicely."

"It could be easy. Sheriff arrests killer."

"A trial brings light to all the dark corners of a crime. Questions that people do not want to have asked will get brought up repeatedly by the press and by your enemies. The Sheriff is the kind of man who accumulated enemies like he's intentionally building a collection of them. If the killer shows up, and if the Sheriff arrests them instead of shooting them in an 'attempted escape', then there will be many long months of very public scrutiny. Unless there's a plan put in place by the boss to keep the wheels of justice moving smoothly. Is there?"

"It is time to go inside."

"I love how you avoided confirming my hypothetical strategy. What does the boss want to see happen? Best case scenario."

"No more bodies. A quick capture with no further casualties."

"The odds on that are low. Very low."

They walked slowly to the front door of the hospital. Falstaff flicked away his cigarette and slipped two pieces of gum in to kill some of the cigarette bad breath.

"Call me deranged, but I would like to have a chance to chat with the killer without a big audience listening. I want to know what led to this collapsing event."

"You would be disappointed. Talking with a murderer reveals much less than most people think."

"Hell of a life you've lived if you can make that kind of statement with authority."

In the foyer, Falstaff spotted 3 gap-toothed, squinty-eyed men wearing ill-fitting scrubs that could only be members of the Sheriff's stakeout team. He nodded discreetly in the direction of the closest one and muttered to Nurse.

"I have considerable doubt that these goons can pull off this operation without bloodshed. Revise my earlier odds of no casualties to 'next-to-fucking impossible'. Keep your eyes on the doors. I hope you're armed."

The Sheriff emerged from a side hall and walked up to meet them.

"What gave you the retarded idea that it was permissible to sit out in the open during a surveillance operation? The perpetrator could have seen the two of you and left."

"Settle down, Dunner. The coast was clear. The killer doesn't know that we exist. We don't look like police. If anything, we look like shady insurance salesmen."

"The two of you will be secured in a meeting room for the duration of the operation. It is too dangerous to let you drive off now."

Falstaff hopped onto the counter and swung his legs back and forth. He peered behind the counter for any signs of the pervert's electronic porn stash but saw only ancient faded issues of Psychology Today.

"First, Sheriff, I am touched by your concern for our wellbeing. Second, I wouldn't dream of leaving now. We're part of this whole mess and we aim to see it through to the end. Third, to that point, I want to watch the proceedings. Put us in a room on the second floor, lock us in if it makes you feel better, as long as we have a window that we can peer through to watch the great Allegheny sting go down."

The Sheriff looked at his watch and scowled. He let out a low growl through his teeth as he yanked Falstaff to his feet.

"Fine. You stay out of the way and be quiet. A word from either of you could compromise everything."

"Sir, yes sir! We will be silent as church mice on Palm Sunday."

The Sheriff personally escorted Nurse and Falstaff up the employee staircase to the second floor. At the end of a series of narrow unmarked halls they arrived at a generic examination room that had sat unused and uncleaned for months. The thick layer of dust over every surface highlighted the general state of the hospital. Falstaff pulled out a chair and the resulting cloud of dust triggered a sneezing fit.

"Charming. At least it has windows."

He took a stack of coarse brown paper towels and scrubbed at the window facing the garden until he could see the paths below. At each of the corners there was a skulking lurker trying not to be seen but doing a terrible job at it. The Sheriff's men were singularly unsuited for reconnaissance work.

"Quite the team you have here, Sheriff. More than a dozen?"

"That is classified" he grunted, but the clench of his teeth told Falstaff it was fewer than twelve and the Sheriff wished he had more.

"Fair enough."

"Stay here, shut up, and do not touch anything."

The Sheriff slammed the door on the way out, pulling violently on it after it was closed to make sure the lock had engaged. They heard his boot heels clacking down the hall in a hurry until he was out of earshot. Down below, the Captain was rolled out in a wheelchair to the center of the garden and left unattended by the orderly who scurried back inside. The Captain sat impassively staring off into an unfixed point in the distance. The rest of the garden was quiet and poorly lit with aging halogen lights. Falstaff crouched down and peered through the partly cleaned window, looking past the garden and into the trees behind.

15 minutes passed by with no activity. Falstaff strained to look through the dark and the branches swaying in the light breeze and was rewarded with a momentary

flicker of light from up in the trees. The light quickly disappeared behind an obstruction.

He stood up and pressed against the door, testing the lock. It was firmly secured and had no visible unlocking mechanism on the inside. The only option would be to batter the door down, which would bring calamity and ruin to the opportunity that was quickly passing by. Falstaff gave up on the door and instead went to the other window in the room. It was long window that faced the back of the property. Below it was the 4-foot strip of dirt and grass between the building and the back fence. Falstaff was frustrated to see a line of poorly applied paint had sealed the bottom edge of the window. He put his back into the effort of pushing the old wooden window up but could not crack the paint sealing it closed.

"Why the fuck is this the only painted wooden window in the whole goddamn building? None of the other windows are like this."

Nurse watched Falstaff flail uselessly at the stuck window and chuckled at the futile exercise.

"It looks like an old window."

"Well no shit. You don't paint new windows, dipshit."

"Old part of building, maybe. They build rest of new building around old building, so this window is from the original. It should not be so hard to open."

Falstaff was sweating profusely and the strain in his shoulders and calves was causing them all to threaten spasms.

"It is hard. Could you maybe lend a hand?"

"You were instructed to stay here."

"And if I do, the fucking killer will get away. I can see something out in the treeline, in that spot where I found the looking post. This is the chance to catch the killer peacefully and quietly, but by all means, keep laughing at my struggle."

Nurse put his massive hand on the top of the window frame and easily pushed it up to the top. Falstaff stumbled to his knees as his stationary opponent was suddenly bested.

"If anyone ever asks, I softened it up for you. Aw, fuck, the opening is barely a few inches high. This must have been a locked down room before, where they put the suicidal nuts and the violent psychos. You are not going to fit through this motherfucker. Guess I am on my own. Listen, lower me down as much as you can so I don't have to fall too far. Then get ready to get out of here and find me up on the hill. The Sheriff has got to come back to let us out eventually."

Falstaff wiggled through the narrow opening head first, regretting that choice as soon as he was hanging halfway out the window. The ironclad grip of Nurse's hand around his ankles was the only reassuring thing in the escape attempt.

He pushed further ahead until he was suspended in midair by his associate in the room behind and above him. Even lowered as far as Nurse could manage, Falstaff had several feet between him and the ground.

He took a deep breath, told himself to go limp, and hissed at Nurse to let him drop.

Falstaff landed in a painful heap in the dirt below. He held in a groan and frantically looked in either direction for signs that he had been noticed. The buzz of the security light on the wall was the only sound in the narrow dirt lane.

He crawled on his belly to the fence. It was too tall to climb without making a lot of commotion, so Falstaff looked along the bottom edge for a gap large enough to crawl through. 10 feet in the opposite direction of the garden, he found an uneven dip in the ground that made a space tall enough to pass through to the other side.

Halfway under the fence he got stuck, the collection of branches and metal tips of the chain link pressing down on his torso and hooking into his clothes. Panic came hammering down onto his heart, but he pushed it aside with considerable effort. Falstaff exhaled fully and used all four of his limbs to scramble through the last few inches of the gap. He heard fabric tearing as he cleared the gap, and he hoped that it wasn't the sound of the seat of his pants being ripped out. He'd hate to meet a killer with his ass hanging out.

Walking crouched over and hiding behind the fence, Falstaff passed the end of the building and the garden. He used the hedge to stay hidden from the watching tree until he reached the brush at the base of the hill. He climbed the small hill as quietly as he could, but he could feel the eyes watching him with curiosity from the perch. His own eyes adjusted to the weak starlight as he made it to the base of the tree. Falstaff looked up to meet the gaze of the woman crouched on the branch above him.

"Hi" he said softly, with his hands held up to prove he was unarmed and harmless.

The woman tilted her head to the right, like a bird watching a nice fat worm pop out of its hole. The low light caught in her eyes turned them into shiny black pools. Her hair was cut unevenly and was a mix of different colors mashed into each other. She stayed still, studying Falstaff intently, until she accepted that he wasn't a threat. She looked back towards the clearing with her right hand lightly touching the trunk of the tree to maintain her balance.

"If I were you, I would have fallen ass over tea kettle by now. You must be part sparrow to keep perched like that."

"You fell like a sack of manure from that window."

"You saw that, huh? I meant to do it, if that counts for anything. I'm not the world's most graceful guy, but I needed to get down here to meet you. I want to apologize to you for lying-Lancelot isn't waking up. He could, if he wanted to. I doubt that he's catatonic at all. He's hiding."

His words set off a maelstrom of emotions that played out across the woman's face. The feelings were intense, conflicting, and shifting so quickly that he couldn't diagnose her specific secrets. His only takeaway was that the woman scared him on a primal level. He let the moment pass by in silence, giving the woman time to process and control her response. He watched the Sheriff's men impatiently moving from their positions to wander the perimeter of the garden.

"It was a shitty stakeout to begin with, and it's only gotten worse. Hey, can I ask you a rough question? I don't ask it to antagonize you, but asking might give me a better idea of what's going on."

She thought about the question for a full minute. The fingernails of her right hand probed the bark of the tree for cracks and picked at the spaces they found as she came to her decision.

"Okay. Ask."

"When did it all go wrong? I mean, everyone arrives at the present moment through a cascading and accumulating series of events, accidents and injuries, but there is always a primary one. The point where your life was derailed, and you had to find a new way to move forward."

The woman looked down at Falstaff, but her mind was far away at a different point in time and space. The memory floodgates were open, and the deluge was overwhelming her ability to speak. She turned her eyes back to the garden and waded against the stream of remembered images to find her words.

"Patrol, through a cleared sector of the occupied settlement. Low visibility was our priority. We were supposed to sweep one last time for combatants, then bug out back to base. Orders were to avoid contact with locals. The village was bombed out. No one was supposed to be there.

In a ruined cinderblock storage structure we found local security forces. They were the ones we were training and arming so that they could protect their own country. The village was off-limits to them, but they snuck in to take a look around. 4 of them, 3 of them barely teenagers, and their commanding sergeant. Upon discovery, they were ordered to identify themselves and explain their conduct. As the sergeant spoke, I heard a moan from behind an overturned table. I investigated and discovered a young girl, maybe 13 or so. Blood at her mouth and groin, naked except for the shreds of her dress around her. My commanding officer demanded that they surrender to him to be tried for rape.

The sergeant claimed the woman was already in that state when they arrived, despite the clear evidence that the men had been in process of raping her when we arrived. Our C.O. refused to accept that and ordered them to bring the woman for medical treatment. The Afghani sergeant shot the girl in the face and laughed. He said there was no more crime, since the woman was dead. 'Problem solved' he said with a smile.

I don't remember who my C.O. shot first, but the room was filled with gunfire. The Afghani sergeant knocked the firearm from my C.O.'s hands. They engaged in hand to hand combat, where the sergeant was killed by strangulation. During the altercation, my C.O. took a blow to the head that rendered him unable to continue command. I assisted him in reaching the extraction point, and I drove us to the field hospital before passing out from the gunshots I had suffered in the firefight."

"Jesus. That is a hell of a story."

"That is what happened" she said with a razor-sharp edge of anger laced through her voice. She needed to believe absolutely that her version of the incident was gospel truth. He had his doubts. There was some big lie in the middle of her account, but she could not bring herself to look at it. Falstaff nodded and moved on to a different topic to avoid the explosion brewing behind the woman's calm demeanor.

"Congratulations for avoiding the Sheriff's incredibly clever trap. To be fair, the part about luring you here was my idea, but that worked just fine. The part where his bumbling toadies corral you into the back of a paddy wagon doesn't look like it's going to work at all. Anyone with a basic awareness of their surroundings could slip past those idiots. Between Sheriff Dumbo and Deputy Fuckstick, there's a whole lot of stupid going on."

Falstaff smiled up at Sparrow, inviting her to laugh with him at the dimwitted police trying to catch her. He was confused by the sudden widening of her eyes and stiffening of her whole body that was accompanied by an odd snapping sound. She pitched forward and fell to the dirt, still rigid as a board. He reached out to her as the snapping sound happened again. Falstaff lost control of his limbs as every major muscle in his body tensed. He fell forward to land on the ground beside Sparrow. His mouth was filled with dirt and leaves.

"Yeah, we're real stupid" the Sheriff drawled from above Falstaff's prone body, as he holstered his taser. Two of the Sheriff's goons ran up with plastic cable ties to restrain the hands and ankles of Falstaff and Sparrow.

"Who's the idiot now?" the Sheriff asked, before kicking Falstaff in the face with enough force to knock him completely unconscious.

27

A jolt from the surface beneath him shook Falstaff awake. He was lying on his side on a cold, hard floor. His face was throbbing from the kick that had knocked him out. Falstaff was confused by the close darkness pressing at the tip of his nose until he realized there was a cheap pillowcase pulled over his head and tied around his neck with a rough length of rope. He gagged as the floor beneath him shook again and pressed the rope into his larynx. The constant rumbling sound made it difficult to get his bearings. Falstaff gave up on understanding the entirety of his situation, and instead he focused on removing his hood.

He started by bringing his knees up to his chest and working his bound wrists around his feet so that his hands were in front of him. The low roof over him and the unidentified masses around him made this an ordeal. When he finally brought his hands up to his throat in triumph, Falstaff was sweating profusely and breathing hard. He yanked at the loose knot in the rope and pulled it free. His hands collided with the unknown object directly in front of him, a wet object that yielded to the impact with unsettling softness. Falstaff discarded the rope and pulled the pillowcase from his head.

The low space around him was dark, smelly and cramped. Another bump made the floor jump. A truck. He was in the back of a truck driving along a rough road. The Sheriff was taking him somewhere. Falstaff reached out to the closest object that was directly in front of him, gently probing it with his fingertips. He caught the even edge of a hard rectangle covered by fabric, and he explored the shape until he found the seam of the pocket that contained it. Falstaff ignored the fact that the owner of the pocket was not responding to the probing fingers jabbing into their flesh. He closed his fingers on the cellphone and brought it close to his face.

He fumbled with the buttons on the phone, nearly dropping it when the truck barreled over a set of train tracks. He woke the phone up but was confronted with the lock screen. Even though he couldn't get into the phone, he could still use the phone screen's dim light to see what his surroundings. He flipped the phone around and directed the light outwards.

Falstaff found himself staring at Nurse's partially crushed face. His one remaining good eye stared blindly at Falstaff. The row of bottom teeth poking through the lower lip mashed into them was the image that sent Falstaff into hysterics. He kicked his feet forward and pushed against Nurse's corpse, desperately trying to get away from it. A strange, high-pitched keening noise was coming from somewhere. A part of Falstaff knew that the noise was coming from his own mouth, a scream that was building in volume and intensity.

He brought his hands back to his mouth and noticed that the wet sensation he had felt before was the blood and viscera transferring from Nurse's mangled head to his hands. The scream changed to a series of short, barking coughs. He was about to vomit. The mass that he backed into moved suddenly, drawing another scream from him. A muffled voice spoke from the lump behind him.

"You should be quiet, or they'll stop and kill us right here."

A second voice from a different spot in the back of the truck gave a low sobbing moan.

"You too. Quiet."

Falstaff focused on the person behind him and ignored the bloody carcass less than 2 feet from his face.

"We have to get out of here. I have to get out of here. I'm nose to fucking nose with a corpse, and I can't take it. They can't leave me back here like this. It's against my rights, to assault me and restrain me and arrest me without reading me my rights or giving me a phone call."

The sobbing voice replied. "This isn't an arrest, its an execution."

"Jesus shitting Christ. Oh fuck."

"At least if we wait until the truck stops, we might escape or something." The first voice said, and Falstaff heard something familiar in its soft tone.

"Is that you, Rennie? The kid trying to buy dope at the gravel pit, right? Do you really think we can escape?"

The sad sob in the second voice was receding to a dull resignation. "It never works like that. They never get away."

The truck hit another massive rut in the road, throwing everyone living and dead around the back of the truck. Falstaff was turned around so that he was facing away from the corpse, but the force of the jolt had pushed him backwards. He was now little spoon to Nurse's big dead spoon. He laughed under his breath as panic settled into his chest and started to bloom.

The truck came to an abrupt stop. Falstaff kicked backwards to keep the dead body from sliding over him, landing both feet into the wide gut of his dead former keeper. The impact pushed the remainder of air from the corpse's lungs, air that exited through the pulpy mashed skin around his mouth with a wet, flapping wheeze. Falstaff started screaming to be let out. A puddle of his own urine spread underneath him.

The back gate of the truck bed was dropped down, and the top was raised up. Rough hands grabbed at the still hooded figures of Sparrow and Rennie. Falstaff's hysteria prevented him from seeing the faces of the men unloading them until he was thrown onto the dirt.

"This one pissed hisself already" Deputy Fuckstick said, with a wide grin and a voice made dull and round by the wads of cotton crammed into his nostrils to keep them from bleeding. The cast that covered Fuckstick's wrist and knuckles was cracked and stained with blood. The Sherriff stood beside Fuckstick and issued instructions.

"That is to be expected, Deputy. But I did think a clever fella like this detective would have been a little bit more courageous. Stand him up."

The deputy roughly pulled Falstaff to his feet and kept a painful grip on his arm as he wavered in place. Falstaff started to beg for his life.

"Sheriff this is a complete misunderstanding and we can fix it. Things go wrong, I know. But it doesn't need to get worse. I can get you money. Lots of money from my employer. He's going to be so fucking excited that the killer has been caught that he'll authorize any expense."

The Sheriff paced the small patch of muddy gravel and mused about the offer.

"Is that so? Your employer won't have any concerns regarding his former employee, your now deceased partner?"

"That guy? Man, fuck that guy. He was a piece of shit. I am glad he's dead. He was just a rented thug who was terrible at his job of protecting me. Seriously, big money. Just let me walk away. I'll find my own way back, and I'll send the money to you."

The Sheriff laughed long and hard at the ridiculous offer. As he stood there laughing, the other 4 goons pulled Rennie and Sparrow to their feet, cutting off the restraints around their ankles and removing their hoods. Falstaff saw a look of equal parts confusion, despair, conflict and contrition on Sparrow's face. She was caught in the middle of some great mental unravelling. He hoped it kept her from being present when things got violent. Rennie was nervously looking in every direction for some route to freedom. Sheriff Dunner finished his laughing fit with a hard, open-handed slap that knocked Rennie to the ground.

"It's time to stop looking for the exits. You're in my neck of the woods and you'll go where I tell you to go.

Now get back up, precious, or you're staying down permanently."

"Hey, what about my offer? Cash. Lots of it!"

"So, if I accept that this scrawny little slip of a girl is the big, bad gangbang killer and the dealer trying to steal my territory, which I do not accept for the record, then I can expect a substantial reward from your grateful employer. And it will arrive in piles of unmarked bills, suitable for spending however I like, in a bag carried by some big-titted whore with an insatiable appetite for my cock. I have heard this speech before. Don't waste your breath selling me something you don't have, son."

"I can get the money. Just have one of the goons drive me to town so I can call the boss."

"We have business to attend to here. We're going on a hike to appreciate the pristine beauty of our state parklands. Unless you would prefer to be put down right here, right now. That seems to be the option young Rennie is choosing."

Falstaff looked at Rennie writhing on the ground, trying to get back up but unable to get their balance with their hands still bound. The Sheriff was watching the display while pulling a pair of gleaming chrome knuckledusters onto his right hand. The base of the duster was wrapped in leather padding to protect the smooth skin of the Sheriff's palm. He didn't want to hurt himself while injuring others. The next punch aimed at Rennie was going to cause grievous harm, and possibly death.

"Oh Jesus, fuck please no, Sheriff. Don't hit me with that thing. I can't bear the pain. I'll do anything. No!"

Falstaff ended his plea with a squealing sob, aiming for maximum pathos. The plea worked. The Sheriff's nostrils flared as he sneered at Falstaff's affected weakness. Dunner walked from Rennie to Falstaff and leaned into a punch aimed at Falstaff's midsection. Falstaff had asked for the punch and received it in due haste. As the punch landed, Falstaff exhaled forcefully, turned his body away from the impact, and tightened his abdominal muscles to lessen the effect. He made sure to add a pretence of pain to his exhalation so that the Sheriff would be satisfied with the attack. The punch hurt but didn't wind him. He doubled over in exaggerated agony and managed to shoot a slight wink and the ghost of a smile to Rennie.

"And how is that? You look like you took that well and good enough. Let's find out if there's anything tough inside of you, or if it's all faggot to the core."

Deputy Fuckstick chimed in to taunt Falstaff, eagerly stepping to his side and yelling down from above him.

"Leave him be, Sheriff. The little faggot is heartbroke over his big fag lover being dead. Got hisself kicked to death, poor fairy. All that muscle don't do no good if you get hit by two Tasers at the same time. He tried to fight back. You should be a proud boyfriend, faggot."

It always came down to accusations of homosexuality. To angry stupid thugs like the Sheriff and his dimwitted deputy, there was no greater insult than to state that a man loved other men. They saw sex with women as rightful male dominance, and sex with another man was a declaration of corrupted weakness. Falstaff pretended to cry weakly as he thought about the biological imperative to procreate and if that shaped their violent bias in some twisted way. To the hateful bigots surrounding him, man was meant to spread his seed to create life and refusing to do so nullified your masculinity. Falstaff had a sneaking suspicion, though, that if he begged for his life with an offer to suck the Sheriff's cock in front of everyone, Dunner would accept. His love of humiliating and dominating someone would win against his homophobia.

Finally, Rennie managed to stand up and remain upright, and gave Falstaff a look of sympathy and gratitude. Falstaff straightened up from his feigned collapse. The Sheriff looked over the three prisoners and nodded.

"Now that we're all ready for a walk, follow me. Deputy, you take the remains and dispose of them."

"Ah, come on Sheriff. Why I got to do the shit work?"

"Because you decided to attack and kill the man when I expressly told you to capture him."

"He charged at me. It was self-defence."

"Sure it was. Retroactive self-defence in response to the way he kicked your ass at the gravel pit."

"It was a bullshit trick he used to distract me."

"And so, you incapacitated him and kicked his face until he was dead. That's why he is your responsibility. End of discussion."

The march into the darker woods began. The Sheriff walked along side the stunned prisoners, rambling on about the tree canopy they passed under, and the animal tracks they came across. He acted like a friendly tour guide leading them to a scenic picnic spot, and his relaxed demeanor told Falstaff that the Sheriff planned to come back without them. Sporadically, when the Sheriff reached a lull in his nature narration, he threw a punch or aimed a kick at Falstaff. Each strike was sloppy, and easy to turn away from to lessen the hit, but they were intensifying in strength. By the time they crested a low hill in the middle of a thick stand of pine and ash trees, Falstaff didn't have to pretend that the attacks were hurting him.

On the other side of the low hill sat a noxious pool of stagnant marsh water. The stench of the murky, rotting marsh rose up to meet them. There were odors mixed in to the smell that raised the hackles on the back of Falstaff's neck. It was a hole where dead things were left to decompose.

"Welcome, freaks, to the asshole of the world. Our local version of it, anyway."

The Sheriff smiled at Falstaff, then pulled back and smashed him in the jaw with his knuckleduster fist. The corner of the knuckleduster's metal bar caught on Falstaff's cheek and punctured it. The metal had enough force behind it that the skin along Falstaff's jaw tore and continued to rip as the punch continued along its course. The end of the tear was slightly downturned, creating a loose flap of skin that dribbled blood from the torn edge as it flopped away from the bone underneath. Falstaff made a gagging sound as he swallowed the blood suddenly appearing in his mouth. He used his left hand to push the skin back into place as best as was possible. He looked at the 4 goons standing at a distance around the hill. They had no intention of stepping forward to stop the conclusion of the death march.

Rennie cried loudly for help and begged to be spared. Sheriff Dunner responded by pulling out his revolver and calmly shooting Rennie in the chest.

Rennie gasped and grabbed at the spot where blood was now starting to soak the thick fleece sweatshirt. Rennie staggered forward a step, then started to fall to the ground. The Sheriff intercepted the fall with his foot and redirected Rennie to the downslope. Rennie fell down the slope into the foul fetid water below and lay still, half-submerged and sinking slowly.

"Shouldn't have tried to do business without me, Rennie. Shame about that."

The Sheriff moved to stand directly in front of Sparrow.

"Now, ma'am. We need to have a chat about your part in this unfortunate business. You've been trying to undercut my distribution network with your drugs. I need to know where the drugs came from, who is running the show, and any other details that may be relevant. Oh, and the identity of the killer would be icing on the cake, I suppose, though I am of the mind to let the FBI deal with that horseshit. Speak up, or things will get rough for you."

Sparrow swayed in an imaginary breeze, leaning first towards the pool of fetid corpse water below, then back towards Falstaff, keeping her eyes unfocused and staring up to the sky above. She was caught in an internal battle that cut her off from the reality of the danger facing her. The rapidly shifting emotions playing out across her face had Falstaff spellbound, and he wanted to see what emerged victorious from the fight. But to do that, he needed to keep the Sheriff occupied and distracted. He sucked down the spit and blood pooled between his wounded cheek and his teeth and called to Dunner.

"It wasn't about the pills. The drugs were a simple way to get control of people, to get them where she needed them to be."

"Oh, the expert speaks. Tell me, oh expert, where did this bony bitch need these people to be?"

"On stage."

The Sheriff turned slightly, to face Falstaff.

"What the hell does that mean?"

"She put them on stage, arranged them in their places, to send a message to the one she loves."

A violent shudder ran through Sparrow's body. It started in her hands cupped in front of her mouth and spread until every part of her was trembling.

"That was what I thought anyway, after the first two murder scenes. But I was wrong, wasn't I Sparrow? You don't love him anymore. He failed you. When you needed him to be the man you loved so dearly, to be the knight you imagined him to be, he refused."

The shudder continued through all of Sparrow's body except for her head. She brought her eyes back down from the sky to drill into Falstaff's, and he saw the darker shape hiding behind her rational thoughts. Rage. Purest, darkest rage burned without limit in the deepest part of her heart. The pretence and ceremony of the murders had kept it partially pacified, but now it was free of that constructed cage and was consuming the shell that had once held it. It was both terrible and majestic to watch it transform her. Falstaff kept eye contact with her but spoke to the Sheriff.

"You know what breaks your heart, Sheriff? Faith. She put all her faith and trust in that catatonic captain, but he let her down. She did everything she thought he wanted her to do, was the person he wanted her to be but, in the end, that didn't make a difference. In pain, she decided to recreate the scene where he failed her, to give him a chance to explain himself."

Past Sparrow, Falstaff watched one of the goons standing at ease 20 feet away from the hill. He didn't recognize the man as a part of the ambush team at the hospital. The goon shifted his weight and held his arms loosely at his sides, comfortable but prepared. It was a pose shaped by a history of discipline and rigor, not thuggish brutality. He also noticed that the goon was only watching Dunner. The Sheriff sneered and grabbed Sparrow in a loose chokehold.

"This little thing killed all those junkies and whores, just to send a message to her ex-sweetheart? I have heard a lot of ridiculous things standing here on judgment hill, but this is the most unbelievable story to date. If you're determined to go to your grave without telling me the truth, so be it. I aim to give you what you want."

The Sheriff dragged Sparrow with him towards Falstaff and sent a pair of kicks at him. The first was aimed at his right knee, causing him to fall to the ground again. The second caught him in the side of his neck. A fresh torrent of blood rolled down from his torn cheek, and he choked and gagged as he writhed on the ground. Falstaff swallowed hard and pushed back against the approaching grey of unconsciousness. He looked up into Sparrow's scared, angry and guilty face. She was still torn between two versions of herself and could not find a path to reconciliation. Something in her eyes told him to help her find that path. So, he gave her an out.

"But you don't have to stay heartbroken, Sparrow. Things change. You don't have to be the person he wanted. Be who you really are, for once in your life."

The change that came over Sparrow was instantaneous. The fire in her eyes burned lower but more focused, and a calm rippled through her body. The Sheriff didn't notice it, but Falstaff did. He also saw that Sparrow had moved her hands to be above her head in an odd pose. Falstaff studied the scene in front of him, a tableau that was about to shift into motion before his very eyes, and he laughed with a gurgling chuckle as he spoke to Dunner one last time.

"Gonna pass out in a second. You kicked the shit outta me, Sheriff. Top notch job. But there's 3 things you should know. 2 are important, the third is going to come too late."

"Go on, dead man. Enlighten me."

Falstaff somehow managed to pull himself up to his knees without passing out. He gestured weakly to Sparrow.

"First, she's been busy. Not only is she the gangbang killer, she's also the devil of the Rust Belt. Those strapping young men she cut apart in the fields were proxies for her disappointing captain."

Sparrow tilted her head to the side with a look that started in confusion, then shifted to admission, punctuated by a narrow little smile as she accepted the truth.

"She had that part of her buried deep in her subconscious and wasn't even aware of it. Huh. Two different murder sprees from the same person. Ah well, she knows now."

"I'm running out of patience for all this nonsense. Finish up so I can shoot you."

"Ha, man has a plan. Point 2: these men watching us, they aren't your men. Take a look. Do you recognize any of them?"

The Sheriff turned his head to look at the closest goon, the one 20 feet away that Falstaff had watched earlier. As his attention shifted to the goon, his grip on Sparrow loosened enough to give her leverage room.

She brought her arms down behind her head to slip her hands under the collar of her shirt. Falstaff was confused by her choice of action until her hands re-emerged with a hunting knife firmly held between them.

Sparrow stabbed backwards and down into the Sheriff's face and neck in three quick jabs. The gleaming black blade cut deeply into the flesh and slid back out with barely any effort. The Sheriff was stunned by the pain and the sudden appearance of a cascade of blood from his neck. He reflexively brought his hands up to the wounds to staunch the bleeding.

Sparrow turned around in the newly available space and slammed her shoulder into Dunner's torso with enough force to topple him to the ground. She followed him down, using the momentum of the fall to drive the knife deep into the Sheriff's gut, two inches above his bellybutton. With a tug to the left she opened his belly and sent his innards spilling out. He screamed for her to stop as he batted at her with his blood-slicked hands, but she only replied with quick surgical strikes that lopped off the offending fingers and severed the tendons controlling his hands. Sparrow continued to butcher the Sheriff with short, quick cuts as the disloyal men stood and watched.

Slumping down and about to pass out, Falstaff held up three fingers and spoke to no one.

"And three, you should have searched your prisoners."

His world went dark to the sounds of meat being hacked to pieces.

28

Falstaff had expected that, if he woke up at all, it would be at the bottom of judgement hill. But instead of slowly sinking into suffocating mud, he was in a soft warm bed surrounded by hushed sounds and stillness. The smooth sheets were cool and comforting against his bruised skin. He blinked repeatedly to clear his eyes and looked down at the state of his being.

A neatly managed array of tubes and wires were attached to his body. An IV stand beside the bed dripped clear fluid in predictable drops continuously through the line inserted into his cephalic vein. The monitors arranged behind the IV played the reports of his continued existence as they watched for a sudden interruption in any of those rhythms. Falstaff reached up with his free right hand and gently touched his cheek. A bandage covered his jawline from the center of his mouth to the edge of hairline. He used his tongue to probe the interior of his mouth and found an evenly spaced line of sutures holding his damaged cheek together. Feeling the stiff protruding points of the sutures made his skin itch. He ran his fingernail under the edge of the bandage and began to pick at it.

"Ah ah" admonished a voice from the left of Falstaff. He turned his head too quickly, sending it swimming with a pain that rose above the sedation in his system. When his vision cleared, he saw that the speaker was the German, sitting comfortably in a wide, luxurious chair upholstered in dark red velvet.

"You are awake. Good. Please lay still until the doctor has examined you."

The German waved his hand and a doctor appeared presently to check Falstaff's condition. His hands were cold but gentle, and the examination was quick. He advised the German that the patient was capable of a brief chat but would need to rest afterwards. The German nodded, and the doctor vanished as quickly as he had arrived.

"We have many things to discuss, Herr Falstaff. Some will wait, some will not. You should be aware of my disappointment concerning your substance abuse. You did not tell me of your addictions, John. They cause an…uncertainty of outcomes. What made you this junkie, John?"

Falstaff looked weakly to the left and the right for a way out or a method of avoiding the conversation. All he found was the rolling table at his bedside that held a cheery orange tumbler with a lid and straw.

"Is that water?" he croaked. The German nodded and picked up the drink. With a carefulness that seemed almost tender, the German held the tumbler for Falstaff as he sipped the cool water inside. When he was finished, the German put the tumbler back and returned to his seat.

"You people made me take drugs. All of you. That 'gift' I have, reading the hidden emotions and intentions that people refuse to admit, it eats away at my sanity. Because everyone is part monster. I cannot have one day of normal interaction without being reminded of the essential shitty nature of humanity. Bad people are easier to handle, because they're acting on their worst impulses. I expect nothing of them, and they deliver. Regular people who think they're good are the ones I want to avoid. But I can't avoid them, not permanently. I can't exile myself from the human race. I get drawn back in, whether I want to or not. So, when I have had too much time with people's secrets, I self-medicate. I numb myself, lift my mood with artificial affection, and above all I stay distracted. If I have to get something done, I take something to wake me up and get me sharp. They give me distance, like I'm seeing myself in a picture but I look removed and far away. Am I physically dependent on all of the shit? Dunno. Maybe. Am I spiritually hooked? Fuck yes."

Giving the speech drained Falstaff's energy and he slumped into the soft stack of pillows behind him. The German gave him a moment to collect himself before replying.

"I confess I do not fully understand your situation, but I accept that it feels very serious to you. Regardless, there will need to be rules and considerations about your drug use. To protect us, and you. On the subject of protection, your associate was not as fortunate as you."

"I warned him. I fucking warned him, but the massive fucker ignored me. He was a completely sadistic asshole to me, but I'm sorry that he didn't listen to me."

"Calm yourself, John, you are not being held responsible for his death. He was a well-trained professional. He should have been better prepared to respond. We are reviewing the mistakes that were made in our planning efforts, so we can correct them, please rest assured. Despite these…challenges, the project was an adequate success. Congratulations are in order."

The air conditioning kicked in, blowing a gust of cool, sanitized air down from the vents to swirl through the room. The cool breeze sent a shiver down Falstaff's spine, which reminded him of the symphony of injuries clambering for his attention. The painkillers they had him on were weak enough to let the bulk of the pain through.

"Success is painful. And for the crooked little Sheriff, our success was lethal. Whatever happened after I passed out must have been astoundingly good to drag the project from 'disaster' to 'adequate success'."

The German held up his right hand and counted on his fingers as he listed the outcomes.

"The killer was identified, located and apprehended quietly."

"Quietly? The dead cop would beg to differ."

"It is relative. The source of the stolen narcotics was identified as the killer's accomplice and victim."

"The fake lieutenant."

"Ya. The narcotics were located and securely removed. And all traces of evidence connecting the killer and her former commanding officer to the illegal incident in Afghanistan has been eliminated, so there is no alarming report that will be made to the international community."

"Wait. The killing of the Afghani soldiers was illegal enough to be an international incident?"

"I cannot discuss that. There are details that will never be confirmed, you must know that by now. But I will ask you why, if it was a simple act of violence committed by a U.S. service member, why was such effort expended to erase it from history? The records of the guilty soldiers, the location of the village, and the village itself, all gone into oblivion. It will never come to light."

"The village was bombed by insurgents" Falstaff said, but as the words came out of his mouth he wondered if he was so certain of that.

"You assume that, yes? Let us leave it there. It would be harmful to suppose otherwise."

"Harmful. Assuming that the bomb was American-made would be the most harmful explanation I could imagine."

The German smiled and wagged a finger at Falstaff.

"Then we leave our imagination to dream of nicer business. Happy times."

"Jesus. Fine. What happened after I keeled over?"

"Oh! It was such a tragic scene. The corrupt Sheriff had a violent falling out with his assistant Sheriff."

"Deputy" Falstaff corrected.

"Yes, deputy. They killed each other quite viciously, in a quarrel over the stolen drugs. The community was shocked to discover that the law men were selling narcotics, and then they were told of the horrifying murders. All drug deal retributions done to punish his rivals. It is scandalous. The deputy shot the Sheriff in a fit of rage before turning the gun on himself. To assist the poor citizens as they deal with this tragedy, Federal assistance funds have been directed to the affected communities."

"Fed money. Is that your doing?"

The German shrugged and continued. "The military commander of the retraining camp has been relieved of his command and is under treatment for his addiction. The army has quietly dispatched a full addiction counselling team to the camp to deal with the prevalent drug abuse."

"I guess you found a few minutes to take care of that too, even though you told me to ignore it."

"Stability, John, is our goal. Anything that stabilizes this country is within our mandate."

Eager to assert his physical independence, Falstaff tried to push himself up to a sitting position and reached for the tumbler of water. He could only manage to flail sideways and grab the glass before flopping back flat on his back. His vision went grey and he came close to passing out, but he buckled back down by jabbing the wound in his mouth forcefully with his tongue. The pain brought the world back into focus.

"Shitty pain meds, by the way. You have me on the weakest stuff imaginable."

"You are an addict."

"Not physically, asshole. And my cheek was a grisly flap hanging in the wind. What's the rest of the damage?"

"The doctors said there was no one serious injury. It was the accumulation of wounds that compromised your health. Bruised internal organs, the cracked ribs you had when we first met in the desert, many surface bruises and contusions, the deep laceration on your face. There will be a scar, I am afraid. The blood loss and continued injuries sent you into shock, and it was all made worse by your lack of proper sleep, food, and the many non-prescribed substances you had ingested."

"A scar to remember the good times. Did you know that fucker you hired to watch over me stabbed my foot with a needle? It was so goddamned painful it still hurts."

"And why did he do that? What medicine did he administer?"

"None of your fucking business. Where's the real killer?"

The German seemed sincerely confused by the sudden switch in conversation topics. He looked perplexed as Falstaff stared accusingly and slurped the last bit of water through the straw.

"Pardon me?"

"You pegged the murders on the Sheriff and Deputy Fuckstick. So, you did not have the young woman who was actually responsible arrested. She also killed those single young men that were found butchered in various fields and ditches around the county. The papers called her the 'Devil of the Rust Belt'. Same person. Did you clean up that part of the mess by putting a bullet in her head and grinding her up into sausage meat?"

"You have a flair for the repulsive, John. I did not know she was also the Devil. That only makes the diagnosis more accurate. The young woman is not well."

"You put her in a secret cell somewhere and threw away the key. Fucking asshole."

Falstaff didn't like the amount of concern for the woman that had snuck into his voice. She was none of his business anymore.

"We have difficult responsibilities, John, but we are not monsters. She is not well, but she can be treated. She has been given an opportunity to get better, in a specialized facility that is best suited to assist."

"Oh shit, let me guess. It's a facility just like this one."

"You are perceptive."

"She's a murderer."

"She is quite skilled, yes."

"Skilled? SKILLED? Oh Christ where is this going? It's a terrible idea to leave her free. She's going to kill again."

The German stood up and patted his leg as he spoke with a heavily patronizing tone.

"Do not upset yourself, John. It will interfere with your recovery. You should think about the success of this first mission, and how you will make the next one even better."

"No next time. I did my best, as poor as that was, and the killer was caught. Done."

"There is more to do, until the work is done."

"I'm too tired to be threatened right now, Kraut. I just want to point out that keeping me under house arrest indefinitely will not improve our working relationship."

"You will be here of your own free will."

"Not fucking likely."

The German leaned over Falstaff's trembling, sweaty body huddled under the sheets and held a tablet in front of his face. The screen had a live stream feed of what seemed to be a support group meeting. There was an official taking notes in the middle of the circle of chairs, as the participants spoke to each other.

"You see them, these people. They are in a treatment program at a very prestigious private institution. Being a patient there is very expensive. None of these people could afford it. How many patients do you see?"

"Uh, who knows? Not counting the admin jerk in the middle? There are five."

"Yes. Four men, one woman. All had an appointment scheduled for next week. That appointment has now been cancelled, because of your efforts. Now they get help for their addictions, with an anonymous donor generously paying the costs."

"They were going to be the next victims."

The German smiled like a saint. "And now they get another chance. Because of you, John. Is this enough reason to stay, my friend?"

"We are not friends, you sack of manipulative shit."

"So angry, so bitter. It will undo you. But will you stay to do some good?"

Falstaff watched the grainy images play out on the screen. One of the men, the youngest looking one, burst into tears. The rest of the circle collapsed on him and held him as he cried. Through the tears, the young man smiled peacefully.

"Fine. Don't think that I believe you care about these people. This is just a transaction to you."

"If so, does that matter? They do not seem to care why I take these actions. So you should not either."

The German gave him another dismissive pat on the leg and sauntered out of the room. Falstaff yelled a parting shot at him as he retreated.

"I don't even believe you're actually German, you phony stack of dicks!"

A chuckle from the other end of the room startled Falstaff. He cautiously and slowly pulled himself to a sitting position in stages, a couple of inches at a time. Finally in a full sitting position, he looked across the room. Diagonal to his bed was another one just like it and laying in the center of the thick blankets and pillows was the slim small form of Sparrow. His arms trembled as he fought to keep himself propped up. She shook her head and chuckled at his effort.

"The bed is automated. Use the controls to raise it up, dunderhead."

He found the control panel for the bed and, after a couple of false starts, managed to raise the bed to an upright position. Sparrow watched him with unending amusement showing in her shiny dark eyes, her head tilted slightly to the side.

"Hello again."

She smiled in response, through the developing bruises and dried blood covering her face. He didn't see any skin breaks on her face or head, so the blood must have come from the Sheriff. She straightened her head without breaking eye contact.

"Hi."

"That was quite the hike into the woods. I still have a few questions. Can I ask them?"

"Of course" she said with an air of complete ease about her. Whatever torment she had been suffering through before had been replaced with a simple peace.

"You killed the Afghani soldiers, right? Captain Lancelot didn't step in to avenge the raped and murdered girl, so you did what he refused to do."

"Yes."

"But you told yourself a different version, so that you could stay in love with him. Deep down, though, you knew the truth, and it made you angry. The angry part of you killed those fellas in the fields. You killed the gangbang actors to send an accusation to Lancelot, to get him to confess. But the devil murders were direct revenge by proxy on him."

"That's not a question."

"I suppose not. Try this-are you going to kill again?"

Sparrow scrunched up her face and seriously considered the question. After a moment, she relaxed, shrugged and smiled again.

"I don't know. The road is long and winding."

Poorly hidden in the smile was a promise of blood yet to come. Falstaff chased it.

"You like killing, don't you? What happens now? Can you give it up and lead a regular life? What kind of life is there for you, or me?"

She stretched and yawned as she settled into the cozy nest piled around her. Sparrow smoothed out the cream white sheets, obviously enjoying the soft smooth texture as it slid under her hand. She folded her hands neatly together in her lap.

"I was sinking into nothingness before I met you. My head was full of noise and confusion. But I found you, Falstaff, and I heard you speak to me. You saw what I was, and you set me free. Now, I think I am going to follow you wherever you go, whatever you do, until the very end."

For the very first time in his life, Falstaff had a fully formed vision. Built on what he saw written on Sparrow's face and what lurked in his own heart, he glimpsed the future made manifest in a single frozen moment hung in front of him. A moment built of fire, and blood that consumed them both before eating the world around them in a blast of jagged white light. He felt his heart stop, triggering a cacophonic scream from the monitors connected to him, then felt his heartbeat return with a hammering thud deep in his chest.

"Oh Sparrow. There's going to be awful trouble, and its going to burn us up."

Falstaff wasn't sure that she was listening. She had a distracted scowl on her face as she scratched away the mess on her skin. Sparrow sucked on her thumb to soak it with saliva, then used it to wipe off the dried blood caked at the underneath her eye. She put her thumb back into her mouth and happily sucked the blood clean. When she finished, she turned her shining eyes back to Falstaff and smiled.

"I like trouble" she said. "It tastes like fun."

THE END

Author Bio

Chris Loblaw is a writer trying to understand the dark parts of the human heart. Jumping from genre to genre and medium to medium, he's landed in this pile of crime novel and he's going to wallow in it for a good long while. He's sentenced himself to 9 Falstaff books, if his sanity holds out long enough to get them written. You can read more of his writing, both fiction and non-fiction, at his website http://www.chrisloblaw.com.